THE BETTER
MOUSETRAP

TOM HOLT

THE BETTER MOUSETRAP

orbit

www.orbitbooks.net
www.tom-holt.com

ORBIT

First published in Great Britain in 2008 by Orbit
This paperback edition published in 2009 by Orbit
Reprinted 2009, 2010, 2011

A CIP catalogue record for this book
is available from the British Library.

ISBN 978-1-84149-504-0

Typeset in Plantin by M Rules
Printed and bound in Great Britain by
Clays Ltd, St Ives plc

Papers used by Orbit are natural, renewable and
recyclable products sourced from well-managed forests and certified
in accordance with the rules of the Forest Stewardship Council.

Mixed Sources
Product group from well-managed
forests and other controlled sources
www.fsc.org   Cert no. SGS-COC-004081
© 1996 Forest Stewardship Council

Orbit
An imprint of
Little, Brown Book Group
100 Victoria Embankment
London EC4Y 0DY

An Hachette UK Company
www.hachette.co.uk

www.orbitbooks.net

For Jan Fergus,
nonpareil of carrier pigeons

CHAPTER ONE

On a hot sunny day, a big blue road sign beside a busy dual carriageway.

Cars swished past. It's in the nature of road signs that they're only ever glanced at. In the time it took, something like a hundred people looked at the sign, but none of them for long enough to see the outline of a door forming in its lower left-hand corner. At first it was just a vaguely suggested rectangle traced by two-dimensional lines, as though someone had drawn them on with a black marker pen and a ruler. Then panels started to press their way through the waterproof cellulose coating, like mushrooms sprouting through compost. A round brass door-knob popped out and, after a moment, slowly began to turn. The lines around the door darkened. It swung open.

A set of foldaway stairs, such as you'd expect on an old-fashioned carriage, flopped out, groped for a moment in mid-air, and found the grass. A man in a long, brown, slightly damp robe, belted at the waist with rope and hooded with a cowl, walked carefully down the steps. Tucked under his arm was a big thin square; hardboard, possibly, or corrugated plastic, but wrapped in brown paper tied with string.

At the foot of the sign the robed man glanced at the watch on his wrist. He set the square thing down on the grass, knelt beside it, untied the knots, pulled off the brown paper, carefully folded it up and slipped it into one of his billowing sleeves. He stood up, facing away from the road, and took from his other sleeve a small clipboard. He checked something, nodded to himself, looked at his watch again. He was counting seconds under his breath.

Something snagged his attention, and he looked up at the doorway in the road sign. Standing on the top step of the stairs, tail wagging, was a small brown and white dog; it shook itself and barked. The robed man muttered to himself and made a shooing gesture at the dog, which took no notice. Behind it, in the gap in nature between the door frame and the door, rain flicked the dog's backside; a few drops trickled down its leg onto the top step of the stairs, and vanished.

The robed man checked his watch again, still counting, and when he reached a certain number he turned round to face the carriageway and advanced five paces, until he was leaning up against the crash barrier. With a broad, friendly smile on his face he lifted the hardboard square over his head. It was white, with two words written on it in big block capitals:

SLOW DOWN

The driver of a red Peugeot, who'd just been about to pull out and overtake, caught sight of the board, frowned briefly, and checked his mirror again. The gap in the traffic he'd intended to pull out into had closed up. He clicked his tongue and braked slightly.

The cowled man watched until the red Peugeot was out of sight, then shouldered his board and walked back to the foot of his folding stairs. The dog wagged its tail hopefully, but the man shook his head and climbed the steps. The door closed behind him, and vanished.

Because everything takes time, even Time itself, there was a pause before nothing happened.

*

'This way,' the manager whispered nervously. 'Mind your head.'

Because she was only five feet tall, she didn't bother to duck. Low ceilings and doorways were one of the few hazards of life that happened to other people and not to her. 'Could we get on, please?' she said, loudly and briskly. 'I'm due in Fenchurch Street at eleven.'

The manager didn't reply, but the back of his neck stiffened. Oh dear, she thought, the public. Still; it was possible that this was his first time, and one had to make allowances. The public had some very funny ideas about this sort of thing. They thought that if you crept along with your shoulders hunched and spoke in whispers, you'd be safe. Probably just as well. If the silly man had any idea of the danger he was in, he'd be halfway to Luton by now, and accelerating.

To put him at his ease, she decided to ask questions. She didn't actually need the data, but the public liked to get involved. Up to a point.

'How long's it been here, did you say?'

'*At least*—' The manager stopped, straightened his neck and dropped the whisper. 'At least two days,' he said, 'possibly longer, we can't be sure. We don't come down here very often, after all. I mean, we've got all that expensive CCTV stuff, there shouldn't be any need. But—'

'I know,' she said. 'I expect it was the temperature that gave it away.'

'Humidity level, actually,' the manager replied. 'We have to be very careful about damp, you see, so we monitor the humidity.' He frowned. 'What I don't understand is, if the damp meter registers that it's there, why didn't it show up on the CCTV?'

'It's technical,' she said, taking a little grey box from her briefcase and looking at it. 'All right,' she said, 'this is as far as you go. I'll take it from here.'

He turned to look at her, and his face was pale grey. 'Are you sure?'

She knew better than to be offended. She was twenty-eight

years old, five feet nothing and slightly built. It was understandable. 'Quite sure,' she said, without snapping. 'There shouldn't be any bother, but if you could please keep your staff out of the lower ground floor until I give you the all-clear—'

The manager was frowning. 'It's just,' he said, 'when we used to use JWW, the chap they sent was – well, taller, and . . .'

She smiled at him. She had a nice smile, under different circumstances. 'Let me see,' she said. 'That would probably have been Ricky Wurmtoter – six foot seven-ish, broad shoulders, lots of blond hair, bit of an accent?'

'That sounds like him, yes.'

She nodded. Normally she wouldn't get heavy with a client, but it was turning into a long day, her shoes were rubbing her heels and she very much wanted to go to the lavatory. 'Ricky and I trained together,' she said. 'He came second in our year, actually. He's dead now,' she added. 'I'm not.'

The manager looked at her. 'Oh.'

'It'll be all right,' she said, as reassuringly as she could be bothered to be. 'If you just go back to the lift and wait for me there, I'll be back as soon as I've finished. Shouldn't take long. If you hear a bang and a loud thump, that's perfectly normal.'

'All right.' He turned, walked away for a few steps, paused and looked back at her. 'So if Mr Whatsisname came second in your year, who—?'

'Me.'

'Ah. Fine.' Pause. 'Sorry.'

She waited until his footsteps had faded, then forced herself to relax. Piece of cake, she told herself. Just another day at the office. She shifted the briefcase into her left hand and carried on up the corridor.

Usually she was able to feed off the chauvinism and the patronising comments. A little tiny bit of anger helped, if used properly. This time, though, instead of fuelling her resolve, the manager's obvious doubts lay heavy on her stomach, like a hot dog with onions at lunchtime. She wasn't sure why. Maybe it was because he'd dragged Ricky Wurmtoter into it, and she'd always loathed Ricky. Maybe. It was, of course, perfectly true that she'd beaten Ricky in their finals by a clear six marks. But in accountancy, not in this.

The smell. Oh *God*, the smell.

With a tremendous effort, she put it out of her mind. They smell: so what? Big deal. The smell never killed anyone. It was probably the only harmless thing about them.

Even so.

She knelt down, laid her briefcase on the tiled floor and flipped open the catches. There was a theory (Ellison and Macziewicz in *New Thaumaturgical Quarterly*, June 1997) that they generated the smell deliberately, to confuse predators and disrupt their concentration. The article she'd read made out a pretty convincing case, but she didn't believe it. She reckoned they smelled bad because they ate a high-fat, low-fibre diet and had no concept of hygiene. To a certain extent, her views had been shaped by her first encounter with one of the loathsome things, in the vaults of the First Mercantile Bank of Cleveland, Ohio. It stood to reason, after all. Any creature who ate Americans was bound, sooner or later, to suffer from chronic flatulence.

She'd originally intended to use the sixteen-millimetre, but a glance at the white encrustations on the tunnel walls and the evidence of her nose made her change her mind and go for the eighteen-millimetre instead. This wasn't a cub or a pricket; it was a big old bull. She stuck the needle into the bottle of SlayMore, drew the plunger back smoothly, and pressed the base until a single amber drop dribbled from the needle's point. Then she laid the syringe carefully down beside her, unwrapped the pound of fresh raw liver she'd bought on the way over, and injected the SlayMore into it.

Piece of cake, she told herself nervously.

She left her briefcase leaning against the wall and advanced slowly and cautiously down the tunnel. The smell was getting stronger – it was like breathing poison custard – and under her feet the tiled floor quivered slightly. That was, of course, how you knew you were coming into olfactory range; the point at which you could feel the beating of its trip-hammer heart through the soles of your shoes.

The vibrations underfoot were starting to give her a headache; not to mention the effect on her unfortunate bladder. Never have a second cup of coffee before going out on a job. She scowled into the grey shadows; this was far enough, her instincts told her. It'll be able to smell the raw meat from here, and then it's just a matter of time. She laid the liver down on the floor, turned and walked back the way she'd just come. Vital, needless to say, not to run at this point. Their huge brains were hard-wired to detect the sound of running feet, and once they'd registered it they had no choice but to pursue, the same way a cat can't help batting at a trailing bit of string.

Back to where she'd left the briefcase. She opened it, took out a two-inch-thick wad of typescript, settled herself down with her back to the wall and began to read.

Ten minutes later, she heard the first groan.

She didn't look up from her paperwork, but she allowed her top lip to twitch into a trace of a smile. From first groan to stone-cold dead was always, invariably, fourteen minutes. You could set your watch by it. You could regulate atomic clocks by it. Whatever the hell the SlayMore people put in the stuff, it was totally reliable. She folded a page over and carried on reading.

(Totally reliable is, of course, just an upbeat way of saying that it hadn't failed *yet*; or at least, nobody had lived to notify the manufacturers of an authenticated case of failure. It's hard to complain when you're a pile of fine white ash on the floor of a bank vault and in no position to draw comfort from the fact that the warranty you never lived to claim under in no way affects your statutory rights.)

Second groan. As the roof of the tunnel shook and flakes of dust and mortar drifted down and settled on the page in front of her, she looked at her watch. Bang on time – good old SlayMore. Without realising she was doing it, she began to count under her breath. She also read the same paragraph five times, without taking in a single word.

It was perfectly natural to be a bit apprehensive at this point, she told herself. After all, she was no more than a hundred yards away from a fully grown bull dragon currently dying of acute indigestion. Everybody in the trade knew that once you'd heard the first groan you were safe. The stuff was doing its job, eating its way through the dragon's intestines; the last thing on the wretched creature's mind at this point would be springing to its feet, spreading its wings and going out looking for a fight. That was what made dragonslaying such a doddle, though naturally you never let the client know that. The client, if he thought about it at all, pictured you hacking away at the monster with a bloody great big sword, dodging plumes of blue fire and elephant-tusk-sized teeth. Mental images like that helped reconcile him to the awesome magnitude of the bill. To the client, dragonslaying was heroism. To the trade, it was just pest control, and the difference between dragons, rats and silverfish was merely a question of scale.

No pun intended.

The third groan was a blast of burning hot air that ruffled her papers and left her face and hands feeling scorched and raw. Exactly on time: six minutes to go. She unwrapped a peppermint and ate it.

The document she was reading was nothing special; still more DEFRA guidelines on the eco-friendly disposal of triffid waste, to comply with the latest EU directive; no more than five thousand kilos to be incinerated per hectare, separate disposal of the stings and venom sacs at designated triffid-elimination depots sited at least five kilometres from the nearest inland waterway, a list of chemical reagents authorised for residue neutralisation . . . She clicked her tongue and sighed. Whoever drew up this garbage lived in a world of their own. Everybody knew that in the real world, you got a JCB and dug a very deep pit and that was that. According to the old-timers, you could grow the most humongous runner beans on the site of a triffid dump; not being a gardener herself, she was prepared to take their word for it.

Five minutes. Ho hum.

If the bards of old had told the truth about dragonslaying – that the worst part of it's the hanging about waiting in draughty tunnels – there'd be a great deal less epic poetry and, quite probably, a lot more dragons. Of course, that wasn't the whole truth; it wasn't just hanging about waiting, it was hanging about waiting while being in mortal peril (because one day a subspecies of dragons on whom even SlayMore has no effect will evolve, at which point expect to see financial meltdown on the currency exchanges and gold going through the roof). That kind of boredom, as any soldier will tell you, is every bit as mind-numbing as, say, accountancy, but with the added mental toothache of cold, bowel-loosening terror lurking a millimetre or so under the surface of the subconscious. There was also the nagging thought that, a hundred yards down the tunnel, a magnificent and highly intelligent animal was dying an extremely painful and protracted death. That was one aspect of the job she tried very hard not to think about; which was a bit like the old gag about not thinking of an elephant. She knew, of course, that Western capitalism simply couldn't function unless dragons were strictly controlled. Their instinct was to seek out large accumulations of wealth and sit on them, carbonising anybody who came within nose-shot; which was why the firm she worked for had such an impressive client portfolio in the banking and art-gallery sector. Even so. There was still a small, idealistic, whale-saving corner of her mind where she couldn't help thinking there had to be a better way. Dragon safari parks, maybe, or *really* long-term designated deposit accounts. But the closest anybody had ever come to making a go of it was the US military's secret trials at Fort Knox; and it had taken the legendary Kurt Lundqvist and two thousand gallons of SlayMore Triple-X-Xtra to sort that one out. No: it was really quite simple, when you looked at it sensibly. Harsh commercial realities. Them or us.

Time. She got up, knocking over her briefcase in doing so. The lid burst open and a load of stuff spilled out of it onto the floor. She sighed and patiently shovelled it all back in, then tried to close the lid. Needless to say, it wouldn't shut. She shuffled the contents around a bit, took out a tube of manticore-rated tranquillisers and stowed it away in her pocket, and tried again. Success.

From her other pocket she took out a small black box, like an old-fashioned photographer's light meter. She turned a dial at the side and watched the needles on the three dials. When a dragon dies, the temperature drops, humidity levels rocket and the ambient Mortensen quotient falls back to a constant 6.339. It was all over bar the dentistry.

Even so.

Other practitioners – taller, more powerfully built members of the profession: men – liked to draw a sword at this point, or at the very least lock and load a fifty-calibre Barrett sniper rifle or a rocket launcher. She knew better than that. If the bloody thing was still alive, no amount of hardware would save her. There'd be a blinding white light, and the last thing she'd hear would be the hiss of her bodily fluids boiling inside her and a soft, reptilian snigger. But the meter said that the dragon was dead, and if there was one thing you could rely on in this business it was a Kawaguchiya XP770 E-Z-Scan. Gripping the briefcase tightly in her left hand, she started to walk up the tunnel.

According to the company's literature, the vaults of the City branch of the National Lombard Bank are the biggest in Europe. They're proud of the fact, the implication being that NatLom have got more money than anybody else, and so need somewhere big to keep it all. She was used to all that sort of thing, of course, having seen and de-infested them all in her time, but nevertheless, the sheer scale of what she saw as she walked through the melted ruin of the massive steel door made her catch her breath. You could have built a cathedral in there, or a railway terminal. The roof was disturbingly high, its proportions emphasised by the shiny white tiles and brushed-steel fittings – what was left of them. The dragon had been busy, ripping out what it couldn't be bothered to melt. Dragons like space, and an absence of clutter behind which their enemies can hide.

She felt something soft under her feet; but she paid it no attention. She was looking at the dragon.

It was, quite unmistakably, dead. In its last throes it had twisted itself up like the rubber band on a balsa-wood aeroplane, its head jammed tight under its left wing, its open jaws pointing at the roof, its claws frozen in the air in a last frantic scrabble. She deliberately froze her emotions and noted that it was indeed a full-grown adult male, somewhere between three and five hundred years old (after three hundred it's hard to tell precisely without careful examination of the claws and the ring of bone at the base of the horn); in any event, it was an old example of a species that improves exponentially with age. The teeth – she counted, then did the mental arithmetic. The teeth were traditionally the dragonslayer's perks; except, of course, that under the terms of her contract, they belonged to the firm, not to her. Annoying, since it'd be her job to gouge the bloody things out. At twelve thousand dollars a tooth . . . She sighed. One of these days, the banks were going to find out how much those things were worth, and then there'd be trouble.

Green scales, she noticed. Who were they using as dragon-knackers these days? Ibbotsons did a quick, efficient job but their charges were vicious. K & J Dragon Removals were quite reasonable, but they were sloppy about details such as acid leakage and blood clean-up, which annoyed the clients. (Understandable: no conscientious employer liked to see its staff dissolving from the feet up, or suddenly gifted with the ability to understand the language of birds.) The last she'd heard, Hancocks had been using Harry Fry, who was the most appalling cowboy. Zauberwerk UK were rumoured to be doing all their disposals in-house. That made sense, given the high value of dragon salvage. There were enough scales on this one alone to insulate a whole fleet of space shuttles.

Under her feet, something soft. Also, something that wasn't there. She knelt down and picked up a handful of fine white ash.

The something that wasn't there, she realised with a jolt that shook her whole body, was money. According to the bank, there should be— She took the briefing memo out of her pocket, counted the noughts and swore. And, as well as the cash, there ought to be bonds, securities, debentures, all that sort of thing. A substantial part of the wealth of the country should be down here, neatly parcelled up in bundles and sealed in wrappers. Instead, there was ash, and a great deal of empty space.

She looked at the dragon. For some reason which she couldn't begin to imagine, the dragon had incinerated all the money, every last note of it. Which was *crazy*. The love of dragons for cash money was, according to all the best authorities, the fiercest, most passionate emotion in the whole world. They scooped it up, nested in it, played with it for hours like happy kittens and, as far as they were concerned, nice soft paper was even better than gold. A dragon would be as likely to eat its own young as to damage a banknote.

With the side of her foot she traced a little furrow in the ash. Unthinkable, she thought. Unless—

She walked slowly across the floor until she was standing next to the vast contorted carcass. She studied the way the ash lay scooped and heaped into dunes around it. She put her head on one side and squinted a little. A bit like a sandcastle, or rather, a ring of sand forts surrounding a citadel. Even in its last convulsive moments, as the SlayMore dissolved its guts and burnt away its heart and lungs, it had been trying to shield something with its enormous bulk.

What, though? She could tell from the lie of the ash that it had done everything it could not to roll on one particular spot, but there was nothing there; just a fine layer of ash covering the white tiles. *Something*: something so valuable, maybe, that as far as the dragon was concerned billions of dollars' worth of negotiable currency was just more clutter to be got rid of, along with the shelves and the cabinets and the surveillance hardware. In which case, something truly beyond price. But there wasn't anything there. Just ash and floor.

Not my problem, she thought; and then it occurred to her that, as soon as she gave the all-clear, the manager would come scuttling down the tunnel expecting to see all that money, and wasn't he ever going to be disappointed. She winced. It wasn't her fault and she'd done a thoroughly professional, efficient job, but she had a strong feeling that the client wasn't going to be happy. Never mind, she told herself. Let's finish up and get out of here, before the ash hits the fan.

Serpentine dentistry is a miserable affair. She got the pliers out of her briefcase, pulled on her Teflon-impregnated gloves and made a start. She had a plastic box to put the teeth in. Mercifully, they came out relatively easily, but her wrists and elbows were still painfully sore by the time she'd finished. The key thing, of course, was to make sure that you didn't drop one . . .

She clipped the lid onto the box, stuffed it into her briefcase, put away the pliers, took off the gloves. Ash powdered under her heel. The next bit, she reckoned, was going to be awkward. She took her phone out of her pocket and thumbed in the number.

'All done,' she said.

'Are you all right? Is it—?'

'Yes.'

'And the— I mean, did it do much damage?'

Deep breath. 'You'd better see for yourself.'

'Not the shelving,' the manager's voice whimpered. 'It was brand new last month. God only knows what the board's going to say if we've got to have all new shelving.'

'I don't think you need worry too much about that,' she said, and rang off.

One last look back at the dragon. It was wrong to feel sympathy for it. Anything that big and powerful that allowed itself to be killed by a squirt of chemical hidden in a gobbet of liver was a disgrace to supernature and deserved whatever it got. But all that money; she'd seen yearling dragon colts fight each other to the death over a Scottish five-pound note. Burning all that money because it wasn't worth anything, because it was *irrelevant* . . . She squeezed her brain for an alternative explanation, but there wasn't one. The only possible reason was that it had found something else buried in the vault; something so valuable that, in comparison, money had no meaning. Even in the last stages of a SlayMore death it had avoided a small patch of the tiled floor, so as not to damage *something*. But she'd looked. There was nothing there.

She was positive there was nothing. After all, she'd looked.

Clearly, not carefully enough. Dropping her briefcase, she sprinted across the floor, kicking up little spirals of ash as she ran. Scrambling over an uplifted scaly leg, she dropped to her knees and scrabbled.

It had burned all the money, just as it had trashed the fittings and smelted the built-in fixtures. Dragons were like that, obsessive-compulsive. When they went broody, everything that wasn't treasure had to go. So if there was anything, anything at all, on that patch of desperately guarded floor, that'd be it, the something. A gemstone, perhaps – no, too bulky. All right, then, a microchip. What about the legendary ninth-generation Kawaguchiya sentient microprocessor prototype, which was believed to be locked away in a bank vault somewhere, waiting for the day when the global economy had grown enough to afford its existence? That'd be a hoard worthy of a really knowledgeable dragon. And it'd be small.

Her fingernails trailed furrows in the ash. Some things are too small to see but big enough to feel. In the distance she could hear footsteps echoing in the tunnel. The manager was coming, and she really didn't want him to find her like this, it'd lead to all sorts of awkwardness. In despair, she made one more sweep with her left hand, and touched something.

A cardboard tube. Just like the ones you find in the middle of toilet rolls.

Oh, she thought.

It didn't matter, she told herself. Whatever it was, supposing it even existed, it sure as hell wasn't hers. It occurred to her that her motive been pure curiosity, because she urgently needed to know why the dragon had destroyed all that money. If she'd actually found it, this notional little thing of inestimable value, there was always the risk that she might have slipped it in her pocket without thinking, the way you do, and that would've been stealing.

She stood up, pocketed the toilet-roll core, brushed five thousand dollars' worth of ash off her knees and walked away.

She met the manager halfway up the tunnel. He was carrying a torch and a big box file.

'All yours,' she said briskly. 'We'll send over the clean-up squad around lunchtime.'

He was looking at her. 'You're all right,' he said. 'You aren't even singed. How did—?'

She smiled at him; and she knew that, in spite of the hurricane of trouble and sorrow that was about to envelop him, it'd be that smile that haunted him as he lay awake in the early hours of the morning. 'Piece of cake,' she said. 'We're professionals. This is what we do.'

'Yes, but you're all covered in—'

'Sorry, must rush. Another appointment.'

She managed to keep from breaking into a run until she was out of the building.

Nobody gets to see Mr Sprague without an appointment. Nobody.

Mr Sprague sat behind his desk, reading. It was a beautiful desk, figured burr walnut, Louis Something, with nothing on it to cover up the exquisite grain of the wood apart from three green telephones and a framed photograph of a sad woman and a plump, scowling girl in jodhpurs. The document in his hands was a report on a horrendous multiple pile-up on the A779, which was going to cost the company something in the region of twelve million pounds, assuming that liability could be established.

Mr Sprague frowned, opened the top drawer of the desk and extracted a single Malteser from the bag.

He'd been in insurance all his working life, and he knew that really it was just a series of bets. You bet people money that they wouldn't set fire to their homes, smash up their cars, fall off ladders or die in their early fifties. Bets like that ought really to be safe as houses (safer, Mr Sprague thought sadly, safer) since the mark had a vested interest in losing, surely. Apparently not. Every minute of every day of every week of every month of every year, some damn fool of a policyholder somehow contrived to win his bet, which meant that the company had to pay him (or, if he'd won the bet really conclusively, his heirs) sums of money which should have gone to the shareholders, or the company reserves, or wherever profits went when he'd finished with them. Mr Sprague really didn't care about that. What concerned him was that there should be profits; huge ones, and bigger every year. It was the only way he had of keeping score, and he had a very competitive nature.

He crunched the Malteser and sucked the honeycomb centre. Yum.

According to the report, some complete idiot of a policyholder had won the jackpot by ramming his nasty little red Peugeot up the tailpipe of a lorry carrying – you had to laugh or you'd cry – fifty thousand gallons of concentrated nitric acid. The lorry had swerved, hit a number of other cars (some of them expensive cars containing even more expensive people), overturned, sprayed acid everywhere; then other cars had hit other cars, which in turn hit the central reservation, blasted through it like a bullet through butter, and spread the general carnival atmosphere to the traffic on the northbound side of the road. Twelve million quid, gone with the wind. It wasn't fair.

Mr Sprague sighed. He was, at heart, a gambler; he knew and accepted the fact. But gamblers come in all different shapes and sizes. Some of them spend their days behind newspapers in bookmakers' shops and sleep under the railway arches. Some of them wear fancy waistcoats with a derringer in the pocket. Not all gamblers are completely honest. Some of them even cheat.

Mr Sprague turned a page and whimpered. The odds against a V-reg Astra leaving the road, cartwheeling twenty yards down the central reservation and completely flattening a brand new Mercedes had to be— As it happened, he was an outstanding mathematician and could calculate the odds to three decimal places, but he knew it'd only depress him if he did. He sighed instead, and ate another Malteser. There were days when Maltesers were the only thing that kept him going.

He was so preoccupied with the report that he didn't see the lines appear on the blank wall opposite the door. First a single black line, where a door lintel would be; then two vertical lines running down at right angles to the first one, forming three sides of a rectangle—

He looked up, frowned; then, as a carefully buried memory broke cover and scampered across his mind, he smiled. It was a rather special memory, since it related to something that hadn't actually happened yet. You got used to that sort of thing after thirty years in insurance.

The outline became a door, with a round brass knob. It swung open, and a young man dressed rather like a monk stepped through it.

'Hello, George,' he said.

Mr Sprague was old-fashioned, and didn't really hold with the first-name stuff, except when angled downwards, from superior to inferior. It was insidious, he felt, so American that it was practically Japanese, and the thin end of a wedge whose back was baseball caps with the company logo and compulsory early-morning t'ai chi on the roof. But he was prepared to make exceptions.

'Hello, Frank,' he replied cheerfully.

The young man grinned at him. Mr Sprague closed his eyes and moved his head just a little before looking down at the pages in his lap. They were blank.

'Thanks,' he said, with feeling.

'No worries,' the young man replied briskly, in a medium-strong New Zealand accent. 'You know me, anything for money. Ten per cent, as usual, right?'

Mr Sprague's face went blank. 'Ten per cent of what, Frank?'

The young man frowned and, when Mr Sprague glanced down at the sheets of paper, they were covered in words again. He sighed. He was pretty sure he understood how the rest of it worked, but he'd never been able to figure out how he did that.

'Sorry,' Mr Sprague said sheepishly. 'But you can't blame a man for trying.'

Frank clicked his tongue. 'Sure, sure,' he said. 'But not every single bloody time.'

Mr Sprague nodded. From the second drawer of his desk he took a chequebook and wrote out a cheque for one point two million pounds, payable to Frank Carpenter. He blew on it to dry the ink and handed it over.

'For what it's worth,' he said, 'you also saved seven lives, not to mention the debilitating injuries, which included—'

Frank shrugged. 'Don't tell me,' he said. 'You know I don't like that sort of stuff.' He folded the cheque and stuffed it in the sleeve of his robe. It always annoyed Mr Sprague intensely when he did that. By way of revenge, he asked, 'Bobby not with you today?'

A scowl flickered on Frank's face. 'No,' he said. 'I left him at—' He stopped short as the door wobbled and a scruffy brown-and-white dog bundled happily through it, tail wagging. 'Yes,' he amended. 'Sit, Bobby. Good dog. Bobby, fucking well *sit*.'

The dog brushed past him, jumped up onto Mr Sprague's lap, turned round three times and went to sleep. Mr Sprague stroked its head gently and smiled.

'I've tried taking him to training classes,' Frank said wretchedly. 'But it's no good. Last one we went to he got expelled.'

'Really.'

'Mphm. Setting the other dogs a bad example.'

The dog wriggled a little and snuggled its nose against Mr Sprague's fly. 'Fancy,' said Mr Sprague. He opened the drawer again, took a Malteser and fed it into the dog's mouth. The dog crunched it without waking up. 'One of these days, you've got to tell me how you came to—'

'No.'

'Ah well,' said Mr Sprague, and to a certain limited extent the look on Frank's face made up for the one point two million. 'Well,' he repeated, and his tone of voice was meant to suggest that he was eternally grateful and would never forget what Frank had done for him, but he did have work that he needed to get on with. 'Another successful mission, then. I expect we'll be in touch again soon. In the meantime—'

'You want me to go away.' Frank grinned at him. 'Fair enough. You know how to reach me. Come on, Bobby. Here, boy, good dog.' The dog opened its eyes, yawned and nestled a little more firmly in Mr Sprague's lap. 'He likes you,' Frank said. 'Anybody can see that.'

'Odd, isn't it?' Mr Sprague said. 'I've always thought of myself as a cat person.'

'So I've heard,' Frank said. 'Especially when there's a full moon. Oh look, bless him,' he added, with extra syrup. 'He's so happy, it'd be such a shame to wake him up.'

Mr Sprague opened his knees. The dog dropped through them like a stone, landed on all fours and wagged its tail. 'Mind how you go, Frank. And thanks again.'

Frank walked towards the door in the wall he'd come in through. 'You know what I always say, George,' he said. 'Gratitude and half a dollar will buy you a— Oh for crying out loud, you stupid animal, leave it. I said *leave it*.' He sighed. 'Oh well. Sorry about that.'

'Not to worry,' Mr Sprague said amiably. 'I was going to get a new one anyway. Of course, that particular example was six-teenth-century Florentine, but what the heck. We're insured.'

Frank made a noise in the back of his throat that communi-cated more than mere words ever could, and pushed open the door. The dog darted between his legs, hurled itself through the gap between door and frame, and vanished in mid-leap. It's just as well, thought Mr Sprague, that my eyesight's so poor these days that I can hardly see at all without (he quickly took them off and laid them on his desk) my glasses. Otherwise my brain might fool me into thinking I just saw a dog vanish into thin air. And that's not possible. Just as well I didn't see it, in that case.

(He frowned. There had been all sorts of reasons why, as a

young man, he'd opted for a career in insurance – earning money, acquiring wealth, getting rich, making a fortune, to name but a few. Expanding his metaphysical horizons and finding out the truth about how the world actually worked didn't feature anywhere on the list; which was unfortunate, seeing that since Frank had entered his life his horizons hadn't been so much expanded as blown to bits, and the truth was no longer safely Out There where he could ignore it, but roaming around inside his living space looking for him with its tongue lolling out. Nevertheless. It was Frank who'd made it possible for him to outperform his rivals and scramble to the top, in the process making him so wealthy that he genuinely no longer really cared about the money, except as the one true way of keeping track of how he was doing. And that, of course, made everything worthwhile: all the strangeness, all the unwanted and intrusive insights, Frank, even the disappearing bloody dog.

Besides, he liked dogs. Not as much as cats. Much, much more than people.)

He tried to concentrate on his work, but he was finding it difficult; not unusual in the aftermath of one of Frank's visits. For instance: open in front of him was a thick wad of papers stapled together at the top right-hand corner, but all the pages were blank. He scowled at them. He knew that, before Frank arrived, there had been words on those sheets (bad words, nasty words) and that Frank had somehow contrived to send them away. As for what those words had been about – the last shreds of memory were stripping away like a dream upon waking, and in the time it'd take to boil a kettle every trace of them would be gone for ever. Splendid. But he couldn't concentrate on anything else, because a part of his mind knew that by rights the full force of his considerable intellect should still be focused on a problem that no longer existed, that had never existed in the first place—

No wonder he got headaches; a bit like toothache in a tooth that'd long since been pulled.

A gentle knock at the door (the permanent one, not the temporary hole-in-the-wall, which had vanished when his visitor left). In came Ms Dennaway, with a thick wad of stapled-together paper.

'The report on the Eccleshaw factory explosion,' she said, putting it down in front of him as though it was a plate of nasty greens that he'd have to eat before he got any pudding. 'Oh, and Mr Cartwright rang. He'd like to talk to you about it before he briefs the loss adjusters.'

Mr Sprague winced. He remembered seeing the TV footage. It wasn't till the next day that he remembered that they covered the Eccleshaw plant. Tentative as an engineer defusing a bomb, he flicked to the last page and read the double-underlined figure at the bottom. So many noughts trailing after the integers. Somewhere in the West Midlands a gambler had just hit the jackpot, though he hadn't lived to enjoy it. Nor, apparently, had a lot of other people.

He sighed. Twice in one day. He thought about ice packs, paracetamol, ibuprofen. He thought about all that money.

His fingers did a little dance on the number pad of the nearest phone. Three electronic burps, and a familiar voice said, 'Hello?'

Oh well, thought Mr Sprague. 'Hello, Frank,' he said.

CHAPTER TWO

After dealing with the Eccleshaw business, Frank Carpenter stepped through a door in a wall in Brierley Hill and came out through an identical door in a builder's hoarding in south London. He closed it behind him, waited as it slowly slid to the ground and rolled itself up, picked it off the pavement and tucked it into a small cardboard tube, which he stowed away carefully in his inside pocket.

Not the most attractive of neighbourhoods, he decided. True, it wasn't one of those districts where you have to look where you're going so you don't slip on a nest of cartridge cases from last night's drive-by shooting, but the security grilles on the shop windows and the burnt-out P-reg Mercedes suggested that this wasn't a happy environment for a shallow, easygoing hedonist like himself. It certainly wasn't the sort of place where you'd expect to find—

But there it was, just across the road and up a floor. Over a chemist's, he noted. How are the mighty fallen, and all that.

(Mum and Dad ought to see this, he said to himself. Most likely they wouldn't grin or snigger, but they'd feel – what? Closure, a necessary turn of the wheel. Dad, anyway. Mum'd probably click her tongue and say *serve them right*. Or maybe not. Where they'd gone, something like this couldn't possibly matter.

It'd be like expecting the moon to care whether Tim Henman made it through to the quarter-finals.)

Below him something snuffled, and he felt the soft assault of a wagging tail against his leg. He sighed. He was pretty sure he'd been alone when he folded up the door, but apparently not. Or maybe (not a notion he cared to dwell on), maybe Bobby didn't *need* the door. They say that dogs will travel hundreds of miles to find their lost masters. 'Oh well,' he said aloud. 'Bobby, *heel.*'

Immediately the dog sprang out into the road, causing a van driver to burn ten quids' worth of value off his tyres and brake pads. It reached the opposite pavement, turned round, looked at him and wagged its tail. Stupid animal.

The stencilled black letters in the window above the chemist's read:

Tanner & Co
Chartered M

From the way the words were spaced, you could deduce that some other letters had faded away or peeled off after the 'M'. Frank grinned. The *chartered* was a nice touch. It was one of those words that the eye skidded off. Behind a word like that, you instinctively thought, works a boring little man whose services I'll never need, and which I couldn't afford in any case. Interest evaporates. Nobody ever lingers in the street looking up and wondering what the 'M' stands for.

There was a side door. The stair carpet was frayed, with flat blobs of spent chewing gum fossilised in the pile. At the top of the stairs, Frank faced a glass-panelled door with a bell-push and one of those boxes you speak into and wait for it to quack back at you before you're allowed in. Somehow Frank got the impression that not many of Mr Tanner's customers were walk-ins off the street.

He pressed the button and said 'Hello,' the way you do. Nothing happened. He tried again. Silence. He was just about to fish in his pocket for the cardboard tube when the box belched static at him and a female voice said, 'Yes?'

'I'm here to see Mr Tanner,' he said.

'Snark wargle squirr appointment?'

'No.'

'Name, please.'

Ah, Frank thought. Of course, he could always lie, just to get through the door. But from what he'd heard about him, he didn't want to start off with Mr Tanner leering down at him from the moral high ground, and quite possibly rolling boulders as well. 'Frank Carpenter,' he said.

'Frank what?'

'Carpenter. As in woodwork. Or Harrison Ford.'

Pause. Maybe a little white lie would've been justified after all. But Carpenter wasn't such an uncommon name. Maybe they'd think that—

Bzzz. He applied gentle pressure to the door and it opened.

He saw a small room with grubby woodchip on the walls and flogged-out carpet tiles on the floor. There was a plain chipboard desk in the middle of it, behind which sat the most beautiful girl Frank had ever seen in his life. Ah, he thought. I've come to the right place, then.

The girl looked at him; eyes like soft blue-black holes. He looked down at his shoes, and noticed that they were splashed with whatever the noxious stuff was that they processed at the Eccleshaw plant. Oh well, he thought. If it burns holes in the carpet, I don't suppose anybody'll notice.

'Is that your dog?'

Inside Frank something growled, but he was a civilised human being, so he nodded. 'I'd like a word with Mr Tanner, please, if he's free,' he said, as pleasantly as he could. The beautiful girl looked at him, and under his clothes he fancied he could feel little dotted lines, like the ones you see drawn on pictures of cows in butchers' shops, to tell you the names of the various cuts and joints.

'Carpenter, did you say your name was?'

'That's right. Frank Carpenter.'

Was it possible to read someone's DNA with the naked eye?

The girl looked as though she was giving it her best shot. 'I'll see if he's available,' she said, and picked up a phone. Into it she recited his name. There was a long, quiet interval; then she put the phone back and nodded at the door behind her. He rather got the impression that if the decision had been up to her, he'd be headed out through the other door. Or the window.

The back office was pretty much like the front, except that the mangy carpet was covered with heaps of paper and buff, red, orange, green and blue folders. At least someone had made an effort to decorate the walls; they were hung with a huge collection of tomahawks, each one with a little card under it to tell you where it had come from and who it'd been made by. Behind the desk, just visible through a haze of blue cigar smoke—

Frank recognised Mr Tanner at once. That was only to be expected. All through his early childhood he'd been told about him: eat your nice dinner, tidy your room, be polite to the visitors or Mr Tanner will come and get you. And when, not unreasonably, he'd asked, 'What's a mister tanner, mummy and daddy?' they'd conjured up for him a mental image of a hunched, evil little man with curly salt-and-pepper hair, huge eyes magnified to disturbing size by massive glasses, wicked sharp teeth, a devilish grin and plumes of smoke coming out of his nose. Young Frank Carpenter's plate was always polished clean and his bedroom immaculately tidy until he reached the age when that sort of fatuous threat no longer worked, and he'd come to assume that Mr Tanner was about as real as the tooth fairy or the Easter bunny.

Apparently not. If anything, his parents' description had been an understatement.

The little man lifted his head and glared at him. 'Well?' he said.

'Dennis Tanner?'

'That's me,' the little man said, in a strong Australian accent. 'Who the hell are you?'

'My name's Frank Carpenter. I believe you knew my—'

'Oh *shit*,' Mr Tanner said. 'No, hang on, that can't be right. Last time I saw Paul Carpenter and Sophie bloody Pettingell was only three years ago, and they sure as hell didn't have a kid, so—'

An embarrassed grin slithered across Frank's face. 'It's complicated,' he said. 'But yes. My mum and dad are Sophie and Paul Carpenter. They send their love, by the way,' he added, because if you climb too far up the moral high ground there are avalanches and yetis.

'Balls,' said Mr Tanner succinctly. 'How complicated?'

'Very.'

Mr Tanner sighed, gusting smoke in Frank's face. 'Park your bum,' he said reluctantly. 'Curiosity's always been my downfall. No, scratch that. Your bloody mum and dad were my downfall. Curiosity's just one of my many nasty habits.' He leaned forward across the desk, peering at Frank through his bulletproof-glass-thick lenses. 'Now you mention it, there's definitely a resemblance. You've got my great-great-grandad's chin, for one thing.' He grinned, suddenly as a shark's jaws snapping shut. 'Your dad mentioned that we're related, did he?'

Frank nodded. 'Distant cousins,' he said.

'That's right. You met my mum on the way in, of course.'

'Oh yes.'

Mr Tanner leaned back in his chair. 'She was very keen on your dad at one time, my mum. Which is the main reason I sent him to bloody New Zealand.' The eyes flared with fear and hate. 'He's not come back, has he?'

Frank shook his head.

'Still over there, then.'

Frank pursed his lips. 'I did say it's complicated,' he replied. 'But as far as I know, he's got no plans to come back to this country again. Ever.'

Mr Tanner sighed, from his boots up. 'Thank God for that,' he said. 'All right, I can start breathing again. So,' he added, lighting a new cigar from the stub of the old one, 'tell me all about it.'

There was no need to give Mr Tanner the full version. He knew better than anyone how Paul Carpenter, Frank's father, had gone to work for J. W. Wells & Co, at that time the leading firm of sorcerers and magical practitioners in the City of London; how, once he'd found out what JWW actually did (he'd originally assumed that they were in shipping or commodities or something), the only reason he'd stayed on was that he'd fallen in love with Sophie, the other junior clerk; how he'd accidentally come into possession of the Acme Portable Door, a wonderful but dangerous gadget that allowed you to travel anywhere in time and space just by unrolling it and pressing it against the nearest available flat vertical surface; how Paul had had the wretched bad luck to get locked in a life-and-death struggle with most of the firm's partners, one by one, and had incredibly prevailed, saving the human race and the fabric of the universe while he was at it but ruining the firm's business in the process. None of that, Frank figured, was Mr Tanner likely to have forgotten.

Instead, he concentrated on what had happened after Paul and Sophie had retired to New Zealand, where they'd acquired (by way of a murderously begrudged gift from JWW) the world's biggest and most profitable bauxite mine. For a while, Frank explained, they tried to live a normal happy life with nothing but each other and an unimaginable amount of money. After twenty-nine years—

'Hold it,' Mr Tanner interrupted, with a bewildered expression on his face. 'That'd be twenty-six years into the future, right?'

Frank nodded. 'Though from my perspective, of course, it's three years ago, although—'

'Do I look like I'm remotely interested in your bloody perspective?'

After twenty-nine years of putting up with a lifestyle neither of them liked very much but which they endured because they thought the other one liked that sort of thing, they came to a decision. Using the Portable Door one last time, they took a trip to a place and time that only the Door could reach, waved an embarrassed and slightly weepy goodbye to their son, and told him to peel the Door off the wall.

It had, of course, been a traumatic parting, but Frank had managed to drag himself through it, ever so slightly buoyed up by the thought of inheriting the bauxite mine. It was only a few days later that he found out that one of his parents' last acts in this reality had been to make over the mine, the company and their goose-liver-pâté-bloated bank account to the New Zealand Trust for Wildlife Conservation. It had been, the lawyer explained, his mother's idea. She knew how much Frank cared about the environment and our natural heritage. She was sure he'd be secretly pleased.

Best-kept secret in human history. After spending a month vainly trying to use the Door to reach his parents' pocket reality, he gave up and considered his position as dispassionately as he could. He had no money, no home (the vast Carpenter mansion he'd grown up in was now the official residence of the Chairman of Trustees, whose first move on taking possession had been to grub up Sophie's thirty-acre endangered orchid nursery and turn it into tennis courts, a golf course and a landing strip for his Lear jet) and no means whatsoever of earning a living. On the positive side, he had a change of underwear, a pair of jeans, a Lizard-Headed Women 2030 World Tour T-shirt and the Portable Door.

All in all, he decided, things could be worse.

'To start with,' Frank went on, 'I set my sights quite low. Materialising inside food stores and clothes shops at two in the morning, that sort of thing. Not really my style, but—' He frowned. 'Are you all right, Mr Tanner?' he asked.

'Mm.' Mr Tanner looked as though he'd tried to eat a whole cow in one bite. 'Sorry. Go on.'

'You're trying not to laugh, aren't you?'

'Me? No. Get on with the story.'

'Well—'

'Snrgff . . .'

The insurance thing had been just one of those bright ideas. It had come to him out of the blue, while he'd been thinking about something else. At first he'd smiled and filed it away in the mental trashcan marked *Wouldn't-It-Be-Cool-If*. But materialising inside shops and helping yourself to merchandise for which you don't intend to pay is burglary, even if you use highly advanced magic instead of a jemmy, and that (Frank decided) was no way to live. He'd actually made a note of everything he'd taken and where it had come from in a little blue notebook, so that some day when he had the money he could make it all right again, but his conscience wasn't fooled that easily. The time had come, he realised with a sinking heart, for him to go out and get a job; or, at the very least, a profession (which is, after all, only a smart word for a job, but with longer hours, better money and a helping of alphabet soup after your name on the printed letterhead).

The time had come – yeah, right. But, he thought, for someone with an Acme Portable Door, time is delightfully flexible. With the Door, when he ran out of money, all he had to do was go back in time to a moment when he'd been loaded, and spend it all over again. Or, better still, what about that crazy insurance idea? After all, it might just work, and if so—

Simple, as the best ideas always are. Insurance companies, he figured, have to pay out huge sums of money whenever there's a disaster; and disasters often start off with some small, avoidable error of judgement – the Great Fire of London, for example, caused by the seventeenth-century equivalent of a chip-pan blaze. Someone with the hindsight of a retrospective hawk who could travel in time could go back to those crucial oh-shit moments, prevent the error and avert the disaster. The fire, explosion, meltdown or multiple pile-up wouldn't happen, the insurance company wouldn't be called on to pay out – true, history would be violated and a brick would be thrown through the brittle surface of reality, but in a *good* way, surely, because people who should've been killed or horribly mutilated would survive intact, wouldn't they? You'd have to be a really callous bastard or a government to find fault with that—

'Your dog,' Mr Tanner interrupted, 'is eating the telephone flex.'

'What? Oh *God*, sorry. Bobby! Bobby, *bad dog*, leave it.' The dog lifted its head and gazed at him. Its deep brown eyes told him that it was hurt and very, very disappointed, but it forgave him. He looked around for something to throw at it.

'It's all right,' Mr Tanner said, 'I don't mind. I like dogs.' Pause, two, three – 'Couldn't manage a whole one, though.'

The joke, Frank realised, lay in the uncertainty as to whether Mr Tanner really was joking.

Being a conscientious young man, Frank hadn't rushed into it. He'd thought it through.

The drill was as follows. Having identified a disaster that he'd be able to prevent (some disasters had horribly complex causes, or were inevitable anyway; or preventing them would be dangerous, or just too much like hard work) he researched the lives of the victims, to see if they were Significant People or just walk-ons in life's pageant, and ran a simulation to find out how their unscheduled survival would affect the ebb and flow of history. To anybody else, that would have involved some extremely heavy maths; but Frank was descended on both sides from generations of ridiculously talented magicians, to the point where his genes practically glowed in the dark. Furthermore, his father had owned a small lump of rock crystal in which, if you got the lighting and the ambience exactly right, you could see all sorts of amazing stuff. He'd kept it hidden from Frank's mother, who didn't hold with anything connected to their previous lives. A Door trip back in time to retrieve it from under the loose floorboard in the attic three days before the Wildlife people took possession of the house, and he had what he needed to run the simulations.

He started small. There is a providence, he vaguely remembered reading somewhere, in the fall of a sparrow. Right on – as he proved with the Door, the bit of crystal and an air rifle. The simulation came out something like eighty-seven per cent accurate; if he hadn't shot it, the sparrow would've been eaten by the Macreadys' cat in any case, and the mother hatched the eggs perfectly well on her own. He felt bad about it for days, and he had a nasty feeling that his mother would've considered the experiment to be Testing On Animals and a mortal sin, but he couldn't bring himself to start fiddling about with the lives of human beings without some sort of trial run. Besides, his views on wildlife in general had changed ever so slightly after the Chairman of Trustees moved into the Carpenter house and turned his old bedroom into a karaoke studio.

Then it was just a matter of establishing contact with Mr Sprague. Actually, he rather liked the man. There was something endearing about the dogged, persevering way he tried to oil out of paying Frank his commission after every successful mission. Also, sometimes when he knew Frank was coming, he laid on tea and biscuit. (Only ever the one: a Rich Tea, from his secretary's private packet. He'd explained that he was in business to make money, not spend it, and he had the shareholders to think of.) Narrowing the focus of his amiability a little, Frank had realised that he liked Mr Sprague because he was just about the only human being he'd met more than once since he'd embarked on his new career. This practically made him a father figure, although when you considered what Frank's real father had been like, maybe that wasn't such a good thing.

'And he pays you money,' Mr Tanner said, after a long pause.

Frank nodded. 'Ten per cent,' he replied.

'And you've been doing this for how long?'

Frank laughed. 'That was supposed to be a trick question, right?'

Mr Tanner frowned. 'What I meant was,' he said, 'you've done several jobs for this Sprague bloke.'

'Forty-seven,' Frank replied promptly. 'Assuming this is the fifteenth of June 2008. Of course, by this time yesterday it could easily be a hundred and six. Or twenty-three. It's complicated.'

'Mmm.' Mr Tanner scowled at him. 'I'll say this for you,' he said, 'you're your father's son, all right. And your mother's too, of course, but that's not quite so bad. I mean, yes, she was a total menace, and if I had that Door thing of yours, the first thing I'd do would be to nuke her in her cot. But your dad—' He shuddered, and grinned. 'What made your dad so very fucking special was the way he trashed the lives of everybody he came in contact with and screwed up the fabric of time and space while always doing the right thing, if you see what I'm getting at. What I'm saying is, you'd go over it afterwards and think it all through; and yes, anybody with a shred of human decency would've done exactly the same as he did in those particular circumstances, absolutely no two ways about it, even though the consequences were pure bloody hell for everybody involved. The choice had to be made, and he made it. It's just, he kept *on* and *on* and *on* getting stuck with that kind of choice, it's like the intolerable moral dilemmas homed in on him across vast distances; and if just once the choice had been up to a selfish, greedy, unprincipled little bastard like me—' He shook his head; there was a miniature snowstorm of dandruff. 'But there you go. Runs in the family, I suppose.'

'Sorry? I don't—'

'Typical bloody Carpenter mentality,' Mr Tanner barked, jabbing with his cigar. 'You go around playing cat's cradle with the lives of everybody on the planet, but it's all OK because you're saving people's lives. And yes, there could be problems as a result, but you've got your little bit of rock that tells you it'll all be fine, so— You know what? That's not just stupid, it's a special, rare kind of stupidity that's so crass it's practically Liberal Democrat. And one of these days, when it all hits the fan—' He shrugged. 'I'd kill you if I thought I could get away with it, but there you go. Enough of that. So: to what do I owe the unwanted pleasure?'

Frank didn't answer straight away. He was hurt. Sure, he'd expected a certain degree of hostility, but this was more than he'd bargained for. 'I'm sorry,' he said. 'I didn't think you'd see it that way.'

'You didn't.'

'No.'

'Figures.'

Frank sighed. 'I only came here to give you some money.'

Mr Tanner froze. Misleading term, in context. Rather, it was as though someone had pressed the pause button and stopped the world for a moment.

'Money?'

Frank nodded. 'I figured that, well, it was partly my parents' fault that you lost the business and everything you'd worked so hard for all your life, and that really didn't seem very fair to me; and I've been doing quite well at this insurance thing I've been telling you about, and to be honest with you I don't really need all that money, it's not like I've got very much to spend it on, and if I did, all I've got to do is go out and earn some more, so I thought—' He hesitated. This was embarrassing. 'Would ten million be any good?'

Mr Tanner's lips shaped the words *ten million*, but no sound came out.

'Dollars,' Frank amplified.

'Pounds.'

'All right, pounds. Would that sort of help you get back on your feet, make a new life for yourself, that kind of thing?'

(Mr Tanner was thinking: yup, he's a Carpenter all right. Bit like what you'd get if you took an atomic bomb and brought it up to be a devout Quaker. Sooner or later you'd get melted pavements and silhouettes on the walls, but it'd have all been with the very best of intentions.)

'Yes,' Mr Tanner said; then he added, 'It'd be a start, anyway.'

Frank frowned. 'A start.'

Mr Tanner nodded, several times. 'A gesture. It's the thought that counts.'

Frank took out his chequebook, opened it, patted his top pocket. 'Excuse me, have you got a pen?'

Mr Tanner gave him one. It was a plain black biro, with extreme tooth-marks where someone had been chewing it.

'Sorry, what's the date today?'

Mr Tanner pointed to the desk calendar.

'Ah, right,' Frank said. 'Only, I lose track – Will just "D Tanner" be all right, or—?'

'That'll do fine.'

Tearing noise. The top left-hand corner had come off, the way it does if you don't tug at it just right. Frank handed the cheque to Mr Tanner, who studied it carefully for a moment, then laid it on his desk and weighed it down with a heavy, old-fashioned stapler.

'My pen,' he said.

'Sorry?'

'Can I have my pen back, please?'

'Oh, right.'

'Not to worry,' Mr Tanner said, taking the pen from Frank and putting it away in a drawer. 'Easily done. Um—' He paused, and a battle seemed to be taking place behind his eyes. 'Want a receipt?'

'What? Oh, no, don't bother about that.'

'Um.' It was as though an invisible dentist was pulling all Mr Tanner's teeth. 'Thanks,' he grunted, then swallowed. 'Yes, well. Thank you.'

Frank smiled. 'My pleasure,' he said. 'Only, it's sort of been on my mind a bit lately, and—'

Mr Tanner had noticed something. He moved the stapler an inch to the left and glanced down. 'I see you bank with—'

'That's right,' Frank said, pleased that the subject had changed. 'Dad always thought very highly of them, and I don't know about finance and stuff, so when I wanted to open a bank account I just kind of took his advice. He said you used to bank with them back in the old days.'

Mr Tanner grunted. 'Yes,' he said. 'Can't say I ever liked them much myself. Good deposit rates, mind, and their charges aren't bad. But I didn't think they did private accounts. Just businesses and so on.'

'It was sort of a favour. Dad told me the chief cashier was an old friend.'

'Mphm.'

Well, then, Frank thought. I've done what I came to do, and clearly he doesn't like me very much. I'd better go.

He stayed.

'So,' he said awkwardly, 'you're still, like, in the trade.'

'It's the only thing I know,' Mr Tanner replied. 'And it's a living. Not like the old days, of course. We had a pretty good client portfolio at JWW, and a good team, even if they were all bastards of one kind or another. We used to make some serious money.'

'Before my parents—'

'—Buggered it all up, yes. Oh, don't look at me like that. You think it's just me bearing a grudge. Fine. Well, when your mum and dad joined the firm, there were seven partners. Let's see, now. Your dad killed Ricky and Theo, he locked Judy up in the Isle of Avalon – bad place, that, you really don't want to know about it – and, oh yes, he turned Humph Wells into a photo-copier, which was probably the nastiest trick of all, because you know what people in offices do to photocopiers. Oh, and if your dog chews up the VAT returns I'm going to turn it into an egg and jump on it, even if you did just give me ten million quid.'

'What? Oh Christ. *Bobby*—'

'So you see,' Mr Tanner went on (he was smirking now, and seemed rather more relaxed, maybe because he felt he'd got the moral high ground back), 'it wasn't just a clash of personalities or nasty bosses bullying the poor downtrodden workers. He *ruined* me. Couldn't have done otherwise, like I said, him being a fun-damentally decent human being, but you know, that really doesn't make it any better, somehow. We had to sell the business in the end. Jack Wells retired, Cas Suslowicz went a bit funny and as far as I know he's working in local government somewhere. Connie Schwartz-Alberich – did your father ever mention her?'

'No.'

'After his time, probably.'

Frank shrugged.

'Screw her, then. As for me, well, you can see where I ended up. Not exactly where I'd have expected to be in five years' time, as they say in the motivational interviews.' He sighed. 'But there we go. Life, and all that stuff.'

'I'm—' Frank hesitated. He felt very sorry for Mr Tanner, but he couldn't help remembering that this was the man who'd terrorised his parents, leaving them scarred for life. He didn't seem so bad – but maybe suffering had mellowed him, or at least drained away his strength. 'Well,' he said briskly. 'The money'll help, won't it?'

'Money?'

'The ten million.'

Mr Tanner went quiet for a moment. 'It's not quite as simple as that. For one thing, I've got debts. From the old days.'

'Ah.'

'Our former landlords, for one thing.'

Frank frowned. 'Dad told me you leased the building from your mother's family.'

'That's right.'

'Surely they'd understand about—'

Mr Tanner laughed. 'Did your dad tell you about my family? *Our* family.'

'Um. Well, he said your mother's a very friendly, outgoing sort of—'

'You leave my mother out of this.'

'He's her son's godfather, isn't he? Her other son,' he said, immediately wishing he hadn't.

'That's right.' Mr Tanner's eyes had grown small and sharp. 'Little Paul Azog, my half-brother.'

'Azog,' Frank repeated. 'That's a Russian name, isn't it?'

Mr Tanner grinned. 'Not quite,' he said. 'Actually, it's goblin.'

'Go—'

'Mphm.' A smile flashed across Mr Tanner's face. 'That's what our family is, on Mum's side. Your dad didn't tell you that, did he?'

'Um.'

The smile was so broad that it crinkled the corners of Mr Tanner's eyes. 'Goblins,' he repeated. 'Little hairy buggers with great big claws and teeth. They live in holes in the ground, and they eat people.'

'Goblins.'

'On my mother's side,' Mr Tanner said. 'My dad's family are from Adelaide.'

'Right.' Frank breathed in deeply. 'Well,' he said, in a rather subdued voice, 'that's – well, I have to say, that does come as a bit of a—'

'Could be worse,' Mr Tanner said.

'Really?'

'Too right. Could've been from Sydney. So, now you know. And yes, the money'll come in handy, pay off a bit of the back rent. Maybe now my uncle Bolg and my auntie Freda won't come after me one dark night and tear out my ribcage with their fingers. Weight off my mind, that, though you never can tell with family. I'm just grateful it was Mum's side I pissed off. Dad's lot are a real load of bastards. But,' he went on, 'if you think for one moment that it makes us all square, no hard feelings, cards at Christmas and why don't we ask cousin Dennis round for a barbie on the lawn, forget it. Not going to happen.'

Frank bit his lip. A substantial part of his brain was still processing the goblin thing. What was left floundered in a pool of well-meaning guilt. 'I'm sorry you feel that way,' he said. 'If there's ever anything I can do—'

'Actually.' Mr Tanner leaned back in his chair and steepled his fingers. 'Actually,' he said, 'there is.'

'Really?'

'Sure.' Mr Tanner nodded. 'Piece of cake for you, as a matter of fact. Right up your alley. All you need to do is go back through that Door of yours to the day your old man was born, and cut his throat. Better still, save you all the mess and bother, go back a bit further and make sure his dad never met his mum, or they had a bloody great row or something. Then your dad wouldn't ever have happened, I'd still be a partner in JWW, and you wouldn't flaming well exist.' He grinned cheerfully. 'I don't call that a lot to ask, do you? And like I said, we're family.'

'I don't really think I could do that,' Frank said, in a very small voice. 'It'd be – well . . .'

'Doing the right thing, if you ask me. I expect your dad'd see it that way.'

'Yes,' Frank said. 'But I'm not him. Besides,' he added, 'that really would upset the fabric of reality and all that stuff. You said yourself, Dad saved the human race and things like that. If he hadn't—'

Mr Tanner waved his hand. 'It's all right,' he said, 'I didn't expect you'd agree. That's the thing about having a really low opinion of human nature, you aren't disappointed. No, you bugger off and enjoy yourself, don't worry about me. I'll get by somehow. I always have. And you told me yourself, you only prevent disasters and right wrongs if you're getting paid. Wouldn't want you working for free, that's not how we do things in the business. Talking of which,' he added with a yawn, 'you may have all the time in the world but I haven't, so unless there's anything else you want to talk about—'

'No, that's—' Frank stood up. 'It was, um—'

'Likewise,' said Mr Tanner.

'– Meeting you, and I really am very sorry. About all the fuss, I mean. And if ever there's anything *else* I can do; look, here's how you can get hold of me.' He took a card out of his pocket. Mr Tanner made no effort to take it, so Frank put it on the desk. 'Just leave a message with Mrs O'Brien, she, um.' He seemed to have run out of words. 'Well, cheers, then. I'll go now.'

His hand was on the door handle when Mr Tanner said; 'Just one other thing.'

He turned round quickly. 'Yes?'

'You've forgotten your dog.'

'Ah, right.' Frank sighed. 'Come on, Bobby – here, boy. Oh, you *stupid* animal—'

Three seconds of dead silence. Then Mr Tanner said: 'Don't worry about it, they needed replacing anyway. I'll just have to keep the window open for a day or two.'

The nastiest thing that anybody had ever done to his parents, Frank reflected as he left Mr Tanner's office, had been meant as an act of kindness. Typical; it had been the sort of present men would die for – quite a few had, over the years – but its only effect, apart from what it said on the tin, had been to make Mum and Dad utterly miserable. In fact, it had probably been the final straw that had prompted them to wall themselves up in their own separate and unreachable tangent of space-time. Good intentions, Mr Tanner had said. Well, quite. The six-lane super-highway to hell is paved, tarmacked, cat's-eyed, signposted, street-lit, hard-shouldered and contraflowed with good intentions. As a Carpenter, he didn't need some goblin to tell him that.

(Goblins, he thought. *Goblins*.)

It had been a Christmas present from Uncle Benny, the only one of his dad's old work colleagues who'd kept in touch. He only remembered him vaguely, as a short, terrifying man with a doormat beard, thick spectacles and a strange laugh. Dad had tried to tell him the backstory once, something about how Uncle Benny had helped him save Mum from the Queen of the Fey, whoever the hell she was. (Dad had tried to explain, but he'd tuned out. He'd only been six at the time.) Uncle Benny used to visit them for a while after he'd retired from the trade. But then he'd given them the present, and after that they'd made it clear, in their kind, tactful, extremely offensive way, that he wasn't welcome in their house any more.

What he'd given them (gruff, kind-hearted, *stupid* Uncle Benny) was the gift of eternal youth. It had come in a card-board box, Frank remembered, like the ones they package computer programs in. There were instructions inside, in seven languages, and a small brown bottle of pills. Mum and Dad had taken two each, after Mum had read the label carefully to make sure they didn't contain synthetic additives or GM ingredients. And that was that.

Irreversible, the leaflet said.

The problem was, Mum and Dad had never quite mastered the knack of being young. Youth hadn't fitted them: too tight in some places, baggy in others, and the sleeves came down to their knuckles. They knew it was something you were supposed to enjoy, a taste you were practically obliged to acquire, like alcohol or extra-mature cheese, and they'd done their conscientious best, but they'd failed, both of them. Middle age suited them much better. It had calmed them down, created a demilitarised zone in the middle of their frantic, hair-trigger relationship in which all the little misunderstandings and presumed slights and routine acts of thoughtlessness didn't really matter all that terribly much. Making them both seventeen again, for ever and ever and ever, was probably the cruellest thing anybody could have done to them. Silly Uncle Benny.

Frank hadn't mentioned any of that to Mr Tanner, though he was sure he'd have been interested. On reflection, that was shortsighted. Mr Tanner was, after all, the first real live magician he'd ever met (apart from Mum and Dad, of course, who didn't count). As such, he presumably knew about stuff like eternalyouth tablets. He'd know if they really were irreversible; and if so, whether there was some other stuff you could take that would override the effects. Frank had his doubts about that. Most likely, he reckoned, it'd be harder to get R&D funding for an elixir of eternal middle age. The point was, Mr Tanner would know if anybody did. If there wasn't one, maybe he could invent it. In return for money, of course, but that at least wouldn't be a problem. If he really could come up with something, some miracle cure that'd make the real world bearable again for his poor, abused parents – well, there was still the small matter of finding them, in a place where even the Portable Door couldn't go. One step at a time.

He looked both ways and crossed the road. Of course, if he did hire Mr Tanner, it might be an idea not to mention to him that it was Mum and Dad he wanted the stuff for. However strong a motivator money might be, Frank had a suspicion that it might not get the job done in this particular case.

Always assuming, of course, that Mr Tanner would agree to see him again. There was definitely a bit of unresolved hostility there. Not to mention what Bobby had done to his phone cables.

Goblins, he thought. *Goblins*.

Quick look over his shoulder, and then he slid the Door out of its tube, held it up against the hoarding, smoothed out the wrinkles with a practised sweep of his hand, and turned the doorknob. He winced as he stepped through, because it was raining on the other side. It always rained there, back home.

(Can the word *home* possibly have any meaning to someone with a Portable Door? Frank had reservations about that, too. The Door changed everything, or at least it turned all the straight lines and edges to jelly. He always went back to these precise coordinates in time and space, in spite of the horrible clammy rain, so presumably it was his home. Strange place to pick; strange moment. He had no idea why he'd chosen it.)

As he pulled the door to after him, he heard a shrill yap. He sighed. 'Come on, then, if you're coming,' he said wearily, and the dog hopped in over his feet, cringed as the raindrops hit the top of its head. He slammed the door and put it away.

On the other side, where a builder's hoarding had suddenly reverted to being blank and featureless, something moved in the gutter. At first it was no more than a trick of the light – or, properly speaking, its absence. Movement defined it, turning it from a vague black blur into a recognisable shape: the two-dimensional silhouette of a dog, complete with frantically wagging tail. After a moment, it sat – sideways, of course, since it couldn't do Up – and its raised head and eloquently expressive nose pointed at the place on the hoarding where the illusion of a door had briefly been. It waited, but the Door didn't come back. The shape of a front paw stretched like bubblegum across the pavement, met the wall and bent at right angles, grotesquely extended, carrying on up the hoarding to where the knob had been. It dabbed at the spot, but there wasn't anything there.

The shadow of a dog can't whimper, so it didn't. The paw shape retreated to the position it had started from. The shadow sat, alert and at attention, like a negative of the HMV symbol. As the hours wore on it moved a little, but only because the angle of the sun changed. It had no mind of its own, needless to say; even less of one than the animal in whose image it had been formed. But the shape knew how to sit, because it had been trained. On some level so obscure and complex that even the most brilliant quantum physicist couldn't begin to describe it, the shape vaguely remembered that there was a connection between sitting and little bits of chopped-up liver.

Concepts of loyalty and patience have no relevance in the context of a patch of concrete where photons can't reach because there's something in the way. Even so; there's a fair chance that it'd be there yet if the shadow of a woman hadn't strolled horizontally towards it, whistled and said, 'Here, boy.'

CHAPTER THREE.

She knew she'd come to the right address when she saw the young man. He was tethered to the reception desk by one of those plastic-covered bicycle chains, and the red glow of shame from his cheeks was bright enough to toast cheese.

'Excuse me,' she asked him, 'but is this Amalgamated Extrusions?'

The young man looked wretchedly at her and shuddered. ''Sright,' he mumbled.

She nodded. 'You're the sacrifice, aren't you?'

'Yes.'

She thought: traditionally it should be a young woman, but this is the twenty-first century. Did it make him feel any better to know that he was an equal-opportunities sacrifice? Probably not. Of course, it didn't say anywhere in the book of rules that the sacrifice had to be a *girl*. The only requirement was that it should be a vir—

'Soon have you out of there,' she said briskly. 'You just hang on, keep very still, and everything's going to be fine. Now, where can I find Mr O'Leary?'

He frowned. 'You're the whatsit? The, um—'

Oh dear. 'I'm from Carringtons,' she said. 'Emily Spitzer, pest control. Do you think you could ring through to Mr O'Leary and let him know I'm here?'

The young man whimpered softly. Emily looked at the security chain, and compared its length with the distance to the phone on the desk. 'No, obviously you can't,' she said. 'Do you happen to know his extension number?'

'Six,' the young man mumbled.

'Thanks.' Surely the whole point of a sacrifice was that it should be something you'll miss when it's gone; otherwise it's simply not entering into the spirit of the thing. She poked in the number. 'Mr O'Leary? Emily Spitzer, Carringtons. I'm in your front office.'

'About time.'

'Sorry?'

'I said, about time. I called your people two hours ago. That may be your idea of a prompt, efficient service, but it bloody well isn't mine.'

Mr O'Leary wasn't to know, because he was sitting in his office six floors up. If he'd been down in reception, the look on Emily's face would've told him that he'd just done a very silly thing; on a par with walking up to a group of off-duty paratroopers in a pub just before closing time and asking them why they were wearing those poncy little red hats. 'So sorry, Mr O'Leary,' she said sweetly, 'I got here as soon as I could. If you could just switch on the system, I can get started.'

The phone went dead. She put the receiver back, stepped away from the desk and turned to face the ventilation grille in the wall. Somewhere far away, a fan began to spin. Emily unzipped her bag and counted under her breath.

She'd got as far as six when the plasterboard surrounding the grille exploded into dust and rubble, and something really rather horrible burst out of the ventilation shaft, hung in the air for a moment, and slithered down from the hole onto the desk.

It's just as well that hydras are mythical creatures and don't really exist. If there really were such things, mankind would have to find a way of coping with a species of giant snake, nearly five times longer and thicker than an anaconda or a boring old boa constrictor, and equipped with somewhere between forty and a hundred heads, each attached to the main trunk by a separate neck, the way grapes connect to the bunch. The number of heads would vary because if you were misguided enough to try and kill the wretched thing by cutting off a head, two more would instantly sprout in its place. Luckily for the human race, the hydra is just a dark-age myth, symbolising winter or redwater fever in livestock, or possibly the kind of problem that just gets worse when you try and solve it.

The sacrifice squealed and started tugging frantically at the lock-up chain, which was only looped round the leg of the desk. 'Keep still!' Emily snapped. It was fortunate that the sacrifice was the kind of young man who's far more scared of girls than he is of ferocious mythical monsters. He did as he was told.

The trick is, of course, to attack strengths, not weaknesses.

Emily popped the lid off the aerosol spray and lifted it. The hydra was holding perfectly still, waiting for her to come within striking range. Mythical or not, it was a snake, capable of moving blindingly fast, inherently practical enough not to waste its energy on a non-viable target. Stay six feet away and you're safe. Five feet, and you're a paragraph in the obituaries column in the trade paper.

Calmly, because hydras are very good indeed at picking up on fear, Emily shook the can. The rattle of the little ball-bearing was disconcertingly loud in the dead silence.

Only a mug tries to deal with an enemy that has an average of seventy self-replicating heads by pruning it. A sensible and experienced person, a professional, takes the view that seventy heads means a hundred and forty eyes, and that her best friend is therefore her spray-can of Mace.

'I suggest you shut your eyes,' Emily told the sacrifice. She couldn't look round to see if he'd obeyed, because of the need to maintain eye contact with the hydra. (Try it sometime, by the way: a ratio of seventy to one. Keep it up for more than ten seconds and you'll completely redefine your concept of headaches.) Very gradually she lifted the can until the nozzle was level with the approximate centre of the thicket of heads.

Schedule D to Section 34 (a) of the Endangered Monsters (Conservation) Order 1998 requires that once a hydra has been blinded with an approved spray (as defined in Schedule D part 2, paragraph (D) (iv) (3)), it's the responsibility of the licensed control practitioner to immobilise it as quickly as possible with a permitted tranquilliser administered by injection or intravenous drip. The hydra should then be removed within two hours (three hours in Wales, Northern Ireland and the Isle of Man) to a holding pen constructed in accordance with the specifications set out in Schedule E part 6, to await relocation to a designated hydra reserve. The only exception provided for in the regulations is bona fide scientific or medical research; in which case, it's permitted to pump twenty ccs of liquid SlayMore into it and hide behind a pillar until it's stopped thrashing about. The pest-control department of Carringtons is on record as being engaged in a long-term research project into hydra toxicology. Their aim is to find out how much SlayMore it takes to kill the buggers and, as far as they're concerned, if you want to end up with good science there's no such thing as too much data.

'It's all right,' Emily said, peering round the edge of the pillar. 'You can open your eyes now.'

'Is it—'

'Yes.'

'Oh.'

It wasn't fair, she told herself, to expect ordinary normal people to be brave. There's a good reason why fear is included in the package of software bundled with every new human being, and a world full of heroes simply wouldn't function. Even so. It'd be nice, one of these days, to meet a civilian who didn't faint or freeze or wet himself while she was in action. For one thing, it'd imply that he trusted her to do her job. Somehow, she couldn't help thinking it'd be different if it had been Ricky Wurmtoter or Kurt Lundkvist or Christian Macdonald wielding the Mace can and the big syringe. That said, there was no call to go taking out her sense of general grievance on the public.

'It's all right,' she said, in her best approximation to a calm, soothing voice. 'I know it was scary and horrid, but it's all over now and for crying out loud stop that ridiculous snivelling.'

(For the record, Emily'd had seven boyfriends, none of them for long. The most recent had been a six-foot-eight rugby international. She hadn't been particularly surprised to discover that he was terrified of spiders in the bath.)

She rang Mr O'Leary.

'All done,' she said crisply. 'Clean-up'll be along in about an hour. Don't let anybody touch anything till they've gone if you value your no-claims. Oh, and you'd better get someone down here with the key to the bike lock. And some Dettol and a sponge.'

I'm probably not a very nice person, Emily reflected as she rattled back to the office on the Tube. A nice person would've have drawn that poor boy's little accident to the attention of his ignorant pig of an office manager. And it's all very well to say that a nice person wouldn't be in this line of business, but does that necessarily follow, or am I only saying it because I'm not nice?

She shook herself like a wet dog. Niceness, she decided, wasn't everything. The lad chained to the desk was probably extremely nice and, if she was honest with herself, she found it hard to believe that he and she belonged to the same species.

Emily filled in the operations report and the travel expenses voucher and attached them to her time-sheet with a paperclip. Wednesday; on Wednesdays she usually had lunch with Marcia and Jane from Snettertons at the pizza place in the Strand, but Marcia was on holiday and she couldn't stand Jane if Marcia wasn't there to hold her lead. Am I *really* not a very nice person? she wondered. Surely not. I have friends – Jane, Marcia . . . (It occurred to her that she didn't actually like either of them very much: one was a bitch and the other was *silly*, that particular blend of calculating frivolity that made you feel uncomfortable all the time. There was something gritty and sharp-eyed about Marcia when she was being silly. She was as sinister as a clown.)

All right, she conceded to herself. I may not like my friends very much, but my friends like me. They couldn't like me if I wasn't basically a nice person. I have redeeming qualities. I'm calm, level-headed, sensible, honest, realistic. I tell it how it is. I don't muck about. I have standards.

She played that last bit back. Dear God, she thought.

Not that it mattered. Emily'd known way back in college that if she intended to make a career for herself in pest control she was going to have to be single-minded about it. There would be sacrifices. (Suddenly she thought of the skinny young man standing on his patch of damp carpet. She smiled.) In pest control, all work and no play meant you might just stand a chance of staying alive long enough to get your money's worth out of a month's rent paid in advance. If you were really diligent, committed, focused and determined, you might even contrive to get the job done and still have your licence at the end of it, in spite of the vast accumulation of brain-pulping Byzantine regulations that you had to comply with in order to slay monsters *legally*. That kind of commitment didn't leave much time for anything else. There was even a saying in the trade: you can't get a life and take one too.

Eight years of that sort of thinking does things to a person. These days, if she had a feminine side, it was probably the Goddess in her aspect as Kali the Destroyer.

Which reminded her: credit-control meeting with Dave Hook at three-fifteen. Bugger. My cup runneth over, Emily thought, and little dribbles are trickling down inside my sleeve.

Dragons can burn you or flay you alive with their claws. Manticores can shred your face with a flick of their tongues; harpies excel at fly-by scalpings, and their prehensile, six-fingered tails can slice the top of your head off like a boiled egg and dip soldiers in your brain. All Dave Hook could do was look at you and go 'Tut.'

I'm brave, Emily thought. Really I am. But the little voice in her head said: no, you aren't, not really. Bravery is defined as facing up to the things that really scare you. Monsters can kill you, but this man can take away your *job*.

Mr Hook put down the spreadsheet, looked at Emily over the top of his glasses, and frowned. 'Tut,' he said. She winced.

'You're doing the work,' he said. 'No question about that. Everything bang up to date. First-class turnaround time. Outstanding feedback from the clients. But those bills just aren't getting sent out, are they?'

'No. Um.'

'We're in this business to make money, after all.'

'Um.'

'There's no point doing the work if we don't get paid for it, is there?'

'Um.'

Mr Hook sighed, and glanced sideways at the framed photograph on his desk. Mr Hook never ever talked about his family, but the woman in the picture was twenty years younger than him and looked as though she'd just stepped off a catwalk. There was also a small nondescript female child, and a dog. 'It seems to me,' he said, 'that we've had this conversation before. Isn't that right?'

'Mm.'

'I have an idea that last time you promised me you'd make a real effort to get the invoices written up and sent out on time.' Pause. His eyes were eating into Emily's soul like shipworms gnawing a keel in the middle of the Sargasso Sea. 'That is what we agreed, isn't it?'

'M.'

'Sorry, I didn't quite catch—'

'Yes. Only,' Emily added quickly, in a teeny-tiny voice that made her sound about the same age as the kid in the photograph, 'there's been ever such a lot to do this month, and I try and keep on top of the paperwork, but it's not always easy, and I get confused about what's zero-rated for VAT and what isn't, and every time I sit down and try and do the apportionments the phone always rings and it's someone with a dragon or a chimera or something and you can't keep the clients waiting, and by the time I get back to the office it's been driven right out of my head, and . . .'

Her words tailed off, like the last few drips from a punctured water-bottle in the desert. Mr Hook looked at her. 'Sorry,' she said.

Those eyes: like those of a crucified spaniel. 'Sorry really isn't good enough, though, is it?'

'N.'

'We really are going to have to buck our ideas up, aren't we?'

'M.'

'This time, when we promise faithfully that we're going to try and do better, we're going to have to mean it, aren't we?'

'Mwf.'

Pause. Oh God, Emily thought, he's about to be nice. I can't stand it when he's nice. It's like having your raw soul scoured with a wire brush.

'I do understand, really,' said Mr Hook. 'You're a hard-working, dedicated young woman who never gives less than a hundred and ten per cent. The profession isn't just a job of work to you, it's a passion. I think that's wonderful, I genuinely do. But.' He stopped and looked at her; that how-do-you-solve-a-problem-like-Maria look that made her feel – that was the wicked, cruel, unbearable thing about Mr Hook's eyes. He could make her feel *sweet*. When his eyes latched on to her like that, suddenly she was a twelve-year-old girl who'd handed in twenty sides of homework that still didn't manage to answer the question. He made her feel like she was playing at the job, indulging herself, instead of doing what she was paid for. Of course, if they'd hired a *man*—

'Now then,' said Mr Hook. 'We really have got to sort this out, haven't we? I'm going to give you one last chance. Bills properly drawn up, sent in on time, credit-control procedures carried out properly. You know you can do it if you try. After all, you're a highly intelligent girl, and it's just paperwork. If you're having trouble with the VAT apportionments, get Clive or Sarah to help you – I'm sure they'll be only too happy to show you how to do it. Get into the habit of setting aside a little bit of time every day – an hour and a half should be plenty – to really get a grip on those invoices and time-sheets and yellow slips. Talking of which, I gather we've been a bit careless about filling out stores requisitions, haven't we?'

Emily nodded. Left undone those things which we ought to have done, and there is no health in us.

'I really don't want to make a big issue out of this,' said Mr Hook, concentrating a billion megawatts of disapproval into the pinpoint lasers of his eyes, 'but we really can't go on just taking stuff out of the stores without signing for it. Let's see, now: twelve kilos of SlayMore, seven packets of detonators, nine boxes of rubber bands, three blocks of Semtex ... It's not just the materials themselves, it's the time and effort it takes to get the books straight at the end of the month, and then of course we've got the licensing and the HSE inspections, and it's getting really rather awkward trying to account for the discrepancies. It may seem like a lot of fuss to you, but it's costing us a lot of money and causing some serious difficulties for us with the authorities, just because you can't be bothered to fill in a few forms and write things down in the book. You do see that, don't you?'

That was, of course, the worst part of it. Emily *could* see. When she thought about it calmly, once the red mist had lifted and the urge to kill and kill and keep on killing had dissipated enough to let her brain start working again, she understood perfectly. Nobody in their right mind would slay monsters for fun; we do it for the money, and we don't get paid unless we send out a bill. And yes, of course we have to keep the stock books and the registers straight, if we don't want the health and safety people and the DEFRA bogies coming down on us like a ton of bricks. Hardly rocket science. It was just—

She slammed into her office, threw her bag at the wall, crashed into her chair and did the long, silent scream. Once upon a time, she could clear her mind just by imagining Mr Hook being torn apart by goblins, but that didn't work any more. No matter how vividly she pictured the scene, these days she tended to see the severed head's lips move and hear the calm, sad voice saying, '*But you know I'm right, don't you?*' And yes, he was. Right, right, right. And yes, you can't eat unless you do the washing-up first, and her room would be so much more comfortable if she tidied it occasionally and yes, she'd be able to find things if they weren't all piled up on the floor in a heap; and yes, they'd have been much better off if they'd hired a man to do her job, even if he'd been useless and she was the best damn dragonslayer in London and quite possibly the whole of Europe; and yes, of course she'd do it all, every invoice and yellow slip and stationery requisition voucher, if only he'd bloody well stop telling her to—

It's me, isn't it? Emily thought. I just don't like doing as I'm told. How silly is that? And I get really angry when people don't do what I tell them, because it's *stupid*. If I say, don't go in there, it's dangerous, and they don't listen and they come out covered in boils or a different species, of course I'm bloody furious, because how could anybody be so dumb? But for some reason, when it's me—

Deep breathing. Calm. Inner peace. And when I've done that, I'll go out and kill something big and scary with enormous teeth, and that'll make me feel better. It always does. Query: would I be able to motivate myself to do this job if I didn't have Dave Hook? Good question. Don't go there.

Emily took a deep breath. It didn't work. She took another, and six more, and one more for luck. Then she got up, dragged an armful of files out of the cabinet, dumped them on the desk and reached for her calculator.

Sodding apportionments. Slaying monsters was zero rated, but you had to charge VAT on materials used (apart from safety equipment and books); and anything that habitually stood upright on two legs – vampires, zombies; orcs, goblins and balrogs were a bit of a grey area – was classed as humanoid and didn't count as a monster for VAT purposes, which meant it had to be charged for. Werewolves were a complete pain: generally speaking they were quadrupeds when you killed them, but they reverted to human shape in the split second before they died, which meant you had to add VAT at 8.75% unless you killed them with a slow-acting poison such as silver nitrate, in which case the rate decreased from 17.5% by one percentage point per day for the period between the first administration of the poison and the actual date of death. And as for shape-shifters—

The phone rang. Emily whimpered and picked it up.

'Mr Gomez for you.'

'What? Oh, right. Put him on.'

Click, pause; then: 'Emily?'

'Yes.'

'Job for you.'

Naturally. Like bloody magic. The moment she picked up a calculator, someone had a job for her.

'Can it wait? Only I've got mounds and mounds of paper-work, and—'

'Emergency,' Colin said. 'I'm at the client's place now, as a matter of fact. Actually,' he added, lowering his voice a little, 'it's the client's mother-in-law. You know Stan Lazek, don't you?'

'No. Who the hell is—?'

'CEO of Dragoman Software Solutions.'

'Oh.' Yes, definitely an emergency, in that case. 'What seems to be the—?'

'Can't talk now,' Colin interrupted. 'Just get over here quick as you can. It's at—' He gave her an address in one of the more opulent west London suburbs. Emily jotted it down on the near-est file cover.

'Look,' she said, 'you need to tell me what it is so I'll know what stuff to bring. Like, if it's harpies I'll just want SlayMore, but if it's a thirty-foot-high one-eyed giant I'll need the 105mm recoilless rifle—'

'Don't worry about that. They've got everything you'll need right here.'

'Yes, but—'

Click. Buzz. *Bastard.*

Colin Gomez was intellectual property, entertainment and media, so it was only to be expected that his grip on reality was one fingertip hooked over the edge of a very tall cliff. Even so. If there was one thing that really annoyed Emily, it was a complete lack of consideration for other people.

Everything you'll need right here. Yeah, sure. But just in case—

She slid open the top drawer of her desk and took out a little canvas pouch. She held it for a moment before dropping it in her bag, as if drawing strength from it. Then she scribbled a note to say where was going, and left the room.

At least, with Dragoman footing the bill, she could take a taxi rather than battling over there on the Tube. As the Embankment shuffled smoothly by outside the taxi window, Emily closed her eyes and tried to figure out what she'd be most likely to find when she got there. Of course, if it was an entertainment-and-media job, there was absolutely no way of knowing. E&M magic was typically flamboyant, wide-dispersal and highly temperamental. If a reality-fiction interface had blown, for example, you could be up against any bloody thing: dinosaurs, skyscraper-climbing gorillas, space aliens, you name it, those cowboys in E&M could contrive a way of getting it over the line and letting it get away from them. A faulty glamour was just as bad. A year or so back, some pinhead in media R&D had developed a sort of cap thing that turned the wearer into whatever he truly wanted to be. Marvellous idea in theory, but if you're going to make stuff like that you really can't go cutting costs at the production stage. If you do, sooner or later something's going to jam, some poor bugger's going to stick like it, and suddenly you've got a junior Home Office minister swooping low over Whitehall on a thirty-foot wingspan shooting out jets of green fire from both nostrils. And Colin reckoned they'd got everything she'd need right there. Absolutely.

Which was why she'd brought the Lifesaver, otherwise known as the Mordor Army Knife. Strictly speaking, she wasn't really supposed to have one, since it had been made in the forges of the Dark Lord and counted as an instrument of darkness. But it had *everything*. As well as the usual penknife, screwdriver, bottle-opener and combination wire-stripper and fingernail-breaker, there was a siege tower, a battering ram, a folding heliograph, a scaling ladder, a high-velocity ballista capable of knocking holes through ten feet of solid rock, a caltrop dispenser, a six-dragon-power welding torch and a pair of scissors that you could actually cut things with. Furthermore, it didn't belong to the firm. It was her very own, which meant she didn't have to write out three pink chits and a yellow requisition every time she wanted to use it.

'Pull up at the top of the road,' Emily told the driver. 'I'll walk the rest of the way.'

An important lesson, one she'd learned the hard way. Unless you know exactly what's waiting for you at the other end, don't jump straight out of a cab and onto ground zero. There're all sorts of things you notice from a hundred yards away that might escape your attention if you're too close. wrecked cars, burning trees, a six-ton adult gryphon perched on a neighbouring rooftop. As she walked slowly and quietly down Chesterton Drive, however, there didn't appear to be anything to see, and her feather-edged professional intuition wasn't picking up anything in the way of bad vibes. She could always tell when something was wrong; but here, everything seemed to be exactly as it should have been. In which case—

You know you're a professional when the hairs on the back of your neck start to crawl precisely because everything feels *right*.

She rang the doorbell: Big Ben chimes, which set her teeth on edge. An elderly woman in an Edinburgh Woollen Mills cardigan opened the door and smiled at her.

'Yes, dear?'

Emily frowned. 'I'm sorry,' she said, 'I think I've come to the wrong house. Only—'

Behind the woman, Colin suddenly materialised. He was one of those men who manage to be very tall without achieving anything in the way of stature. 'There you are,' he said, in a voice that suggested that he'd had a long and uncalled-for day. 'I was wondering where you could've got to. This is Mrs Thompson. This is Emily Spitzer, who works with me at the office. Now, if you'll excuse me, I'd better be making tracks. Clients coming in at four-thirty, mustn't keep them waiting.'

Colin slipped past Mrs Thompson and disappeared up the path in a sort of coherent blur. He was just in time to catch up the taxi she'd arrived in. E&M people could do that sort of thing. It was very impressive, until you realised that it was no more than the power of applied arrogance, harnessed through a few simple focusing techniques. If you sincerely believed the world was there entirely for your convenience and you knew the magic words, more often than not it turned out that you were right.

Bastard, she thought. He could at least have hung around long enough to brief her on what needed doing, instead of leaving her to extract the information slowly and tactfully from someone who was quite definitely The Public. She hated all that: trying to explain things in terms that lay people could understand, and which wouldn't blow their minds. She took a deep breath.

'What seems to be the problem?' she said.

'What, dear? Oh yes. It's Barney.'

'Barney.'

'My cat.'

'Your—'

'Didn't Mr Gomez explain? Poor Barney's got himself stuck in the apple tree in the back garden, and I'm so worried he might fall out and hurt himself.'

For perhaps as long as a second and a half, the world seemed to flicker. At first it felt as though nothing was real, as though Emily was standing in the void waiting for the Creator to turn up. And then there was anger.

'Your cat's stuck up a tree,' she said.

'That's right, yes. Now, Mr Wilcox at number sixteen's got a ladder, but he may have gone out, it's his day at the clinic, but Mrs Palladio at number twelve might have one, only I don't know her terribly well, she only moved in a few months ago. Or I suppose you could try John at number twenty-four—'

'Excuse me.'

'Yes, dear?'

And then she thought: no. I don't destroy old ladies, even old ladies with cats, because in the final analysis they aren't the real enemy. I shall be as nice as I possibly can to the old bat, I might even rescue her bloody cat, and every precisely quantified milligram of niceness I expend on her will be another red-hot skewer with barbed wire wrapped round it when I get back to the office and see Colin—

Emily smiled.

'That's all right,' she said. 'You just leave it to me and everything'll be just fine.'

Mrs Thompson pursed her lips. 'Are you sure? Because—'

You can read eyes after a year or two in the profession. *Because, after all, you're only a girl, I'd have thought Mr Gomez would've got a man to do it, after all, climbing up ladders* – Emily broadened her smile. All the king's horses, Colin, she thought, and all the king's men. 'Why don't you show me where the tree is and then go and make us both a nice cup of tea?'

That must've been the right thing to say, because Mrs Thompson nodded and led the way through the house and into the back garden. There, sure enough, was an apple tree, with a fat ginger blob sticking like used chewing-gum to one of the spindly upper branches.

'You sure you don't want to borrow Mr Wilcox's ladder, dear?'

'No, I'll be fine. Now, how about that cup of tea? This won't take a moment.'

'You will be careful, won't you? Only Barney can be a little bit wary of strangers.'

Emily waited till the back door was safely shut; then she took the Mordor Army Knife out of her bag, thumbed out the scaling-ladder attachment, dropped it on the ground and jumped back.

She didn't know how it worked, and couldn't have cared less, but she'd learned the hard way to give it plenty of room. The little metal thing like a comb which she'd hooked out of the body of the knife seemed to blur for a moment, as though it had gone out of focus. When it resolved itself again, it was a twenty-foot aluminium ladder. She frowned at it and said, 'Shorter.' The adjustment was instantaneous. When she picked the ladder up it was warm, just about bearable to the touch. She leaned it against the nearest substantial branch to where the cat was, wiggled it about a bit to check it was stable, and began to climb.

'Here, kitty,' she said through gritted teeth. She wasn't a cat person, in the same way petrol doesn't have a soft spot for naked flames. The cat, which was licking its paw, lifted its head and looked at her.

'Don't start,' she said grimly. The cat's left ear flickered. She felt her tights catch on a projecting twig. Colin Gomez, she promised herself, was going to spend the rest of his abbreviated life paying for this.

Three more rungs and Emily reckoned she was in comfortable grabbing range. She put together a plan of action. Left hand off rung, reach out, form grip on cat's collar, secure cat firmly under left arm, then back the way we came. No bother. The key to success would be smooth, controlled movements.

The cat hissed at her and stood up, its tail stiff and straight as a pine tree. At this point, it occurred to her that all her training and experience had been directed towards killing animals rather than saving them; which was fine, bearing in mind the sort of animal she tended to deal with, but maybe in this case she was a trifle out of her depth. She glanced over her shoulder to see if Mrs Thompson had emerged from the house; no sign of her, and she wouldn't be able to see what was going on up the tree from her kitchen window. She grinned.

'Go on,' she said, 'make my day.'

The cat made a growling noise that it had inherited from ancestors who hunted mammoths for a living, and edged a little further along its branch. Emily recognised the tactic: deliberately fall off, get yourself killed, land me in serious trouble with your owner, the feline equivalent of suicide bombing. All domestic animals are terrorists at heart. The secret is, never negotiate.

'Go on, then,' she said to the cat. 'You fall off if you want to.

I've got reflexes like a snake – I'll catch you by your tail or something, it'll hurt like hell and I'll have *won*. Or you can hold still, we can go back down together in comfort, and then I can go back to the office and make Colin Gomez eat his own legs. You decide. Your choice. Oh and by the way, the Knife's got a built-in safety field extending three feet in all directions from its base, so even if I miss you, you'll just bounce. So go for the big gesture if you want to, but it won't do you any good.'

When you talk to animals it's all in the tone of voice. The cat gave Emily a look of quiet disgust and walked calmly along the branch until it was well outside her reach. Then it made a sort of chirruping noise and started washing its ear with the back of its paw.

Emily sighed. You don't negotiate, and when they raise the stakes you don't back down. Carefully she took one foot off the ladder and pawed the empty air until she felt something reasonably solid under her sole. Gradually she applied weight to it until she was satisfied it wasn't going to break off, and repeated the procedure with her other foot. It was, she realised, a bit like going after nesting harpies in a bell tower, except that there was a better choice of footholds and she wasn't burdened with cumbersome heavy weapons. On the other hand, there was plenty of tree left for the cat to move to. She thought about the Knife's safety field; she knew it was there because she'd read about it in the owner's guide, but she'd never actually had occasion to put it to the test. How high up was she, exactly? Twelve feet? Fifteen?

She thought of something else she could say to Colin Gomez, and the thought gave her the strength to proceed. Equalising her weight on both feet, she reached out towards the cat's neck. It was only a few inches from her hand. She reached a little further and felt her elbow brush against a branch.

There was a click, like a door opening.

The tree disappeared.

Fifteen feet up in the air, with nothing to hold on to except an absence of tree. Don't try this at home. You could do yourself a mischief.

Half a second later, the tree was back again, pretty much exactly as it had been – it had rotated through something like six degrees clockwise, which was an acceptable margin. Too late, of course, to do Emily any good, at a speed of thirty-two feet per second per second. The last thing she heard was her own neck snapping.

A full two seconds later, the cat shimmered back into existence on its branch. It arched its back, yawned and scampered down the trunk, landing neatly and comfortably next to Emily's outstretched left arm. Sniff, sniff; nothing to smell here, folks. With a slight wave of its tail, it walked lazily towards the back door and slid through the cat flap.

CHAPTER FOUR

Mr Sprague sighed deeply, put the file down on his desk and rang through to his secretary. 'Hello,' he said, 'please put a message through to Frank Carpenter. You'll find the contact details in—'

A shadow fell on Mr Sprague's face. He looked up.

'Twice in one week,' Frank said. 'That's unusual.'

Mr Sprague closed his eyes and slowly opened them. '*Please* don't do that,' he said. 'You know I find it extremely disconcerting.'

Frank shrugged. 'Sorry,' he said. 'From that, I take it that you haven't actually sent for me yet.'

'No. I was just about to—'

'Ah. Slight miscalculation, then.' Frank closed the Door, caught it as it slid off the wall, rolling itself up as it went, and tucked it into its cardboard tube. 'It isn't easy, you know, plotting these things to the exact moment. Anyhow, I got your message – well, obviously I did. And the file.'

He was holding a green wallet folder. Mr Sprague tried not to look at an identical folder sitting on his desk; identical, that was, apart from the fact that the version Frank was holding contained a ten-page briefing document that hadn't been dictated or typed out yet. It was things like that, Mr Sprague decided, that made him question the wisdom of hiring Frank Carpenter: little things that get lodged under the dental plate of the unconscious mind, long after the big, vague issues have been chewed over and swallowed.

'That's all right, then,' Mr Sprague said. 'So you know the background?'

Frank nodded. 'Actually,' he said, 'there's a few things about it that seem a bit fishy to me. Not that it matters, I suppose, if I'm going to make it so that it never happened.'

'Fishy?'

'Well, I thought so. I mean, think about it for a moment.' Frank was hovering next to a chair. He never sat down unless invited. Mr Sprague nodded, and Frank took a seat. Somehow, every chair Frank sat in seemed to fit him *exactly*. 'There's this woman, right? She's a professional pest controller, monster hunter, whatever you choose to call it. Did you know my dad was one of those, by the way, when he was in the trade? Wasn't terribly good at it, so he said. Only ever killed one dragon, and that was by sitting on the poor thing, by accident. Anyhow . . .'

'Your father was in the—?'

'Didn't I mention it? Oh yes. Aeons ago, back in the – sorry, about three years ago. J. W. Wells & Co. They've gone bust since then. Anyhow, that's beside the point. She's a professional dragon-slayer, so you'd think she'd be fairly – well, agile, fit, good at climbing things, you know? And then she gets herself killed, falling out of a tree, trying to rescue some old dear's cat.'

'Accidents happen,' Mr Sprague said, with feeling.

'Maybe,' Frank said. 'But I remember some of the stories Dad used to tell me about his old boss, Ricky something. Quite the action hero, always jumping out of windows and scaling tall buildings and stuff. I can't imagine him falling out of a tree.'

Mr Sprague frowned. 'Never heard of him,' he said. 'I don't know, maybe she got overconfident and careless. Showing off. To be honest with you, I'm not all that concerned about how it happened or why. All that concerns me is that her employers had her insured for eleven million pounds, which I'm going to have to pay unless you can go back and stop it happening. Not the most challenging assignment I've given you, I wouldn't have thought.'

'Fine.' Frank held up a conciliatory hand. 'None of my business, I entirely agree. You just leave it with me and I'll see what I can do.'

Mr Sprague sighed. A great many things about Frank Carpenter irritated him unbearably, but so far he'd never failed to complete an assignment. Nine point nine million pounds which would otherwise have drifted out of his life like lost orphan lambs weren't likely to be going anywhere after all. Mr Sprague arranged his face in a tolerably close imitation of a smile.

'Splendid,' he said. 'Usual terms, of course.'

'Um,' Frank said.

Mr Sprague knew all about that Um. It meant Frank was about to make difficulties. 'Was there something?' he said.

'Well, yes.' Frank got so coy when he was about to ask for more money. 'Thing is – well, you know that before I do a job I run the projections; just to make sure I won't alter history and start a war or cause a plague epidemic or anything.'

Mr Sprague nodded. 'What about it?'

Frank clicked his tongue. Mr Sprague was familiar with that one, too. It was generally even more expensive than an *Um*. 'Well – actually, it's all a bit technical, really. All to do with, um, magic and things.'

'Oh.'

'Because she's a – well, because she's in the trade. You see, tracking component variables and extrapolating data for my projections, it's all based on the assumption that, well, people are *normal*. Normalish, anyhow. I mean, they've got to be a bit different or they wouldn't try overtaking on the inside at ninety miles an hour or nipping behind the bulk-hydrogen tanks for a quick smoke and all the funny little things that people do. But stupidity's perfectly normal. I mean, it's a defining characteristic of the species, so it's dead easy to allow for it in the synthetic projection matrix.'

Mr Sprague looked at him. 'The what?'

Frank flushed slightly. 'Oh,' he said, 'sort of maths stuff. You don't need to bother about it.'

'I happen to have a doctorate in pure mathematics from the Sorbonne,' Mr Sprague said frostily. 'But I don't seem to remember anything called a synthetic—'

'Synthetic projection matrix?'

'That's it. Of course,' he added, 'my attention might have been wandering at that point in the lecture, or maybe I was in bed with a cold or something. Unlikely, though.'

Frank's ears were glowing pink. 'Actually,' he said, 'I don't think it's been discovered yet. In fact, I know it hasn't because it's, um, one of mine. Little something I knocked up so that I could do these projections, you see.'

'I see – *one* of yours?'

''Fraid so. Started off as something I had to deal with to get the simulations up and running, turned into a bit of a hobby. In fact, I only just missed out on the Nobel prize the year before I – in twenty years' time. Pipped to the post by a very clever old bloke from Malaysia – would you believe he's managed to calculate the square root of—' He hesitated. 'Um,' he said. 'Better not go into that, might be letting the cat out of the bag. Anyway. Yes, I like to dabble a bit here and there. I got algorhythm, you might say.' He frowned. 'Sorry, what were we—? Oh yes. People in the trade. Point is, they're bloody hard to plot. They keep nipping in and out of alternative realities and post-sequential subordinate time-lines and all sorts of aggravating stuff like that. Makes tracking them a bit like catching a gnat with a butterfly net. And the bottom line is, lots more sums to do. Which means lots more work, which in turn calls for—'

He didn't say *lots more money*, because it wasn't necessary. Mr Sprague pulled a sad face. 'What did you have in mind?' he said.

Frank shifted uncomfortably. 'Would twenty per cent be really greedy?' he said. 'Only, I'll probably have to invent a whole new methodology for calibrating the self-cancelling resonances, plus I'll need to do all the calculations in base eight and base twelve as well as base ten, because of the – because of a lot of stuff that I'd better not tell you about, because if it gets discovered before the next US presidential election, there's likely to be this sort of global-holocaust thing, so you're just going to have to—'

'Thirteen.'

'Fifteen.'

'Agreed,' said Mr Sprague; and then he added, 'Base *eight*?'

'You really do need to forget I said that. Just think,' Frank added, with rather more cunning than he'd have credited himself with, 'of all the insurance claims there'd be if Plymouth got wiped off the map by a cryomolecular bomb.'

'Cryo—' Mr Sprague's eyebrows disappeared into his hair. 'Oh,' he said. 'Fine. Fifteen per cent, then. After all,' he added, with a mild shudder, 'it's not as though I have a choice.'

'Not if the poor woman's already dead,' Frank said sympathetically. 'Forces your hand rather, I can see that. And I promise, it really is just because of the extra calculations. I mean, for the run-of-the-mill jobs, I've always considered ten per cent is more than fair. Anyhow, there it is. Sorry.'

Mr Sprague sighed. 'It's a deal, then,' he said. 'I'll look forward to—' He stopped. He'd just noticed something. 'No dog today, then?'

Frank nodded. 'Actually,' he said, lowering his voice to a whisper, 'I think I may have given the wretched thing the slip.'

'Oh. You mean – I thought you *liked*—'

'Me?' Frank shook his head industriously. 'Not a bit of it. Don't like dogs, and as a general rule dogs don't like me. Usually it's ears back and deep growling as soon as they clap eyes on me. Which is fine,' he added. 'Nothing harder than trying to be friends with someone you can't stand just because *they* happen to like *you*, and even more so with bloody dogs. Mind you, he's wandered off before, and just when I think it's safe and I can carry on with my life, I go through the Door and there he is, curled up on the other side and *waiting* for me, you know, the way they do.'

Mr Sprague grinned unpleasantly. 'You'll miss him,' he said.

'No chance,' Frank said quickly. 'Doglessness means not having to go around with a pocketful of plastic bags, not to mention eating food that hasn't got a wet, snuffly nose in it. You know what? For the first time in ages, I feel like I really have a *future*.'

Mr Sprague nodded. 'You more than most people. Several, in fact.'

Frank smiled bleakly. 'Time-travel jokes,' he said. 'When I retire, I'm going to put them all in a book, provided there's still enough rainforest left to provide that much paper. Anyhow, mustn't keep you, I know you're a busy man. Although,' he added, grinning faintly, 'by the time I meet you again, this little chat won't have happened, so I needn't feel quite so guilty about it. Be seeing—'

'Hold on,' Mr Sprague said, frowning as an unpleasant thought occurred to him. 'What you just said. Does that mean – well, does it mean there's great chunks of my life, when I'm talking to you, or working on cases that you end up making never happen . . .' His mouth was unaccountably dry, though he did his best not to let it show. 'What I mean is, what *happens* to them? And what about the man who's talking to you right now? Do I get, well, *rewound* or something, and then recorded over after you've—?'

Frank beamed at him. 'You know,' he said cheerfully, 'you always ask me that. Cheerio.'

The Door opened in a red-brick wall in a dusty courtyard shaded from the oppressive sun by an ancient fig tree. It disturbed the concentration of a big stocky man with a long grey beard as he sat under the tree sketching a design for some sort of machine. He looked up, recognised Frank Carpenter and nodded.

'How's it coming?' Frank said, in a somewhat archaic dialect of Italian, although of course the words had been modern English when he framed them in his mind. One of the things he loved about the Door was its attention to detail.

'Bloody thing,' the man replied. 'I mean, birds don't have this problem. They just hop off the edge of the nest and it *happens*. They don't have to give themselves headaches figuring out surface-to-weight ratios.' As he spoke, he was doodling a man's head in the margin. 'The way I see it, if God had meant us to fly he'd have given us—'

'Imagination,' Frank said. 'And a pair of opposable thumbs. Stick at it and you'll get there in the end, you'll see.'

The man glanced down at his piece of paper, then looked up. There was a faint gleam of cunning behind his eyes. 'Of course,' he said, 'you know all about this stuff, where you come from.'

'*When* I come from,' Frank corrected him. 'And yes, *we* know, but *I* don't, if you follow me. Specialisation, it's the curse of our age. Whereas your lot – we have a saying, in my time: Renaissance man. Means a man who can do pretty much anything if he sets his mind to it.'

The grey-bearded man muttered something vulgar, crumpled up the sheet of paper and threw it away. 'Oh, come on,' he said. 'One little hint wouldn't kill you.'

'Not *me*, maybe.' Frank sighed. He didn't like saying no to people, particularly those he'd admired for as long as he could remember. 'Look at it this way,' he said. 'If I told you, it'd be *cheating*. You'd miss out on the wonderful sense of achievement that you only get from doing it all yourself.'

'Fine. As opposed to missing out on a hundred thousand Florentine ducats.' A thought occurred to him. 'Thir— twenty per cent of which could be yours,' he said, 'if only you didn't have such fine principles.'

Frank shook his head. 'You'll get there in the end,' he said.

The grey-bearded man said something which the Door translated perfectly, which was a pity. Frank shrugged, and watched him stomp off in a huff. When he was out of sight, he picked up the discarded ball of paper and smoothed it out. It was, of course, horribly tempting; and what harm could it do?

He looked at it again, sighed, and dropped it. He'd read the book and seen the film (though he didn't think it was quite as bad as everybody made out). The last thing he wanted to do was be responsible for a sequel.

He settled himself down under the shade of the fig tree, looked round to make sure he was alone, and flipped open the cover of his palmtop. Nowhere and nowhen quite like fifteenth-century Tuscany, he always reckoned, for doing really heavy maths. It was the clean air, or the scent of the lavender, or something. He pressed a button and the screen began to glow.

Cheating, Frank thought. It could be so easy. It could be something as simple as taking this perfectly ordinary Kawaguchiya XPK-36 back to a computer-hardware manufacturer in, say, 2005 and letting them salivate over it for a minute or two before naming his price. Thirty years' difference; close enough in time that the potential buyer would realise what it was and, eventually, be able to figure out how it worked and how to copy it. But thirty years in the electronics biz is the same sort of gap that separates – well, the space shuttle and Leonardo da Vinci. One little act of betrayal and he could have, if not all the money in the world, then at least a substantial proportion of it. But even his poxy little Kawaguchiya palmtop (last year's model; practically an antique) had enough computing power to run the simulation that'd show him how catastrophically disastrous that move would be. Cryomolecular bombs would be coloured lights and candy floss compared with what'd happen if a turn-of-the-century caveman got his hands on post-Enlightenment technology. Which was why it was so essential, he reckoned, that the Door either stayed hidden in a very deep, dark place, or else came to live with just the right sort of person. Someone with principles, yes; but principles in moderation. The thought of the utter carnage that would result from the Door falling into the moist little hands of an idealist, someone who Only Wanted To Make The World A Better Place, was enough to melt your brain until it started dribbling out of your ears. Frank Carpenter was realistic about his own intellect, talent and worth, but he couldn't help feeling that he met the Door's ownership criteria fairly well: moderately bright while being intelligent enough to know that a great many people were cleverer than he was, selfish enough to have a vested interest in keeping it secret and safe, shallow enough not to be tempted to use it for the betterment of mankind, and with just enough traces of decency clinging to the bottom of the barrel to care about the consequences.

He read through the dead girl's biographical information for the fourth time, and set about the ticklish job of reducing it all to numbers. It was maths, sure enough: no insight or intuition required. You read the words and translated them into figures, as simple and scientific as that. But he couldn't help feeling there was a little bit more to it and that, for some reason he couldn't quite understand, it wasn't something that just anybody with a postgraduate degree and a calculator could do. Even though he'd proved the formulae over and over again, to the point where he was completely satisfied that they were right and they worked, this stage of the job always struck him as a cross between number-crunching and playing pinball with a blindfold on.

Frank concentrated. Maths was one of the few things he could actually concentrate on. It hooked his mind in a way that mere words or events somehow never could. Gradually, the shapes began to form; lines intersected like a worm-eaten Underground map, clusters formed and clotted, paths bifurcated, ran parallel and rejoined. What he hadn't told George Sprague was that he'd failed to get his Nobel prize because, compared to him, the judges had only just mastered the six-times table. The silly thing was, he was entirely self-taught. Dad belonged to the nine-ten-lots school of numeracy, and at the progressive school that Mum had insisted on sending him to maths was even more optional than all the other subjects. Indeed, there were moments during his occasional outbreaks of self-doubt when he wondered whether it was really the Door doing all these clever sums, the way it translated languages and sometimes supplied him with memories of relevant historical and geographical data that he knew for a fact he'd never learned. It was possible, but he doubted it. Three-in-the-morning thinking, and even he knew better than to pay it much attention.

He stopped. The numbers—

Frank thought about it for a moment, then went back and did the last three sets of equations again, this time in base eight. It made no difference. He frowned. The numbers—

Yes, of course it sounded ridiculous, when he tried to put it into words. Nevertheless. The numbers simply weren't working. It was as though someone had switched off the gravity, and suddenly everything was in free fall, without mass or density; as though all the numbers had suddenly become interchangeable, with six having the same value as nine.

Frank sighed. Magic, of course. It wasn't a subject that had ever interested him much, mostly because it refused to obey the laws of mathematics. Dad had told him the stuff came in two basic sorts, Effective and Practical; the difference being that when a Practical magician turned a policeman into a frog, the result was a genuine frog, whereas if an Effective magician did the same trick, what you got was a policeman who believed he was a frog, a belief shared with everybody else in the world. Generally speaking, both types got the job done efficiently enough for the file to be closed and an invoice sent, which was all the bosses cared about. One of the few differences was that maths took no notice of Effective magic, while Practical messed it up good and proper. Faced with an instance of Practical magic, maths was a wheel spinning in mud, unable to grip.

Which put him in an awkward position. If he couldn't do the maths, he couldn't run the simulations; in which case, he couldn't accept the assignment. That would mean going back to George Sprague and breaking it to him that this time he was going to have to pay out on a claim, something that he had an almost religious objection to doing. And Frank *liked* George Sprague. He was the closest thing Frank had to – well, a friend. It'd be the first time he'd failed. He really didn't want to do it.

But if he couldn't run the simulation—

Deep inside his mind, something small and rather ugly woke up. Thinking about it later, Frank couldn't help personifying it as the little bit of goblin he'd apparently inherited from his father's side of the family. *Go on*, it whispered, and its voice was soft and appealing. *What harm could it possibly do?*

Frank shivered. It was a phrase he'd taught himself to react to, the way a woodland animal reacts to the sound of a breaking twig.

Besides, the voice went on, *it's not as though you'd be doing it for yourself. You know you aren't in this for the money, not really. Do it for good old George. Your pal.*

Yes, but—

He tried to get a grip. He tried to concentrate on the fact that he'd beaten George up from ten to fifteen per cent on this job, so it stood to reason that if he took the risk, it'd be because of the money, because of greed. It almost worked.

And then there's the girl, hissed the soft voice. *Only twenty-eight, poor kid.*

I'm not lis—

You could save her.

And that, regrettably, was really all it took. The other reasons, which he quickly gathered round him like a hedgehog rolling in dry leaves, were only there for decoration: *you don't really know what's going to happen, even if you do run your daft simulations; you think you're God's gift to calculus, but really you're just guessing; history heals its own wounds, it must do or else all the other jobs you've done would've made a real mess.* His inner goblin was chattering away, but it needn't have bothered. It'd nabbed him with a damsel in distress, easy as twitching a bit of string under a cat's nose.

Frank stood up. It was funny about the dog, but he wasn't going to argue with a stroke of good luck. The thought made him frown. He didn't like dogs, but he was too soft-hearted to take active steps to get rid of one. He'd even parted with money when ferocious women had shaken collecting tins under his nose in the cause of various homeless-dog shelters. It always came back to his strong sense of duty. If someone or something liked him, he was morally obliged to like them back, even if he didn't.

The sun was viciously hot and bleachingly bright: mad-dogs-and-Englishmen weather. He stepped out from the shade of the fig tree and hurried back to the Door. As he opened it, something prompted him to look back over his shoulder. He paused. Something was missing. He couldn't identify it, but he was aware of that moment of deadly vulnerability that a man gets when he doesn't know for certain where his car keys are. Quick as a snake he patted his pockets, then remembered that he didn't actually own a car. Couldn't have been that, then. Nevertheless, the feeling was dangerously strong. He'd lost or forgotten *something*; but he couldn't figure out what it was.

Maybe it was just the dog. In which case—

Far too hot to linger out in the open without a hat; but he went back into the shade of the tree and carefully searched the place where he'd been sitting. Nothing. He carried out the mild obsessive's standard kit inspection – the Door's cardboard tube, wallet, house keys, palmtop, mobile, all present and correct. He tried to remember if he'd been carrying anything else. The file; yes, got that.

The feeling was very strong.

This is silly, Frank thought. I've made sure I've got all the important stuff, so whatever I'm missing, by definition it's not something I'll miss. And, of course, the occasional flash of misplaced instinct was perfectly normal for someone who spent his time whizzing backwards and forwards in time via the Door. There were all manner of annoying and bewildering side effects, ranging from mild and vague déjà vu to being able to recite huge chunks of dialogue out of movies he'd never seen, often because they hadn't been made yet. As for detective stories and thrillers: forget it. He always knew who'd done it as soon as he opened the cover or saw the opening credits.

He caught himself checking his pockets yet again, his fingers groping for a shape and a texture that he was unable to specify. Searching for an absence of something is a really bad way to spend time, a bit like trying to play darts blindfold in zero gravity. He *ordered* himself to stop doing it. He mutinied.

And while I'm at it, he thought, I'll keep my eyes peeled for the invisible man.

Somehow Frank managed to get a fragile fingernails-only grip, and made long strides back to the Door. Doesn't matter, he told himself; because if he really had lost something important and found out later what it was, he could always return through the Door to the moment just before he arrived, and leave himself a note to remind him to take care not to lose it. There, you see? Nothing to worry about. Go home.

He stepped through the Door, closed it behind him and caught it as it rolled down his bedroom wall.

You could call it home, but only like estate agents call Swindon the Cotswolds. Really, it was just a shed; to be precise, a temporary shelter for shepherds during the summer grazing season in one of the remotest parts of New Zealand's North Island. Frank had chosen it precisely because it was miles from anywhere, or anyone. The sheep station it had originally belonged to had been derelict since the mid-twentieth century. Nobody came here, not even the movie people; it was practically the only place on the island that hadn't doubled for Rohan or the Shire. He'd bought it, all legal and above board, just to be on the safe side, but he needn't have bothered. Nobody else in the world could possibly live there, except the owner of the Portable Door.

He kicked off his shoes and flopped down on the bed. He had a job to do, but he couldn't summon up the energy. Not like him at all. His motto had always been *there's no time like the present* – completely meaningless for him, of course, but nevertheless. Mostly it was just that he hated sitting still. That was why he'd chosen the hut; it was an ideal home for someone who was always out. He yawned.

This is no good, he told himself. You've made the decision, and now there's a poor dead girl out there for you to bring back to life. Get up. Busy busy.

Frank closed his eyes. Something was missing and until he'd worked out what it was and got it back, he wasn't going to feel *right*. Once again, he toyed with the rather appalling notion that it might just be the dog, but mercifully that didn't ring true. Not the dog; but possibly something not totally dissimilar. Something that was always there. Something that followed him about, whether he liked it or not.

It could well be something like that; except that his life didn't contain anything that fitted that description. He had no bodyguards, disciples, groupies, cameramen or sound crews. As far as he knew he wasn't being tailed by the police or the CIA or even the VAT people. His defining characteristic was that he was a table for one. So that couldn't be right, could it?

Forget it, he told himself as he opened a cupboard and took out a plate and a spoon and dropped them into a carrier bag. Can't be important. Let's get this job of work done and out of the way, and then – well, then there may be another job to do, and George Sprague was very good at keeping him busy. The main thing was not to stop too long in any one place, or any one time. My life, he decided, is the very antithesis of a posh restaurant. Absolutely no ties.

He picked the Door out of its tube with the nails of his thumb and forefinger, and slapped it onto the wall. The familiar outlines spread and grew a third dimension. He concentrated on the target location and turned the handle.

One thing Frank found hard to predict, even when entering a place he knew well, was what the Door would choose to open out of. Nine times out of ten it was a wall; other useful surfaces included billboards, hoardings, road signs, cliff faces. Once he'd had to materialise in the middle of the Gobi Desert, no vertical surfaces in ten square miles. On that occasion, the Door had turned into a manhole cover, and he'd had something of a shock when he'd tried to walk through it and tumbled head over heels into the sand. This time it was reasonably straightforward. He stepped out of a doorway in a garden fence onto a flower bed.

There in front of him was an apple tree, with a ladder leaning against its branches. The object of his mission wasn't hard to spot. She was halfway up the ladder, stretching out her arm towards a fat, annoyed-looking cat. Frank cleared his throat and said, 'Excuse me.'

She didn't look down. 'Yes?' she snapped, in a go-away-I'm-busy voice.

'Excuse me,' he repeated, 'but that doesn't look terribly safe. Would it be all right if—?'

'Who the hell are you?'

George Sprague's briefings were always delightfully rich in minor details. 'Kevin Thompson,' he said, 'I'm, um, Mrs Thompson's nephew. It's the cat again, isn't it?'

'Yes. Look, do you think you could just shut up and let me do this? I don't mean to be rude, but I do need to concentrate.'

'Actually—'

'Go away.'

Oh well, Frank thought. And you'll never know I'm just about to save your life.

He took the plate and the spoon out of the carrier bag. She'd be furious, of course. She'd assume he'd done it to make her look stupid. It didn't matter, needless to say. He'd probably never have anything to do with her ever again, so who cared what she thought?

'Here kitty,' he sang out, tapping the spoon against the edge of the plate. 'Here kittykittykittykitty.'

The cat lifted its head and looked at him.

'Kittykittykitty.' Tap, tap, tap. 'Din-dins. Here, kittykitty.'

The cat gave him a look that'd have scarred a more sensitive man for life, but it got to its feet, ran lightly along the branch, hopped down onto a lower one, darted past the girl, brushing her face with its tail as it did so, and ran down the tree trunk to the ground. He put the plate and spoon back in the bag. The cat trotted past the foot of the ladder and vanished through a cat flap in the back door.

'Oh look,' Frank said. 'He's come down all by himself.'

The girl still had her back to him, which was probably just as well. He had an idea that she wouldn't be happy when she came down off the ladder. He turned to go, and took a long stride onto the flower bed, trying hard not to tread on any intentional vegetation.

He heard a thump.

There are some noises that aren't good, ever. The thump was one of them.

He looked back. The girl was lying on the ground. The angle of her head to her spine was definitely wrong, as though she'd been drawn by a clumsy amateur. She was lying on top of the ladder, which was flat on the ground. There was no sign of the tree.

Oh, Frank thought.

He tried to remember the original storyline, as set out in George Sprague's briefing. The old lady was due to come out of the house at any moment; probably not a good thing if she saw him there.

He glanced quickly at the back door, but couldn't see it. The reason being, there was a tree in the way.

It was back.

Oh, he thought.

Part of his brain said: got to be Practical, then, rather than Effective. Effective magic could make her think that the tree had suddenly vanished, causing her to topple off the ladder and fall to her death, but it wouldn't be able to persuade the ladder. But the ladder's lying on the ground with her on top of it. Therefore, someone must have physically removed the tree and then put it back a split second later. Furthermore, put it back about ten inches off to the side, so it wouldn't zap back into existence on top of her dead body. Definitely Practical, then, rather than Effective. Also, according to what Dad used to say about the two different types of magic, extremely difficult to do and a lot of effort to go to when a perfectly simple bit of Effective would've achieved the same result.

The rest of his brain said: Oh Jesus, she's dead. And the tree just sort of *vanished*—

Frank heard a door open, and crockery smash. Time – he felt really guilty about running away like this, but you had to be sensible – he wasn't there.

CHAPTER FIVE

'**M**urdered', Mr Sprague said slowly. And then: 'So what?'

Frank frowned. 'I thought it might be – well, you know. Relevant.'

'She's still dead, even if it wasn't an accident. We've still got to pay out. Or have we?' A flicker of hope lit up Mr Sprague's face, and he scrabbled through the pages of the policy document. 'Bloody small print,' he added, reaching for his glasses. 'Ah, here we are. Sod it, no, it says here they're covered against homicide. Makes you wonder what sort of business they're in, really. Still, pest control and all that. I guess some of the, um, things they have to deal with are technically human – vampires, I suppose, werewolves.' He sighed. 'Oh well,' he said. 'You'll just have to try again.'

Awkward silence. Money was about to sour their otherwise pleasant relationship.

'Of course,' Frank said, 'I won't be expecting any additional payment.'

Mr Sprague looked at him like a prisoner on Death Row who sees the state governor coming through the door when he'd been expecting to see two guards. 'You won't?'

'I get paid by results,' Frank said calmly. 'A percentage of money saved. I haven't saved you any money yet.'

'Ah.' Mr Sprague sighed rather beautifully. 'Well, yes—'

'And,' Frank went on, 'I think it'd be only fair if I waived the extra five per cent. After all, there's the delay and so forth. Time is money.'

He waited for the joke, but it didn't come. That told him he'd got Mr Sprague genuinely off balance. But in a good way, he hoped.

'Glad you see it like that,' Mr Sprague said, rather breathlessly. 'Though of course—' He paused. He'd been about to point out the logical flaw in Frank's argument. 'Glad you see it like that,' he repeated. 'Always a pleasure doing business with you.'

'Likewise,' Frank said happily. He yawned. 'Better go back and have another stab at it, I suppose,' he said. 'But I think perhaps you should just mention it to her employers,' he added. 'If someone's murdering their staff, it's possible that they might be interested.'

Mr Sprague thought about that. 'Yes, but once you've fixed it up, none of this'll ever have happened, so—'

Frank shook his head. 'I don't think it works quite like that with, um, people in their line of work,' he said. 'Dad used to say, it's a bit like companies that keep two sets of books.'

'You mean they—'

Frank nodded. 'I believe it gets very complicated,' he said. 'Keeping track, and everything. Some of the bigger firms have specialist bookkeepers. Time and Motion, they call them.'

Mr Sprague nodded. It was a gesture designed to show that he didn't understand and didn't want to. 'You never thought of going into the family business, then?'

'Me? Heavens, no. Dad said it was utterly miserable. Boring.'

'*Boring?*'

'Oh yes. Apart from short intervals of being horribly frightened. He got killed, too.'

'Ah. I hadn't realised. I'm sorry—'

'Three times,' Frank went on. 'Or was it four? Can't remember. Anyhow, he got quite friendly with the man in charge at, you know, the other end. But even that got to be a bit of a drag after a bit, he said. Going where no man has gone before is all right the first time, he used to say, but when you're practically commuting—'

Mr Sprague did the nod again. He was getting quite fluent at it.

'Besides,' Frank went on, 'it's – well, it's proper *work*, isn't it? It's getting out of bed at half-past six every morning of your life and going to the office and having to do as you're told all the time. Office politics. Not my style at all. I mean, I can stay in bed till noon if I want to, and I can still be there bright and early for a six a.m. start.'

Mr Sprague was looking at him. There was a sort of unspoken agreement between them, so fundamental that it was practically the Constitution and the Bill of Rights. Mr Sprague didn't ever ask about the Door – what it was, exactly, how it worked, how Frank had come by it – and Frank never volunteered enough information to make Mr Sprague's carefully suppressed curiosity into an unbearable itch. 'Right,' Mr Sprague said. 'Well, mustn't keep you. I expect you want to be getting on with it. And thanks.'

Frank dipped his head in graceful acknowledgement. 'Don't mention it,' he said. He stood up.

'Still no dog, then.'

If Frank winced, it was just the slightest of movements. 'So far so good,' he said. 'Really, in this life that's the best you can ever say, isn't it?'

This time, for some reason, the Door opened in the back wall of the house, right next to the real back door. Frank nipped through, took it down and put it away, and scuttled off behind the cover of a large bush.

He'd got here earlier this time. If the girl (Emily Spitzer; names weren't his strongest suit) was going to be killed by a van-ishing tree, the sensible thing would be to solve the problem before it happened. He looked up into the branches and located the cat. It was washing its ears with its paw, the way they do. Relaxed, happy cat. Everything's so much easier if you avoid stress and melodrama.

Frank took the plate and fork out of the carrier bag and said the magic words. The cat's head went up, its ears twitched forward. Frank repeated the performance – oh come *on*, you wretched animal, I haven't got all day – and the cat did its hopping-from-branch-to-branch routine as before. Then, at the point where it was due to run down the tree trunk, it stopped, looked down and yowled.

Oh for crying out loud, Frank thought. Bloody creature. *I* could get down from there, and I'm scared stiff of heights.

The back door opened. He couldn't see the two women come out, because of the stupid tree. But he could see the cat. As soon as the door's hinges creaked, its ears flattened against its skull and it shot back up into the branches, ending up higher and more precariously perched than it had been to start with. It stopped, realised where it was, and let out a faint mewing noise that would have softened the heart of a Chief Constable.

Frank didn't swear, not very often. 'Fuck,' he said.

The old lady was standing under the tree, pointing. The girl was looking bored and cross. After a bit, the old lady went indoors. The girl produced a ladder, apparently out of thin air, and started to climb.

'Excuse me,' Frank called out.

On reflection, it was perhaps a misguided thing to do, calling out like that when he was quite well hidden behind a bush. The girl started, shaking the ladder. The thin branch it was resting on snapped. There was a thump. One of those thumps.

Oh, Frank thought.

The bushes screened the back fence from the back door. He left, quickly.

'Good morning, sir,' said the sales assistant in the hardware shop. 'What can I—?'

The young man looked at him in a way he didn't like.

Nevertheless, the customer is always right, even when he might just be completely barking.

'I want a chainsaw,' the young man said.

Frank stepped through into Mr Sprague's office, caught the Door as it rolled off the wall, and flopped into a chair without waiting to be asked. He had sawdust all over his clothes and he was looking unusually frazzled.

'Got there in the end,' he said, before Mr Sprague had a chance to speak. 'Nipped in there before the damned cat had a chance to get stuck, said I was from the council and the tree was blocking the neighbours' satellite reception and it had to come down. I've never cut down a tree before – it's very complicated and rather scary. If your lot does the old biddy's house insurance, I'm afraid you're going to have to cough up for a new fence and a couple of windows. But tell you what, you can knock it off my commission.' He smiled, made himself calm down, and went on: 'Sorry, George. I know perfectly well that you haven't got the faintest idea what I'm talking about, but you know what it's like when you've had a stressful time, it helps to talk to someone about it even if they— Anyway. Job done, and here's the—'

Mr Sprague was frowning. Frank was holding out a blank sheet of paper.

'Oh,' Frank said.

'Though I'm glad you've dropped by,' Mr Sprague said, his voice just a little strained. 'I was just about to call you, in fact.'

'You were? I mean, oh, that's good.'

Mr Sprague nodded. 'I've got the file here all ready. Ought to be quite straightforward. There's a fair bit of background I won't go into now, but basically there's a young woman who got herself killed trying to rescue a cat stuck on a roof.'

The Door opened.

Frank had considered fifteenth-century Tuscany, but it wouldn't have been quite right. Tuscany was for maths, and this wasn't really a maths problem, though he felt sure that complex calculations were going to figure in it quite heavily before too long. He'd considered going home and lying on his bed staring up at the rafters for a very long time. He'd even thought about dynamite – sure, if he blew up the old dear's house so there'd be no roof for the cat to get stuck on, Mr Sprague's company would have to pay to have it rebuilt, but he'd still be saving them money. But something told him it wouldn't end there. Except for Emily Spitzer, of course.

Which was why he was here.

He climbed the stairs and pressed the buzzer. 'Frank Carpenter,' he said, when the door squawked at him. 'To see Mr Tanner.'

Long pause, and then the door opened.

There was a different girl behind the reception desk. If anything, she was even more bewilderingly gorgeous than the one who'd been there last time.

'Mrs Tanner, isn't it?' he asked politely.

The girl gave him a long, hard stare. 'You've got a nerve,' she said.

'Yes,' Frank replied.

She sighed. 'So,' she said, 'how's your dad these days?' The stare became a grin. 'I always got on *very* well with your dad, back in the old days.'

'No, you didn't,' Frank said. 'You tried to, but—'

'Told you about me, did he?'

Frank nodded. 'Warned rather than told, yes. Oh, while I think of it, how's your son? Your other son, I mean. Dad's godson.'

The grin became a genuine smile. Frank couldn't help feeling touched. 'Little Paul Azog,' she said. 'Coming along very nicely, thanks for asking. He'll be three in September. He's doing very well at play school. Last week he ate a hamster. Caught it himself and everything.'

'Jolly good,' Frank said. 'Can I see Mr Tanner now, please?'

'Mphm.' The beautiful girl picked up the phone and said,

'He's back again.' Frank could just make out some of the string of curses that made up the reply. 'He says, go right in,' she said.

'Thanks.' He hesitated. 'Um,' he said.

'Yes?'

'The, er, appearance thing. Are you really a shape-shifter?'

She smiled sweetly at him. 'Your dad said that, did he?'

'Yes.'

There wasn't anything to see, not even a blur. But five seconds later Frank had seen fifteen different girls sitting in the receptionist's chair: all different shapes and sizes, all outrageously beautiful, all sharing the same feral grin. 'I suppose I am, yes,' she said. 'It's a goblin thing. Sort of a trick we evolved into, so we could sneak up on our prey.'

'Ah,' Frank said. 'Very impressive. So,' he went on, 'if I'm part goblin, could I—?'

She shook her head. 'Our Dennis can't, either,' she said. 'Only pure-bred goblins, you see.'

Frank nodded slowly. 'So,' he said, 'presumably that's a kind of Effective magic.'

Her eyes were suddenly as cold as last night's chow mein. 'I'll pretend you didn't say that,' she said. 'And just so there's no confusion, no, it bloody well isn't. Goblins don't do that stuff. When we change shape, we change shape, every single bloody molecule. The other thing – what you just said – that'd be *cheating*.'

'I see,' Frank said mildly. 'Thanks. And, um, sorry.'

'No problem,' said the beautiful girl. 'You weren't to know, were you?' She grinned at him. It was getting to the point where, even if he never saw it again, he'd have no trouble picturing that grin with his eyes shut for the rest of his life. 'And you didn't answer my question,' she added. 'Your dad. Not still hanging round after that frigid little thin—'

'My mother, you mean.'

She sighed. 'Oh well,' she said. 'But apart from that, he's happy enough, I take it? Enjoying life, all that?'

Frank pursed his lips. 'You could say that,' he replied. 'Look, I don't want to keep Mr Tanner waiting, so—'

'Go on, then.' Another burst of the grin. 'We can have a nice chat later, after you've finished with our Dennis.'

Frank smiled. He pictured Mr Tanner's office. Four perfectly good walls he could spread the Door up against. 'I'll look forward to it,' he said, and went through into the back office.

'That's it?' Mr Tanner said.

Frank nodded. 'As far as I know,' he said. 'I've just got what was in the file to go on, of course.'

Mr Tanner drew heavily on his cigar and blew smoke in Frank's face. 'All seems perfectly straightforward to me,' he said. 'Someone in the trade wants this Emily Whatsername dead. The mechanics of the thing are no big deal,' he went on. 'What we in the biz call a Better Mousetrap.'

Frank thought about that for a moment. 'Mousetrap?'

Mr Tanner nodded. 'Nothing flash or showy,' he said. 'Just thorough, and it works. Invented by a man called Petersen, in Norway, back in the late seventeen-hundreds.'

'Mousetrap?'

'What? Oh, right. The idea is, a really good mousetrap doesn't just kill the mouse in this variant of the space/time continuum, it kills it in every possible alternative reality in the multiverse. We used to get them mail order from the States. Just over seven thousand dollars each, if you ordered them by the hundred.'

'Ah.' Frank nodded slowly. 'So,' he said, 'how do you stop it working?'

'You can't.' Mr Tanner stubbed out his cigar and lit another one. 'That's what's so good about them – well, I say good, depends which end of them you're on, I suppose. Efficient, if you prefer. Also easy to use, reliable and at a sensible price.' He leaned back in his chair and blew a smoke ring. 'Looks like you're going to have to tell your insurance bloke he's going to have to eat it on this deal.' He frowned. 'What did you say this female's name was, again?'

'Emily Spitzer.'

'Spitzer, Spitzer—' Mr Tanner's small, smooth face screwed up. 'I used to know a Clive Spitzer,' he said. 'Head of alchemy at Langsam, Chang & O'Brien in Toronto. Come to think of it, I seem to remember he had a daughter or two.' He scowled for a moment. 'Pity,' he said. 'Old Clive was a bit of an arsehole, but – well. All flesh is grass, as they say. Specially in this business. Practically silage.'

Frank looked at him. 'I was wondering about that,' he said.

'What? Oh yes.' Mr Tanner nodded. 'Very competitive, the spell trade. Very much into the cut and thrust of the market place, with the added factor that you don't get any strife from the authorities, the way you tend to in other lines of work. We keep ourselves to ourselves, see. Wouldn't occur to any of us to go whining to the cops, and if we did who the hell would believe us? Also, there's hardly ever a body, or at least, not enough of one to notice. Naturally we have a code of conduct, and we come down like a ton of bricks on anybody who goes too far. In theory,' he added.

'In—?'

'Well, you know how it is in business,' Mr Tanner replied with a yawn. 'At the end of the day we're all in it for the long haul, and you can't go starting feuds with people you'll be working with for the rest of your life. Got to be a bit pragmatic. Besides, the way we see it, looking after your own skin, taking simple precautions, that's your responsibility. Anybody who gets it was probably too careless or too stupid to be in the trade anyway.'

Frank considered that. 'Is that true?' he said.

'No,' Mr Tanner replied. 'But it makes it easier. People get hurt from time to time, that's how it goes. It's a bummer if you've spent a lot of time and money training someone up to the point where they're actually more help than hindrance. But looked at from the other point of view, for an ambitious youngster trying to make his way in the world, when it comes to dead men's shoes, the profession's a bit like Imelda Marcos's wardrobe, if you get my meaning.' He rolled his chair back and put his feet up on the desk. 'I don't suppose they're exactly crying their eyes out over at Carringtons right now.'

Frank nodded. 'And Clive Spitzer? Your old friend?'

'Never liked him much anyway.'

Business, Frank thought. Just business. And the girl had been – well, he'd only spoken to her once, and she'd been rude and unpleasant to him, when all he was doing was trying to save her life. Even so—'

Fine knight in shining armour you turned out to be.

He knew the little voice was just trying to wind him up; he knew it, and he knew perfectly well that if that really was why he was letting himself get involved, then it was a bloody stupid reason and he ought to be ashamed of himself. It was a great big fiery Thou Shalt Not: you don't go helping people just because it makes you feel good – or, in his case, makes you feel slightly less of an insignificant little tit. That kind of motivation was the very worst kind of eight-lane blacktop, last-petrol-before-Eternal-Damnation good intention.

Analyse, he ordered himself.

Why?

Well—

– Because otherwise George Sprague is going to have to fork out money, and he *hates* that. And George is my friend.

– Because I accepted the contract, and I like to see these things through.

– Because an accident is one thing, but this is murder, and that's nasty and shouldn't be allowed.

– Because of a million US dollars. (Good one. We approve of that one.)

– Because— Well. Because it's there. Because.

He ran the checklist, and found it wanting. Those aren't the reasons, he made himself confess. You know what the real reason is, and it's very bad. We *don't do* damsels in distress. Why don't we? Because only *heroes* do that stuff, and we're not a *hero*. We're not a swinging-in-through-windows, Milk-Tray hero, nor are we the meek, quiet hero with hidden depths who comes through when the chips are down. We aren't any kind of hero. We're just us. Me.

Got that?

'Fair enough,' Frank said mildly. 'It's just a pity, that's all.'

Mr Tanner shrugged. 'Yeah, well—'

'Because I was going to use the fee from this job to pay off a bit more of what I owe you, but since you say there's absolutely nothing anybody can do—'

(Got that? Apparently not.)

Mr Tanner stayed perfectly still, apart from his eyes. They flicked round in their deep-set sockets and focused on him like an advanced targeting system. 'Is that right?' he said.

'Never mind,' Frank replied. 'I expect there'll be another job along in a bit, and I can pay you then. Assuming Mr Sprague still wants me to do stuff for him. I had a hundred per cent success rate, you see, up till now.'

Mr Tanner wasn't fooled, he could tell. He could see the silly little bit of string being dangled in front of his nose. His problem was, he really, really liked string.

'Hundred per cent, eh?'

'Satisfaction guaranteed,' Frank said. 'Someone you can rely on. But it doesn't matter. Mr Sprague's a reasonable man. And surely everybody's allowed to screw up once.'

The flash of a paw, as the string moves. 'You think so?'

'Well—'

'It's pretty obvious you've never been in business, then,' Mr Tanner said. 'It doesn't work like that. *Oh well, you did your best* is one of those phrases you just don't hear in the challenging environment of the modern market place.'

Keep the string moving. For both of us. 'Oh, I don't think Mr Sprague's like that. He's more of a friend than a boss, really. He'll understand, I'm sure.'

'Yeah, right.' Mr Tanner was grinning at him. 'Until the day comes when some other kid comes into his office with a Portable Door, or something else that does the same thing; and then he'll have to ask himself, *who can I really trust to get the job done and the shareholders off my back?* Fat lot of good personal rapport and cards at Christmas are going to do you when that happens.'

'All right,' Frank said slowly. 'But it's all academic, isn't it? Because you said yourself, there's nothing at all anybody can do about it.'

Mr Tanner looked up at him. String, set and match. 'Well,' he said.

In the very heart of the City of London, wedged in between two dizzyingly tall glass and steel towers, snuggles the Cheapside branch of the Credit Mayonnaise. The building is extremely old, one of the very few survivors of the Great Fire of 1666; which means, among other things, that it's so heavily listed, you'd need a dozen licences just to open a window. Most of its business is something abstruse to do with turning one sort of money into another, but it also has a modest cellar, which houses a number of safe-deposit boxes.

Cellar, please note; not vault. There are no time-locked steel doors, because the Environment wouldn't stand for it; likewise, no pressure pads, infra-red beams or cunning sensors capable of registering the slight change in temperature caused by the heat of an unauthorised body. A moderately enterprising burglar could probably break into it armed with nothing more than a tyre lever and a garden trowel, although he'd have to be careful not to scratch the paint if he didn't want to spend the rest of his life hiding from the enforcers from English Heritage. Besides, no burglar would bother. There's nothing valuable down there; just a load of old papers and some empty boxes.

A tall middle-aged woman in a smart dark suit walked up to the window marked *Securities*. The clerk knew her by sight, of course, and had her key ready before she'd said a word. She smiled at him. A security guard opened a door and stepped aside to let her through. He didn't go with her. She knew the way.

Down a flight of old stone steps. The cellar was cool, very slightly musty, impeccably clean and dust-free. She stopped in front of an ancient oak door studded with big, blacksmith-made nails, and rang a little bell. The door opened slowly on well-oiled hinges. A small bald man stood up from behind a desk and said, 'Good afternoon, Ms Carrington.'

'Derek.'

The man walked over to a set of beautifully polished library steps and wheeled them over to the back wall, which was covered from floor to ceiling with shelves: a cross between a stately home library and an old-fashioned ironmonger's shop. Every shelf was crammed with black sheet-metal boxes, each of them just about big enough to house a pair of wellington boots. The man knew his way around the shelves without needing to look at the faded gilt numbers. He picked up a box, tucked it under one arm and came down again.

'Keeping well, Ms Carrington?'

'Fine, thanks. And you?'

'Can't grumble.' The man put the box down on the desk and walked to the door. 'Just call out when you're finished,' he said, and the door closed behind him.

The woman fitted the key into the keyhole in the tin box and turned it. There was a squeak, followed by a click. She lifted the lid carefully and stood back.

The box expanded. You could try and explain how it did that by talking about film of a courgette growing into a marrow, played at extreme speed. Such an explanation would be hopelessly misleading, but it'd be something that a human brain could accept without overloading, which is what would inevitably happen if you told it how it really was.

The tall woman got out a powder compact and made a few trivial repairs to her face.

When she'd finished and put the compact away again, the box had grown large enough to accommodate a set of steps, a bit like the wheeled stairs you leave an airliner by, but in reverse. Leaning against the table, she slipped off her two-inch-heeled court shoes and tapped each of them in turn with her forefinger. They flickered for a moment and turned into hairs, exactly the same colour and length as the hair on her head. She added them to her fringe. They stayed put.

The stairs, which had been growing steadily, reached the floor and stabilised. A handrail materialised; first the rail hanging unsupported in mid-air, then the struts to hold it in place. She sighed (all this fuss; honestly!) and climbed down the stairs into the box.

At the foot of the stairs was a large, spacious reception area, roughly the size of a football pitch. Expensive carpet compressed under her stockinged feet as she walked towards a large, rather magnificent reception desk, where a smartly dressed girl was answering a phone.

'Carringtons, how can I help you?' she said.

The tall woman walked past her, through the middle of three fire doors, down a long corridor lined with regularly spaced office doors. At the end of the corridor was a huge room, its walls lined with books, most of its space taken up by a large, immaculately polished conference table. A dozen men and half a dozen women were seated round it, but the chair at the top of the table was empty.

'Sorry I'm late, everyone,' the tall woman said, in a voice conspicuously lacking in sincerity.

She sat down at the head of the table and looked round. Everybody had stopped talking and was watching her closely. She reached up, tugged three hairs from the crown of her head and blew on them gently; they became a mobile phone, a laptop and a briefcase.

'Sorry for the inconvenience in getting here,' she said briskly. 'I do hope it wasn't too much of a bore, but in the light of recent events I felt we'd better go to yellow alert for the time being.' She glanced round the table. 'Just in case any of you didn't get the memo, I've closed off realspace access until further notice. Anybody who's got meetings with clients scheduled for the next few days, either arrange to meet somewhere else or use the service elevators.' She paused and counted heads. 'Anybody know what's happened to Fritz?'

'He asked me to tell you he's been held up,' said a small, ginger-haired woman at the far end of the table. 'Apparently there was a mix-up at the Strasbourg branch of the bank, and they've lost the key to the box. He says he's jumping on the 11.06 flight to Geneva, and he'll use the box there.'

The tall woman clicked her tongue. 'Oh well,' she said. 'Can't be helped. Now, then.' She frowned. The tension level around the table went up a degree or so. 'What are we to make of all this, then? Armando?'

A thickset silver-haired man in full cardinal's regalia cleared his throat nervously. 'We've made a preliminary examination of the site, and initial findings would seem to suggest—'

'Armando.'

The cardinal swallowed. 'It's a mystery,' he said. 'No idea. Sorry.'

'Ah.' The tall woman tapped her fingers on the table top. 'All right, then,' she said, 'let's just run through what we *do* know. Emily Spitzer, junior pest-control associate at London office, was killed by a Better Mousetrap at –' she glanced down at her laptop '– four-fifteen p.m. on Friday the seventh of June at number 47 Waverley Drive, Kew, south-west London.' She looked at the screen again. 'Twice,' she added. 'No, scratch that. Three times. So far,' she said, her eyebrows bunching gracefully. 'Though the Mortensens seem to suggest there'll be further activity. Anyhow,' she went on, in a voice that nobody round the table seemed very comfortable with, 'that's part one. Colin, maybe you could fill us in on part two.'

Colin Gomez wriggled nervously in his seat. 'I'm not even sure it's connected to – well, what happened to her,' he said. 'Could just be a coincidence. But—' He took a deep breath. 'We had a break-in here at London office. Obviously it's hard to be precise, but as far as we can tell, it was some time after one a.m. on Saturday. They got the petty cash and a few computers, which turned up on Sunday in a lay-by just off the A34. One of them had a wooden stake hammered through the CD port, so I'm guessing that whoever nicked them must've switched them on. We're making discreet enquiries around the mental hospitals, so it won't be long before we know who did it. These things happen,' he added, 'and it's just as well they didn't go snooping about in the closed-file store, because getting rid of bodies is a real pain. The thing is,' he went on (and his voice became a little higher and less sure of itself), 'they also turned over a couple of the offices. Drawers pulled out, papers chucked on the floor, that sort of thing. There's a photocopier missing that we know of, and some other stuff – garbage, really; office supplies – pencils, Sellotape, ink cartridges, paperclips, staples, a few boxes of envelopes. But one of the offices they had a go at was Emily Spitzer's.'

Long, thoughtful silence. Then a slim blonde young woman said: 'Surely it's too obvious. Look, we know somebody murdered the girl. Somebody in the trade, because of the Mousetrap. Assuming it wasn't just some personal vendetta, it must've been work-related. Well?'

The tall woman frowned. 'Go on.'

'Immediately after, there's the break-in. A lot of trouble to go to, burgling London office, particularly since there's nothing in here worth stealing, unless you're in the trade. But apparently none of the – well, the specialised stuff was taken, just worthless junk. Which is as clear a way of saying *this isn't an ordinary burglary* as you could possibly think of, bar sky-writing. Well, it's obvious, isn't it? Someone wants us to think they've been through the Spitzer girl's stuff and taken something – papers or a tape or a magic ring that makes you the ruler of the universe or whatever; and if they want us to think that, it clearly can't be true. But,' she went on, 'if it's that obvious that it's not true, maybe it *is* true; and now we're into double bluffs and triple bluffs and all that sort of stuff, and I for one really don't want to go there, because it always gives me migraine. I mean, if they want us to think that they don't want us to think that they *intend* us to think that—'

The tall woman cleared her throat. 'Cecily.'

'Yes, Mum?'

'You've made your point. And it seems to me that the likeliest explanation for that is that whoever did this just wanted to confuse us. And, of course, they may also have wanted to get hold of something from Ms Spitzer's office. All right, dear?'

'Yes, Mum.'

'Fine. But,' the tall woman went on, 'since we've got no way at all of knowing if that's the case – and if it *is* the case, even less of a clue whether or not they found what they were looking for – I really can't see any point in speculating about it; not, at least, until we've got a bit more hard data to go on. Well?'

Nodding heads all round the table, to the extent that a casual observer might have thought he was in Hollywood. After a while, however, the small ginger-haired woman said, 'That's all very well, but it doesn't alter the fact that someone killed one of our people. With a Mousetrap, what's more, which makes it pretty well certain that it was someone in the profession—'

'Unless that's just a quadruple bluff.'

'*Quiet*, Cecily, you aren't helping.' The tall woman pulled a hair from her fringe and blew on it. It turned into a pencil, which she turned over in her long fingers a couple of times before deliberately breaking off the lead against the side of the table and fixing her stare on the ginger-haired woman. 'Sorry, Consuela. What you're saying is, if they didn't get what they wanted they might kill again. Is that right?'

'Well, it needs thinking about.'

'Oh, I agree. That's why we've moved to yellow alert, of course. And naturally we're doing everything we can. I've asked the forensic department from Rio office to see if they can piece together what's left of the Mousetrap to the point where we can at least find out who it was made by; a batch number or a date stamp would be a wonderful bonus, but I'm not holding my breath. I know the ID markings on Mousetraps are supposed to be indelible, but we all know there's ways round that. Hutchinsons have promised to lend us their morphic resonance amplifier, and Bert Schnell from Zauberwek AG says we can borrow Friedrich for a day or so, just in case they've been careless about time signatures – well, you never know, everybody makes mistakes. No, pulling up the drawbridge and minding our backs for a week or so isn't really the problem, and if it was just a security matter I wouldn't have dragged you all out here.' She paused, to make sure she had their undivided attention. 'I should've thought it's obvious, actually, what the real puzzle is. It's not that someone killed the girl. It's that someone's been trying to bring her back.' The tall woman paused again. 'Not someone in the trade, because a professional would know all about Mousetraps; but someone with the knowledge and the equipment to try, three times. Now that, I put it to you, is cause for genuine concern. Not to put too fine a point on it, there's someone out there meddling in the affairs of wizards, and until we've found out who it is and applied the traditional ton of bricks I think we're going to have to take this very seriously indeed.'

CHAPTER SIX

Emily Spitzer thought of something else she could say to Colin Gomez, and the thought gave her the strength to proceed. Equalising her weight on both feet, she reached out towards the cat's neck. It was only a few inches from her hand. She reached a little further and felt her elbow brush against a branch.

There was a click, like a door opening.

The tree disappeared.

Thirty feet up in the air, with nothing to hold on to except an absence of tree. Don't try this at home. You could do yourself a mischief.

Emily fell. As she did so, her entire life flashed before her eyes, just the way it was supposed to. Having been trained in all aspects of her trade, including death management, she realised what the slide-show meant, and thought, *Nuts*. After all, it was such a silly way to go; and the thing about the life flashing in front of her eyes wasn't just that it had been unfulfilled, pointless and so very short. Mostly it was that she hadn't finished with it yet. It was as though the waiter had brought pudding and then snatched it away from under her nose before her fingers had closed round the handle of the spoon. Not bloody well fair.

Thirty-two feet per second per second; good old Isaac Newton, or was it Galileo? Like it mattered a damn.

Falling out of a tree is a bit like life itself. It all goes swimmingly until the end, and then bad stuff happens. Since she knew she wasn't going to survive this one, there was no point bracing for impact. An awfully big adventure, wasn't it supposed to be? But she'd spent her working life battling dragons and staking vampires. Adventures? Yawn.

All in all, she just wanted to land, die and get it over with.

Emily landed; and the first observation she made was that death didn't hurt. Since a large slice of humanity spends a lot of time worrying about that, it'd have been nice if she could have passed on the good news – sent them a postcard, maybe, or an e-mail – but presumably that wasn't possible or someone would've done it already. Death, in fact, didn't seem to be bad at all. It was dark – no, that was because she had her eyes closed.

Pause. If she still had eyes to close, how could she be dead?

She opened them, and a waiter handed her a menu.

Saving others is its own reward, which is just as well. You can't expect gratitude. Even so, Frank had secretly been hoping for something along the lines of '*My hero*' or '*You saved my life, how can I ever thank you?*' Instead, when Emily Spitzer opened her eyes, what she said was, 'This isn't death, it's Paris.'

Factually accurate, but there are times when you want to hear a little bit more than just the truth. 'Yes,' he said, very slightly nettled. 'I can recommend the lobster.'

'It's bloody *Paris*,' Emily said, sitting bolt upright in her white plastic chair and staring past him. (As though he wasn't there; great.) 'Look, that's the Eiffel Tower, for God's sake.' Then, apparently, she noticed him; she swivelled round in her seat like a tank turret and gave him a scowl that would've scorched asbestos. 'What the *hell* is going on here?' she snapped. 'And who are you?'

'Frank Carpenter,' Frank said. 'Or if you don't fancy lobster, there's the crêpes Suzettes. My treat,' he added. 'I can get it back off expenses, so we might as well—'

'But I *died*.'

'No,' Frank pointed out emphatically, 'you didn't. Not this time. All the other times, oh yes. Whee, thud, splat, call a doctor, no, don't bother, over and over again. This time, though,' he added, with a certain fierce pride, 'you made it. So we're having lunch. To celebrate.' He nodded at her defiantly, then raised the menu and made a show of studying it. '*Oeufs en bricotte avec fleurs du matin*. What on earth is that supposed to be when it's at home?'

For about a second, Emily sat perfectly still, tense as a guitar string. Then she slumped back into her chair and began to sob.

Oh *God*, Frank thought. He glanced furtively round. People were staring.

'Look,' he hissed, 'if it's something I said then I'm very sorry, and I understand that this must be rather disconcerting for you and you've got every right to be upset. But do you think you could possibly not make that fucking awful noise?'

She shook her head. 'I'm sorry,' she snuffled. 'It's just, for a moment there I thought I'd died, and I must've been really, really bad and wicked in my life, or why would God have sent me to France . . .' She stopped, and sat up. You could almost hear the click, as all the pulled-together parts of herself locked back into place. 'Who are you?' she said.

'I just told you, Frank Carpenter.' He hesitated. 'That's my name,' he added, then heard what he'd just said, and went on, 'I, um, save people.'

Emily frowned. 'What, you mean, like Superman?'

A stray tendril of the concept tickled the edge of his mind, but he ignored it. 'Not really, no,' he said. 'I do it for money, actually. I work for an insurance company.'

'Oh.' For some reason, the words *insurance company* made Emily feel a whole lot better. There's something so wonderfully mundane about insurance. It's so solid you could build sky-scrapers on it. 'But how—? You were standing under the tree and you caught me?'

Frank twitched. 'Sort of.'

'Ah. But in that case, what're we doing in France?'

Shrug. 'Like I said, I thought it called for a celebration. You know, you not being dead and everything.'

Silence. A long interval, during which Frank buttered a piece of bread and ate it.

'But I fell out of the tree like, two minutes ago. How did we get here?' A look of panic spread across Emily's face. 'I've been in a coma, haven't I? Or did I get amnesia from the bash on the head, and—?'

'Nope,' Frank interrupted. 'Look, if you can't make up your mind I'll order for both of us, all right? Only I'm hungry. Missed breakfast.' He waved at a waiter, who immediately homed in like a Scud missile and took down an order for two lobster salads. That alone made Emily realise that supernatural forces were at work.

'This is magic, isn't it?' she said quietly.

'Of course,' Frank said. 'You're in the trade, I'd have thought you'd be used to— All right,' he said, holding his hands up by way of supplication, 'I can see I'm possibly not handling this as well as I might have done. Begin at the beginning?'

'Yes, please.'

'You died.'

'Oh.'

Frank smiled. 'Yes,' he said, 'but luckily your employers had the good sense to insure your life with Beneficent Mutual for eleven million quid. My boss – George Sprague, nice bloke when you get to know him – he could no more pay out eleven million quid on a claim without a fight than walk to Mars without a spacesuit. So he hired me to save you. And I did.'

'Ah.' Emily looked at him as though she was wearing fogged-up glasses. 'So I didn't die after all?'

'Oh yes, you died all right.' Frank paused to crunch some more bread, and wipe crumbs off his shirt. 'Broken neck, punctured lung, massive brain trauma. I read the autopsy report, it was practically instantaneous, so you didn't suffer, but it was a genuine all-the-king's-horses job all the same.' He grinned. 'George Sprague suffered, though. I imagine they could hear him groaning on Alpha Centauri. So he sent for me. It's what I do. When there's a particularly expensive accident giving rise to a claim, I go back in time and make it not have happened.'

Long silence. Then she said, 'That's impossible.'

'Yes,' he said. 'I think it's worth mentioning that you gave me more hassle than any other case I've handled. I had three goes at it, no, scratch that, four, and on each occasion you snuffed it. A lesser man would've given up,' he added with a gentle smile that he later realised must've been quite insufferable, 'but not me. I was baffled. Until, of course, I figured out what was going on. Well, actually,' he conceded, 'I went and asked someone, and he explained it to me. You see, you were the victim of a Better Mousetrap.'

The look on Emily's face told him that he wasn't going to have to explain what that meant. It also had the useful effect of sobering Frank up. He'd been showing off, he realised. Not good.

'Sorry,' he said.

'That's all right,' Emily replied quietly. 'But – look, you're sure about that, are you? The Mousetrap, I mean. Only—'

'Someone was trying to kill you, yes. I'm—'

'Sorry, I know, you said.' She was angry; he could understand that. Actually, the way she snapped herself out of it was quite impressive. 'But if it was a Mousetrap – I mean, they're infallible. They always work, and there's nothing anybody can . . .' She stopped dead, like someone who's just realised they've missed their turning. 'You can go backwards and forwards in time?'

'Yes. Also impossible,' Frank said. 'Unless you're lucky enough to have a Portable Door.'

The look on Emily's face was worth paying money to see. Eventually, she whispered, 'You're kidding.'

'Straight up.' For some reason, Frank felt absurdly pleased that she was so impressed. 'The only one in existence, as far as I know. Belonged to my dad.'

'You've got a Portable Door. That's amazing.' She made it

sound ever so much cooler and more impressive than, say, boring old saving someone from certain death. 'So that's how you brought me here, then. The Door.'

'Yes,' Frank said smugly. 'Like I said, I asked someone how to beat a Mousetrap. He said, the only thing stronger than a Mousetrap is the Door; because it can take you anywhere, you see, anywhere in time and space. And then I remembered, Dad used it to get out of death once – long story, and I'm not sure I ever really understood it – so, well, why not give it a go? And it worked.'

'Oh,' she said. 'So how did you—?'

There are times when you can't stop a grin. You've just got to step back and let it rip. 'Quite simple, actually. I snuck up quietly while you were playing about up the tree with that cat, and spread the Door out on the ground exactly where you were going to land. Then, when you fell, I quickly opened it. You fell through the Door; I jumped through after you and told the Door to bring us here. Piece of cake, really. Ah, here's lunch.'

The lobster was a bit rubbery and the tomatoes didn't actually taste of anything much, which was a bit of a disappointment. The restaurant guide Frank had found this place in had particularly recommended the lobster salad. Still, not all magic works. And Emily didn't seem to mind, or to have noticed. She ate quickly and efficiently, like a jet liner refuelling in mid-air.

'So you're in the trade?' she said.

'Me?' Frank swallowed a chunk of fennel. 'No, not really. My parents were.'

'Oh.' Complete lack of interest. It could be that she was thinking about something else: not being dead, maybe, or who it was that had tried to kill her. Frank decided that it probably wouldn't have made much difference if the lobster had been all the guidebook cracked it up to be. It was awkward. It'd have been nice to talk to her (that was something Frank found he had strong views on: when had that happened?) but finding a subject wasn't going to be easy. Probably best if he left that to her. But she just went on eating, as though it was a chore she had to get through; and when she'd run out of things to eat, she looked at him and said, 'Now can you take me back, please?'

Oh, he thought. 'Sure,' he said. 'Where do you want to go?'

'Home,' she replied. 'I mean, the office.' Interesting slip there. 'I've got to get back and find out who tried to kill me.'

Well, there's that. 'Have you got any idea?' Frank asked.

Emily shook her head. 'Not a clue,' she replied. 'I mean, it's not exactly unheard of in the profession. We're pretty much a law unto ourselves, if you see what I mean. Partners – well, the office politics can get a bit intense sometimes.' She frowned. 'But I can't see why anybody'd want to get rid of *me*. I mean, I'm not anybody. I'm right down at the bottom of the ladder, not even on the letterhead, so it can't be someone who wants my job; and outside of the firm, I can't think of anybody I could be a nuisance to. It doesn't make sense, really.'

Frank rubbed his chin rather self-consciously. 'Revenge?' he said. 'I don't know, the family of a vampire you slew, something like that?'

'Unlikely. The things I get rid of, everybody's only too glad to see the back of them. Besides, nobody outside the profession would've known about Mousetraps, or how to get hold of one, or how to make it work. And vampires and werewolves and ogres and trolls and suchlike aren't really in the profession. I mean, they don't do magic themselves, usually they aren't bright enough, for a start. Goblins, maybe; but I've never had a job with goblins involved. But if it's not office politics—' Emily paused. 'Anyway,' she said, 'that's my problem.' Hesitation. Embarrassment, even? No, not really. Just another chore she was about to get out of the way. 'I'm sorry,' she said, rather primly, 'I haven't thanked you yet for—'

'Forget it,' Frank said, rather too quickly. 'Like I said, I get paid. And now I've got this job out of the way at last, I can get on with something a bit less complicated. Usually it's just road traffic stuff, the occasional industrial accident. Most of it you could do in your sleep.' He waved his hand again, and a waiter materialised with a bill, like a Klingon battlecruiser decloaking. He plonked a card on the tray without looking.

'That's amazing,' she said. 'How do you do that?'

He frowned. 'What?'

'Attract waiters like that. Is it some kind of psychotelekinesis, or are you using a modified form of Lexington's Hook?'

It took Frank a moment to figure out what she was talking about. 'Oh, I see. No, it's not magic or anything like that. I just sort of look hopefully at them and they come.'

'Really.'

'It's just a knack, I suppose,' he said. 'I've never thought about it.'

'That's—' Emily was looking at him; for the first time since they'd met, looking at him as though he was actually visible. 'I just sit there hoping they'll notice me. And they never do. And I hate sitting around after the meal's finished, waiting for the bill.'

Frank was disconcerted, he found, by how disconcerting he found her sudden interest. A great deal was happening all of a sudden, and he wasn't sure he was keeping track of it. 'Never been a problem with me,' he mumbled, thinking: a moment ago, she was in a hurry to get back to the office. 'Not that I'm a great one for eating out anyway. I generally just have a—'

'How about getting served in pubs?'

He shrugged. 'I walk up to the bar and someone asks me what I want.'

'Oh.'

'Is that unusual?'

'A bit.' Emily was staring – no, gazing – into his eyes, as if trying to read something written on his retina in tiny letters. 'I can stand there for ten minutes and nobody sees me. Sometimes I wonder if I'm invisible.'

'Really?' He was about to say that he found it strange that people didn't notice her; fortunately for his peace of mind, he stopped himself in time. 'I'd have thought that, you know, in your line of work, an assertive personality—'

'It's not that, I don't think. I mean, I can stand up for myself and all that. I don't know, maybe I've just got myself into the habit of being inconspicuous—'

'So that you can creep up on dragons without being seen and stuff?'

'Well, sort of. Actually, you try not to get in a position where creeping up's necessary, if you see what I mean. Dragonslaying's not like that, as a matter of fact, not if you do it properly.'

Frank frowned. 'Sorry if this is a frequently asked question,' he said, 'but how do you go about something like that? I mean, Dad talked about it occasionally, but he never went into any sort of detail. He did say he killed one once himself; a very small one, though. He sat on it.'

Emily nodded, as though this was a perfectly normal conversation. To her, of course, no doubt it was. 'A wyvern, probably,' she said. 'They're pretty fierce, but they've got very fragile bones. Very thin bone walls, to save weight, for flying.'

'Ah.'

'That's right. With wyverns, a percussive approach is often the best way, because they've got an amazing poison tolerance, for their body mass.' Frank got the impression that she was comfortable talking shop. 'And as for shooting them, you can forget it. Their muscles have a low water content, so ordinary hydrostatic shock just doesn't seem to get the job done.' She paused for a moment, then said, 'Which firm was your father with?'

'J. W. Wells,' Frank replied. 'They went bust.'

'Heard of them. But you didn't go into the trade.'

Something had changed; and it wasn't the sort of effect you got with the Door, where a neat, surgical intervention altered history. It was – well, rather more remarkable than that. A moment ago, she'd been – well, bewildered to start with, understandably enough, then eating busily, because death gives you an appetite and you need to keep your strength up; and after that, she'd wanted to get back to the office . . . Something had changed; and if it meant listening to her talking shop, because that was the sort of talking she felt comfortable with, he didn't really mind.

Bloody hell, Frank thought.

(But by the time you think that, it's generally too late.)

'Me? No.' He could hear his own voice, and it didn't sound very familiar. 'Mum and Dad didn't actually like the magic business very much – they were glad to get out of it. They came into some money, you see.'

'Oh.' He'd disconcerted her again. Probably, not liking the profession was heresy. 'My father was in the trade, too,' Emily went on, and she was being careful not to make it sound like a reproach. 'It was what I always wanted to do, since I was little. I can't imagine doing anything else.'

In Frank's mind, sirens wailed as the damage-control teams swung into action. 'I imagine it can be a really interesting job,' he heard himself say, and made a mental note to save up and buy some decent words, instead of tatty old ones like *interesting*. 'I mean, you must get to deal with some fascinating stuff—'

'It's boring, mostly.' Emily frowned. 'When it's not terrifying, I mean. But it's half a per cent blind terror and the rest is just being in an office. Funny, actually,' she said, after a heartbeat's pause. 'I'm in the magic business and I do mostly tedious, repetitive clerical chores. You travel through time and save lives, and you're in *insurance*—'

'Mostly maths,' Frank said quickly. 'Got to calculate the exact moment of intervention, you see. For every minute of actual fieldwork, there's two hours of quantum calculus and probability crunching. Actually,' he added – it hadn't really occurred to him before – 'it may sound rather dashing and weird but it's just work, really. I kid myself it's not, because if it was work, that'd mean I'm all grown-up and responsible, but when you take a long, hard look at it, it's not that easy to spot the difference.'

Silence. Not so much a pause as a rest, like in music. You have to stop occasionally to allow the changes to take effect.

'I suppose I should be getting back to the office,' Emily said. 'They'll be wondering where I've got to.'

Especially the ones who're trying to kill you? Best not to go into that. 'Not a problem,' he said, with a bit of grin left over from his earlier bumptiousness. 'The Door, remember? If I try hard I can land it on a quarter of a second. Marvellous thing,' he added. 'Sometimes I really wish I knew how it works.'

'You don't know?'

'Not a clue.'

'Well—' She stopped. 'I can tell you, if you like, but it probably won't make much sense. It's a bit – well, technical.'

Frank made a fine-by-me gesture with his hands. 'Try me,' he said.

'Yes, but—' Frown. 'I get carried away when I start talking about work stuff. I have an idea that listening to a long speech about things you don't understand can be a bit boring.'

Frank shook his head. 'I grew up in New Zealand,' he said. 'If you live there for any length of time and you're not interested in sheep or the movies, you learn boredom management as a basic survival skill. Also, it might be quite useful to know how the thing works, since I make my living out of it.'

'Well—'

Actually, Emily was quite right. It was boring, very boring indeed, and she had the rare ability to reach inside a basically uninteresting concept and bring out the deeply buried latent tedium that the casual observer could so easily miss. The curious thing – very strange indeed, stranger than time travel or dragon-slaying or mysterious assassins lurking behind suburban apple trees for no apparent reason – was that he really didn't mind. Listening to her explaining about Z-axis bipolar simultaneous shunts was a bit like opera: you can't follow the plot and the words are rubbish even if you can make them out through all the caterwauling, but if you relax completely and let it all wash over you like the lava flow from a volcano, it's actually rather soothing. More to the point, Frank realised (and the realisation made him sit up in his chair as if he'd been poked in the bum with a sharp nail), he'd rather be bored by her than interested by anybody else. Which is about as perfect a definition of the L-word as you can get—

'And that's about it, basically,' he heard her say. 'Mostly it's just Shirakawa's Constant, but with a guidance system and stable superconductors. The only difficult bit is how anybody ever managed to make one in the first place, because of the reverse exit instabilities. If you've already got one, of course, then in theory you could duplicate it using—' She paused, and seemed suddenly to be aware of how long she'd been talking for. 'You didn't really want to be told all that,' she said. 'Sorry.'

'Don't apologise,' Frank said immediately. 'It was fascinating. I learned a lot,' he added, neglecting to state what it was he'd learned a lot about. 'Look, would you like some coffee or something? Ice cream? Boat trip down the Seine? You don't have to worry about getting back,' he added quickly. 'I can have you standing outside your office door any time you like, in about thirty seconds.' He stopped and noticed that he'd run out of words and breath. Whatever she said next, he knew, was going to be very important indeed.

'I'd better not,' Emily replied; and he'd been right. It was a very important, highly significant statement, easily up there with the Gettysburg Address and *Ich bin ein Berliner*; not so much because of the words, but because of the way she'd said them. 'I mean,' she went on, 'quite apart from the stacks of work I've got piled up on my desk, there's this whole someone-trying-to-kill-me business, and until I've got that sorted out, it's kind of hard to give my full attention to anything else. But—' (It was at that moment that *but* became Frank Carpenter's all-time favourite three-letter monosyllable.) 'I don't know, would you like to have lunch sometime? If you're not busy or anything. So I can say thank you properly, when my mind's not all clogged up with weirdness and stuff.'

'Love to,' Frank said. 'I know this nice, quiet little Italian place in 1976. They do really good pasta, and it's a well-known fact that anything you eat before you were born isn't fattening.'

The Door whisked them away to Cheapside, where it opened in the side of a parked Transit van. Emily was clearly impressed by the foldaway stairs. When it was rolled up back in its tube, Frank said, 'See you here tomorrow, then, twelvish', and she nodded, smiled, and walked away. Not long afterwards, a door, an ordinary glass office door, swallowed her up and left him standing alone on the pavement.

The temptation to unroll his little square of plastic sheet and issue the command *Here, tomorrow, twelvish* was almost too strong to bear, but he managed it somehow. Instead, he walked slowly down the street, turned left and right a few times, and arrived at the entrance to Mr Sprague's office.

'That's unusual,' George Sprague said, when Frank had been shown in. 'You came in through the door.'

'So?'

'Instead of the wall. Nothing wrong, is there?'

'What?' Frank woke up out of a distinctly soppy daydream. 'Oh, no, everything's fine. Just fancied the walk, you know.'

Mr Sprague shrugged, waited a few seconds, and said, 'Well?'

'Well what?'

'To what do I owe the pleasure?'

'Oh.' Frank shook himself like a wet dog. 'Sorry,' he said. 'Miles away. The job. Done.' He fished about in his top pocket and produced a folded piece of paper. Mr Sprague read it, shuddered slightly, and put it in his in-tray. Then he reached for his chequebook.

'Aren't you going to check it out first?'

'That's all right,' Mr Sprague replied. 'I trust you.'

But Frank shook his head. 'If you wouldn't mind,' he said. 'I just want to make sure everything's worked out all right. So if you wouldn't mind—'

'If you like,' said Mr Sprague, and he prodded at his keyboard with a fingertip. 'There you go,' he said. 'No matches found. No record of any claims involving Emily Spitzer. Who is she, by the way? I mean to say, eleven million pounds. Someone must think pretty highly of her.'

Frank looked at him, then nodded. 'Yes,' he said.

The first thing Emily did when she reached her office the next morning was grab her diary and write down *lunch, twelvish*, on tomorrow's page. When she'd done that, she looked at the words for rather a long time, as if wondering how the hell they'd got there.

The opening of the door brought her out of suspended animation. Nobody ever knocked at Carringtons.

'There you are,' said Colin Gomez, and the white glare of the fluorescent strip lighting flashed off the shiny top of his slightly pointed head. 'How'd it go? Everything all right?'

For a split second, Emily couldn't think of what she should say next. 'Fine,' she managed to grunt. 'No problem.'

'Excellent.' Colin Gomez loomed in the doorway like a large shapeless bag full of something. 'Keep the clients happy, that's the ticket. How about Mrs Thompson? Glad to get the moggy back safe and sound, I expect.'

Emily looked at him as if he was one of those puzzles where you have to find words hidden in a random jumble of letters. Try as she might, though, she couldn't make out *murderer*. Lots of other words, perhaps, nearly all of them offensive to some extent, but not that one. 'I didn't get a chance to talk to her before I left,' she mumbled. 'Just got the cat and came away.'

'Oh.' Frown. His forehead made her think of a mop, the sort where you push a handle and it squidges up. 'You should've waited and spoken to her, made sure everything was all right.'

'Sorry.'

The mop unsquidged. 'Never mind,' said Mr Gomez. 'Can't be helped. I'll phone her. Old biddies like the personal touch. Just rang to see if Tiddles is OK after his nasty experience, something like that.'

'Good idea,' she replied. 'Actually, I was wondering—'

'Got another job for you,' Mr Gomez went on, blundering through the last words of her sentence like a stray elephant through a bazaar. 'Giant spiders. Nest of the buggers, in the main computer room at Zimmerman and Schnell in Lombard Street. Turned up out of the blue early this morning and started spinning webs everywhere. Probably quite well established by now, so you'll need rubber overalls and some kind of cutting torch.'

Emily sighed. 'Fine,' she said. 'It'd have been nice if they'd called us in a bit earlier, though. Those webs are a pain.'

Mr Gomez clicked his tongue. 'They said sorry for that,' he replied. 'But it's taken them this long to unravel the office manager, and apparently he's the only one who can authorise bringing in outside contractors. They haven't started laying eggs yet, though, so it's not so bad. I said you'd pop over there as soon as you got back from your other job. Take a taxi,' he said, with the air of a prince scattering gold to the urban mob. 'Save you lugging all the gear about on the Tube.'

'Thanks. That'll make all the difference in the world.'

Colin Gomez nodded. Irony had a tendency to bounce off him, like gravel off a battleship. 'Splendid. Oh, and one other thing.'

Oh for crying out— 'Yes?'

'You'd better take the new man with you. Show him the ropes, give him a feel for how we do things here. Nothing like plunging in at the deep end, after all.'

The final step of the escalator, the one that isn't there. 'New man?'

Mr Gomez frowned again. 'Didn't you get the memo? Oh, right. Yes, we've taken on a new trainee. Splendid chap, very highly qualified, we were lucky to get him.'

'Oh.' Emily snatched a fraction of a second to consider that. Nothing wrong with taking on trainees, of course, though the last she'd heard was that the partners reckoned the firm was overstaffed and there'd have to be Rationalisation unless productivity per capita could be jacked up to some impossible level. Still, since when was management consistent? 'Sure,' she added. 'Only – well, giant spiders, it could get a bit awkward. I'm not sure it's such a terribly good idea, taking along a novice. The client might not like it,' she added quickly.

But Mr Gomez waved his hand in that vague of-course-I-know-best-I'm-a-partner way she'd had to get used to over the years. 'It won't be a problem,' he said, in the manner of a bald pop-eyed god saying '*Let there be light.*' 'Just keep an eye on him,

he'll be fine. I've told him he'll be working closely with you for
the next six weeks. He seemed very pleased.'

'*Six weeks?*'

Mr Gomez beamed. 'I know you've had a lot on your plate
lately,' he said, 'what with the Credit Mayonnaise job and the
Dillington Fine Arts business. Having an assistant'll take some
of the load off your shoulders.'

'Yes, but—'

How could someone with such big ears be so deaf? 'All I ask
in return is that you help him get settled in, take a bit of time to
show him the routines, a bit of on-the-job training, no big deal.
All right? Splendid. I'll get Julie to send him down and introduce
himself.'

The appalling thing, Emily thought, as Colin Gomez's ele-
phantine footsteps receded down the corridor, the truly
appalling thing is that he honestly thinks he's helping me. But
what's actually going to happen is, I'm going to have to nurse-
maid this clown, show him how to blow his nose and tie his
shoelaces, keep him from getting eaten or fried, and still find
time to get my work done. And to think: when Gomez came in
here, the worst I thought him capable of was trying to have me
killed. You can be so wrong about people.

By way of a counter-irritant, she turned her mind back to the
Mousetrap and its implications. But her thoughts wouldn't cut
into it; they kept glancing off, like a knife on glass, and sneaking
back to her rather bizarre lunch hour. Frank Carpenter: every
time she tried to concentrate on motives and opportunities, he
kept floating back into her mind's eye, like the people who stand
behind celebrities being interviewed in the street and wave idi-
otically into the camera. That was disturbing, rather more so
than the alleged Mousetrap or even her brush with death.
Emotional entanglements – Emily liked the expression, it always
made her think of brambles, coils of rusty barbed wire, hopelessly knotted balls of string: dangerous, tiresome things that
got in the way, held you up and could cut you to the bone if you
weren't very careful how you handled them. A sort of World War

One scenario; even if you made it over the top and across No Man's Land, you still had to cut your way through the emotional entanglements before fighting it out hand to hand in the enemy's trenches. *Not fair*, she protested to the universe. Bad enough getting saddled with the newbie for six whole bloody weeks. Love as well as nursemaiding was just plain insufferable.

Her mind froze; then, quite calmly, she played back that last thought. There it was, the L-word, like something nasty showing up on an X-ray. Unwelcome, scary, changing everything if you let it, but if we stay calm and practical, maybe we can figure out what to do about it before the panic sets in—

I actually agreed to have lunch with him tomorrow. No, excuse me, I damn well *suggested* it. I must've been out of my tiny—

Spend too long in the magic trade, and you start thinking differently from other people. Her first thought was: J. W. Wells, didn't they use to market the best love philtre in the business? Bastard! He must've laced my salad with it; only, no, both meals came at the same time and anyway, you fall asleep for ten minutes before it takes effect. All right, then, while I was in transit, between Kew and Paris, maybe there was some way he could've—

Or maybe, Emily told herself, you just quite liked the guy. It's possible. Maybe (heresy warning: secure all fragile preconceptions and evacuate sensitive areas) it'd be quite nice to meet someone, have a life outside work, access a few of those human feelings you've been carrying around all these years, like the mysterious gadget you find in the car's tool kit and can never figure out the use of. Maybe. It's all very well being the job, and her job was one that demanded absolute focus and paid for it in narrow-band self-esteem; in the words of the great Kurt Lundqvist, the man who's tired of killing is tired of life. But.

She scowled. Something she was scheduled to do in the near future was making her feel apprehensive, and she had a feeling it wasn't exterminating giant spiders—

'Emily Spitzer?'

She looked up. Standing in front of her was a tall young man, ginger-haired, with glasses. 'That's me,' she said. 'Who are you?'

A smile you could've defrosted pizzas with glared in her face. When the dazzle abated and she could see again, she was aware of an outstretched hand pointed straight at her, like a weapon. It took her a moment before she realised that she was supposed to shake it.

'Erskine Cannis,' the young man said and, since he kept a straight face as he did so, Emily guessed he must be entirely immune to embarrassment. 'I'm the new trainee, and I'd just like to say how excited I am at the prospect of working with you for the next two months. It's been—'

'Hold on,' she interrupted, letting go of the hand and fighting the urge to wipe her palm on something. 'Six weeks. That's what Colin Gomez told me.'

The tiny spasm of Erskine Cannis's eyebrows translated as *does not compute*. 'Two months,' he corrected her. 'As part of the firm's trainee-induction programme. It says all about it in the brochure.'

Brochure? 'But that's not – I mean, I think there's been some confusion here,' she mumbled. 'But that's OK, I'll sort it out with Colin, and—' She listened to herself, and the get-a-grip lights came on inside her head. Sort it out with Colin; sure. 'So,' she said, flattening herself against the back of her chair, 'you've joined the firm. Well. Good to have you with us.'

'It's great to be here.' It came back at her like a tennis shot. 'This is a very special moment for me, and I want to thank you for—'

Emily held up a hand for silence. 'You're not American by any chance, are you?'

'No.'

'Ah. My mistake. Listen,' she said quickly, before he could start again, 'we've got a job to do.'

He nodded, like someone trying to shake cocktails in his mouth. 'Mr Gomez told me,' he said. 'As you can imagine, I'm pretty damn thrilled about it. Of course, I haven't absolutely committed to the pest-control track quite yet, naturally I won't be making a final decision about specialisation-option selection until I've completed all the legs of the induction programme, but I think I can say that right now, pest control's definitely heading up my shortlist, particularly since I got a distinction in both theory and practice in my finals. Talking of which, what are your views on depleted uranium versus traditional mercury as regards exploding projectiles for ogre management?'

Contrary to what everybody tells you, counting up to three in your head doesn't really help. 'You stay here,' Emily said firmly, 'while I get the stuff. Sit down, and don't play with anything. All right?'

'Absolutely.'

Induction programme, she thought, as she fiddled with the sticky lock on the grenade locker in the hardware store. Specialisation-option selection. Depleted uranium versus boring old traditional mercury. The brochure – what brochure, for crying out loud? When I joined up, they stuck me in front of a desk and pointed at the filing cabinet, and it was three days before I found out where the ladies' toilet was. Where the hell did they get this exhibit from, anyhow?

Emily stuffed two more grenades into her plastic carrier for luck, then signed for the gas bottles in the weapons register. Two months, she muttered to herself. Two months of dedication, enthusiasm and motivation, unless she broke first and killed him. After killing Colin Gomez, of course. With a Better Mousetrap, just to be sure—

She paused, her fingers clamped tight on the handle of the poisons drawer. Better Mousetraps.

She wasn't paranoid; of course not. But wasn't it just a teeny-tiny bit odd that the tight-fisted, cost-hyperconscious firm should've hired a new trainee, one who by his own admission had pest control right up there on the frozen summit of his shortlist, at a time when they should be facing an unexpected vacancy in the dragonslaying sector? If the Mousetrap had worked – and it had never been known to fail before; in front of her eyes danced a mental image of Colin Gomez, bleating '*Of course, we must do everything to minimise workload disruption and inconvenience to established clients, I know, let's take on a trainee—*'

Bastards, she thought. It really must be them, then.

Emily drifted across the room and sat down heavily on a crate of 105mm armour-piercing shells. That doesn't make sense, she thought. If they want to get rid of me, all they've got to do is fire me. True, that'd mean paying redundancy, and they wouldn't want to do that; but they'd find a way round it somehow, something that wouldn't actually involve homicide. And a Better Mousetrap: complete overkill, dark and slightly hysterical pun intended.

At least it answered one question. Why had they hired this clown? Because he was all they could get *at short notice.*

All right, fine. They really are out to get you; in which case, vitally important to decide what I'm going to do about it, and quickly, before they try again. Resign; they want rid of me, indulge them. But that wouldn't do; see above, under firing, ease of. Run away? Leave the country, one-way ticket to Nova Scotia, change name, retrain as an aromatherapist. Emily shook her head; so naive. In her office on the eighth floor, she knew for a fact, Amelia Carrington had a mirror that could show you anything you wanted to see, anywhere. True, she'd buggered up the central processor unit by asking it 'Who's the fairest of them all?' and kicking it round the room when it flashed up Kate Moss instead of her, but even so, it wasn't a viable business risk to assume that it couldn't still do simple things like finding runaway employees. And there were other ways they could track her down, if they wanted to. Running and hiding were strictly no dice.

Unless—

The thought made her wince, but she forced her eyes open. Hiring the trainee was so typically *them*; it made it believable, real, serious. In which case, she was going to die. Again. And again and again, if needs be, until the job was done and signed off. Unless the one man in the universe who could save her was prepared to help.

Emily sighed, and pulled a face. My hero, she thought.

CHAPTER SEVEN

Dennis Tanner was reading his obituary when the call came through.

He'd found it eighteen months ago, in the back of one of the trade journals, while looking for a piece on applied demonology in the petrochemicals industry. Dennis Norman Azog Tanner, 1880-1997, and a list of his various discoveries, publications and achievements. At the time he'd been bewildered, terrified and extremely annoyed that they'd left out his 1989 Gandalf award (the bauxite find at Wayatumba; still the biggest on record). Now it was just a useful reference for dates and names.

'Call for you from Carringtons,' his mother said. 'That pushy tart.'

Coming from her, that was praise indeed, and it could only refer to Amelia Carrington – his god-daughter, for what little it was worth. She'd been a revolting child, he remembered; top of the class in everything, played six musical instruments and kept winning rosettes at gymkhanas. Of course, the winged horse was an advantage.

'Fine,' Dennis Tanner said, closing the journal and putting it away in his desk drawer. 'Put her through.'

Click, pause; then, 'Uncle Dennis.'

He frowned. He was only Uncle Dennis when she wanted

something, and anything the managing partner of Carringtons wanted from a sole practitioner with an office over a chemist's shop couldn't be good. 'Hello,' he said. 'How's tricks?'

'Pretty good.' That low, husky voice, Marlene Dietrich with her mouth full of chocolate. Pure effective magic, of course. Unadjusted, she sounded like a mouse on helium. 'Reason I'm calling, I've got something that's rather in your line, and I thought it might be fun if we looked at it together.'

Being mostly humanoid, Dennis Tanner didn't have the wonderfully expressive ears of his goblin ancestors. If he had, they'd have been right back, like a worried cat's. 'Something in my line,' he repeated. 'You mean minerals.'

'Bauxite, yes. Jerome Hernandez in our Christchurch office thinks he's on to something, but apparently there's high levels of ambient thaumaton radiation, which means he can't get a clear reading. I seem to remember something in that April '76 article of yours in the *Gazette* about cutting through thaumaton interference, so I thought I'd give you a shout.'

Dennis leaned back in his chair and groped for a cigar. Very flattering, of course, that she'd read his article, even though it was groundbreaking stuff and still the last word on the subject. But if she remembered it, including the date and everything, why didn't she just look it up, instead of ringing him? Letting a trade rival know that there was a whiff of a big bauxite find in – Christchurch office, did she say? Presumably not Hampshire, so New Zealand somewhere. Not the sort of thing a sensible person would do. And for all her many faults, Amelia was sensible. Smart as a smart bomb, in fact.

'Thaumaton radiation,' he said slowly, playing for time. 'Well, basically, it's caused by the decay of compromised magic particles in a powerful Effective field. Eberhard and Chang—'

'I know all that, Uncle Dennis,' Amelia interrupted, and her voice changed slightly: a shark's fin breaking the surface of an ocean of dark brown honey. 'What I need to know is, what can we do about it? I mean, Jerome's a nice enough boy and very sound on basic scrying, but if what he's saying about the scale of the thing's anything to go by, we need to cut to the chase on this one, start out the way we mean to end up, you know? So, naturally, I thought of you.'

Quite, Dennis said to himself; and if that's right, it's the first natural thought you ever had in your life. 'I'd be interested,' he said carefully. 'What's the deal?'

'Joint venture.' Dennis nearly dropped the phone. 'Your expertise, we do the legwork and the boring stuff – the legal side, contractors, all that. Obviously we'll organise the money. Basically, you find the stuff, we dig it up and flog it.'

Joint venture. Dennis tried to light his cigar and scorched the tip of his nose instead. It was his experience, painfully and often bloodily acquired, that anything that seems too good to be true is probably too good to be true. And as far as trustworthiness was concerned, Amelia Carrington was a British government dossier. Even so.

'Sounds good,' he managed to croak. 'When are you free?'

'Right now.' Alarm bells. Amelia I-can-window-you-five-minutes-next-January Carrington, free right now. An urge to grow a beard and flee the country gripped Dennis Tanner like a mole wrench, but he suppressed it. There was an old goblin saying: your enemy is never more vulnerable than when he's trying to be clever. And if there was one resource Dennis Tanner had every confidence in, it was his own cleverness. 'Fantastic,' he said. 'Your place or mine?'

'Here, I think.' Amelia's voice had just the right modulation of distaste. 'No disrespect, Uncle Dennis, but I think our facilities are just a tad more cutting-edge than yours.' Slight pause. 'Shall I send a car, or—?'

'Thanks,' Dennis replied through gritted teeth. 'The bus'll do me fine. See you soon, then.'

'Ciao.'

He sat for a while with the phone in his hand, thinking serious thoughts. Old Tosser Carrington, for example. A complete idiot blessed with ridiculously good luck and just enough vicious low cunning to survive; back in the nineteen-hundreds they'd been good mates, two young newly qualified magicians trying to make it in the merciless cut and thrust of the Canberra sorcery trade. When they'd quit Oz to give the old country a go, they'd had some kind of vague idea of setting up in partnership: Dennis on corporate magic and minerals, Tosser handling the private-client and pest-control side. But within a few weeks of getting here, Tosser had been practically handed an apprenticeship at Mortimers on a plate, leaving Dennis to fend for himself. True, the first job he'd applied for had been at J. W. Wells, and the rest was history, as his obituary was at pains to point out. Nevertheless, the old resentment was still there, logged and ticketed and archived in Dennis's monumental grudge collection. The thought that, now he was down on his luck and scratching a living in inner-city Nowheresville, Tosser Carrington's equally obnoxious daughter was going to wave a magic wand and make him rich and famous once again was a bit too much to swallow.

A trap, then. Well, she was perfectly capable of it, but why bother? If she meant him harm, why go to such ridiculous lengths? Damaging people, getting rid of them entirely, was easy-peasy for someone like Amelia. Which reminded him of something. Carringtons. Better Mousetraps.

Dennis's nostrils flared. He believed in coincidences to the same extent that the Pope believes in Odin. The possibility that this stuff was somehow Carpenter-related gave him a pain in his midriff. He scowled, rebuking himself for his own dimness. Lights should have gone on when Amelia had mentioned New Zealand: last known address of Paul and Sophie Carpenter, location of the vast bauxite deposit with which he and his erstwhile partners had paid those two unmitigated pests off after the nasty business with Theo van Spee and custardspace. He shivered. He could feel dark, slimy tendrils of Carpenter curling softly around him, poised to crush him into pulp.

Yes, but a joint venture with Carringtons – Dennis Tanner knew all about tides in the affairs of men, and he was Australian enough to know that any tide can be ridden if you're handy enough with your surfboard. And, of course, he had one special weapon that

Amelia had almost certainly underestimated and quite possibly clean forgotten about. He frowned, then grinned the great, unique Tanner grin. Then he rang through to the front office.

'Mum,' he said, 'get your coat. We're going out.'

In the bottom left-hand corner of the big screen, which at that precise moment was filled with Russell Crowe's hugely amplified armpit, a door opened.

Luckily, it was the mid-afternoon showing, so nobody noticed as Frank Carpenter stepped out from under Russell's coat, nipped smartly down the Door's foldaway stairs and darted up the centre aisle. Thanks to Mr Sprague's excellent report on the Catford multiplex blaze, he had no trouble finding the small patch of smouldering carpet. He jumped up and down on it a few times, emptied the bottle of Evian he'd brought with him over the embers and retraced his steps. Job done.

The Door opened again in the back wall of a Marks & Spencers in west London, and Frank stepped out, looking unusually grave. Putting out the fire, saving several lives and many millions of pounds: *morceau de gateau*. Now he was going to have to do something really difficult and scary. He was going to try and buy a shirt.

He had shirts, of course – three of them. One of them was a sort of blotchy off-white, with frayed cuffs and collar. One of them was yellow, with a striking Paisley motif, a birthday present from his mother. He'd been wearing the third for three days now, and even when it was pristine from the launderette it was hardly a thing of beauty. When a man's got a date with the girl he thinks he may be in love with, he may well find himself having to reassess his entire shirt philosophy. Also, he decided, trousers. And socks. And stuff.

Of course, Frank thought as he wandered in through the door, I could be really daring and hell-for-leather go-for-it and buy a suit. Probably that's what Alexander the Great would've done, and possibly also Napoleon and Robert E. Lee. Also, with a suit you get a jacket as well as the trousers, which'd be two birds with one stone. On the other hand, there's no point in overdoing it. I mean, suppose it doesn't work out and I haven't met the girl of my dreams?

Then I'd be broken-hearted and all alone in the world, *and* stuck with a useless set of clothes I'll never wear again. You've got to be practical, play the odds, have a fall-back position; like Hannibal, the Duke of Wellington or Field Marshal Montgomery.

An escalator took Frank up two floors, and he found himself in a place where there were shirts. Lots of shirts. Everywhere he looked, shirts pressed in on him like the souls of the dead in the underworld, each one seeming to reach out to him, begging him to take them out of there into the light. The reckless courage that had got him in through the Door was ebbing fast. There were too many of the damned things, and how could anybody be expected to choose between them? By one set of criteria, they were all practically identical – two sleeves, collar, buttons, everything a boy could ever need in terms of weather exclusion neatly contained in one simple-to-operate package. Looked at from the other relevant perspective, the variety was stunning. Patterned and plain, stripes going up and down and side to side, colours representing every conceivable fragmentation of the spectrum, *combinations* of every colour imaginable; and the bitch of it was, some of these shirts were right and some of them were wrong, and he had no idea of how the rules worked. All he knew was that if you got it right, you looked a million dollars and lovely women melted into your arms like ice cream on a hot day, and if you got it wrong, children pointed at you in the street. It was, he couldn't help thinking, a bit like the other incomprehensible scary thing, the one he was buying the shirt for. Finding the right one, having the wit to know it when you'd found it, keeping it, looking after it properly, never letting it go. Washing it occasionally. Ironing. Life is so much easier, of course, if you never bother.

That had been easy enough back in Wayatumba, South Island, where Frank had lived in a pretty remote place and had never got opportunities to meet many shirts. Here, though, they were everywhere you looked. You couldn't ignore them, sooner or later you had to bite the bullet and find a way of coping, unless you wanted to have nothing to look forward to but a lonely old age wearing nothing but vests and polo-necks. And sometimes, when life steams up your mind's glasses and you can't see the pattern that governs your destiny, you just have to trust to providence and synchronocity and take a chance. Frank pulled himself together, clenched his muscles till the tendons twanged, and grabbed the first shirt that came to hand. It was pink.

So much for providence and synchronicity. He put it back with the strained delicacy of someone handling something dead, looked again and gave up. It was too difficult. Given, say, three shirts to choose from, he could probably reach a decision if he took his time. Three hundred, however, was too many.

I don't actually have to do this, Frank told himself. I could Portable Door back home, wash, dry and iron the shirt I'm wearing and still be in good time for lunch. And yes, all right, using magic so I don't have to do a perfectly simple thing that everybody else but me can cope with may be a bit pathetic and sad, but so what? Surely magic's there for the pesky little things in life rather than the great big important stuff that only matters to governments and multinational companies; or if it isn't, it damn well should be.

He played that thought back, and sighed. Well, quite; and while you're at it, feed the world and give peace a chance. All in all, it was probably just as well he'd never been tempted to go into the magic business. Just think of all the damage he could've done, even in the very short space of time he'd have been likely to survive.

The hell with it, he thought. Quick look round, then into the changing room, where he spread the Door over the full-length mirror and stepped through.

Mr Sprague was mildly surprised to see him.

'Not business,' Frank explained quickly. 'Need a favour. Won't take a minute. Please?'

'Not business,' Mr Sprague repeated, as if speaking a foreign language he didn't understand.

'No. Personal. Look, it'll take longer to explain than to do it, so—'

'All right.' Mr Sprague scowled. 'You don't expect me to go into that thing, do you?'

'What? Oh, the Door.' Frank laughed. 'You don't want to worry about that. Perfectly safe. And if you're really, really busy—'

'Yes?'

'I promise I'll get you back here one second after we leave. Deal?'

'Um.'

'One second *before* we leave.'

Sigh. 'Well, if you really insist—'

'Thanks.' Frank held the Door open. 'After you.'

'Are you *sure* that thing's—?'

'Positive. I use it myself, every day.'

Head bowed, fingers crossed, eyes screwed shut, Mr Sprague edged through the Door and disappeared. Shaking his head, Frank followed him, and walked out into the M&S changing room. 'There,' he said, closing the Door and catching it as it fell off the surface of the mirror, 'you see? Safe as—'

His mouth froze. He looked at the curtain in front of him, the mirror behind, the narrow space in between. Then he ripped open the curtain, plunged through it and stood for a moment, completely stunned.

No sign of Mr Sprague. Vanished. Gone.

When she was a little girl, Emily Spitzer was terrified of spiders. Her father, being that sort of man, refused to deal with them when she came sobbing. Life, he used to say, is full of scary things. The sooner you learn how to deal with them for yourself, the better. You'll learn to be resourceful, self-reliant. You have nothing to fear but fear itself.

Not knowing any better, Emily took him at his word; and, since she was the sort of person who has to do everything well, she quickly transformed herself from a perfectly normal junior arachnophobe into the champion spider-hunter of the Home Counties. She learned how to approach quietly, not making sudden movements that'd be likely to spook them and send them scuttling away into their inaccessible fastnesses under the skirting board. She learned the quick, wristy swat with a slipper heel or a rolled-up teen-fashion magazine, the precise amount of forward allowance to compensate for the last-second panic scuttle. By the age of ten, she was squashing spiders for her friends and their parents, at 25p a time. When she passed the entrance exam for magic college and had to choose a specialisation, it was almost inevitable that she'd opt for pest control; after all, it was no more than spider-hunting on a slightly larger scale, but with access to vastly more efficient forms of slipper heel. If she doubted her decision, it was only because pest control wasn't one of the fast-track disciplines that got you a partnership before you were thirty, unlike, say, Media & Entertainment or spiritual conveyancing. The danger aspect of it didn't bother her in the least, since she knew all about fear and how easy it was to overcome. Piece of cake, she thought. Line up those supernatural monsters and let me at 'em.

Her first encounter with giant spiders (*arachnis grandiforma Atkinsonii*) changed all that. It was, perhaps, unfortunate that the class tutor who was demonstrating basic giant-spider-management skills got his head bitten off, leaving Emily to lead the rest of the tutor group to safety through a thousand acres of Atkinsonii-haunted forest. As the goblins say, though, it's the burned child who fears the baptism of fire. On her return from that memorable field trip, as soon as she was out of intensive care, she amended her father's first law of survival by adding to it three small but very important words. Henceforth, it went –

You have nothing to fear but fear itself and scary things.

As the taxi stopped outside the offices of Zimmerman and Schnell in Lombard Street, it was in Emily's mind to share her guiding principle with Erskine Cannis. She had an idea that it might help him survive until, say, next Wednesday. She wasn't prepared to rate his life expectancy any higher than that, mostly because by then she would almost certainly have killed him herself.

'I think you'll find,' he was saying, as the taxi drove off and left them at the kerbside, 'that section 47, paragraph 5(c) of the third schedule to the Endangered Species Preservation Order 1997 includes all three of the major European subspecies of Atkinsonii as category 6, which means you can't destroy them with Class B explosives in a metropolitan district or the Isle of Wight without express permission from the secretary of state. Of course, if they turn out to be *arachnis grandiforma Atkinsonii erythrostomata*, there is a general licence during March and April—'

'We're here,' Emily said, loudly and clearly. 'Now then—'

'The distinguishing marks of *erythrostomata*, as I scarcely need to remind you—'

'Shut your face and carry the bags.'

The woman at the front desk asked them their names and the purpose of their visit; Emily replied, 'Pest control,' and the woman gave them each a little plastic badge. Then they sat and waited for a long time, until Mr Ahriman from Maintenance saw fit to come down and claim them as his own.

'Big bastards,' he said, in the voice of someone who's seen rather more than he wanted to. 'Big hairy bastards with ten legs—'

'Ah,' said Erskine, smirking, '*arachnis grandiforma Atkinsonii pachythorax*. In which case, schedule four applies.'

Mr Ahriman shot him a terrified glance. 'What's he talking about?'

'No, it doesn't,' Emily said firmly. 'And even if it did, we aren't going to start letting off nukes in the middle of the City of London, so you can forget about that for a start. Technical stuff,' she told Mr Ahriman blandly – he'd gone ever such a funny colour – 'nothing for you to worry about. You just leave everything to us and we'll have them out of there in a brace of shakes. Oh, while I think of it,' she added, 'we'll need some dust sheets and a couple of big rolls of sticky tape. Could you possibly organise that for us? Thanks.'

Mr Ahriman left them outside a door on the third floor marked *No unathorised entry* and scuttled back into the lift. When the doors had closed behind him, Erskine said, 'What are the dust sheets for?'

'Nothing,' Emily replied. 'It's just to give him something to do, let him feel he's contributing. And another thing,' she said. 'When we're on a job, don't you ever talk about trade stuff in front of the punter again. Got that?'

'Of course.'

She sighed. Rebukes, even when pitched at bollocking level, just seemed to soak away into Erskine, like water into sand. Instead of cringeing or taking offence like a normal human being, he was *grateful*. That was too much. It wasn't natural. It was inhuman. 'Good,' she said weakly. 'Glad we've got that sorted out. Now, then.'

Her mind had gone blank. She couldn't think what she was supposed to do next.

Of course, Emily said to herself, I'm used to working solo. Having someone else along flusters me. Even so; it wasn't good. On the other side of the door was an unspecified number of giant spiders (the ten-leg variety; oh, joy): lightning-fast, bodies as big as cows, legs like scaffolding, stings that went through five-mill Kevlar like it wasn't there, venom sacks holding more poison that a party conference – dammit, she needed to be focused, tuned, in touch with the grimly single-minded little girl with the torch in one hand and the slipper in the other who feared nothing (except fear itself) and who *got the job done*. And instead, here she was, mind like a teenager's bedroom, dithering.

'Right,' she snapped, her voice a trifle shrill, 'prime the stun grenades, and – no, scratch that, set up up the Everleigh scanners and *then* prime the grenades. Or is it the other way round?'

Panic.

Emily had heard the stories, of course. Everyone in the trade had heard them. Hugo van Leipzig, winner of five consecutive Siegfrieds, suddenly freezing in the middle of a routine manticore clearance. Gordon Shirasaya, five hundred and seven authenticated vampire stakings, taken down by a poxy little Class Seven because he lost the plot at the critical moment and dropped his tent peg. It was the thing you dreaded and never ever talked about in the bar at seminars, the sudden, unexplained onset of crippling fear in the course of a piece-of-shit milk run. It happened, everybody knew that. Basically, if you'd already lasted more than eighteen months in the trade, you knew for stone-cold certain that, sooner or later, that was how you were going to die. *But this isn't that*, screamed a voice inside Emily's head; she thought about it, as dispassionately as she could, and had to agree. It wasn't fear, she'd know it if it was. She'd feel the twisting in her stomach, the vicious twinge in the bladder, the loosening of the bowels. Not fear, then: something worse. It was – it was just woolly-mindedness, plain and simple. Somewhere in her head a door or a window had been left open, and she couldn't concentrate.

'Grenades first, isn't it?' The voice just behind her had lost that insufferable cockiness. Erskine was *worried*. Not good. 'Then the scanner, and then—'

'Then the thunderflashes, masks on, and then the gas bottles.' Emily was almost sobbing with relief as she said it. Her mind was clear again, and of course she knew what to do. 'Sorry about that,' she heard herself say. 'Just had a funny five seconds. Got those primers in, have you?'

'Nearly. Look, are you feeling all right? Only—'

'Of course I am, I'm fine. And get a move on with those primers. If we stand out here chatting all day they'll register our body heat and then we'll be really screwed. Or didn't they tell you that at college?'

Erskine handed her the first grenade in dead silence. Oops, Emily thought. Not making the most brilliant first impression here. Not, she added quickly, that it matters a flying fuck what that young stick of celery thinks. Even so.

'Right,' she said; and, with the fluency of long practice, she breathed in deep and out again, and kicked open the door.

After that, it was all a bit of an anticlimax. The stun grenades made the whole building shake, and in the complete dead silence that followed she fitted together the three parts of the Everleigh scanner as coolly as if she was putting the little brush thing on her vacuum cleaner at home. Thunderflashes – ho hum, yawn; slip the mask on, turn calmly round to make sure that Erskine's mask was clipped down properly, then out come the cyanide-gas bottles, twiddle the valve screws, close the door, sit down on the floor, set the timer, get out the latest Robert Harris and chill for ten minutes while the gas does its work—

'Excuse me,' Erskine said. 'What are you doing?'

Emily looked up from her book. 'Reading,' she said.

'But—' Shocked expression, as if she was doing something disgusting. 'Shouldn't you be monitoring life signs on the Everleigh scanner?'

'Nah.' She yawned. 'You can, if you like. Personally, I find watching a digital readout counting down from three thousand doesn't really light my fuse. Tell you what,' she said pleasantly. 'Why don't you go and find someone to make us a nice cup of tea? Milk and no sugar.'

'I – Certainly, right away.' For a split second, she honestly believed he was going to click his heels.

When Erskine had gone she tried to read, but her eyes just seemed to skid off the page. She shut the book, leaned her back against the wall and closed her eyes. Whatever had happened to her back then – not fear; not fear of death, anyhow, but there are other scary things in the world – it hadn't been any fun at all, and she needed to figure out what it was before she went any further. Was it, Emily asked herself, just that she'd been working alone for so long that any disruption to her customary procedures was enough to thrown her off balance? Or was it Erskine's unique ability to create irritation and self-doubt? She considered the evidence – no problem at all concentrating now – and reluctantly decided that it was none of the above. True, it was the first time she'd had a trainee tied to her tail, but there'd been plenty of times when the client, or the office manager or the head of security or some other pest had tagged along and got under her feet, and on those occasions she hadn't gone all soft in the head. Quite the reverse: the annoyance had only made her more focused, as she'd sublimated the irritation into cold, grim determination to do the job and get out of there before she murdered a customer. No, it was something else, something she couldn't isolate and label. She hadn't frozen, or let annoyance distract her. Instead, there'd been a moment when she hadn't been herself, almost as if—

The monitor beeped, and Emily glanced down. All the indicators were flatlined, and the infra-red showed nine large stationary biomasses, cooling steadily at the appropriate rate. She checked the toxicity level and used her E-Z-Teek telekinesis remote to tap into the building's environmental controls and set the extractor fans running. Simple, routine magic. Another day at the office.

Three minutes later, Erskine came back carrying two mugs. One had *The World's Greatest Boss* written on the side, and the other one was decorated with dancing cartoon pigs.

'Just waiting for the gas to clear,' she said brightly. 'You'd better ring Ibbotsons and tell them we're ready for clean-up. There were nine of them, so they'll probably need two skips.'

'Oh.' Erskine's face fell. 'I missed it.'

'What?'

He shrugged, rather ostentatiously. 'Doesn't matter,' he said. 'I'll ring Ibbotsons. Straight away.'

Emily felt an urge to jab the air with her finger and bark out 'Make it so,' but she fought it down. 'No rush,' she said. 'Ten minutes before we can go in there. Loads of waiting about in this game,' she added. 'You really should bring something to read.'

This time when Erskine went away she had no trouble getting into her book; in fact, it was rather nice to have an obedient gofer to do the phoning and fetch the tea, and she found herself wondering what on earth all the fuss had been about. So yes, she'd had a funny turn; but it had happened before the serious business started, it had only lasted a second or two, and once she'd got back into the swing of things it had faded away completely. Lot of fuss about nothing, she reassured herself; you're just a bit wound up because of having the idiot along.

'I called Ibbotsons,' Erskine reported, sounding as though he'd just come back from being the first man to reach the South Pole. 'They're sending two skips and a crane, just in case.'

Emily frowned. 'You weren't to know,' she said, 'but the crane's a scam. Means they can charge an extra ten per cent, and they know perfectly well they won't need it. You've got to watch them like a hawk or they'll fatten the bill like a Christmas turkey.'

'Oh.' He looked so very guilty and sad that she cheered up considerably. 'Shall I call them back and—?'

She shook her head. 'Don't worry about it,' she said. 'Client pays out-of-pocket expenses, so it's no skin off our nose. I just don't like to let them get out of hand. Word gets around if you're not careful.' Her monitor bleeped again; she closed her book and stood up. 'Right,' she said. 'That's the all-clear. We can go in now and check that everything's OK, and then we can sign off and go back to the office.' She grinned. 'Welcome to the pest-control business. What do you think of it so far?'

'Well—' Erskine said, and she opened the door.

He was bleating something about objective verification procedures as she peered into the darkened computer room. For a moment, the darkness puzzled Emily, until she glanced up and saw the swathes of dense black cobweb hanging like curtains from the ceiling. Even if the lights were still working, there was no way that stuff would admit the passage of a single photon. She sighed and pulled out her pocket torch.

The first spider she saw was about five yards from the door, curled up in the classic folded-legs configuration that meant it was no longer a problem. Just to be on the safe side, however, she monitored it for life signs with her Kawaguchiya XZ7700 SpydaSkan. Dead as the proverbial hammer. Next.

Emily edged forward, prodding her way with a telescopic probe. Even if the spiders were all dead, getting caught up in a patch of web was still something to be avoided. The revolting stuff ruined any article of clothing it came into contact with, and as for hair . . . She shuddered. Scary she'd learned to cope with, but there was no real, permanent defence against yucky. As a stray wisp snagged the back of her hand and welded itself to her skin, making her whimper as she pulled it away, it occurred to her that a routine check like this should really be left to junior staff – a trainee, say. Valuable hands-on experience, and cheaper for the client, too. The only factor that put her off the idea was the likelihood that Erskine would jump at the chance and quite possibly thank her afterwards, and she wasn't sure she could stand that.

Seven more dead spiders. They'd made a thorough mess of the computers. *Atkinsonii* are classed as sentient-intelligent, and some veterans of the trade reckoned they were considerably brighter than most non-humanoid monsters once you got to know them, though their world-view was crude and violent and their love of country-and-western music was predictable but sad. One thing on which all the authorities agreed, however, was that they were extremely literal-minded, which meant that once they started hearing rumours about humans building a worldwide web, they abandoned their usual habitat in dark, remote forests and started making a serious nuisance of themselves. Monitors and CPUs cracked open and with their wiring wrenched out littered the floor, and there was even a small, rather droopy proto-cobweb made out of modem cables slung between two desks in the far corner of the room.

Seven plus one makes eight; Emily stopped, and flicked the beam of her torch through the shadows. Another feature of *Atkinsonii* behaviour was their urge to crawl under something to die, so she knelt down and looked under the desks and tables. Nothing. She killed the torch beam and stood up, instinct ordering her to keep perfectly still. There had been nine quite distinct blips on the Everleigh, but so far she'd only found eight folded-up corpses. Of course, there was no way anything could have survived in there while it was pumped full of cyanide gas, and the Everleigh had also shown her nine perfect flatlines. At the back of her mind, a memory flickered: something about *Atkinsonii acrodontis* being able to slow down its bodily functions to simulate death and fool a scanner. These weren't *acrodontes*, they were *pachythoraces*, but maybe the research was incomplete . . . Emily's intestines prickled, and she called up the floor plan of the room in her mind's eye, with special reference to the distance and vector of the doorway. If her theory was correct, it'd be nice to live long enough to write a short piece for the *Gazette* about it.

'Hello.' Bloody Erskine's voice. 'Are you all right in there?'

One of the few really useful things she'd learned in second year at college was that, ninety-five times out of a hundred, you make more noise going *Sssh!* than the person you're trying to silence. Something about sibilants carrying further than dentals, labials and all the other types of articulated sound. She tried to remember if the article she'd read had mentioned whether *pachythoraces* understood English. *Atkinsonii acrodontes* were only fluent in Spanish, she recalled, while *leptopodes* were bilingual in Gujarati and (by some extraordinary quirk of evolution) Esperanto. But if the article had mentioned *pachythoraces*, she couldn't remember what it'd said—

'I said hello,' Erskine bellowed. 'Is anything the matter? Can I do anything to help?'

Dropping dead would be a good start, Emily thought. She did her best to edit his voice out of her mind. Was that a very faint rustling sound, such as two-inch leg bristles might make as they rubbed against the leg of a desk? Needless to say, she'd gone in without anything even remotely resembling a weapon, unless you counted the Mordor Army Knife (one of whose more puzzling features was the lack of any kind of cutting edge; she could only assume that the users it was designed for had perfectly good claws and teeth for that sort of thing, so there wasn't any call for a blade). Unleashing a twelve-foot collapsible ladder under its rapidly moving mandibles might disconcert the bastard for a moment or so, but would that be long enough for her to reach the doorway? Probably not. The RSPCA website recommended clapping your hands loudly and saying 'Boo!' as a humane, non-lethal alternative to blowing *Atkinsonii* to hell with rocket-propelled grenades, but she had a suspicion that the recommendation wasn't the product of what she'd consider as valid hands-on experience. Emily took a very careful step backwards, and felt something brush against her shoulder.

Nuts, she thought.

The stickiness and strength of *Atkinsonii* gossamer makes it a revolting nuisance when there aren't any live spiders around. In a spider-rich environment, it's just a tad more significant. With exquisite delicacy, she moved her shoulder until the tendril started to tug on the fabric of her jacket. If, as was often the case, the web-builder was sitting up there in the centre seat of its creation, the slightest twitch on a strand would tell it everything it needed to know about her. That meant wriggling out of the jacket could prove fatal. On the other hand, staying put until the spider did its regular patrol was a guaranteed trip to Eternity. Under those circumstances, it was probably worth taking the risk that *pachythoraces* didn't know English—

'Help,' Emily whispered. 'I'm stuck.'

'You're not, are you?'

'Yes.'

'Oh.' The surprise in Erskine's voice was very mildly flattering, implying that he was reluctant to believe that a skilled, highly trained professional like her was capable of getting into trouble of any kind. 'Are you sure?'

'*Yes.*'

Pause. 'But surely, if you recalibrated the XZ7700 to scan for gossamer fragments, like it says you should do in the office procedures manual, it ought to have picked up any stray bits of web, and you shouldn't have got caught. In which case, I don't understand how—'

'I didn't.'

'Excuse me?'

'I didn't do that,' she hissed. 'Reconwhatsit the scanner. I should've done but I forgot, all right? Now, at the back of the tool kit there's a zip-up compartment with a neon-acetylene cutting torch in it. I want you to adjust the flame till it's—'

'No, there isn't.'

'What?'

'In the zip-up pocket. No torch. There's half a roll of extra-strong mints, if that's any use.'

It was a nasty blow, but Emily had handled worse. 'All right,' she said. 'Prime three more concussion grenades and pitch them in here, and then I want you to come in and haul me out while the spider's counting stars. You'll need to watch out for—'

'Spider?'

'Hphm.'

'You mean there's still one left alive in there?'

It was the constant, cumulative bombardment with snippets of the blindingly obvious that wore you down in the end. 'I have reason to think so, yes. Now prime the bloody grenades like I told you, and then—'

'We're out of grenades. Sorry.'

Wince. Erskine was quite right, of course. She'd only brought four, and they'd all been used up in the preliminary strike. 'All right,' she whispered. 'So what have you got? Cattle prod? Taser? Come on, for crying out loud, there must be something in the bag we can use, even if it's just a poxy magic sword.'

Pause; then, 'No, terribly sorry, nothing like that in here. This is very bad, isn't it?'

If she had a knife, of course, or better still a pair of scissors, she could cut the cloth away from around the gossamer and be home and dry. Scissors. Scissor attachment on the Mordor Army Kn—

Emily froze. Now that definitely was a movement, somewhere in the darkness above her head. A tactical disaster, but at least she knew where the horrible thing was, whereas there was a chance it hadn't made her yet, or why hadn't it—?

Another movement. A big one, this time, and so fast that she never really had any chance of reacting to it. Swinging on a gossamer rope like five Siamese-twin Tarzans, the *Atkinsonii* swooped down on top of her. She felt its boot-leather belly slam into her face, breaking her nose. Without thinking, Emily cringed away, right into the thick of the gossamer net, which held her like a magnet. She filled her lungs with air for a really loud, pathetic, betraying-everything-she-stood-for B-movie scream, but she never made it that far. By the time her larynx had adjusted itself to the required shape, the spider had bitten her head off.

CHAPTER EIGHT

For Amelia Carrington, magic meant never having to eat celery.

Today, she'd ordered in steak and kidney pudding, followed by chocolate mousse with whipped cream, with a bottle of good claret to help it down. Her father had always maintained that she ate like a man, and maybe he was right. Regardless of that, she had the satisfaction of knowing that her daughter couldn't borrow her clothes because they'd be too tight.

She ate a mouthful of suet and gravy, and smiled. Cecily, whose weakness was cream cakes and boxes of Thorntons chocolates, relied on Effective magic to undo the ravages of comfort eating. That was all well and good, in its way. Everybody who met her saw a lithe, slender figure, so the reality didn't matter; the only way she'd be found out would be if she happened to stand in front of an imp-reflecting mirror, an annoying Chinese invention that shows you as you really are, and at the last count there were only seven of them in London, one of which snuggled at the bottom of Amelia's handbag. True, another one was built into the top of Carrington's boardroom table, disguised as a really good French-polish finish: Amelia had paid top dollar for it at the J. W. Wells bankruptcy sale, partly because it was always helpful to know exactly who (or what) you were negotiating with, but mostly to annoy her daughter. Even so: Effective magic was a perfectly adequate response to Cecily's weight problem. Good, straightforward professional thinking, if a little deficient in imagination.

Amelia, on the other hand, used Practical magic. It was a hell of a business, since every atom of surplus bulk had to be magically removed; it took a long time, and the process was inherently dangerous. Magic is strictly Boolean in its applications, and it'd be far more logical to lose two pounds by dematerialising a kidney than by stripping off small deposits of adipose fat. The point was, though, that whereas Cecily just looked thin, her mother really was thin. Another excellent reason for buying JWW's conference table.

Amelia was just scraping the last smears of chocolate mousse off the sides of the dish when the buzzer went. Dennis Tanner was here to see her. She frowned, vanished the dirty plates, and adjusted the room slightly. Normally, it looked out over the back courtyard, a small, overshadowed concrete square where they put the dustbins out. But it'd be far cooler to have a panoramic view out over the City, so she rotated her floor of the building through ninety degrees and widened the window by six feet. Not bad, but the façade of the Credit Mayonnaise partly obscured the dome of St Paul's. She toyed with the idea of vanishing the bank, but somebody'd be bound to notice and make a fuss, so she contented herself with raising her own building by forty feet. As a finishing touch, she turned the nice comfy old chair she was sitting in into genuine Louis Quinze, and gave the visitor's chair an annoying squeak. Then she leaned forward and toggled the intercom.

'Send him up,' she said.

'Right away. Oh, and he's got someone with him.'

Amelia paused, fingertip on toggle. 'What sort of someone?'

'Assistant, I think. He didn't say.'

Amelia frowned, then brushed the consideration aside. For all the difference it made, Tanner could have brought along a regiment of heavy cavalry. He was still small fry. 'Fine,' she said, and released the toggle. With a tiny movement of her head she added another chair, very straight-backed and spindly-legged; then, as an afterthought, she lengthened the lift shaft to compensate for the extra height of the building. Detail, detail, detail, as her father used to say. Well, indeed.

The someone Dennis Tanner had with him proved to be a nineteen-year-old bimbo with legs up to her armpits and an expression so vacant you could've dry-docked an oil tanker in it. Which meant precisely nothing, of course. It could be that Tanner was vainly trying to impress Amelia by dragging along his latest trophy PA; but, given his goblin connections, the dolly-bird could just as easily be his uncle. She smiled, acknowledging the small tactical victory. Of course it didn't matter who he or she was, but the fact that Amelia had had to stop and think for a moment represented a point scored. Clever old Uncle Dennis. Aggravating as usual.

'Dennis.' Smile. The only proper response to the enigmatic bimbo was to ignore her entirely. 'Great to see you. It's been ages. Sit down.' She twitched her head slightly, and a table with a large rectangular box on top of it appeared next to the squeaky chair. 'Have a cigar.'

'Thanks,' Dennis grunted, flopping into the chair, taking a cigar from his top pocket and lighting it. He didn't seem to have noticed the squeak. 'Nice place,' he said, wriggling backwards and forwards in the chair a few times and producing a noise like a cage full of breeding mice. 'I was just thinking, I haven't been in here since old Toss— your father passed away. How long's that been, now?'

'Seven years. And I do believe you're right. In fact, wasn't the funeral the last time I saw you?'

'Could be.' Dennis Tanner sucked in a mouthful of blue fog. She waited for it to come out again, but it didn't. 'Anyhow,' he said, 'what's all this about a major bauxite strike?'

The bimbo, Amelia noticed, was staring right at her. Correction: not at her in general, but a needle-sharp focus on the underside of her chin. Instinctively she lifted her forefinger and prodded furtively, but of course there was nothing there, no unsightly weal of flab she'd inadvertently missed out of her daily reduction. Another point scored, she conceded, though with rather worse grace this time.

'Take a look at these.' She levitated a buff folder across the room and onto the cigar-box table. 'Taken by our satellite last week. Have a poke about, tell me what you think.'

One of the very few advantages of having a face like Dennis Tanner's was that it was relatively easy to keep – well, not straight, it could never be that; impassive, then. Poker-perfect, not an eyebrow twitched or a lip-corner tweaked. As he ran a fingertip over the glossy surface of the photos, it was only the slightest shiver of his neck that gave him away, and she wouldn't have noticed that if she hadn't known him practically since she was born.

'Could be something there,' Dennis said, putting the pictures back on the table.

Amelia cocked her head a little on one side. 'Only *could* be, Uncle Dennis?'

He grunted. 'Fairly high probability,' he said, 'but I'd need seventy-five-by-nineties to be sure.' He looked up at her. 'You can arrange that, presumably.'

She nodded. 'Assuming it's what we think it is,' she said. 'What do you reckon?'

He shrugged. 'I'm impressed,' he said.

'Bigger than Wayatumba?'

Minimal nod.

'How much bigger?'

Another shrug. 'Fifty, maybe sixty per cent.' He paused to draw on his cigar, and found it had gone out. Amelia lit it for him with a glance. 'Of course,' he went on, 'there's other things to consider. How far down it is, geological formations, dangerous contaminants. But assuming it's viable, then yes. Nice strike.'

'Splendid.' She flashed him a big smile. 'And just as well, in the circumstances. I bought the land earlier this morning.'

Dennis grinned. 'Just like your dad,' he said. 'Did he ever tell you about the twenty thousand acres in Zaire he bought, thinking it was diamonds, and it turned out to be a coal seam, too deep to get at?'

Amelia nodded. 'How we laughed,' she said. 'Though as a matter of fact, we've just finished building a safari complex on it. Hotels, pools, a clubhouse. Quite a good investment, seeing as how he got the land so cheap. Coffee?'

Dennis shook his head. The bimbo was looking out of the window.

'So,' Amelia went on, 'we've got the land, and we're pretty sure—'

'Fairly sure.'

'—Fairly sure there's bauxite in there. Well, now, you're the expert. How should we go about this? Last thing we want to do is let everybody know what we've got. Once the market gets to hear about it, the price'll go through the floor.'

Dennis didn't reply straight away. He appeared to be thinking about it, though she was sure it was just acting and that he already knew what he was going to say.

'Do we know,' he asked, 'who owns Wayatumba these days?'

She nodded. 'New Zealand Ethical Minerals Inc,' she replied. 'Which is just a corporate front for a trust fund – furry animals and stuff – set up by some people called Carpenter. I wasn't able to find out anything about them.'

'Doesn't matter.' Dennis's face stayed as still as Buster Keaton posing for a photo, except that the tip of his nose twitched. Probably he wasn't aware he did that. She filed it away for future reference. 'My idea is,' he went on, 'we buy out New Zealand Ethical. Then, when the new strike comes on line, initially we pass it off as increased production from Wayatumba. Use the first proceeds to buy out as many of the other consortiums as we can.'

Amelia raised an eyebrow. 'A monopoly, you mean?'

'With hotels on Mayfair,' Dennis answered casually. 'Corner the market, you can set your own price. Then, when the truth about the big strike comes out, there's sod-all anybody can do about it.'

For a moment, a Planck's Constant fraction of a second, Amelia was tempted. It was, after all, rather a good idea. It'd mean a huge investment, but it'd work, and then there'd be all the money in the world, and nobody would have to die after all. But, on reflection, she resolved to go with her original idea. Not that it was all that much better; but it was hers, so she liked it more. 'OK,' she said cautiously. 'With you so far. What if these Carpenter people won't sell?'

'Oh, I think they might.'

Carpenter: the name rang a bell. Wasn't there a Carpenter mixed up in the spectacular decline and fall of J. W. Wells & Co? That needed checking. 'All right,' she said. 'For argument's sake, let's say they sell. It's still an awful lot of eggs in one basket, and minerals—' She shrugged. 'To be honest with you, it's more of a hobby with us. I know it was always your big thing, so naturally you're inclined to take the broad, ambitious view. But I don't think my partners'll be too happy about committing so heavily to what's basically a fringe thing for us. Sorry,' she added sweetly. 'Nice thought, though.'

Not a trace of a reaction from Dennis, but the bimbo smiled so broadly you'd think she was baring her teeth. 'No worries,' Dennis said. 'So what did you have in mind?'

Very delicately, Amelia made herself two inches shorter and seven years younger. Time to be daddy's little girl for a bit. 'Like I said, Uncle Dennis,' she said, 'you're the expert. Could we pretend the strike's much smaller than it is? Then it won't upset the price.'

Victory; a tiny gleam of a patronising grin. 'Doesn't work like that,' Dennis replied. 'You can't keep stuff like this secret very long. Soon as we start digging, you can bet the other companies'll have Mason and Schmidt or Zauberwerke on the case, and they can scry a photo just as well as I can. They'll know, trust me.'

'Awkward.' Amelia synthesised a baffled look. 'I suppose we could just sort of sit tight and wait to see what happens.'

Dennis shook his head. 'Bad idea,' he said. 'If word does get out, the others'll know we're sitting on a major find, which means we could flood the market at any time. The bauxite price'd crash, and we'd be no better off. That's why a monopoly's the only safe way to go. But if that's not practicable—' He shrugged. 'Maybe you should consider selling to one of the big companies,' he said. 'A nice little Dutch auction, maybe. All the main players'd have to join in, just to stop their rivals getting it. Nice return, no outlay, get shot of it and move on. If you're not really into minerals, it'd be the sensible thing to do.'

He was calling her bluff. Loathsome little man. No wonder Dad had liked him. He always hero-worshipped people who were smarter than himself – his own offspring excepted, of course. 'Perhaps you're right,' Amelia said, making herself sound just a bit disappointed. 'It'd be a pity, though, wouldn't it? I'm sure we'd make ever so much more if we mined it ourselves, just so long as we could control the silly old price.'

Dennis stifled a yawn; a genuine one, damn him. 'I think you may be worrying too much about that,' he said. 'Even if the price goes splat, there's still money to be made out of it. I've been in this business over a century, and if there's a way of out-smarting the market I haven't found it yet. Try being too clever and you'll end up with footprints all down your back. Anyway,' he added, stubbing out his cigar, 'we don't yet know for sure that there's anything worth having down there. Get me those seventy-five-by-nineties and then we'll have a better idea of what we're dealing with.' He stood up. So did the bimbo, simultaneously. 'Great to see you again,' he said. 'Give me a shout when you've got the pics, and then we'll talk.'

After he'd gone, and she'd conjured up demons to empty the ashtray and spray the room with air freshener, Amelia sat for a while and thought about her plan – no, her grand design. Clever Uncle Dennis, she thought; he'd come within a long gobshot of stumbling on the truth, and she wouldn't put it past him to figure out what she really had in mind, given time. She'd known he was smart – he had to be, to have survived the savage office politics of JWW for nearly a century – but maybe she'd under-estimated him; it made her wonder what sort of diabolical genius the Carpenter man must've been, to have outsmarted him and the rest of the JWW brains trust. It'd be annoying, to say the least, if he did manage to work it all out for himself. Maybe – she frowned as she contemplated it – there would have to be a tragic accident in Uncle Dennis' near future. A probability mine, per-haps, or even (hang the expense) a Better Mousetrap. It'd be a pity, of course, because he reminded her of her childhood, and there was a sentimental streak buried deep inside her, like a small, uneconomic-to-exploit bauxite deposit. But there. Cruel world, and all that.

She'd have to think about it. If Dennis Tanner could be allowed to survive without jeopardising the project, nobody would be happier than her; if not, well. Meanwhile— Amelia snapped her fingers, and a cloud of small, burning flies appeared in mid-air. They swarmed for a moment, then split up, swirled around for a couple of passes and formed themselves into a flow chart of the project so far. A third of them turned green – things already done – while the rest stayed blue: things still to do. She studied them for a while, then disappeared them, picked up the phone and thought of a number.

'Honest John's House of Monsters, this is John, how can I—?'

'Amelia Carrington,' she snapped. 'Is it ready yet?'

The sound of air being sucked in through teeth. 'Ah yes,' said the voice at the other end of the line. 'That one. Been meaning to give you a call.'

'Is it ready yet?'

Pause. 'Remind me,' said Honest John, 'how long did we quote you?'

'Six weeks, and that was five weeks ago.'

'Mmm.' A tongue, unseen and distant, clicked. 'Could've been a shade on the optimistic side there. It's the hot weather, basically. Throws out their whatchercallits, biological clocks. Hold on a tick, I'll go and have a look in the tank.'

'Now just a—' Too late. Click, and the phone started warbling

Aretha Franklin in her ear, apparently through a megaphone stuffed with socks. She scowled. It was well known in the trade that anybody who put Amelia Carrington on hold and made her listen to music was unlikely to live long and prosper, but clearly Honest John hadn't been on the Cc list when that memo did the rounds. She clenched her fingers into claws, and told herself to be calm.

'Thought so,' Honest John said, after what seemed like a very long time. 'Probably we're looking at another three, maybe four weeks, call it five and you won't be disappointed. Sorry,' he added – very much an afterthought – 'but there you go. Can't rush Mother Supernature, after all.'

Amelia took a deep breath. 'Now listen to me,' she said (Penelope Keith and Margaret Thatcher and just a hint of the Goddess in her aspect as the Destroyer). 'We have a contract, and if you care to look at clause 7(c), you will see that time is of the essence. Do you know what that means?'

'Yes, of course I do.' He sounded just a little bit rattled. Brave man. 'But like I said, you can't rush things in this business. I mean, you're dealing with livestock here, not machines, and if the ewe's not in the mood, there's really not a lot I can—'

'Seven days,' Amelia said. 'At the end of which, I expect a delivery. Failing which, I shall have you killed, eventually. Do we understand each other? Splendid. So nice talking to you – good-bye.'

It is, after all, just another kind of magic. Tell someone to do something impossible and back it up with a credible threat, and somehow it always seems to get done. It did occur to Amelia that maybe she'd been a little bit hard on the poor man, given the nature of his business. She resolved to make it up to him by sending him a card at Christmas, assuming he was still alive.

Eventually Frank decided to go with plain white with a button-down collar. It was, he felt, what George would have wanted him to choose.

He felt awful about it, of course, but what could he do? As far as being resourceful went, he was the proverbial one-trick pony.

If time travel could put it right, he knew how to cope. Other stuff – flat tyres, chip-pan fires, basic first aid – was beyond him, and he knew it. And in the matter of the disappearance of George Sprague en route from Cheapside to Marks & Spencers, Marble Arch, he couldn't see how the Portable Door would be of any use. If he went back in time to try and prevent it, he'd have to confront himself in George's office and somehow convince himself that he ought to choose his own rotten shirts without outside help, without actually mentioning what would happen to George otherwise. The hell with that. Even thinking about it made him feel timesick.

Feeling guilty, miserable and frustrated, he nipped back home to New Zealand, had a quick shower and changed into his new shirt. It didn't suit him at all, and the thought that his good friend George Sprague was now missing presumed lost in time just so that Frank Carpenter could look like a waiter made him even more depressed. No, he couldn't just leave it and hope it'd fix itself. He had to do something about it. What, though? That was the question. Pound to a penny magic was involved in it somewhere. He cursed his own ignorance, not to mention the arrogant stupidity of using magic without having the first idea how it worked. Nothing for it, he decided, he'd have to ask someone. Someone in the trade. Such as—

Well, Emily, of course.

Frank sagged with relief. Emily would know what to do. You could tell just by looking at her that she was good at her job. Besides (he felt slightly ashamed of the thought, but not enough to be put off it) it'd be a splendid opportunity to get to know her better. She'd come across as the kind of person who'd quite like showing off her professional expertise to a prospective boyfriend, a touch of the knight in shining armour embarking on a quest for his lady's sake. Silver linings, he thought.

And then he thought, Shit, the time—

The panic didn't last long. He took out the Door, spread it on his cabin wall, thought in the arrival coordinates and stepped out into Cheapside precisely on time, to find she wasn't there.

No big deal. She was a busy professional, he reminded himself, she could easily have been held up by a last-minute phone call or an emergency call-out to an infestation of basilisks or something. Not everybody, he reminded himself primly, has a Portable Door. Most people have to go the long way round, via linear time. He leaned against the builders' hoarding he'd just walked through and tried to relax.

One drawback to having a Door is that you quickly get out of practice when it comes to being bored. No more arriving half an hour early and having to kill time wandering up and down looking in shop windows; just fast-forward through the tedious, unproductive bits and cut to the chase. But he couldn't do that on this occasion, and as three minutes became five and then ten, he started to feel distinctly uncomfortable. His feet were hurting, for one thing, from the unaccustomed labour of standing still. Also, he was sure that people were looking at him; and nobody likes the thought that maybe they've been stood up. Fifteen minutes: it was sheer torture, especially with the George business still painfully unresolved at the back of his mind. Even if Emily'd changed her mind and didn't want to spend the rest of her life with him after all, he still needed the wretched girl to help him find George. Bloody woman, he thought. Talk about inconsiderate—

Twenty minutes. Thirty. *Forty*—

If it hadn't been for George, he'd probably have given up; walked away, reset his mind and heart to zero, made a note on the file not to fall in love again, gone home. But he needed a magician to help him save his friend, and apart from Dennis Tanner, who'd be unsympathetic and either refuse to help or charge him money, Emily was the only one he knew. Frank walked across the street and into reception.

'Hello. I'd like a quick word with Emily Spitzer, if she's free.'

The woman behind the desk looked at him. 'Oh,' she said. Not on the list of reactions he'd been expecting. 'Are you family?' she asked.

Oink. 'What?'

'Are you family?'

I got all my sisters and me? No, that didn't seem to be what she was getting at. 'You mean, am I a relative?'

'Yes.'

And then it struck Frank that there's only one set of circumstances where they ask you that.

Another thing the Door had taught him was how flexible time could be. Given the right equipment, you could bypass a hundred years in a few seconds. Or, given exactly the right kind of shock, you could live a year in the time it took to blink twice.

Something bad had happened. Yes, and if he said he wasn't a relative, they'd tell him – politely, of course – to take a hike, and he'd have no way of knowing what had happened to Emily, and he wouldn't be able to do anything about it. 'Cousin,' he heard himself say; then, as it occurred to him that maybe a cousin wasn't a close enough relative, '*First* cousin. What's going on?'

The receptionist's eyes told him that she wasn't paid enough to do things like this. 'I'm really sorry,' she said. 'She's dead.'

Don't be silly, Frank was about to say; and then he remembered. Apple tree, Better Mousetrap. He couldn't say, 'Don't be silly, people her age don't just die,' because of course she already had.

She already had; and afterwards, he'd asked her out to lunch. He wriggled slightly, pressing the Door's tube gently against his ribs. It was there in his pocket. Dead, he said to himself, right. We'll see about that.

'How?' he snapped.

The receptionist looked away. 'Maybe it'd be best if you saw Mr Gomez,' she gabbled. 'I'll just ring through and see if he's—'

'*How?*'

No nonsense from anybody; he was rather impressed. The receptionist wavered for a moment, and he treated her to a big stare. Apparently it worked. Frank was surprised but pleased.

'She was killed. By a giant spider. It bit her head right off.'

'Yes, fine, I see. Where? And when?' he added sharply. 'It's important.'

Startled, she told him.

'And you're sure about that? Twelve forty-five precisely?'

'Pretty sure,' the poor receptionist whimpered. Frank felt guilty for badgering her, but it couldn't be helped. 'I heard Mr Cannis – that's the new trainee, he was there when it happened – telling Mr Gomez and he said twelve forty-five, I'm sure he did. If you want, I can ask—'

'No, that's fine. What was the address again? No, write it down for me. Thanks. Sorry, is that a P or an R?'

No time to think, because thinking would mean he'd have to address the issues raised by the words *giant spider* and *bit her head right off.* Frank had never faced physical danger before, unless you counted being driven in a beat-up old Fiat by Lucy Henderson. Giant spiders that bit off people's heads . . . He found a wall, not caring if anybody saw him, spread out the Door and lunged through it.

He came out in a corridor. The carpet underfoot was deep and springy, like spring grass, with a monogram woven into it; very corporate. There was a door a few yards down, a proper door, non-portable, with *No admittance* written on it. He hesitated. If that door led to the room where the spiders were, where she'd died, was about to die, he really didn't want to go inside; unless he'd arrived a little bit too late and she was in there already—

Calm down, he ordered himself. If she's in there getting decapitated, there was nothing he could do; he'd just have to reset the Door and come back again, this time five minutes earlier. No, not chicken, just sensible. He wouldn't be in any position to save anybody if the spider got him. Headless chicken. Quite.

Frank heard voices; one of them was hers. Relief and joy washed out his mental processes for a moment or so, and then he realised he hadn't figured out what he was going to say. No time for that, though; she'd just walked round the corner.

He stood up straight and smiled at her. 'Hello,' he said.

Emily looked at him. Confused, slightly embarrassed, but not hostile – 'Hello yourself,' she said. 'What're you doing here?'

For a moment he couldn't speak; then he remembered that if he screwed it up this time round, he could always try again. And again, and again. Somehow that made it much easier, and he felt himself relax a little. 'Well,' he said. 'You remember I told you what I do for a living?'

'Friend of yours?' Frank hadn't noticed the man with her until he spoke. Her assistant, he remembered the receptionist saying. Mr Cannis, the trainee.

'Yes,' Emily said. 'Erskine, do me a favour.'

'Certainly.'

'Go away.'

'Right you are.'

The trainee retreated back round the corner; quite the human sheepdog. 'You've got him well trained,' Frank said.

Emily pulled a face. 'Don't blame me,' she said, 'I think he's always like that. Stuck like it or something. What did you mean by what you do for a living?'

Oh well, he thought, here goes. 'I was round at your office just now.'

'Oh yes?'

Nod. 'When I say just now,' he went on, 'I mean about an hour and a half in the future. You hadn't shown up for our lunch, you see, and I was . . . Well, anyway, I asked if you were in your office and they said no. Actually, they said that you'd been killed.'

She took it quite well. True, her eyes widened and her mouth fell open like the tailgate of the lorry off the back of which all good things fall, but she didn't faint or scream or any of the things he was fairly sure that he'd have done in her shoes. 'Oh,' she said.

'The spiders got you,' he went on. 'Apparently you'd done the business with the cyanide gas and the readings all showed clear, but there must've been a fault in the equipment or something, because one spider was still alive, and it . . . Look, do you want to hear the details, or shall I just skip them?'

'I think I get the general idea,' Emily said quietly. 'Listen, are you quite sure about all this? Only, it's a bit hard to take in, if you see what I—'

'Quite sure,' Frank said firmly. 'It's what your receptionist told me, anyhow, and she didn't strike me as someone who'd make stuff up.'

Emily dipped her head, conceding the point. 'So basically,' she said, nodding at the door, 'if I go in there I'm history, is that it?'

'Yes. Well, not necessarily. But in the version of events I've just come from, one of the spiders doesn't get killed by the gas, that's all I know.' He smiled thinly. 'I guess it's a bit like getting a peek at the question paper the day before the exam. You know what the questions are going to be, but it's still up to you to answer them.' He yawned. 'Sorry,' he said, 'but it's been quite an interesting day, and I reckon I've had about as much as I can take without a sit-down and a rest.'

'Well, quite.' She frowned. 'All right,' she said, 'I'll double the gas exposure and recalibrate the Everleigh for brain activity rather than heartbeat and respiration. Will that do it, do you think?'

'Don't ask me,' Frank said, just a little sharply. 'You're the professional. I just save you when you die.'

'Yes, quite. Sorry.'

'That's quite all right,' he said gravely. 'Tell you what. You get on with whatever it is you're going to do, and I'll meet you for lunch, same as we agreed. No, belay that,' he added quickly. 'We can't meet where we'd planned, I'd be there already.'

She smiled. 'Good point,' she said. 'All right, how about the pub on the corner? Cumberland Arms or something like that.'

'Fine. And if you're more than twenty minutes late, I'll know you've been, um, held up, and I'll come back and—'

'Try again?'

Frank nodded. If at first you don't succeed; like Robert the Bruce and the— 'Anyway, don't worry about that,' he said, rather wearily, 'we'll get it sorted out one way or another.' He unrolled the Door and slapped it on the wall. 'You don't mind if I don't stick around and watch,' he said. 'Only, I've got this thing about spiders.'

For some reason that seemed to amuse Emily, but in a nice way; she smiled, and said, 'Me too. See you later, then. And, um—'

'Don't thank me.' He cut her off abruptly. 'You may still be dead for all I know, I won't know till I get back to the present.' He thought about what he'd just said and screwed his eyes up tight for a moment. 'I'm sorry,' he said, relenting. 'Anyhow, you've got spiders to kill, I'd better go home and change my shirt. Which reminds me,' he added, 'I've got a favour to ask. Tell you about it later.'

'If I survive.'

'Indeed.' Frank unrolled the Door and opened it. 'Oh, and take care, all right?' he mumbled, and stepped through into the one bleak room of his cabin. There he changed his shirt, scrambling frantically even though being late clearly wasn't an issue, brushed his teeth, combed his hair and hopped back through the Door, which opened inside a pub lavatory. Fortuitously, the man who saw him arrive was drunk; he shook his head, as if to say he wished he'd listened to his mother, and stumbled away up some stairs.

Emily was waiting at a table when he reached the bar. He let out the lungful of air he'd inhaled in New Zealand forty seconds ago and walked over, rather shakily, to join her.

'You're all right, then,' he said.

She nodded cheerfully. 'Piece of cake,' she replied. 'Spiders all dead. I left the waste contractors loading them onto a lorry.'

'What about your sidekick?' he asked. He hadn't intended to use such a pejorative word. 'Did he suspect anything?'

She shook her head. 'I told him you're Mr Arkenstone from our Salt Lake City office, and you'd just popped by to borrow a pack of detonators. He gave me a sort of none-of-my-business look and we didn't discuss it any further.'

'That's all right, then,' Frank said. 'In that case,' he went on, 'if it's all right with you, I'm going to get myself a drink.'

Emily stood up. 'Stay there,' she said, 'I'm buying.'

'Thanks, I'll have an orange and bitter lemon. No ice.'

She raised an eyebrow. 'Let me guess,' she said. 'Alcohol in the bloodstream can turn volatile in a strong temporal field.'

'No, I just don't like the taste of it very much.'

While she was away, he sank back into his chair, like cheese melting into bread. Now he came to reflect on it, he hadn't actually stopped to think since the receptionist had told him she'd been killed. At that moment, he'd known exactly what he had to do, and he'd gone and done it. Better Mousetraps, screwing up the time-lines, the implications of Mr Sprague's disappearance hadn't even crossed his mind. Probably, he told himself, doctors act like that all the time; except, of course, that they know what they're doing. Big *except that*.

'Would it be OK if we just got a sandwich or something here?' Emily said, putting down Frank's glass and resuming her seat. 'Only I don't feel like a big lunch. I think it's probably the spiders.'

'Fine,' he replied. 'I'm not hungry either. Zipping about in time plays hell with your body clock.'

For a moment they sat and didn't look at each other, like two cats on a fence. Then she cleared her throat and said, 'I'm going to thank you for saving my life now, all right?'

'OK.'

'It was very—' Emily sighed impatiently. 'Look,' she said, 'I don't know what to say, it's not like writing to your aunt on Boxing Day to thank her for the nice soap. I'd be dead right now if you hadn't—'

Frank shrugged. 'It's what I do,' he said. 'For money.'

'The first time, maybe.' She took her gaze off the salt and vinegar bottles in the middle of the table and looked at him. 'The second time, though: did your insurance man call you up and tell you to come and rescue me?'

He hesitated. 'No,' he said.

'Right.'

'Though I expect he would've,' Frank said quickly. 'I mean, you're still insured, so—'

Emily nodded. 'So,' she went on, 'if you were just in this for the money, when you found out I'd been killed, you'd have waited till he sent for you, and then you'd still have saved me, but you'd have got paid for it. Yes?'

Frank hadn't thought of that. Well, of course not. Mr Sprague was missing. But he hadn't thought of that, either. 'What're you getting at?' he said irritably.

'Just that this time, you rescued me because – well, you wanted to, not just for money. So I need to thank you.'

'Ah.'

'Thanks.'

'You're welcome.'

She smiled. 'There,' she said, 'all done, have a rinse away. Didn't hurt, did it?'

There were no *arachnides grandiformae Atkinsonii* in the bar of the Cumberland Arms. Even so, Frank had the distinct feeling that he was all caught up in something strong and sticky, and the more he struggled, the worse it'd get. Better, in that case, not to struggle. 'Sorry,' he said. 'I just didn't want you to – well, get the wrong impression or anything.'

Emily frowned. 'What, you mean like you saved me out of sheer malice, something like that?'

'Not sheer malice, no.'

'Got you.' She picked the slice of lemon out of her drink, fiddled with it and flicked it on the table. 'Shall we drop that subject and lay barbed wire and a minefield round it?'

'Better had,' he replied. 'Let's order some sandwiches instead.'

Emily had cheese and pickle; Frank opted for simple ham. The bread was slightly stale, and they came with lettuce and the inevitable ring-and-a-half of onion that nobody ever eats. 'This favour,' he said.

She looked up. 'Something professional, I take it.'

'I think so.'

'All right. Fire away.'

Frank paused for a moment to crowd his thoughts into a huddle. 'Well,' he said, 'this morning, before I went to meet you, I popped into Marks to buy a shirt.'

'The one you've got on now?'

'Yes.'

Emily frowned. 'Doesn't suit you. Makes you look like a waiter.'

He smiled thinly. 'Yes,' he said, 'I thought so, too. Anyway, I got there and looked round, and I couldn't decide, so I thought I'd get George Sprague – you remember, the insurance man I do the jobs for – to come and help me. But then—'

'Just a moment. You took your boss along to help you choose a shirt?'

'Yes. Why? Is it significant?'

'Probably,' she said, in a rather odd tone of voice. 'Sorry, you were saying.'

So Frank told her what had happened; and when he'd finished, she looked at him again and said, 'And after all that, you went and bought a shirt anyway?'

He blinked. 'Well, yes,' he said.

'I see.' Pause. 'Next time you go clothes shopping,' she said, looking closely at him, 'maybe I'd better come with you.'

'Right. To recreate the sequence of events, you mean.'

'No.' Emily shook her head, as if trying to clear dust out of it. 'Right,' she said briskly, 'let's just go back over that, shall we? For – well, for reasons that made sense at the time, you took this Mr Sprague with you through the Portable Door—'

'Yes.'

'And he went in at his end but didn't come out again at yours.'

'Exactly.'

'I see.' She thought for a moment, then said, 'And you've phoned his office to make sure he's not turned up there?'

Oink, he thought. 'Well, no,' he said.

'You haven't?'

'No. I assumed—'

Emily smiled, rather nicely. 'I do that, too,' she said. 'I think it comes from being around weird stuff too long.' She fished her phone out of her bag and turned it on. 'What's his number?'

Frank told her and she keyed it in. 'Could I speak to George Sprague, please?'

Muffled, like a mouse inside a wellington boot, but he heard a voice saying 'Who's calling?'

'Carringtons.'

'Putting you through.'

A definite smirk on her face, there was no getting away from it. But so what, she'd earned it. 'Like I said, happens to me all the— Oh, hello, is that George Sprague?'

Frank heard a grunt; Sprague for yes.

'My name's Emily Spitzer, from Carringtons. I have Frank Carpenter for you.'

'Who?'

She raised her eyebrows and handed him the phone. He grabbed it and said, 'George?'

Pause. 'George Sprague here. I'm sorry, I don't know you.'

'Frank,' said Frank. 'Frank Carpenter.'

Silence.

Emily shrugged at him across the table. 'You know,' he said feebly, 'Frank. I was in your office just now. I asked you to come and help me choose a shirt.'

'A what?'

'Shirt. We went through the Door together, but—'

Click.

Frank sat still and quiet for two seconds, then handed her the phone. 'He's playing silly buggers,' he said. 'Probably getting his own back because of the shirt thing. That'll be it.'

She nodded. 'He's got a lively sense of humour, then. Practical jokes, that kind of stuff.'

'No.'

Emily was looking at him oddly again, but this time it was a different kind of oddness. 'So you tell me,' she said, 'that you saved my life because you get paid by this Mr Sprague.'

'That's right, yes, but—'

'Who reckons he's never heard of you.'

'Yes, but—'

Thinking about it, the earlier oddness had been quite nice. Not so the new form. 'And you turn up just now telling me I've been killed by spiders, but – well, I've only got your word for that. Well, haven't I?'

It was a bit like using the windscreen washer on a very cold day; as soon as it hits the glass the water freezes, and suddenly you can't see anything. 'You don't believe me,' Frank said.

But Emily shook her head. 'I know you rescued me the first time,' she said. 'I can remember falling out of that damn tree, and thinking, well, this is it; and then I was in Paris—' She frowned. That was *yesterday*, for pity's sake. It seemed like ten years ago. 'And I know you've got the Portable Door, because we went through it. So yes, I know you can travel through space, but the time thing—' She pulled a face. 'Everyone says time travel's impossible, except for the Door. You have no idea how hard it is for me to come to terms with you having that thing. It's like . . . I don't know, like looking down at the foam cup your milk shake came in and finding it's the Holy Grail. It's just *weird*—'

'Fine. But do you believe me?'

She looked at him. 'Well, that's the funny thing,' she said. 'Yes, I do. I think that either you or the universe is telling lies, and somehow I don't think it's you. I mean, why would you? I've only known you thirty-six hours, and in that time you've saved my life at least once. And maybe Sir Ian McKellen could act bewildered as convincingly as you've been doing, but I don't think you could. I think you're probably a rotten liar.'

'No, I'm not.'

'See? I'm right.' Emily smiled at him. 'So, if you're not lying—'

Frank had no idea why a sudden flare of joy lit up inside him when she said that. Well, maybe a vague hypothesis—

'—Then what the hell's happened to Mr Sprague?'

CHAPTER NINE

O n his return to the office, Erskine Cannis went to his room, took off his coat and sat down at his desk. He knew it was what he was supposed to do, and he did it well. He was getting the hang of this. He was proud of himself.

The female, Emily, had told him that she wouldn't be needing him till two-fifteen. He glanced at his watch – they were really very easy to use, not at all confusing – and worked out that he had over an hour before then. Plenty of time.

Erskine Cannis analysed the phrase, and it made him smile. It implied that the stuff somehow gathered in pools, like rainwater, whereas he knew perfectly well that it was an unceasing linear progression, with its active component (the present) never more than one second long. Sort of like a one-millimetre-long conveyor belt. They, on the other hand, seemed to think of it as a form of chewing gum, something that could be softened and stretched and set hard, played for, wasted and even killed. He wasn't sure how he felt about that. Really, it was rather silly, and he had an innate mortal fear of silliness. But, somehow, you couldn't help liking them. They had a sort of quirky charm that was hard to resist.

Plenty of time, then. The other prerequisite was not being disturbed.

He looked down at his desktop and noticed a small pot. It was made of clear plastic, and inside it were paper clips, red and green and white and black. He frowned, momentarily distracted. Why all the different colours? He could conceive of a reason – colour-coding, for instance, red for clipping together letters, blue for receipts, green for internal memos – but he knew intuitively that that wasn't it. They manufactured them in lots of different pretty colours because it made them *fun*. That word was a brick wall across the fast lane of his mental processes. It meant he had to slow down, stop and find a way round, and just now he had better things to do. He realised he'd picked the pot up while he'd been thinking about paper-clip colours, and for some reason he felt an urge to shake it, just to hear the noise it made. He put it down again, the urge denied (Why? Wouldn't have done any harm just to shake a plastic pot. But no, it would've been *silly*) and tried to remember if it had been there earlier. No, it hadn't. In which case, someone must've gone out of his or her way to put it there, believing that the new trainee would sooner or later need coloured paper clips. He frowned. Would that be an office procedure or some kind of quasi-religious ritual? No, stop it, he ordered himself; leave it. Fascinating though this environment undoubtedly was, crammed with strange new worlds, new life and new civilisations, he wasn't here to explore it. He was here to work. The God depended on him – he kept letting that slip out of his mental focus; how could he *do* that? – and he had no time for idle curiosity.

The God. Even now, Erskine Cannis's mouth went dry at the thought of her. It's given to very few sentient entities to be so close to their God, in the same building, with the possibility, likelihood even, of actually seeing her, three or four times a day. His kind, he knew, was uniquely blessed in that regard, and the consideration for that blessing was duty. Work, he told himself. Snap to it.

He moved his hand to open the desk drawer, and in doing so knocked over the plastic pot. It fell on its side and rolled. Quick as lightning, Erskine Cannis slammed a hand down on it and closed his fingers tightly. Then he frowned, let go and gently stood it upright.

From the desk drawer – basically a rectangular storage compartment riding on an ingenious arrangement of runners and rollers – he took a small cloth bag, loosened the string round its neck and shook it over his palm. A few grains of light grey dust spilled out; he closed his hand on them, put the bag away safely and unclenched his fingers. The grey specks made his skin itch.

He tried to remember how to do this.

It wasn't complicated, but it was only his second day. With his other hand, Erskine Cannis searched in his pocket and took out a cigarette lighter; next, he carefully dropped the dust onto a piece of scrap paper (a memo about reducing Sellotape wastage; obviously important, but he'd read it and taken its message to heart, so the actual paper was expendable), creased it down the middle to keep the dust from spilling, and set light to it. The paper flared for a moment, then crumpled into black ash. He felt the tips of his fingers burn, but that couldn't be helped. Any moment now, he thought.

Bright white light scorched his eyes; he closed them (lacking a secondary eyelid) and, when he opened them again, a small green creature was perching on his knuckles. It looked vaguely humanoid, in a toadlike sort of way. Its most striking feature was its big round red eyes.

'Put me down,' it said.

'Sorry,' Erskine said automatically. Very slowly and carefully, he moved his hand down to desktop level, until the little creature could comfortably jump down.

'Quite all right,' the creature said pleasantly. It sat on the cover of Erskine's desk diary, fished behind its ear and produced the stub end of a very small roll-up, which it lit by snapping its clawlike fingers. It took a long, deep drag and said, 'Report.'

Erskine took a deep breath. 'So far, so good, I think,' he said. 'I've been assigned to assist the female, Emily Spitzer—'

The creature waved its cigarette at him impatiently. 'We know all that,' he said.

'Sorry. This morning, we went to a place called Zimmerman and Schnell . . .' He paused. Not the right time to ask, but curiosity had been gnawing at him all morning. 'I was wondering about that, actually. If it's a place, why's it got the same name as people? Only places are called things like America and Leicester and Tottenham Court Road, but Zimmerman's a person name. And isn't Schnell the German for "quickly"?'

The little creature sighed. 'It's technical,' it said. 'Look it up on the Internet in your spare time. You went to Zimmerman and Schnell.'

'Yes.' Erskine winced. He was being inefficient; in fact, verging on *silly*. 'We went there. We had to exterminate a nest of giant spiders.'

'Mphm.' The little creature dabbed a tiny speck of ash off the tip of its miniature fag. 'And?'

'We succeeded,' Erskine said, with a hint of pride. 'Having sealed the infested area and run Everleigh scans, we introduced cyanide gas—'

'Yes, yes, you can skip all that. Anything odd happen?' The creature seemed to be making an extreme mental effort. 'Anything – well, out of the ordinary.'

Erskine shook his head. 'No,' he said. 'We killed the spiders, called in the clean-up squad and came back here. Oh, and Mr Arkenstone from the Salt Lake City office stopped by to borrow some detonators. That's it, really.' Pause. 'Did I do all right? Only—'

'Hold it.' The creature raised a claw. 'Mister what from where?'

'Mr Arkenstone from the Salt Lake City office.'

The creature scowled; at least, that was the likeliest explanation for what it was doing with its face. 'We haven't got a Mister Arkenstone. Come to that, we haven't got an office in Salt Lake City.'

For a moment, Erskine's mind went blank. He hated it when that happened. 'But the female told me—'

'Ah.' The creature sat up. 'Let's go through this one step at a time. What happened?'

'Well.' Erskine took a moment to shepherd his thoughts. 'We took the lift to the sixth floor – that's where the infested room was – and when we got there, this man was standing outside the door, waiting for us. He said hello, and Ms Spitzer said, hello yourself, what are you doing here—'

'Just a tick.' The small creature frowned. 'Just say that again.'

'Hello yourself, what are you doing here?'

The creature sighed. 'Inflection,' it said. 'Emphasis. No, fine, all right. Did she say, what are you *doing* here, or was it more like, what are *you* doing here?'

'The second one.'

'Got you. Go on.'

Erskine had lost his place. He wasn't making a very good job of this. He felt ashamed. Still, he could put that right by doing much, much better. 'Then the man said, you remember I told you what I do for a living. Then Miss Spitzer told me to go away. So I did.'

The small creature studied him for a moment, and Erskine couldn't help feeling that this wasn't at all good. To have failed on only his second day—

'All right,' the creature said slowly. 'You went away.'

'Yes. There was a bend in the corridor. I went round that, so I'd be out of sight and earshot. I – well, I assumed she didn't want me to see or hear anything.' Pause. 'Was that wrong?'

The small creature waved its hand. 'Don't worry about it,' it said, and Erskine's heart blossomed with relief. He hadn't failed after all. 'So, how long did you stay there?'

Erskine thought. 'Fifty-one seconds,' he replied. 'I didn't know how long I was supposed to be away for, you see, she didn't say, and there was nothing in the training sessions or the accompanying written material—'

'And then you went back.'

'Yes.' Erskine bowed his head. Now he came to think about it, his actions had been irrational and arbitrary; instead of asking how long he had to go away for, he'd just relied on his own intuition and *guessed*. He made a solemn vow never to let anything of the sort ever happen again.

'And?'

'The man had gone,' Erskine said. 'Miss Spitzer told me he was Mr Arkenstone from Salt Lake City, and—'

'She told you. You didn't ask.'

Oh no, Erskine thought, I got that wrong as well. 'No,' he confessed.

'Fine.' Having found him out and made him confess, the creature didn't seem inclined to make anything of it. 'That's interesting. Right, yes. Well done. Keep up the good work.'

Erskine couldn't believe what he was hearing. 'You mean I did all right?'

'What?' The creature was stubbing out its roll-up on its thumb claw. 'Oh, yes, great stuff, keep at it. Report again tomorrow.' He tucked the roll-up stub back behind his ear and stood on tiptoe, which meant he was about to dematerialise. But Erskine couldn't let him go without asking—

'Excuse me.'

'Mm?'

He could hardly bring himself to say it. 'Will you—?' Go on, say it and get it over with. 'Will you have to tell Her about it? About all the – well, the mistakes I made? Only, I know they were pretty bad, some of them, but really, I've learned a lot today, and I promise I'll make absolutely sure I don't do anything like that again, so if you could possibly . . .' He ran out of words, sagged and waited. The creature looked at him.

'Get a grip, son,' it said, and vanished.

When Emily got back to the office after lunch, there was a message waiting for her at reception. Mr Gomez wants to see you, ASAP.

She pulled a terrifying face, which the receptionist ignored through long practice, and stalked through the fire door and up the stairs. By the time she got to Mr Gomez's room, she'd calmed down a little; you could've melted brass on her, but not iron. She whacked the door with her knuckles and went in.

'Ah, there you are.' Why was it, she wondered, that no matter how quickly she responded to his call, how legitimate her reason for not instantly materialising when summoned, there was always that note of mild, indulgent reproach in his voice when he first spoke to her? 'Good lunch?'

Of course he didn't give a toss. He just said stuff like that to show you what a warm, caring employer he was. 'No,' she said.

'Fine. Now, we've got a bit of a situation with San Cristobal Plastics.' He frowned. 'Turns out that one of their board of directors is a troll.'

'Know the feeling.'

'Sorry?'

'Nothing.'

'Beats me,' Mr Gomez went on, 'why they didn't notice it earlier. I mean, they're a very well established firm, very big in injection moulding, turnover up twenty-six per cent last year, and it's a highly competitive market these days. Doing particularly well in the Far East, too. Still, there it is, nobody's perfect.'

He paused, reflecting on the basic treachery of the universe. Usually, Emily would have let him indulge himself, but not today.

'So?' she said.

'Hm?'

'So what do they want us to do about it?'

Mr Gomez frowned. 'Well, kill it, of course. Get rid of it, before it eats a customer.'

'But—' Emily took a deep breath. 'You said it's a director of the company. You can't go around knocking off members of the board just like that.'

'Oh, it's all right, they've had a vote. Some trouble with the small investors, but the insurance companies and trust managers pushed it through. So they want it taken care of before the news reaches the market. They're in a delicate enough position as it is, with the Koreans pushing them. And there's rumours of a hostile bid from—'

'Fine,' Emily said. 'I'll go and do that, then. You'd better give me the details.'

Mr Gomez gave her a little smile, the sort that a harassed mother might give to a teenager who'd finally consented to put away her newly ironed clothes. 'Here's the address,' he said, handing her a sheet of paper. 'They're expecting you. Just go to the front desk and ask for Mr Pickersgill.'

'Mphm.' She nodded. 'He's the head of security, then.'

Slight frown. 'No, he's the troll. And this time, please remember to get the work order countersigned. You know we can't raise an invoice without a completed work order.'

Emily kept her teeth clamped together. She turned to leave, but Mr Gomez called her back. 'You'd better take young Erskine along with you,' he said. 'The more of our established clients he meets, the better. If they can put faces to names—'

'Have I got to?' She hadn't meant it to come out as a whine, but there wasn't really any other way of saying those particular words. 'Look, it's going to be a pretty delicate job as it is. If I've got to babysit Erskine while I'm at it—' She closed her mouth. Complete waste of time. 'I'll take Erskine with me,' she said. 'It'll be good experience for him.'

'Splendid. Let me know how it went when you get back.'

As Emily walked back down the corridor, her mind was a three-lane highway. In the fast lane, the ethics of killing company directors just because they happened not to be human. In the middle, the practicalities of offing a troll (skin like Kevlar, bones practically unbreakable, immune to all major poisons; daylight usually fatal, but these days, with high-factor barrier creams—). Not just killing one, but doing it in broad daylight, in its *office*, and without turning most of SW1 into a radioactive desert. A challenge. Which left the slow lane, in which the problem of what had happened to George Sprague still chuntered quietly along, going nowhere in particular but draining her already overtaxed reserves. All that and Erskine too. What joy.

When she barged into his office without knocking, she found

him sitting at his desk reading a file. 'What've you got there?' she snapped.

'The Piedmont Technologies case notes,' he replied pleasantly. 'I was just admiring the way you handled the infestation of three-headed giant bats. Though, strictly speaking, the use of dioxin in an environmentally sensitive area—'

'Put it away,' she said irritably. 'And get your coat.' She paused, sat on the edge of the desk. 'Tell me,' she said, 'how would you go about killing a troll?'

It was like pressing an on-switch. 'Built-up area or open countryside?'

'Horseferry Road.'

Dip of the head to acknowledge the data input. 'In that case – oh, sorry, daylight or night-time?'

'Right now.'

'One-oh-five millimetre recoilless rifle and a molybdenum steel projectile,' Erskine said promptly. 'Assuming we can establish a danger area not less than eight hundred by six hundred metres—'

'In his office,' Emily said sweetly. 'Probably in an interview room, but we may have to do it in reception. Oh, and without making him suspicious.'

'Hm.' The look on Erskine's face was thoughtful, but with overtones of suppressed enthusiasm. 'Presumably a suicide attack isn't an option.'

She shrugged. 'You'll be doing it.'

'Me?' He stared at her as if she'd just told him he'd been made king. 'Really?'

'Mr Gomez thinks the experience will be good for you.'

'Gosh.' Pause, as self-doubt cut in. 'You'll be there, though, won't you? In case anything goes wrong, I mean. Only—' Hesitation; then the big confession, all in a rush. 'Only I've never actually done a solo trolloctomy, not in practice. I mean, I've done computer simulations, but—'

'Of course you haven't, you fool.' Emily sighed. 'Neither have I, come to that. You don't get many trolls south of the Malverns these days. And yes, of course I'll be there – you don't think our insurance'd stand for letting trainees loose killing things without proper supervision? So,' she went on, pressing her fingertips to the side of her head, 'how are you going to go about it? Decided yet?'

Erskine thought for a moment – not explosives, not poisons, recoilless rifle not available, golly, tricky one – and suddenly the answer was there, staring him in the face. But it was so – well, so amazingly *cool* that he hardly dared suggest it—

'M-magic sword?' he said breathlessly.

Emily nodded sadly. 'Magic sword,' she repeated. 'Worse luck.'

'But—' This was so exciting; he felt he was about to burst. 'I mean, I didn't think people really used them any more.'

'Oh, they do.' Emily pulled a face. 'Believe me. It makes you wonder if there's really such a thing as progress in this business. I mean, we can put a man on the moon and take out fully grown manticores with satellite-mounted high-energy lasers, but there'll always be some prick who can't resist the urge to chase after wildlife with a bloody great knife. Distinctly Freudian, if you ask me. Anyway, I told them when I joined, I don't do swords unless I've really got to, and it strikes me you're just the sort who'd *enjoy* it, so yes, the gig's yours. Nip down to the stores and sign one out. See you in reception in ten minutes.'

As soon as she'd gone, Erskine was on his feet and tearing down the corridor towards the lift. As he ran, he accessed his mental plan of the building. Edged weapons were stored in the stationery cupboard on the third floor, in a locked steel cabinet whose combination was 1415 (easy to remember: battle of Agincourt). When he got there, he burrowed through stacks of green chit pads and time-sheet books until he'd cleared a way through to the cabinet door. He picked the tumblers round with his fingernail and opened the door.

Tsk, he thought. Why do these people have to be so untidy? Spears, axes, cutlasses, crossbow bolts, all jammed in together any old how; he was going to have to take the whole lot out if he wanted to get at the stuff at the back, and all those sharp edges piled up like that was just begging for someone to do himself an injury.

Right at the back, behind a stack of mildewed whaling pikes, he found it: a simple black scabbard, flecked with white mould. A simple steel cross-hilt, with a brown label dangling off it on the end of a bit of white string. The label read *E77931542 Mgc Swrd Class 2b*.

Erskine finagled it out past the pikestaffs, wiped the mould off with his sleeve, and laid his right hand very gently on the wire-wrapped grip. It felt icy cold, and when he pulled his hand away sharply, small patches of skin stuck to it and ripped off.

I don't know you, said a high, shrill voice in his head.

'I'm Erskine Cannis,' he said aloud.

Your name is not important. What are you?

Intuitively, Erskine knew he was going to have to choose his words very carefully. After all, the thing had already tasted his blood; didn't that give them some sort of power over you? He was beginning to wish he hadn't accepted the honour of carrying out the mission.

'I'm a junior trainee,' he said.

Very good. What are you, junior trainee?

He thought hard and quickly. People who lied to these things tended to have short, unhappy lives. On the other hand, he didn't think he'd be much better off telling it the whole truth.

'Scared,' he said.

Silence; then the voice in his head laughed softly. *Nice answer*, it said. *Bear in mind that I am permitted three questions.*

'Are you?'

You didn't know that?

Erskine tried a little smile. It came out droopy and sad. 'Like I said, I'm a junior trainee. We were going to do magic swords in my second year at college, but we ran out of time.'

Unfortunate. What are you, scared junior trainee?

He managed to drag his stare off the sword and onto his watch face. 'Late,' he said. 'My boss is waiting for me upstairs, so if it's no trouble—'

Very well. The risk is yours to take, if you insist on it. Please note that Weyland Metal Industries and its successors in title accept no liability in respect of death or injury incurred as a result of false or misleading answers, for further details see handbook. Pause. *Your last chance. Is there anything you'd like to say at this point?*

Erskine swallowed hard and licked his lips. 'Um,' he said.

Um?

'Can we go now? Only, Miss Spitzer did say ten minutes, and I've still got to put all this junk back in the locker.'

He listened for a moment, but the voice had gone, and all he could hear was his own heart pounding. Well, he said to himself, got away with that, then.

So far.

Erskine shuddered and started stuffing weapons back inside the cabinet. His hands were bleeding where he'd lost the patches of skin, but they were still so cold and numb he couldn't feel any pain. It took him a long time to reset the combination, with fingers that felt like huge overripe bananas.

'There you are,' Emily said as he scuttled through the fire door into reception. Of course, she couldn't quite give it Colin Gomez's unforgivably patronising tone. Presumably that only came when you were real management. 'You found one, then.'

Erskine nodded. 'Here,' he said. 'In the golf bag.'

'Fine. Really inconspicuous, he won't suspect a thing.' She sighed. 'I was going to take the Tube, but if you insist on lugging that thing around with you, the firm can bloody well pay for a taxi. We'll be about an hour and a half,' she called out to reception, who made a note in the going-out-and-coming-in book. 'Come on, you,' she said to Erskine. 'And if you can make it look like you're not with me, that'd be something.'

Like the Delphic oracle or a crystal ball, Frank's ham sandwich with Emily had answered some questions and raised an uncomfortable quantity of others. As he peeled the Door off the cabin wall and lay down on the bed, he made an effort at correlating the results.

Questions definitely answered. Yes, she was now an unmistakable and unavoidable issue, something he was going to have to deal with, one way or the other. It wasn't an issue he particularly wanted to face, because love is like consumer credit: a refusal often offends. He'd always had a tendency to believe what people told him, and ever since he could remember, his parents had given him the impression – in the nicest, most loving way imaginable – that he was neither use nor ornament, and nothing he'd done or experienced since leaving home had given him cause to question their assessment. It was logical, therefore, to assume that any girl he offered his heart to would find it about as desirable as junk mail; and then there'd be all that tiresome lovelorn mooning-about to get through before he could draw a line under the whole business and move on to something else. Certainly, if God had come to Frank in a dream and asked him what he wanted for Christmas, he wouldn't have put true love at the top of the list. Come to think of it, he'd probably have ended up asking for socks and soap on a rope, because as far as he knew he'd never really wanted anything – which explained why at one stage he'd had ten million pounds in his bank account, and never spent it on anything except underwear and convenience foods.

Yes, but doesn't everybody want true love? Everybody else. He had the advantage over them of having seen it in action, close up. His parents had been utterly devoted to each other, he knew that for stone-cold fact; for one thing, his mother was under the influence of J. W. Wells & Co's universally acclaimed love philtre, guaranteed to ensure true love for ever, and Dad – well, dosing him with the stuff would've been like pouring bottled water into the Great Lakes. A fat lot of good true love had done them, though; true love and unlimited wealth and even the Portable Door, but if you had to sum them up in one word, it'd have to be *miserable*. Why else, after all, would they have built their own pocket universe and retired into it? That, Frank recognised, had left him with a rather jaundiced view of love, not to mention money and magic. As far as he could tell, all three were in the same category as satellite TV and broadband: everybody says you've got to get it, so you do, and then it either doesn't work or turns out not to be worth having. In which case, why bother?

Not the most constructive world-view, he was perfectly ready to admit, but it was the one he was stuck with, and there didn't seem to be a lot he could do about it. Take away love and money, though, and what were you left with? All he could think of was Doing Good; and somehow he'd never been able to get himself particularly worked up about that. He had no quarrel with other people; most of the other people he'd met had turned out to be quite nice, on balance. But the thought of spending his life doing nice things for them had never really grabbed his enthusiasm. The insurance thing, with Mr Sprague, had been the closest he'd been able to get. It was Doing Good, because people who would've died or been horribly mutilated didn't and weren't. Also, he got paid money for it, and (most important of all) it hadn't called for any real effort on his part. Nip through the Door, hold up a bit of cardboard with some writing on it, nip back, the rest of the day's your own. True, there was also the heavy maths, figuring out precisely when and where he had to intervene, but he'd never really minded that. He hadn't enjoyed it, but it had been a not-too-irksome chore; somewhere between a little light dusting and ironing while watching something good on TV.

Fine; not much of a life, all told, but a hell of a lot better than working for local government. Now, though, it looked like all that was about to go up in smoke, thanks to the question answered and the question posed; yes, I'm in love, and what the hell happened to Mr Sprague?

Well. There wasn't a lot Frank could do about the question answered. Like a man trapped in a subterranean cavern rapidly filling with water, he was just going to have to wait and see what happened on that score. Mr Sprague, though: different kettle of fish. He didn't know much about these things – and Emily, for all that she was now officially the most wonderful person on earth, hadn't been much use at all – but it did seem quite likely that the George Sprague thing was because of him, and quite possibly his fault. In which case, it was up to him to do something about it. The problems of others which weren't his responsibility might not have interested him much, but he was red-hot on clearing up his own messes. It was, he recognised, about all the character he had. When he was fourteen, his bedroom had been tidy. It was that bad.

Frank rolled off the bed and stood up. He hadn't a clue where to start, so the only option open to him was to go and ask someone. And, since he couldn't think of anybody else to ask –

He spread out the Door and walked through it into Mr Sprague's office. This time, to be on the safe side, he didn't go straight into Mr Sprague's actual inner lair. Instead, he chose a patch of wall in a corridor halfway between the secretary's office and the toilet. Luckily there was nobody about, and he rolled up the Door and put it away. Then he presented himself before – what was her name? He'd heard George say it many times, but he hadn't taken it in. Luckily, he'd never actually met her; the most she'd been was a squeaky voice at the other end of a phone line.

'Hello,' he said pleasantly. 'Any chance of a quick word with George?'

She looked at him, whatever her name was. 'How did you get in here?' she said.

'Front door was open,' he replied, innocent as a lamb, 'so I came on up. Is he in? I can come back if he's not.'

Deep frown. 'He's not expecting you, then.'

'No.'

'And your name?'

'Frank Carpenter.'

Where he'd got the charm from, he had no idea. Definitely not from his parents, who between them had enough of that precious quality to fill a very small acorn cup. Dad had once told him he guessed it must be from the non-human side of his family tree, a remark that had puzzled him a lot until he'd met Mr

Tanner's mother. One drop of her personality diluted with, say, the Pacific Ocean, and you'd probably get charm. Anyway, regardless of where he'd got it from, he had it, occasionally, mostly when dealing with harassed middle-aged women. Right now, he guessed, it was the only thing stopping him from being slung out into the street.

'I'll ask,' the secretary said. It was clearly a huge concession, but Frank doubted whether it'd be enough. He liked George, but he had an idea that he suffered fools and time-wasters as gladly as fire does water.

'Thanks,' he said gloomily. Then, on the off chance, he turned the charm tap till it jammed and added, 'Sorry, can you spare me a second?'

She hesitated, hand on intercom switch. 'Well?'

Big frown. 'Not quite sure how to put this.' (And that was no lie.) 'You'll think this is a very strange question, but—' Another hesitation. Bank up the suspense, engage her curiosity. Then just blurt it out, as though you've tried not to ask the question and failed. 'Do you think George has been acting a bit oddly today?'

Frown. 'What makes you say that?'

Interesting reply. 'Oh, I don't know. Maybe I'm imagining it. Only – well, I spoke to him on the phone earlier, and I couldn't help thinking he wasn't—'

'Quite himself?'

(Bingo!)

'Exactly,' Frank said gratefully; no need to act there. 'And I was a bit worried, so I dropped everything and came straight over.'

The secretary considered him as though he was a crossword clue. 'You're a friend of his, then?'

'Oh yes. Friend of the family, really. Uncle George. He's known me since before I was born.' Which was true, of course. 'I don't know,' he added quickly, 'I expect I'm making a great big fuss over nothing. I think I'd better go – I know how busy he is and I don't want to be a nuisance.'

'No, don't do that,' she said; and Frank thought, if I really did get it from the goblins, then thank you, little scaly people, for sharing your DNA with me. 'Actually, he's not that busy right now. I'll tell him you're here, and you can go right in.'

'Actually.' Don't screw it up now, Frank ordered himself. 'I think it'd be better if I just went in unannounced. It's this game we used to play when I was a kid. Pretty childish, of course, but you know what it's like in families.'

Pure babbling, of course; but if she hesitated, it was only for a moment, until he'd given her a winning smile. It wasn't an expression he'd had much experience with, and without a mirror handy he had no idea how it'd come out. But it must've been good enough, because she smiled back and said, 'You go on, then. Shall I get you both some coffee?'

'That's very kind, but it gives me the most dreadful indigestion.'

'You should try decaff.'

Sad smile. 'Makes no difference, I'm afraid.'

'Oh dear. Would you prefer tea?'

'Tea's worse.' He reached for the door handle, gave it a twist as though wringing its neck, and dived into the office.

Mr Sprague was sitting behind his desk; well, where else would he be? The odd thing was, he had his feet up on the desktop, and was reading a newspaper. Upside down.

As soon as he saw Frank, the paper collapsed like a tent in a hurricane, and the feet were whisked off the desk. 'What the hell are you doing here?' Mr Sprague barked at him, but his voice sounded scared. 'I mean, who are you?'

There hadn't been many sudden flashes of insight in Frank's life, and he found the sensation bewildering. Nevertheless, when he replied, his voice was surprisingly steady.

'You know perfectly well who I am,' he said. 'Where's George?'

The owner of Honest John's House of Monsters wasn't really called John. That harmless deception aside, however, he generally did his best to earn his self-awarded adjective. When he'd told Amelia Carrington that her order wasn't ready yet, he'd been telling the truth. His mother had always insisted that the truth, rather like major credit cards, is accepted everywhere.

Fine.

He reached down and grabbed hold of the lid. Properly speaking, it was too heavy for one man to lift on his own, but Neville the trainee had already gone home and the winch was bust. He leaned back against the weight and heaved, ignoring the strongly worded communiqué from the muscles of his back.

The problem as he saw it was that, by all accounts, Amelia Carrington shared his single-minded sincerity. If she said he'd be killed if he didn't deliver on time, she meant it, and there was precious little he could do about it.

The lid lifted eight inches. Then the strain on his fingers and elbow tendons got too much for him, and he let go.

Needless to say, the problem lay with the livestock. He had a very good breeding ewe – possibly the finest in the country: Best of Show at Smithfield last year, and Best In Class at the Bath & West three years running – and a thoroughbred drake with a better pedigree than the Duke of Kent. The problem was, they didn't like each other. Nor was it one of those quirky, Bogard-and-Hepburn love/hate relationships, which only takes a gentle pressure on the right levers to convert it into a fiery romance. The ugly fact was, the last time he'd managed to coax the drake into the ewe's pen, she'd tried to eat him.

Technical problems, as they say in the trade.

So, with Amelia Carrington's not so oblique encouragements very much on his mind, Honest John decided it was time for a little lateral thinking. It was sheer luck, he couldn't help thinking, that he had a Plan B.

He tried again. This time, he raised the lid a full fourteen inches before yelping with pain and letting go.

It had to be a very heavy lid, of course; half-inch high-tensile steel plate, and that was the lightweight version. The regulations specified a full twenty millimetres for Class 4 species, and you had to have four padlocks to BS 8867 and an alarm system.

Honest John's operation couldn't run to that (the EU will be the death of small business in this country) so he made do with what he'd got. Right now, that included a lid he couldn't lift and a (no pun intended) deadline.

Years ago, before he'd been Honest John's House of Monsters, he'd had a short and colourful career as Honest John's House of Clones. He'd managed to blot most of the details out of his memory, but he still had a few mementos: stuff the liquidators hadn't found, or hadn't considered worth the expense of taking away. One of them was the large, built-in cast-iron vat that took up most of the floor space in Number Six shed. He hadn't used it since he'd been hounded out of the cloning biz; he wasn't even sure if the rich green goo that filled it was still functional. Only one way to find out. Unfortunately, that would involve lifting the damn lid.

The pyramids, he thought. Stonehenge. They'd managed to shift bloody great big heavy things using muscle power alone. Technologically speaking, what did they have that he didn't? Apart from thousands of conscripted labourers, of course.

Honest John clambered down and took an armful of bricks from a pile in the corner. With these, he was able to wedge the gap each time he lifted the lid, until at last it was big enough to let him get his arm through. Shivering a little, he groped about until his fingers made contact with the surface of the goo. He fished out a sample and studied it.

Yuck was, of course, his instinctive first reaction. It was slimy, green and smelly, but that was how it was supposed to be. There were traces of some kind of yellow mould, but presumably it was either inert or non-organic. Just as well. Thinking about it, he cursed himself for his negligence. A mildew spore finding its way into that lot could easily have evolved into sentient life inside a week; a fortnight, and it'd probably have discovered nuclear fission.

Fool's luck, he thought. But the stuff felt and smelled right; it even (don't try this at home, kids) tasted right. He remembered some of the stories he'd heard about Amelia Carrington over the years, hopped down and scuttled over to his bench. Busy, busy.

On top of the bench was a small fridge, the sort you daren't open in hotel rooms unless you're a millionaire on expenses. Inside was a rack of test tubes. He filled a pipette with foul-looking yellow gunge from one of them, and shut the fridge door.

Halfway to the vat, he paused. Was this a sensible, responsible thing to do? No. On the other hand, living to regret it would nevertheless be living, and by definition preferable to the alternative. He climbed up onto the rim of the vat, stuck his arm out as far as he could get it, and squeezed the little rubber bulb. Then, moving faster than he'd done in years, he dragged the bricks out until the lid slammed shut, and hopped clear like a startled frog.

He landed awkwardly, hurting his ankle. Silly, really. Even under optimum conditions, it'd take seventy-six hours. In cold, crud-encrusted goo, you could add another six to eight hours, assuming it was going to work at all. The light-blue-touchpaper approach was simple hysterical melodrama. He got up slowly, hobbled over to the bench and switched the kettle on. He hadn't had a brew for hours, and his throat felt like sandpaper.

Either the ewe would have to go, Honest John mused, or the drake. No bloody use at all having them if the buggers didn't get on. He thought it over. Sound business principles dictated that the ewe was the one to get shot of. With her pedigree and stallful of rosettes, she'd be worth a fortune. Tierkraft AG and Cincinnati Lifeforms had both made him tempting offers for her. The drake, on the other hand – well, he was worth money, but not nearly as much. Even so, it'd be a wrench to say goodbye to Daisy, even if she had eaten three DEFRA inspectors and a Ministry vet . . .

A sound like the booming of an enormous gong startled him out of his meditations. He looked round, then down at his watch. Twenty minutes. It couldn't have come from the vat, then. Must've been something else. Concorde going over, maybe.

He sipped his tea. Stone-cold. He preferred it that way.

Only, hadn't they grounded Concorde years ago? He couldn't remember. Served him right for not reading the papers. To fill in the time, he opened a dog-eared box file and made a start on the monthly accounts. Now, then: feed receipts.

Boom.

Not Concorde, even if it was still flying. Not unless it was taking a short cut through the shed. Once his head had stopped spinning, he stood up and took a few steps towards the vat. Then he changed his mind. If it was the vat . . . He had an idea there'd been an article in the trade mag a while back; something about what happened if the goo was left so long that it began to ferment. Hugely accelerated development, Honest John seemed to recall, but really bad stuff happened to the DNA coding.

Um.

He could go back to the vat and investigate. Or he could nip outside, get in the van, drive very fast to Heathrow and hope like hell that Concorde (a) was still in service and (b) could outfly whatever was beginning to stir under that lid.

His twisted ankle held him up rather, and he stopped to get his coat. But for that, he might have made it.

Instead, he'd just laid his hand on the door handle when a third boom knocked him off balance. He staggered and fell, just as the lid flew off the vat like a frisbee and took out the far wall. For a moment, his eyes were filled with brick and plaster dust. When he'd wiped them clean, he looked at the vat and saw a single huge green claw rising up and digging its talons into the rim.

Cast iron is brittle old stuff. It went *ping* as it crumbled.

Oh well, thought Honest John. He searched in his pocket for his mobile phone, and prodded in a number. He gave his name, asked to speak to Amelia Carrington and was put through straight away.

'Your order's ready,' he said.

'Good.'

'One thing, though.'

'Well?'

The claw was snaking upwards, on the end of a massive green-scaled leg. The talons flexed, and something made a deep growling noise that set the building vibrating.

Honest John took a deep breath. 'Do you think you could possibly collect?' he said.

CHAPTER TEN

'George?' said Mr Sprague. 'Who's George?'

'You are.'

'Oh, I see.' Mr Sprague looked down, and Frank couldn't help being reminded of a small boy who's been caught out in an obvious lie. 'What a silly question,' he said. 'I'm here.' Then, as if he'd just remembered that he was the injured party: 'What do you mean by bursting into my office like this? I have no idea who you are. Get out right now, or I'll call the police.'

Frank clicked his tongue. 'You're not very good at this, are you?'

Mr Sprague's face fell, and again, Frank got an impression of extreme youth. Odd, since Mr Sprague had to be at least fifty-five. 'I don't have to talk to you,' Mr Sprague said. 'Go away. Immediately.'

'Not until you tell me what you've done with George.' Frank took a step forward; Mr Sprague jumped out of his chair and retreated behind his desk. 'Oh for crying out loud,' Frank said wearily. 'It's bloody obvious you're not him.'

'Isn't.'

'It is.'

'Isn't.'

Frank Carpenter wasn't a violent man. He preferred to

resolve conflicts by quiet, rational argument or (better still) by running away. There are times, however, when even the gentlest soul can be goaded into fury. Frank lunged, stretching across the desk, and grabbed the lapels of Mr Sprague's suit jacket in both hands. '*Is!*' he roared, and at precisely that moment, Mr Sprague disappeared, leaving Frank baffled and empty-handed.

Not quite. As he stood and stared at the place where Mr Sprague had been, he noticed something sticking to the palm of his right hand. It was a single long blonde hair.

'We're here to see Mr Pickersgill,' Emily said.

The receptionist looked up at her. 'Have you got an appointment?'

'No.'

'Just a moment, I'll see if he's free. Who should I say—?'

No harm in giving her name, or the firm's. After all, she was here because the board – the *rest* of the board – were paying for her to do a job. 'Emily Spitzer,' she said. 'Carringtons.'

'I'm afraid he's on the phone right now,' the receptionist said. 'If you'd care to take a seat, I'll ring through as soon as his call's finished.'

This time, Erskine had brought something to read; well, he would have, wouldn't he? It had been a suggestion rather than a direct order, but obviously he'd taken it to heart, considered it and seen its self-evident merits; probably written it down in a notebook. The book he'd selected was Hasdrubal and Singh on banshee management; Emily'd been told to read it for her final exams, but she'd never managed to stay awake past the introduction. Erskine, she noticed, was two-thirds of the way through, and was using a pink requisition slip as a bookmark.

Needless to say, she'd forgotten to bring a book of her own. She glanced down at the selection of classic issues of *Country Life* and *The Times* colour supplement, all of them so old she was surprised they weren't bound in vellum and chained to the table. Not for her, she decided. Instead, she half-closed her eyes and tried to run scenarios for the job ahead. It was what you were supposed to do when you were waiting on a mission like this. She'd never managed to get the hang of it.

Instead, she thought: how the hell can you have a troll on your board of directors and not notice? A goblin, now; that'd be quite understandable. Goblins were natural shape-shifters. Ditto dark elves, gnomes and the Fey. Even giants – there were some very short giants, and some of the full-sized ones had techniques for shrinking down to normal proportions for up to seventy-two hours; a really smart giant with access to the right equipment could probably pass for human indefinitely, or at least until his morphic signature began to break down under the strain. But trolls? No. Sunblock and dark glasses helped them cope with the daylight issue, but there wasn't really anything they could do about their size, their shape, or the fact that their mouths were full of precious stones instead of teeth. You'd notice something like that, surely.

(Without taking his eyes off the page, Erskine reached in his top pocket, took out a small notebook, and wrote something down. Emily hated him.)

Yes, of course you'd notice. In which case it stood to reason that the other directors had noticed, probably long before Mr Pickersgill was promoted to the board, and they were fine about it – no silly prejudice, no bigotry, this is the twenty-first century after all. It therefore followed that if they now wanted their colleague terminated with extreme prejudice, it wasn't because of his inhumanity. There'd be some other reason – a difference of opinion over a takeover offer or a recapitalisation issue, or maybe they had a buy-back option over his shares and wanted to get them cheap from his executors before higher than anticipated mid-term profits sent the share price soaring. All sorts of possible reasons; and it was all quite legal and legitimate, since Mr Pickersgill happened not to be human. You can't murder a monster, you can only kill it, and provided you abide by the requirements of the Supernatural Vermin (Welfare) Regulations 1977 and the various EU directives, they can't have you for it. Which, Emily had to concede, was generally fine by her. Ninety-nine per cent of the creatures she dealt with in the course of her professional life were ruthless instinctive killers who had to be disposed of in order to make the planet habitable for small, weak, squishy human beings. The other one per cent – well, omelettes and eggs. No room in this business for sentiment or Disneyeqsue anthropomorphising.

Even so. She did what she always did when she reached this point, and thought about something else. Frank Carpenter – no, we won't think about him. All right, then, his problem. The disappearance of Mr Sprague.

That was all right. It was challenging, interesting, and sufficiently remote not to bother her. Emily considered the facts as she knew them.

The laws of metaphysics categorically state that people don't just vanish. They can be changed into something else (Practical magic) or made to look like they aren't there (Effective magic); in the latter case, they can even be made to believe themselves that they aren't there, a useful trick if you can do it. They can be transported from one place to another (telekinesis). They can be killed and their component molecules instantaneously dispersed (Gardner's Hammer); they can be banished to the interdimensional void through Probability Snares, Better Mousetraps and Consequence Mines, or retuned to super-low intensity frequencies that mean they can only be detected with a Kawaguchiya RF7000 oscilloscope and three-way litmus paper. Any one of these processes can give you an effect indistinguishable to the layman from vanishing. But people don't just vanish. Doesn't happen. Can't be done.

Simple, then. She had to get into Sprague's office with an RF7000 and take readings. That'd tell her what had happened to him, and thereafter the mystery should solve itself. It wouldn't be difficult, not for Frank and his Portable Door; when everyone had gone home, and there was nobody to worry about apart from cleaners and night security. And then they could have dinner, to celebrate—

Emily's train of thought skidded on the wet leaves of shock and ploughed into the embankment of shame. She wasn't quite sure why. She'd do him a favour, naturally he'd want to thank her, they could discuss her findings over Thai chicken with lemon grass, and what was so very wrong about that? She couldn't put the reason into words, but then, she didn't have to. It'd be – what? Betrayal? Surrender? Prostituting her craft in order to worm her way into the affections of her mark?

Oh, come off it.

But. She scowled, and Erskine, happening to look up from his book, intercepted her ferocious glare and shrivelled like a salted slug. Good, she thought; serve him right for – well, for whatever it was he deserved to be punished for. Existing, for example.

'Mr Pickersgill's free now, if you'd like to go through.'

Who the hell was Mr Pickersgill? Oh yes, the troll they were here to kill. Emily stood up abruptly and marched towards the open door, Erskine trailing behind her like the tin cans behind a newly-weds' car.

As soon as the door closed behind them, her mind reverted to tactical mode. They were in a small, bare room – interview room – with a plain table and three chairs; one door, but there was a nice old-fashioned sash window (sealed shut with nine or so coats of paint) and they were on the ground floor. She glanced through it and saw a grubby, overshadowed courtyard, empty apart from a colony of wheelie bins. Escape route, in case things went wrong. She ticked Priority One off her mental list, and relaxed very slightly.

'Where should I sit?' Erskine hissed at her.

Stupid question, she thought; no, scrub that, it's a very good question, since he'll be doing the sword work. She stared at the backs of the two visitors' chairs, her mind a sudden blank. For sure, one of the chairs was better, strategically speaking, than the other, but just then she didn't even know how to set about deciding which. 'That one,' she snapped, pointing at the space directly between the two.

'Right,' Erskine said, in a clipped, efficient voice, and took the chair furthest from the window. Well, of course. It placed him on the victim's left, so he'd have space to use his right arm.

Assuming he was right-handed. Emily realised she hadn't bothered to notice.

The door opened, and a troll walked in.

Other than his size – eight foot two, at a guess – there was nothing remotely intimidating about Mr Pickersgill. He was broad in proportion to his height, but cheeks like slices of grey spam and a veritable harem of extra chins dissipated the effect of his bulk. He was bald, with a shiny, pointy head that rose through a chaplet of fuzzy white hair like a mountain through clouds. He wore thick-lensed, gold-rimmed spectacles and a plain dark blue suit with the sort of tie that only gets bought by children for Daddy's birthday.

I can't kill that, Emily thought.

Mr Pickersgill smiled. It was a pleasant smile, faintly apprehensive. 'Ms Spitzer?' He held out a big, soft hand. She shook it. 'Sorry to keep you hanging about, call from one of our suppliers. Now then.' He waited for them both to sit down, then lowered himself carefully into his chair. 'What can I do for you?'

Erskine was looking at her. He was practically quivering, like a dog watching a rabbit. She gave him a tiny frown. Oh God, she thought.

It was, she realised, all about spiders. As a little girl, she'd squashed spiders because she was terrified of them. Really, there wasn't anything else she could do. She couldn't leave them be, in case they ran up her leg – unthinkable, yuck. She couldn't catch them alive and put them out the window, because that'd mean touching them. She didn't have the dexterity or the quick reactions to trap them in matchboxes. But a swift, decisive blow with a long-handled hairbrush turned them into a smear on the wall, and that was the problem solved. The killing aspect – an inoffensive living thing brutally and arbitrarily crushed to death – never crossed her mind. Then, later, she killed spiders because they scared other people, and by then she was hardened to it. After that – spiders, dragons, vampires, manticores, harpies, the world was a better place without them. An article of faith, and no grey areas. A few brown, sticky ones, maybe, but no grey.

Mr Pickersgill, on the other hand, wasn't a spider, not even by Emily's extended definition. He was just a rather large man whose skin happened to be the colour and texture of pumice. He didn't invalidate the spider principle; it just didn't apply to him, that was all.

Which left her in an awkward position, with only one way out. She took a deep breath.

'I work for Carringtons,' she said.

He nodded. 'Excellent firm,' he said. 'By the way, how's old Colin Gomez these days? He did a marvellous job for us once. Infestation of pixies at our Swansea plant. Had 'em all cleared out in no time, we hardly lost any production.'

She thought about the pixies. The recommended method was cyanide gas.

'It was Mr Gomez who sent us,' she said. 'On behalf of your fellow directors.'

She'd hoped that that would be enough to send the penny tumbling through space. But he just looked mildly puzzled. 'Oh yes?'

'That's right. They hired us to kill you.'

Mr Pickersgill froze; all apart from his eyes, which turned round and huge. Magnified by his glasses, they looked like fried ostrich eggs.

'Because,' she went on, 'you're a troll. And, as you probably know, trolls count as supernatural vermin, which means they can be killed – well, any time, so long as you obey the regulations.' She paused, to give him a chance to digest what she'd just said. He seemed to be having trouble with that.

'Killed,' he repeated. 'Heavens.'

'Now,' Emily continued, and to her surprise her voice sounded level and calm. 'You can tell by the fact you're still alive that – well, I've got a few issues with this assignment.'

'Issues.'

She nodded. 'The way you people run your company is none of my concern,' she went on, 'but I'm assuming they want you out of the way for some other reason besides you being a—'

'Quite. Yes.'

'Fine. On the other hand –' (help me out here, damn you) '– you've got to appreciate my position. If I go back to my bosses and tell them I didn't do the job because I don't like the thought of killing someone because they're a nuisance to their business colleagues, I'll quite probably lose my job. And – no offence – my career means more to me than your life does.'

'Perfectly reasonable view,' Mr Pickersgill mumbled. 'Perfectly reasonable.'

'So.' She was making terribly heavy weather of all this, she knew. 'I'm asking you if you can think of any way I can not kill you, without disobeying a direct order and being told to clear my desk by half past five.' Pause. 'I'm open to any sensible suggestions, but I'm afraid I'm going to have to hurry you along a bit. I'm sorry, but I've got a whole load of paperwork to catch up on when I get back to the office—'

'It's all right.' Mr Pickersgill held up a doormat-sized hand. 'I do apologise. This has come as something of a shock, but I think I can see a way. Would you mind very much waiting here for a moment, while I see to something? I'll get Denise to bring you in some coffee and biscuits.'

The biscuits turned out to be ginger nuts and Rich Tea. Emily watched Erskine eat one of each and not die of arsenic poisoning, then helped herself. The coffee was good, too – proper filter coffee, not instant.

'Excuse me.'

'Mm?' she replied with her mouth full.

'With all due respect,' Erskine said, and you could believe he actually meant it, 'should you have done that? I mean, warn him and—'

'No.'

'Oh.'

'No, I should've let you chop his head off with the magic sword. Then we'd have got the work order signed by one of the other directors, and gone back to the office. But I didn't feel like doing that, so I didn't.'

'Ah.' Short, thoughtful silence. 'This is one of those ethical things, isn't it?'

Emily sighed. 'Listen,' she said. 'Actually, you may want to write this down. Ready?'

Notebook out. 'Fire away.'

'Good. In this business,' she said slowly, 'we don't do ethics. As far as we're concerned, ethics is southern East Anglia pronounced with a lisp. Got that? You can call it Spitzer's Law if you like. By the same token, we don't go around scragging company directors, either. It's—' She paused, trying to think in Erskinean terms. 'It's beneath the dignity of our profession. We have an understanding with the Mafia. We don't rub out people's business rivals, they don't tamper with the fabric of perceived reality. It's perfectly simple. And it's I after E in "perceived".'

'Right.' Erskine reversed his pencil, erased a few letters with the rubber end and made the correction. 'So what do we do?'

Emily frowned. Good question. 'We drink our coffee,' she said.

There was a long, pensive silence after that. It lasted until the door opened and Mr Pickersgill came back in. He was smiling and holding an envelope. There was blood all round his mouth.

'I've discussed the matter with my colleagues,' he said, 'and we won't be requiring your services after all. I've signed a cheque for your wasted time and call-out charges; I've left it blank, perhaps Colin Gomez would be kind enough to fill in the correct amount. Please give him my regards, by the way.'

He put the envelope on the desk. There was a big red thumbprint on the back flap.

'Your colleagues—' Emily said quietly.

Mr Pickersgill burped and apologised. 'My *former* colleagues,' he said. 'Thank you so much for your sensitivity and discretion. I'm sure we'll be doing business again in the near future.' He took the handkerchief from his top pocket and dabbed at the blood around his mouth. 'I'll see to it that the new board puts all our supernatural work your way in future, it's the least I can do.' He winced sharply and put a hand on his chest. 'Dear me,' he added, 'indigestion. My doctor did warn me about eating between meals.'

Erskine, she noticed with a small degree of pleasure, had gone ever such a funny colour. 'That's all right, then,' she said. 'We'll be getting back to the office. Nice to have met you.'

'The pleasure was all mine.' Mr Pickersgill beamed at her. 'Let me show you out.'

He led the way back to the front office. Emily followed, with Erskine trailing nervously after her, hugging the golf bag in his arms like a baby. At the street door she shook hands once again with Mr Pickersgill, trying hard not to see what was under his fingernails. Then he reached inside his mouth with a forefinger and thumb and tugged at something. She heard a brittle snapping sound; then he reached for her hand and pressed something in it. 'A small token of thanks,' he said. She hesitated, then glanced down. It was slightly damp, about the size of the top joint of her thumb, and it sparkled. 'They grow back,' Mr Pickersgill assured her with a pleasant smile. Then he noticed Erskine, who was standing there looking fuddled. 'And one for your colleague, of course,' he added.

'Really, you shouldn't,' Emily started to say, but by then Mr Pickersgill had broken off another tooth and pressed it into Erskine's hand. He stared at the troll as though he'd just kissed him on the mouth, then looked at what he'd been given, yelped and dropped the golf bag. It came open at the neck, and the magic sword slid out like a landed fish.

Mr Pickersgill looked at it with an expression of extreme distaste. 'Yes, of course,' he said, in a slightly strained voice. 'For the— Well, you'd have had to, I can quite see that. Allow me,' he added, as Erskine went to retrieve it. He stooped down – an impressive performance, given his size – and took hold of the sword's hilt. It screamed.

'I'm so sorry,' Emily heard herself say, as embarrassment flooded her mind. 'They're programmed, you see, and technically you're a—'

The scabbard fell off the blade, and it twisted in Mr Pickersgill's hand until he dropped it. The sword fell to the floor, nicking his trouser leg on the way down. Mr Pickersgill hopped out of the way with an agility hard to credit in such a large creature. 'I do apologise,' he mumbled, his eyes fixed on the sword, which was still quivering a little as it lay on the carpet. 'Thoughtless of me, I do hope I haven't damaged it in any way. If there's anything like that, you must send me the bill, I insist.' The sword shuffled half an inch towards him across the carpet, its edges shining blue. Magic swords will cut through anything, but they're criminally lacking in tact.

'Put it away,' Emily hissed, but Erskine was frozen solid. She darted forward and grabbed the sword like a mother pulling her child out of a fight. She was prepared for it, but even so; as her hand closed round the hilt, she was filled with an urgent need to strike, send the troll's head spinning off its shoulders— Without stopping to think, she snatched up the scabbard and ran the blade down into it. She felt the sword shiver, then relax.

'Oh *dear*,' Mr Pickersgill was saying. 'Now you've cut your finger. Lorraine, plasters and disinfectant, quickly, please.'

News to her; Emily glanced down and saw a little red line on the pad of her middle finger, like a paper cut. Instinctively she put the finger to her lips and licked it. 'Please don't bother,' she said loudly and clearly. 'It's just a—'

But the receptionist was already there, with enough medical supplies to equip a hospital. Emily gave up, and held her hand out obediently. As she did so, she had the strangest feeling. It was very faint, and it was definitely centred in her hand, though gradually starting to creep up her arm; but the nearest thing she could compare it to was the wonderful clarity of hearing you get just after you've had wax syringed out of your ears. Silly, of course, because you don't hear with your fingers—

'There you are,' the receptionist said brightly. 'Good as new.'

That was what she said, and Emily heard it perfectly clearly, every word. At the same time, though, just as if someone else was speaking simultaneously, she could just make out the same voice—

– *Load of fuss about nothing, as if I didn't have enough to do—*

– only very quiet, just on the threshold of her hearing. She stared at the receptionist, who smiled pleasantly, gathered up her first-aid stuff and went back to her desk.

'Thanks,' Emily muttered. 'Now we really must be going. Goodbye, Mr Pickersgill. Come on, you.'

'Goodbye, Ms Spitzer.' *Horrible, vicious creature. Get rid of it, make it go away.* 'Safe journey.' *Hope it falls under a bus, serve it right, vicious, nasty.* 'See you again, I hope.'

By the time she'd reached the pavement outside, her head was spinning, and her whole body felt like one enormous, bloated ear. She staggered across to a lamp-post and leaned against it, desperate to get a grip. Voices in her head; they warned you about that in college. An occupational hazard, particularly in pest control. If you're lucky, they go away again after a bit, but whatever you do, don't listen to them or do what they tell you, and most especially, don't be tempted to raise an army and drive the English out of Aquitaine— But no, it wasn't that kind of voice. It wasn't telling her to do anything; it wasn't really a voice in that sense. It was more like – yes, that was it; more like the simultaneous translations they have at the UN or Brussels, but without the slight time-lag. When the receptionist and Mr Pickersgill had spoken to her, she'd heard them *twice*; the words said out loud, and a translation—

Oh, Emily thought. That.

'Are you all right?' Erskine was peering into her face, intruding unbearably into her space. 'You're acting very strange. Shall I call an ambulance?'

'Shut up, Erskine.' Yes, she knew exactly what this was. She'd read about it, years ago, in mythozoology. Except, she hadn't . . . She screwed up her eyes, as though peeling onions. The sword. She'd cut herself on it, after it had fallen on Mr Pickersgill's leg and cut him first. Could it really have happened like that? It seemed so unlikely. But the effect; she most definitely wasn't imagining it.

Bloody hell, she thought.

'Taxi,' she snapped. 'Come on, don't just stand there. And watch what you're doing with that stupid *thing*.'

Erskine scuttled away, leaving her feeling weak but some-how – lightened, as though someone had turned the gravity down by a third, just for her. Because if she was right, and it was what she thought it was . . . She blinked three times in a row. It was amazing. People had *died* trying to achieve what she'd just done by accident, and just think of the advantages.

And the drawbacks, she reminded herself. The drawbacks.

Erskine had caught a taxi; it was sitting purring at the kerb, its door invitingly open. She managed to wobble across the pavement, nearly banged her head on the door frame, and flopped into a wonderful, comfortable seat. She heard the door slam, and the driver said 'Where to, miss?'

(*Nice arse, tits too small, bit on the chunky side but—*)

'Cheapside,' she snapped angrily. 'And you're disgusting.'

'Oh. Right you are, miss.'

The taxi jolted along steadily for a while. Emily didn't feel like talking, and Erskine just kept turning the diamond tooth over and over in his hand.

'Is this worth a lot of money?' he asked eventually.

'Yes.'

'Oh.' Pause. 'Do you think – I mean, are we allowed to keep them? Or—'

'Depends,' she said, too weary to bother looking at him.

'Ah. I mean, depends on what?'

'Oh whether you're stupid enough to tell anyone you were given it.'

'I see.' Another pause. 'But don't you think we should?'

'No.'

'Right.' And another pause. 'I'm sorry about what happened. With the sword.'

Emily sighed. 'Forget it,' she said. 'Just try not to be so clumsy next time.'

'I will, definitely. Um, what did happen with the sword?'

'What? Oh, I see what you mean. Well, basically, it's allergic to trolls. And goblins and dark elves and vampires. Instruments of darkness generally. It's so the bad guy can't take your sword off you in a fight and use it against you. Assuming the bad guy isn't human, of course.' She grinned. 'That's the sort of assumption they tended to make, back when magic swords were in fashion. Naive, or what?'

'I understand, thank you.' Erskine took a long last look at his diamond and put it away. 'That troll,' he said.

'Mr Pickersgill.'

Nod. 'Did he—?'

'Yes.'

'What, all of them?'

Emily shrugged. 'I don't know. Presumably he took out enough of them to make sure he had the majority shareholding. He may have had to leave one or two alive to make up a quorum at a board meeting, so he could vote himself managing director. I'm afraid I don't know much about company law.' She frowned. 'Have you got a problem with that?'

'Me? No. Well.' Erskine pulled a thoughtful face. He looked like someone on his way to a fancy-dress party, dressed as Thoughtful. 'I mean, he's a troll, right?'

'Yes.'

'But, on the other hand, the other directors can't have been very nice people, or they wouldn't have wanted to kill him just to get control of the company.'

'Yes.'

'Which is what he just did,' Erskine said. 'By killing them.'

'Yes, but—' Emily hesitated. Yes, but they started it. Yes, but he was polite and nice. 'Look, the customer's happy and we got paid. Nothing else matters. All right?'

He looked at her as though she was a burning bush. 'I understand,' he said. 'Thank you.'

Aaargh, she thought.

The taxi stopped. She let Erskine pay, since she didn't particularly want to communicate any further with the driver. 'I'll fill out a yellow chit so you can get it back off expenses,' she told Erskine as they walked into the front office. 'Would you mind doing the report? I've had about enough for one day.'

'Of course. Thank you for trusting me with the responsibility.'

'My pleasure. Now put that stupid thing back where you got it from.'

Erskine trotted away, and Emily wandered slowly back to her room, closed the door behind her and dropped into her chair. There was the usual wadge of While-You-Were-Out notes and yellow stickies on her desk, but she couldn't be fussed to look at them.

The advantages, she thought. And the drawbacks.

The phone jarred her out of her contemplations. She snatched at it and snapped, 'Yes?'

'Call for you.' *Aren't we in a mood, then?*

'Fine. Who is it?'

'Frank Carpenter. About Mr Sprague.'

Oh, she thought. 'Put him through.'

'Connecting.' *What did your last slave die of?* Click, then Frank's voice, saying 'Hello.'

Emily froze. If she was right about what had happened to her at Mr Pickersgill's office, she really didn't want to talk to Frank right now. It could be—

'Hello? Are you there?'

'Sorry, can't talk now,' she said quickly. 'Meet me after work?'

'Yes.' *Yippee!* Oh God, she thought. 'Where?'

'That pub. Westmoreland or something.'

'Cumberland Arms?'

'Yes. Quarter past six. Bye.'

Emily rammed the phone down as though plugging a leak with it. Hell, she thought, this is going to be so *embarrassing*. Unless, of course, there was some way of controlling it.

There had to be. She jumped up, pulled Bowyer & Leong's *Foundations of Magic Procedure & Practice* off her bookshelf and dived into the index. Telepathic communications, reception, suppression of: 12, 78, 566, 819ff.

When she'd read all the references, she put the book back, sat down again and said 'Bugger,' out loud and very clearly. There was a procedure, right enough. Basically, it consisted of saying nursery rhymes over and over in your head when you didn't want to hear what someone else was thinking. With enough practice, the book reckoned, it became automatic, so you didn't have to do it consciously. Eventually you'd be able to filter out what you wanted to hear and ignore the rest. Eventually.

Emily looked at her watch. Quarter to five. She didn't have time for eventually.

There must be another way. She tried the *New Oxford Thaumaturgy*, which said the same as Bowyer & Leong. Likewise O'Shaugnessy's *Theory & Practice* and Morrison's *First Steps In Commercial Sorcery*. With a sigh, she turned to her last remaining resource, *Magic For Dummies*. It too recommended nursery rhymes, though in rather less formal language . . .

– But hey, who can be bothered with all that, right? So instead, try 2ccs of lithium cryptosulphate on a sugar lump. Works a charm, and you don't have to share your head with Mary's lamb.

A greatly underrated book, Emily said to herself as she pulled open her desk drawer and took out her bare-essentials stash of chemicals. She didn't have anything to measure the lithium cryp with, but she was a good guesser: two drops on a cube of Tate & Lyall's best, and down the hatch.

Count to five; then pick up the phone.

'Yes?' reception answered.

'Could you be awfully sweet,' Emily said, 'and just nip over to the closed-file store and get me everything on the Skallagrimson job? 1982, I think it was, but you may have to dig down a bit. Some time in the Eighties, anyhow.'

Pause. 'All right.'

'No rush. Any time between now and half past five.'

'All right.'

Emily kept her mind closed for the 'all', then opened it on the 'right'. The result made her sit up very straight in her chair, but it proved conclusively that the lithium cryp was doing its job, but hadn't wiped out the effect completely. Far from it. She wondered where Nikki on the front desk had learned how to swear in goblin.

'Thanks ever so much,' she said, and put the phone down. That was all right, then. If she could control it (was the lithium-cryp effect permanent, or did you have to keep it topped up? She'd find out soon enough), she was definitely onto a winner. All advantages, no drawbacks, and wouldn't it look good on her CV? If, of course, she chose to mention it to her employers, future or present . . .

She sat back in her chair. The thought hadn't occurred to her before; but if there was someone at Carringtons trying to kill her – because of work; what other reason could there be? – wouldn't the simplest, safest thing be to resign and get another job? She could do that. Just think: no more Colin Gomez, no more credit-control meetings with Mr Hook. No more waking up in the mornings and thinking, *Oh shit, I've got to go to that place again today*. And, of course, no more people trying to kill her. Werewolves and dragons and *Atkinsonii* and dark elves, yes, but not her colleagues. Presumably.

Emily frowned. It wasn't as though she liked it at Carringtons; but it was her job, and she felt strangely reluctant to part with it. Silly, really; actually, stupid verging on suicidal. Even so; *her* job, *her* office (her beat-up filing cabinet with the sticky top drawer, her frayed carpet, her chair that went *sproing* if you leaned too far back, her overflowing in-tray, her Too Difficult pile, her sheaf of While-You-Were-Outs, her fluorescent-tube ceiling light that flickered very faintly all the time and guaranteed a headache after forty-five minutes). Her life.

There's an old saying in the magic biz: all work and no play makes Jack a junior partner by age thirty. She wanted that; not a desperate, dream-haunting longing, but as much as she'd ever wanted anything. It'd all be different, after all, when she was on the letterhead. No more being ordered around by idiots, told off about her late invoices, badgered into ripping off the clients to meet some wildly overblown quarterly target. Her destiny was the centre seat, command, a starship of her own to roam the galaxy in. If she changed jobs, it'd mean starting all over again, settling herself into a new and probably hostile hierarchy, learning a whole new set of people.

Excuses, Emily realised. I'm just too lazy.

My life, she thought; and for some reason that conjured up a mental image of Frank Carpenter, of all people. Someone she'd only met once or twice (that she could remember . . .), someone she hardly knew. Someone she couldn't really have much in common with, since he wasn't even in the trade. Someone.

Oh for crying out loud. Shaking her head, she reached for the stack of notes and stickies and shuffled through them, dividing them into piles – Not Now, Maybe Tomorrow, Sometime, Never. For a moment, she was tempted to sweep the whole lot off her desk onto the floor in a grand gesture; but she'd only have to pick them up again later, so why bother?

Indeed.

Now she was feeling guilty. So she picked out a note at random and looked at it. Mr Allenby at English Nature, please call back re application to cull giant spectral hound on Dartmoor within a site of special scientific interest. Silly. Someone had to go and dispose of the wretched thing before it ate a tourist, but she was going to have to grovel and plead and be made to feel she was being done an enormous favour by a stupid little man who'd probably wee in his pants if she saw so much as a single fluorescent footprint. Wouldn't it be better, she caught herself thinking, if people could be made to deal with their own spiders? Probably not. If you left that sort of thing to the general public, bless them, the spiders'd probably end up squashing people.

So she rang Mr Allenby, who was actually very nice and helpful, and promised to push the paperwork through as quickly as possible so she'd have her dispensation order before the autumn rains started and the moor turned into impassable bog. No trouble, that's what we're here for.

Emily thought about that. Just when you've squared up to the solemn realisation that life is a bitch, it turns round and does something nice, just to confuse you.

At twenty-five past five, Nikki staggered in with an armful of dusty old files and manila envelopes. 'What've you got there?' Emily asked her.

'Skallagrimson files,' Nikki grunted. 'Where do you want them?'

Of course she'd forgotten all about that. 'Oh, on the floor, anywhere,' she mumbled guiltily. 'Thanks.'

''Salright.' Nikki dumped the files on the floor, wiped cobweb out of her eye, and left. *Yes, but it was a necessary experiment*, Emily told herself. *Like Bikini Atoll.* She got up and shifted the pile so she wouldn't trip over it all the time. So much for command. Now she thought about it, maybe she wouldn't like it so much after all.

Dutifully she made a file note of her chat with Mr Allenby, filled in Mr Pickersgill on her time sheet, wrote a memo to Colin Gomez and paper-clipped Mr Pickersgill's cheque to it; and then it was five past six. Doesn't time fly when you're doing tedious chores while racked by deep-rooted existential doubt? She switched off the plugs, turned off the lights, hurried upstairs to the stationery cupboard and signed out an RF7000 scanner.

'Sorry I'm late,' she panted, as she slid into a chair in the front bar of the Cumberland Arms a quarter of an hour later. 'Got held up. Not a problem you ever have to face, I expect.'

Frank smiled at her. There was a glass half full of what looked like orange juice in front of him on the table.'Quite,' he said. 'Partly because of the Door, but mostly because I don't have an awful lot to do most of the time. I guess you rush about a lot.'

My life, Emily thought. 'Yes,' she said. 'It's called earning a living – you should try it some time.'

He looked at her. 'Should I?'

Shrug. 'Maybe not. I don't think it'd suit you. I'm not sure it suits me, actually, but I don't have much of a choice.' No, not where she wanted the conversation to go, even with a head full of lithium cryp. 'You said you wanted to talk to me, about your Mr Sprague.'

Frank gazed at her for a moment, then said, 'I went round there.'

'To his office, you mean?'

Nod. 'I sort of slipped in,' he said.

'And did you get to see him?'

'Yes and no.' Frank hesitated for a moment. 'I saw something, but I'm not sure what it was.'

'Ah.'

'I mean,' he went on quickly, 'it looked just like George, but it definitely wasn't him. More or less admitted it, even. But when I tried to—' He smiled feebly. 'Actually, I sort of made a grab at it, and it vanished.'

'I see.'

'And all I was left with,' he went on, 'was this.'

From his pocket he took an envelope; a New Zealand stamp, Emily noticed, and for a moment she wondered what it must be like, living with the Door. He picked out a single human hair. 'I grabbed at him,' he said. 'Actually got a grip on his collar, and then *phut*, like turning off a light. And I'm pretty sure this wasn't in my hand before. I mean, I don't know anybody with long blonde hair.'

'Except me.'

They looked at each other for a moment. Then she leaned forward and picked the hair up, tweezering it between thumbnail and forefinger. 'That's not mine,' she said after a short, rather tense silence. 'For one thing, it's your actual movie-star blonde, as opposed to—'

'Mouse?'

'Mellow light brown. Hang on,' she added, pulling the scanner across the table towards her. 'Just as well I brought this.'

Frank's eyebrows huddled. 'What is that?'

'Technology,' she replied. 'Don't worry about it. But it might—' The little screen flickered and the annoying welcome message came up. 'Come *on*,' she growled, and the screen went blue. 'It takes a minute or two,' she said.

'Ah. A Microsoft product.'

'No, but almost as bad. Right, here we go.' Emily picked up the hair and laid it on the screen. 'Well,' she said, 'it's human, for what that's— Natural, no signs of chemical treatment, but it has been subjected to an intense transmorphic field at some time in the last forty-eight hours.' She prodded some buttons, swore at the screen as a little hourglass icon popped up, prodded another button and twiddled a little rollerball thing. 'If it says *program not responding*, it's going to get an unscheduled flying lesson . . . Ah, that's better.' She studied a clutter of symbols that Frank didn't recognise, then looked up at him. 'I'll hang on to this,' she said, sweeping the hair back into the envelope. 'Just a hunch, but I think I may have an idea about this. It's perfect, you see.'

He gave her a puzzled look. 'Perfect?'

She nodded. 'Absolutely perfect. Hair any woman would die for. No colour, no conditioner or jojoba-root essence or moisturiser or any of the crap we spend billions of dollars a year on as a species; just perfect, natural hair. Doesn't that strike you as just a bit suspicious?'

'Um,' Frank said. 'Well, no.'

Emily glanced at him. 'That's because you're a man,' she said. 'But you can't help that.' She tucked the envelope away in her bag and switched off the scanner. It chimed at her, and she winced. 'You don't happen to have your friend George's home number, do you?'

'No.'

'Pity. Because I'm prepared to bet he won't be there if I call him. Or at the office. Or anywhere. First thing in the morning, give him a ring. I'm ninety-nine per cent sure he won't be at his desk tomorrow, not unless— Where are you going?'

'Won't be a tick. Don't go away.'

'All right. Would it be OK if I got myself a drink? Only, this is supposed to be a pub, you see, and it's been a long day.'

'Fine,' Frank said, and scampered off in the direction of the lavatories.

Emily got herself a drink with plenty of gin in it. By the time she returned to the table Frank was back. 'You were right,' he said. 'Not there.'

'You phoned him?'

'At the office,' he replied. 'Tomorrow morning. Mr Sprague won't be in today. Well, tomorrow.' He shook his head. 'I know, it confuses the hell out of me sometimes, too. So,' he went on, leaning forward a little, 'how did you know that?'

She smiled. All right, he could nip off to the toilet and Portable Door into the future to make a phone call, but she knew things. 'It's magic,' she said.

'Ah.'

'It's a Chinese invention,' she went on, 'like most things, really. You can take a bit of yourself – hair's the usual choice, for obvious reasons, though a bit of toenail clipping will do, or even a gob of spit – and turn it into a replica of yourself. Sort of like cloning, only magic, so cheaper, quicker and you don't need specialist equipment or a licence or anything. If you're really clever, and there's only a few people in the trade right now who can do this, you can turn it into a copy of someone else.'

'Oh,' Frank said. 'That's—'

'Quite.' Emily frowned. 'It has its limitations, of course. The replicant is usually pretty basic. They're not generally very bright, for one thing. They've only got a very limited memory capacity, and you can get the appearance fairly exact, but the personality's usually a bit sketchy. If you want to do a thorough job of replacing someone, you're better off transfiguring a whole animal or making a golem. For a quick and dirty job on the fly, though, it's a useful technique.'

Frank wallowed about in the unfamiliar concepts for a moment. 'You think that's what this is?'

She nodded. 'When you grabbed at him, I guess you overloaded the programming and it broke down. Turned back into a hair. Hence, no Mr Sprague at the office tomorrow. And if I'm right about where that hair came from—'

'Yes?'

She shook her head. 'Let's not jump the gun,' she said. 'And don't you dare go forward through that Door thing of yours and find out. If I'm stuck in boring old linear time, I don't see why you shouldn't be too.'

'OK,' he said, rather solemnly. 'And thank you. I think I'd be dead from bewilderment poisoning by now if it wasn't for you.

Which only goes to show,' he added, 'how high my bewilderment threshold is, since I didn't actually understand a word of what you've been telling me. But that's all right,' he added quickly, as she opened her mouth. 'Just so long as one of us knows what's going on, I'm not all that fussed if it isn't me.' He pulled a face and nodded toward the scanner. 'What is that thing, anyway? And don't say technology again.'

Emily smiled. 'It's a scanning device,' she said. 'Just as well I brought it along, wouldn't you say? Talking of which . . .' She hesitated, then said, 'Have you got any plans for the rest of the evening?'

A look came over Frank's face which she had difficulty interpreting. 'No. Why?'

'Well,' she said, 'I thought we might go over to your Mr Sprague's office and take some readings, see if we can pick up any morphogenic residue-decay signatures.'

'Oh. I mean, yes, if you think it'd help, that'd be great. Wonderful. Thanks ever so much.'

Again, she wasn't quite able to read his expression, and for just a moment she was tempted to override the lithium cryp and listen in . . . But no, she couldn't do that. It'd be unethical and a gross violation of his sentient rights. Also, she was a bit afraid of what she might hear.

'Right, then,' Emily said, finishing her drink and standing up. 'Let's get going.'

For some reason, Frank didn't seem as enthusiastic as she'd been expecting. Odd; after all, he'd asked her to help him solve the Sprague mystery and here she was, all energy and do-it-now, and he seemed – disappointed? Not quite. But almost, as he swilled down the dregs of his orange juice and got to his feet. 'We'll use the Door,' he said.

'I assumed we would.' She said it ever so casually, but in spite of everything – years in the trade, seen it all, done it all – a tiny part of her was squeezing its hands and hopping up and down in excitement. (Look at me, everyone, I'm going through the actual Portable Door, isn't that just so amazing?) Colin Gomez had never been through it, or Mr Hook, or even Amelia Carrington herself. So cool—

(And, even further back in her mind, in the grubby back streets where she preferred not to go, a little voice said: you know, a thing like that, it's wasted on him. I mean, not even in the biz, doesn't know how it works, could be really dangerous in the hands of the clueless. But if *we* had it . . . And then the rest of her mind reflected that when a part of you starts talking in the plural like that, it's only a matter of time before it starts mucking up its grammar and saying 'precious' a lot. She closed her mind to the little voice and it crept away to its lair in the guilt stacks.)

There was a convenient alleyway behind the pub, with a nice broad brick wall. Emily watched Frank tap the Door out of its cardboard tube and flick it against the bricks like a veteran flyposter. She hadn't really watched closely before, not enough to observe the fine details with a professional eye; the way the lines went so subtly from two to three dimensions, the way it flowed rather than popped into existence. There was enough material for a doctorate, and he hadn't even turned the handle yet—

He opened it, and over his shoulder she saw into the room beyond: an office, dark but faintly lit by the lamps in the street below, shining up through the window. It was the sort of perspective that creased your mind, and instinctively she looked away; but he was hissing 'Come on' at her, and she felt ashamed. She followed him, heard the Door click; and then he leaned past her to catch it as it unrolled off the wall.

We wants it, yes, precious, we wants it for our own—

Stop that, Emily ordered herself. Even so; there was a line in the marriage service that referred to worldly goods. Whether the Door counted as worldly was perhaps a moot point, but if – well, if they somehow metamorphosed into a *couple* (in her mind's ear the word sounded strange, bizarre, even faintly obscene), surely Frank would have no objection if she wanted to borrow it, just now and then, for a specially demanding job.

She shook her head, rattling the voice about until it shut up.

'Switch the lights on,' she snapped irritably, 'before I fall over something.'

A moment later, there was a click and a wash of bright white light from the overhead tubes. Mr Sprague's office turned out to be just another enclosed space for making money in; the desk was bigger than hers, maybe, the chair a bit more sumptuous and commanding; but the framed photo of Anonymous Wife And Child was in almost exactly the same place on the desktop as its counterpart in Colin Gomez's room, and the two people in it wore exactly the same long-suffering expression. It's a basic law of magic that all places are one place, and where offices are concerned it's literally as well as metaphysically true.

'I'll set up the scanner,' Emily said.

'Great,' Frank replied awkwardly. 'Anything I can do?'

For a moment, he could have been Erskine: a superfluous life-form with the potential to get under her feet and impede her in the execution of her duties. 'What? No. I mean, yes,' she added quickly, because he wasn't Erskine. 'Keep watch, let me know if anyone's coming.'

'Right.' Hesitation. 'How, exactly?'

Good question. She'd said it because that's what they say in films; and then the spare character goes offstage somewhere while the hero does his stuff with his impressive techy gismo. 'Just keep still and don't interrupt,' she said, because every meaningful relationship is founded on total honesty. She was both surprised and impressed when he did exactly as he was told. In her experience, men were creatures who stood over you, saying 'What does that bit there do?' and 'Are you sure you've got that the right way up?' Maybe, Emily thought, he really is the only man in the world for me.

The screen flickered. The annoying chime made her jump. She pulled down the functions menu and tapped the little pad with the tip of her forefinger. A shoal of Mortensen data flooded the screen, and she frowned and ran the cursor across to *Analyse*.

The screen went dark.

Technology, she thought; oh well. Nothing for it but to reboot and start again.

'How's it—?'

'Shh.'

'Sorry.'

The flicker. The bloody stupid chime. The little dancing hourglass that she hated so much. The functions menu. The Mortensen numbers—

'Now we're getting— Bloody hell,' she said, as the numbers vanished. The screen flashed brilliant white two or three times, and then filled with an image she'd never seen on it before: a single sea-blue eye, gazing straight at her.

Under different circumstances, she'd have assumed it was a practical joke, a virus, an Easter egg, something of the kind. Sad, technically proficient members of the profession had been known to play funny games along those lines, though the screen-filling eye was invariably red and usually bordered with darting flames. Intuitively, she knew this wasn't anything like that. For one thing, CGI doesn't jam your windpipe or turn your knees to aspic. The eye on the screen was too real. It wasn't just pixels dancing on the face of a tube. It was alive, and looking at her with amused, malicious interest.

Emily had a nasty feeling that she could put a name to it.

How long she sat there staring at it, she had no idea. It was only when an arm reached across her and hit the off-switch that it occurred to her that she might have been there for quite some time.

'It's not meant to do that, is it?'

Erskine – no, Frank. Frank's voice, calm but worried. The eye was still there on the screen.

She tried to say 'No, it isn't.' Her lips moved, but someone had pressed the mute button, and no sound came out. She couldn't turn her head, either.

'Hold on.' She heard rustling, somewhere outside her field of vision; then a page from a broadsheet newspaper came between her and the screen, and she pulled away as though she'd been burned, overbalanced her chair, wobbled and fell off it onto the floor.

'Are you all right?'

Emily scrabbled for a moment like a beetle on its back, then found her feet and jumped up. The eye was still there, in negative, a black oval with a burning white centre, printed on her retina. She massaged her eyelids, and it gradually faded.

'The bitch,' she said.

'Sorry?'

'The miserable cow.' She groped her way to the desk and sat on the edge of it. 'What a mean, nasty—'

Frank was there, standing in front of her. 'What's wrong?' he was saying, looking so wretched that she nearly laughed. 'That picture—'

She felt a lot better. 'Booby trap,' she said, as her heart started beating again. 'Bloody Amelia Carrington. To stop people borrowing the firm's kit for private work, I guess.' She shuddered. 'I know we're not supposed to, but even so, that's a bit extreme. It scared the life out of me, staring at me like that. Like she was looking right at me—' She broke off, as a horrible thought struck her. 'She *was* looking at me,' she said. 'I'm going to be in so much trouble in the morning.'

Frank was gazing at her, a pictorial dictionary's definition of *mortified*. This time, Emily couldn't help it. She giggled. 'Sorry,' she said quickly, 'but really, you should see your face.'

He frowned; still tortured by guilt and remorse, but a bit hacked off, too. 'I've gone and landed you in it,' he said. 'I'm really sorry, if I'd known—'

'Forget it,' she sighed. 'It's not your fault my boss is a miserable, sadistic cow with a warped sense of humour.'

'But you could lose your job—'

'Big deal.' The words came out before the thought took shape in her mind. 'Face it, would you want to work for someone who'd pull a stunt like that? Putting a lock on the stationery cupboard door, that's one thing, but scaring people half to death, that's got to be harassment or something like that. Not that it'd do me any good,' Emily added ruefully. 'We don't do industrial tribunals in our profession. Last person who tried it ended up relocating to a lily pad. No, if they want to fire me, let them. But they won't. I do a good job and bring in money. I'll just get a bollocking, that's all.'

'Well, that's bad enough,' Frank said. 'Come on, let's get out of here, before it gets any worse.' Before she could argue, he'd spread the Door on the wall and turned the handle. 'Where to?' he added. 'I can drop you off anywhere you like.'

Anywhere she liked, just say the word. Venice, Acapulco, Barbados, the Alps, the Serengeti. She remembered something they'd made her read at school, when she was a little girl, about the cat who walked by herself and all places were the same to her. Sure, everybody wants to travel. But this would be too easy. Like giving in.

'Just drop me off outside the office,' Emily said, forced-casual. 'I'll get the bus home from there.'

Frank looked at her, but all he said was, 'You sure?'

No, of course I'm not, you stupid man. You're supposed to say, don't be ridiculous, I can take you direct to your doorstep. She waited, a whole two-thirds of a second, but he just stood there looking blank. Not a word out of him, not so much as a muted squeak. He couldn't have declared his lack of interest more plainly if he'd taken a thirty-second prime-time slot on ITV.

'Fine,' she snapped. 'Right, is this thing ready?'

He nodded and she pushed past him, nudging him out of the way. As her elbow prodded his solar plexus – accidentally; a happy accident, you might say – she heard his voice saying 'Ow.' And, at the same time, it said: *I love her, but obviously she's not the least bit interested, she'd rather take the bus home, well, fine, serves me right, won't be making that mistake again in a hurry.*

Hell of a time for the lithium cryp to wear off.

Emily froze in mid-step, but her weight was over her front foot, carrying her forward, under the two-and-a-bit-dimensional lintel of the Door. 'Actually, you're wrong,' she blurted out; but by that time she was over the threshold. She jammed her heels down, wobbled, caught her balance and spun round, to find herself an inch or two away from a blank, featureless wall.

'Shit,' she yelled.

Calm down, she told herself. Any second now, the Door will open in this wall, he'll come through, I'll tell him – well, I'll say something, any bloody thing just so long as it stops him thinking like that; and then we'll have a calm, sensible talk about things, and it'll all be fine. It's nothing two rational human beings can't iron out in a minute or two, and then we'll both know where we are, and—

She shoved past him and lunged through the Door. Frank stepped smartly back to get out of her way. The Door slammed, then unrolled and fell off the wall.

Fine, he thought. Be like that. I can take a hint, particularly if it's ferocious enough to make the floor shake and bits of loose plaster come off the ceiling.

He stood quite still for a moment, thinking about his life and its general futility. No change there; except, for the first time ever, there was something he wanted, and now it was pretty clear that he wasn't going to get it.

The hell with it, he thought. The hell with love, and happiness, and waking up each morning to greet the unlimited promise of a new day. The hell with all of it. The hell with her.

Frank stooped wearily, picked up the stupid Door, slapped it hard against the wall, opened it, went through, shut it, caught it, put it away and flopped onto his hard unmade bed.

No Door. No thin black lines forming on the whitewashed plaster. Emily frowned. What was keeping him? Naturally he'd come after her. Ordinary common politeness—

Oink, she thought. Whitewashed plaster wall. Not many of them in Cheapside.

Whitewashed plaster *interior* wall. Forming part of a dimly lit, musty-smelling room. No windows. No furniture, apart from a single chipboard and square-section steel table, with a thermos flask and a plate of sandwiches on it. Aside from that, and Emily Spitzer of course, no contents of any kind.

And no door.

Oh, she thought. That's not right. Got to have some kind of door, of the everyday, small-case-first-letter kind, or how the hell are you supposed to get into it? Or, come to that, out again? Magic?

Oh.

I'm being stupid, Emily thought. There's got to be a door, but it's in the shadows somewhere. I've just got to look for it, and there it'll be.

She looked. Didn't take long.

No door.

CHAPTER ELEVEN

Mr Tanner's mother sat at the front desk of her son's poky little office, knitting.

Well, of course she did. Knitting is one of the things mothers do. In her case, she was using 6mm high-tensile steel winch cable, and her drop-forged chrome molybdenum needles were bent like saplings in the breeze as they took the five-hundred-kilo strain required to keep the line taut. It was going to be a baby-grow for little Paul Azog.

As her needles hummed – knit one, purl one, knit two together, and a quick tack-weld at the end of the row – she reflected on her other son, with particular reference to his gulli-bility and general naivety. No more idea, she told herself, sternly but fondly, than next door's cat. Just as well he's got me to look after him.

The welder sparkled, showering her knees with white-hot spatter. Instant ruin to tights, but since they were simply an extension of her morphogenic field, no harm done. She shape-shifted into a similar but different auburn-haired beauty wearing an unblemished pair of sheer silk tights, and cast on the next row.

On balance, she decided, she'd rather have a son who was a bit thick and a bit soft but who still had time for his old mum,

206 • Tom Holt

than a hard-nosed, no-nonsense, streetwise offspring like, say, Amelia Carrington. Of course, she didn't believe the rumours about her; and even if they were true, she wouldn't have cared unduly. Tosser Carrington always was a waste of resources, and if his daughter had seen fit to turn him into a hedgehog and dump him on the hard shoulder of the M3, no great loss to the profession or the species. But Dennis would never dream of doing anything like that. He was fond of his mother. And scared shitless of her, of course, but also genuinely fond. Which counted for more, she felt, than all the brains in Seattle.

Even so.

Trouble was, the boy wouldn't be told. She'd tried dropping a few hints on the journey home from the meeting – you do realise she's going to have to kill you, I wouldn't trust that skinny cow as far as I could sneeze her out of a blocked nostril, that sort of thing – but Dennis had just looked smug and declared that he knew what he was doing, at which point she'd lost patience with him and resolved to save her breath to cool her porridge. Well.

Mr Tanner's mother glanced down at the pattern, sighed, and reached for the wire-cutters.

Amelia Carrington, she thought. It seemed like only yesterday that she'd been eating strained pear off a spoon and strangling snakes in her cot. It's a shame they have to grow up.

Obviously, she was up to something; well, that went without saying. Knowing her, something big and flashy, probably some kind of take on world domination; something involving bauxite, at some level or other. The part that puzzled Mr Tanner's mother, though, was why she needed to involve young Dennis.

That was a mystery; it was also pretty much the only clue she'd got. Fortunately, it was a significant one. For all that she was his mother, she had few illusions about her son. He was a perfectly competent private-practice magician with an undoubted flair for scrying, but that was all. His rise to a partnership in J. W. Wells & Co he owed to the slender but tenacious streak of ruthlessness that he'd inherited from her side of the family. The other, human side had made him sloppy, soft and sentimental, though to do him credit he hid it well. His worst fault was his own unshakeable faith in his own cleverness. It wouldn't have mattered too much if he'd been stupid. Idiots with delusions of intelligence never climb up high enough to hurt themselves badly when they fall. It's the level-eight smar-tarses who think they're level tens who come badly unstuck; which was what had happened, of course, to Dennis.

The other problem caused by his most significant flaw was that when he fell, he hadn't fallen quite far enough. If he'd been left broke and destitute after JWW crashed, he'd most likely have quit the frontline magic business and found some nice quiet backwater of the profession in which to live out the rest of his days. But he'd been just sufficiently clever to salvage enough from the wreck to set up this two-rooms-over-a-chemist's-shop business of his own, and he was doing just well enough at it to harbour dangerous dreams of getting back into the big time, as and when the one lucky break came along. Hence, presumably, the Carrington bitch's interest.

It had to be scrying, Dennis's mother thought, as she twid-dled the knobs of the oxypropane torch. It was what he was best at, so it had to be something of the sort. Even so; Amelia Carrington had two dozen scryers on her staff who were almost as good, and (more to the point) the scheme she'd told them about didn't actually need the best in the business—

Pause. Was Dennis the best in the business? No, but a lot of people in the trade believed he was, or pretty close to it. A frown crossed her face and for a moment the auburn-haired temptress flickered, and you could have caught a glimpse of the underlying goblin. If Dennis Tanner said there was bauxite under some mountain in New Zealand, that'd be good enough for anybody. But what if there wasn't any?

Yes, she thought, but that doesn't make sense. The reason everybody would believe him if he said the new strike was the biggest yet discovered was that he wouldn't say it if it wasn't true; and he'd know if Amelia Carrington was trying to trick him, he was definitely good enough for that. That was another defect in his character: integrity. Not that he wouldn't lie and cheat for money and steal a child's teddy bear from its cot if he knew someone who'd pay him money for it. But as far as scrying was concerned, he told the truth. Everybody knew that.

In which case, that had to be the scam; that Carrington bitch must've come up with something that'd fool even the great Dennis Tanner into guaranteeing a strike that didn't exist. Except that that was impossible. Grr.

The phone rang. Talk of the—

'Amelia Carrington. I'd like a quick word with Dennis, please.'

'Putting you through.' She put her on hold and rang Dennis. 'It's that cow on the line,' she said.

'What?'

'Amelia bloody Carrington. On the phone for you.'

'Oh, right. For a moment I thought you were talking about railways.'

She sighed. 'You want to talk to her or not?'

Pause; then, 'Yeah, why not? Put her on.'

Mr Tanner's mother would never have dreamed of picking up the phone and listening in on her son's private conversation. With goblin hearing, she didn't need to.

'Dennis,' said the Carrington female. 'Good news. We've got the satellite pics.'

'About time.'

'Yes, well. Anyhow, they're here on my desk right now. How soon can you come over?'

The hesitation that followed was so slight that only a mother would have detected it. 'I'm a bit tied up right now. Could you have them sent over here?'

Good boy, thought Mr Tanner's mother.

'I'd rather not, if it's all the same to you. No offence, but somehow I doubt your security's up to our standards. I'm probably being over-fussy, but the last thing I want right now is for these pics to fall into the wrong hands. I'm sure you understand.'

'I just wanted to save time, that's all,' Dennis replied, so convincingly that his mother almost believed him herself. 'The earliest I can get there is – what's the time now, half-six; call it eight-fifteen, too late for New York or Tokyo.' (Nice touch, Mr Tanner's mother conceded; doesn't actually mean anything, but just convincing enough to throw Amelia Carrington off balance for a second or two.) 'If you rush them over here in a taxi right now, we'd still be able to catch Riyadh and possibly New Delhi.'

'No, sorry. I sort of gave my word I wouldn't let them out of my sight. Look, I'll send a car for you, OK? See you soon.'

Followed by a click, meaning end of discussion. Fair enough. When you're Amelia Carrington you don't need to be subtle, in the same way elephants don't need wellington boots. A moment later, the dividing door opened and Dennis came in. He was wearing his coat.

'You got all that?' he asked.

She nodded. 'You're not going, are you?'

'Looks like it. Bloody woman,' he added with feeling.

Mr Tanner's mother turned off the gas bottle and stood up. 'I wish I knew what she was up to.'

'Only one way to find out.'

It's annoying when your son, your own flesh and blood, turns out to have a point. 'We won't wait for the car,' she said. 'I'll get a taxi.'

He grinned at her. 'You're coming, then?'

No need to answer that. She transformed into a coat-wearing blonde, flipped on the answering machine and reached for the door handle—

'For crying out loud, Mum.'

'What?'

Sigh. 'You can't go out looking like that.'

Not the first time they'd had this argument. Her first instinct was to ignore him – do him good, make him lighten up a little – but the prospect of him sulking at her all the way there and back again was too tiresome to contemplate. She relented and lengthened her skirt an inch. 'There,' she said, in her best humouring-with-extreme-prejudice voice. 'Is that better?'

'No. Look at yourself, will you?'

Scowling, she grabbed her mirror from the front desk. Pause. 'Oh,' she said.

'Yes.'

Two points in one day. She sighed. 'Coincidence,' she said.

'Really.'

'Yes.'

'You turn into the exact spitting image of Amelia Carrington, and it's a coincidence.'

'All right, then, it's subconscious. I must've been thinking about her, and—'

'Whatever.'

Just to spite him for being right, she changed into a geisha. 'Satisfied?' she said.

'If you insist.' That resigned tone she knew so well. 'Actually, it'll bug the hell out of Amelia, so yes, why not? Get the taxi.'

If he hadn't known Amelia since before she was born, Dennis wouldn't have had the satisfaction of being proved right. The slightest flicker of the eyelashes, the faintest widening of the eyes thereby enclosed, and that was his lot as far as provoking her was concerned. In context it was enough. In fact, it was a triumph, and as always, Mother had known best.

'Dennis, at last,' she said, waving him into a chair and pretending that his exotic companion was invisible. 'Well, here we are. The photos.'

There they were indeed. They looked like nothing at all; your best guess would've been black and white abstract painting by an avant-garde artist with absolutely no imagination. To Dennis Tanner, of course, they were aerial views of a large tract of landscape, taken from a satellite so high up that no man-made feature was large enough to register. He drew one of them across the desk with a fingertip and looked at it.

Like being hit across the face with a bike chain. He did his best to mask the shock, but he knew he was too late. Amelia would have seen the brief but extreme look of amazement on his face and appreciated it for what it was. Dennis Tanner, the whole world knew, wasn't easy to impress.

'Something there, Uncle Dennis?' in that sweet-little-girl voice that made him want to puke. No point trying to dissemble now.

'Too bloody right,' he said, with deep feeling.

'Is it big?'

'Yes.'

'Bigger than Wayatumba?'

'I haven't looked at the rest of the pics yet,' he said, hedging.

'But?'

'Give me a chance.' Dennis reached across and grabbed a few more prints at random. It was a bit like catching hold of a live electric cable, but he held on, gritted his teeth and, after a suitable pause, muttered, 'Yes.'

He could have done without the peal of silvery laughter. To distract himself from the surge of irritation washing through his mind, he tried to recall what little he knew about Amelia's mother. According to Tosser, she'd been a wood nymph he'd come across while she was bathing in a remote pool somewhere in the Welsh mountains. Trade scuttlebutt reckoned otherwise, of course; in any event, she must've inherited her flair for the infuriatingly dramatic from her mother's side. Tosser's idea of drama was the last act of *Hamlet*: dead bodies everywhere and a horrible untidy mess for someone else to sort out. Besides, were there still wood nymphs in rural Wales in the Sixties? He vaguely remembered something about Macmillan having them all relocated to Swansea.

'Excellent,' Amelia was saying. 'Our people were pretty sure about it, but I wanted to have it verified by the leading authority before we went any further. Well, thanks ever so much, Uncle Dennis. We really must have lunch sometime.'

The penny, dropping, never landed. It fell so fast it burnt up in the atmosphere, sprinkling Dennis's mind with droplets of molten copper. 'No worries,' he managed to say, nevertheless. 'Now, about our partnership—'

'Not the P-word, Uncle Dennis.'

'All right, then, our joint venture. Don't take this the wrong way, but before we go any further, I'd like to see some paperwork. A draft contract, something like—'

'Uncle Dennis.' Such a sweet, sad smile. 'You may be the greatest scryer in the world, but when it comes to business, you're just an old silly.' Ominous growl from the corner of the room; Amelia shot a startled glance in that direction, recovered quickly and went on, 'Really, you know, you should've mentioned it earlier, before you carried out your side of the bargain. Be fair,' she added, 'you don't really expect me to cut you in on a deal this size in return for services already rendered. I'm very grateful, of course, and I know Daddy would've been, too. But there it is. If you will go doing jobs for people out of the kindness of your heart, no wonder you've ended up in that squalid little office.'

The growl became a roar, at more or less the same moment that the geisha turned back into a fully grown adult female goblin. Amelia instinctively shrank back in her chair, then rallied gloriously and smiled at her. 'Uncle Dennis,' she said. 'Aren't you going to introduce me to your friend?'

'My mother, actually.'

'Of course.' The smile widened, until it threatened to engulf the planet. 'Auntie Rosie, how silly of me, I didn't recognise you.' She leaned forward a little and peered. 'You've done your hair differently, haven't you?'

Like spiders, goblins can move horribly fast. Before she could get within claw's reach, though, Dennis reached out and caught hold of her wrist. 'Forget it, Mum,' he said.

'But that bony little cow—'

'Forget it.'

Mr Tanner's mother quivered for a moment, then dissolved back into the geisha, demurely smiling and, as far as Amelia was concerned, non-existent. 'Look,' Amelia said, 'I don't want to be stingy or anything. Tell you what, I'll give you a quarter of a per cent of the net profits, for old time's sake. It's what Daddy would have wanted, I'm sure. Take it or—' Shrug, which set her golden hair dancing like Wordsworth's daffodils. 'It's more money than you'll ever see in your entire life,' she said. 'And all you had to do for it was prod a photograph. That's not a bad evening's work, when you think about it.'

Dennis Tanner sat quite still for four seconds, breathing through his nose. 'That's true,' he said. 'Actually, between you and me, I was planning on retiring sometime soon, in any case.'

'Splendid idea.' Amelia nodded sharply. 'High time you got away from the stresses and strains of the business. You can relax, chill out, garden, play golf.' Glance towards the back of the room. 'Spend more time with the family. A nice little nest egg's just what the doctor ordered.'

Dennis sighed and stood up. 'That's right,' he said. 'I must be getting old. Lost the knack of judging character, and once that's gone you're not fit to be let out on your own in this trade. Well, time we were going.' He paused at the door, and looked back at Amelia. 'You've done pretty well for yourself,' he said. 'Your dad would've been proud.'

He opened the door; and then his mother said, 'Aren't you going to say thank you to the nice lady, after she's given you such a lovely present?'

Dennis stopped, and grinned. 'Thanks,' he said. 'I won't forget it in a hurry.'

'My pleasure.' Amelia beamed at him. 'Enjoy your retirement, Uncle Dennis.'

Dennis and his mother didn't say anything to each other until they reached the street and found a taxi.

'What the hell,' Dennis said eventually, 'was all that about?'

His mother thought for a bit before answering. 'She wants to provoke you into doing something,' she replied.

'I know that.' Dennis scowled at the back of the driver's neck, giving him a headache that lasted for three days. 'What, though? Bloody woman,' he added petulantly.

'Whatever it is,' his mother said firmly, 'don't do it. Which means,' she added, 'don't do anything. Forget all about it. Otherwise, it'll all end in tears, you mark my words.'

He gave her a don't-you-start look. 'I'm guessing,' he said, 'that what I'm supposed to do now is try and double-cross her, to get my own back. Buggered if I can see how, though.'

She nodded. 'Just as well. You don't want to go messing with that one, our Dennis. She's cleverer than you.'

'Mum—'

'She is,' she said firmly. 'And she's the head of Carringtons, and you ... Well,' she went on, 'anyway. Don't do anything. Don't give her the satisfaction.'

Dennis snarled. 'Next you'll be saying I really should think about retiring.'

'Don't be stupid,' his mother said reassuringly. 'And you'll get her back, one of these days. Just not now, all right? Look, whatever she's got planned, she's relying on you doing something predictable. My guess is, her whole plan depends on it. So don't do anything. Then either she'll have to give the whole thing up, which'd really piss her off, so that's all right, or she'll come back and have another go; and that may tell us a bit more about what she's got in mind. At the moment, we know bugger-all, so anything we do'll be playing right into her hands. You do see that, don't you?'

Dennis grunted. 'I never liked her,' he said. 'Do you remember, I bought her a cuddly lion when she was four, and she never did say thank you.'

'That's right.' His mother nodded. 'She brought it to life and it ate a plumber before young Ricky Wurmtoter managed to get rid of it. Always had a nasty streak, that one.' She sighed. 'Like I said, you don't want to mess with her. Leave well alone, is my advice.'

Dennis stared out of the window for a moment or so. 'We won't see a penny of that money,' he said.

'Well, of course not.'

He yawned. 'I suppose you're right,' he said wearily. 'Forget all about it for now and see if she comes back. Though,' he added doubtfully, 'for all we know that's exactly what she's expecting us to do. You're right about her being cleverer than me, but has it occurred to you that she may be cleverer than you as well?'

Mr Tanner's mother shook her head. 'No,' she said firmly. 'Nobody's cleverer than me. It says so in the rules somewhere.'

When they'd gone, Amelia Carrington made a few calls.

Yes, they told her, it was settling in nicely; eating well (very well), sleeping most of the day, hadn't burned down any more buildings, should be ready to deploy any day now. That made her smile.

No, they told her, he's not in the office right now, he must have gone home already, they'd leave a note on his desk to say she'd called. That made her frown, but it couldn't be too important.

Yes, they told her (and could she speak up, it was a dreadful line), all the legal guff was sorted out, apart from final registration with the Mining and Minerals Commission, and they were pushing that through as fast as possible. No worries. That made her nod and say, 'Fine, carry on.'

For crying out loud, they told her, did she realise what time it was? Oh, sorry, didn't recognise her voice there for a moment. Yes, all going ahead as per schedule; finished the heavy blasting and ready to start pouring the concrete, as soon as the health and safety people had signed off on the plans. Yes, they were being a bit awkward but no more than usual. Maybe she could get her people to have a word with them, smooth things over a bit. Attention of Mr Donaldson. That'd be really helpful, thanks.

Yes, they told her, this is the health and safety executive, Donaldson speaking, who the hell gave you my home number and rivet rivet rivet.

No, they told her, she's not home yet. No, she hadn't said where she was going after work.

I'm sorry, it told her, there's nobody here to take your call, please leave your name and *aaargh*.

Amelia put the receiver back, yawned and tapped her fingers on the desktop. So far, apparently, so good; the look on Uncle

Dennis' face . . . It's so nice, she felt, to deal with people you know you could rely on. And Auntie Rosie, too. Never did like her very much.

She frowned. Auntie Rosie was clever, though not nearly as clever as she thought she was, and naturally Dennis would do exactly what his mother told him to. She tried to reconstruct the conversation they'd be having at that moment. Somehow she fancied the words *don't give her the satisfaction* would come into it somewhere. True, she hadn't actually factored Auntie Rosie into her calculations, but that didn't matter. She knew exactly what line she'd be taking, and the only effect would be to make Dennis react the way he was supposed to, only slightly faster and with even more grim determination. Well, you would, with something like that nagging away at you all day long.

Amelia tried Mr Sprague's office again, but they'd all gone home and the switchboard was down for the night. Which reminded her. She reached for the phone and called Colin Gomez.

'Colin,' she said briskly, 'why hasn't that Spitzer girl been killed yet?'

Pause. 'She has,' he replied awkwardly.

'No, she hasn't, Colin. I know for a fact she's still alive.'

'Well, yes, she's still alive. But I've had her killed. Twice.'

'Ah.' She clicked her tongue. 'Well, you know what they say. Third time lucky.'

'Certainly, yes, I'll get on to it right away.' Pause. 'Actually, I was thinking—'

'Yes?'

'Well.' Pause. 'Since she will insist on coming back to life again, I thought maybe a slightly more oblique approach, possibly slanted more in the getting-her-out-of-the-way direction, as opposed to actual life termination—'

'Don't be silly, Colin. Look, as of now I'm authorising the use of extreme measures, up to and including tactical nukes. Things are starting to move at the New Zealand end, that stupid prophesy's hanging over me like the Sword of Whatsisname, and I don't want to be held up and lose out on a rising market because of a silly little girl. Do you understand?'

Amelia didn't need to see him to know what expression he had on his face. Poor Colin. He could be so sweet sometimes. 'Yes, certainly, of course. Right away.'

'Excellent. What's her status at the moment?'

'I've got her in a Tomacek trap. She's in holding, down in the basement.' Pause. 'Do you want me to—?'

'Yes.'

'Of course. Right away. Certainly.'

'That's very nice of you, Colin, thanks. Ciao.'

In his office two floors below, Colin Gomez pushed away from his desk and shuddered. In his view of the universe, all it took to make the world go round was for everybody to work hard, pull together for the good of the firm, keep the clients happy and always charge slightly more than the job was worth. Management philosophies based on the balance of greed and terror had never appealed to him much, however fashionable they might be in the world at large. Employees, he reckoned, were like tubes of toothpaste: there to be squeezed, but only from the right end. He tried not to browbeat or bully, if he could help it. As for actually killing junior members of staff, it was something he preferred to avoid whenever possible. However tactful and discreet you were about it, inevitably it led to tension and bad feeling in the workplace, which in turn reduced output and efficiency and encouraged a distrustful us-and-them approach which was the exact opposite of the way things ought to be.

But a direct order from the senior partner wasn't open to question, and if Amelia Carrington wanted the Spitzer girl disposed of, that really ought to be good enough for him. He sighed, thinking about her for a moment. True, she was a good worker, professional, got the job done with a minimum of fuss. But her attitude towards the clients had never really quite come together, he couldn't help thinking; she'd never quite understood that a client was like a beautiful fruit tree, to be nurtured, cared for, pollinated and pruned. She'd always given the impression that clients were just another nuisance arranged by the malevolent universe to make her job slightly more awkward. Which just went to show: the senior partner always knows best. The secret of survival in middle management is the ability to recognise the new truth, even when it was heresy and sin only ten minutes ago.

Colin Gomez had been a partner in Carringtons for twenty years. When the boss told him something, he *believed*.

In which case, Emily Spitzer had to go. A pity. Omelettes and eggs. The only remaining question was, how?

There are proverbially more ways of killing a cat than drowning it in cream. Sure. The problem in this case was persuading it to stay dead. Cagliari's Marvellous Tree hadn't managed to get the job done (which reminded him: it was still under warranty, so at the very least he should be able to get the money back). A rogue *Atkinsonii*, kitted out at ruinous expense with a cynanide-gas-proof cybernetic breather unit hadn't cut it, either. More to the point, the Better Mousetrap, which should've guaranteed immunity from all this now-she-is-now-she-isn't nonsense, had failed spectacularly. He sighed and scratched his head. They have a slightly different version of the proverb in the magic biz. If drowning in cream is what it takes, buy a cow.

Easier said than done, when the cat has at least nine lives and can swim. Colin Gomez was a methodical, analytical sort, not given to wild swoops of intuition, but perfectly capable of digging away at a mystery until he'd unearthed the tap root. If Emily Spitzer kept coming back to life again, it could only be because (a) someone was protecting her, and (b) that someone had access to some pretty impressive technology. Trying to figure out who the someone was would, he felt, be difficult and take too long. The technology, on the other hand, ought to be reasonably easy to identify.

When you don't know the answer, look it up. He leaned across his desk and picked up his copy of the Carringtons office-procedures manual. Index: death, avoidance of.

Ten minutes later he had a shortlist.

Hiroshige's quantum chicane; possibly. The chicane allowed you to zip backwards and forwards between alternate realities – it was basically the same technology that had enabled him to keep track of Emily's deaths and resurrections without getting hopelessly confused, although he had the Read-Only version, rather than the one that actually took you there. Even so; it was really only an observation-and-research tool, with academic and tourism potential. You could look at alternate futures or even visit them, but you couldn't change anything while you were there, and you certainly couldn't reprioritise the defaults and replace your own time-line with a different one that happened to suit you better. So, unless the mysterious someone had found a way of banjaxing the safeties and reconfiguring the entire feed mechanism, it couldn't be the chicane.

Mississippi Micro Industries Synthetic Angel: a distinct possibility. Using advanced wish-fulfilment technology which some authorities declared was still only theoretical, the Angel allowed you to rewind unsatisfactory episodes in your life and record over them inside a bubble of very high-resolution synthesised reality that overlaid your original time-line. It meant you could go back and edit out your mistakes, even potentially fatal ones, but with the significant drawback that you had to spend the rest of your life isolated in a world of your own; and if you wanted to do that, there were easier and cheaper ways. What you couldn't do (as far as Colin knew) was transfer the effect to anybody else. Which more or less ruled out the Angel. Oh well.

The Acme Portable Door.

The what? Oh, right. *That.*

Colin Gomez had heard of it, naturally. Everybody in the trade had. He just wasn't quite sure he believed in it. If it really did exist, then it shouldn't. It broke all the fundamental rules of the business, and to a serious practitioner like Colin, it was virtually an insult to his years of training and patient study. If there really was such a thing, of course, and if some irresponsible idiot had got hold of it and was using it to mess about with time-lines and raise the dead – well, it fitted all the known facts, you could get the job done with it. And there weren't any other possibilities. Therefore, as Sherlock Holmes would have said—

Index again: Door, Portable. He found the place and started to read.

The Carringtons office-procedures manual devoted forty pages to the Portable Door. Eight of those pages were a closely reasoned explanation of why the Door couldn't possibly work and therefore had to be mythical. A further twelve set out in considerable detail the letters you had to write and the file notes you had to make in order to notify the firm's insurers if you came across one. There were nine pages of awful warnings, ways in which careless use of the Door could spell the end of sentient life in the galaxy, and ten more setting out the firm's procedure for getting the senior partner's written approval before using it, should you ever get your hands on one. The remaining page gave a very sketchy history of the thing: how it had been developed in total secrecy by the brilliant maverick and former J. W. Wells partner Theo van Spee, late professor of magic at the University of Leiden, how he'd originally made two (using the prototype to copy itself; but see page 277, note 3) but only one had survived, and its whereabouts were currently unknown, although there were unsubstantiated rumours connecting it to a former JWW employee (name unknown) who had used it to defeat the Fey and unmask and then defeat Professor van Spee himself. Anomalous Mortensen readings had been interpreted by some authorities to mean that the Door had recently been used somewhere in New Zealand (but see page 1,866 and Appendix 12), although their findings had been disputed by other researchers in the field.

There was a final paragraph, in bold type:

It is the policy of the firm that the Portable Door does not exist. Any member of staff coming into possession of it, or having information concerning its location or recent Door activity, should notify the senior partner without delay.

Not many grey areas there. If he was right, Emily Spitzer was being helped by someone with the Door – whether she was aware of it or not was another matter entirely – and the book said, quite explicitly, *recent Door activity*. A memo, at the very least, seemed to be called for. Colin reached for the microphone of his dictating machine and cleared his throat.

And hesitated. Because Amelia Carrington was much, much more intelligent than he was, otherwise she wouldn't be the senior partner; in which case, it stood to reason that she must also have applied her noble mind to the problems he'd just been chasing round his mental mulberry bush, and had reached the same conclusions. In which case, if she'd figured out that the Door was involved, why hadn't she seen fit to brief him on the subject? He obviously had a need to know if he was supposed to get rid of Emily.

Oh dear, he thought.

Colin didn't phrase it more strongly than that, because you don't swear at the senior partner, even in the privacy of your own mind. It took significant effort to restrain himself, though. For one thing, it didn't make sense. Why on earth wouldn't she tell him about something so important? Clearly she wanted the Spitzer girl disposed of – she hadn't said why, but was under no obligation whatsoever to provide reasons, just as the brain doesn't have to justify itself to the hand. But the brain doesn't tell the hand to reach out when it knows perfectly well that there's an armoured-glass window in the way.

Pause and rewind. The brain wouldn't do that, sure; but it might order the hand to pick up a lump of metal it knew was red-hot, and not tell the hand because it suspected the hand might not feel like getting burnt.

Colin Gomez believed in the divine right of management. Part of that right was sacrificing the occasional pawn in the interests of the grand strategy; all very well, assuming you're not a pawn. He liked to think of himself as a bishop, though if he was going to be realistic, a castle would be nearer the mark; in any event, a major piece, as opposed to cannon fodder. Expendable, though; somehow, he'd never quite imagined himself as that. Other people, yes. Himself, no.

He was jumping to conclusions, he knew that. Even so. Why else would Amelia Carrington keep him in the dark about the wretched Door thing? All right, maybe it wasn't necessarily as sinister as he was assuming. But even if he wasn't for the chop . . . terms such as scapegoat, fall guy, cat's-paw, deniability, unwitting tool splatted like summer flies on the windscreen of his mind. He frowned, and upgraded *Oh dear* to *Damn*.

Slowly, very reluctantly, he got up from his chair. This wasn't right. Part of him was bitterly ashamed of the rest of him for thinking this way. Instead, it should be saying something along the lines of 'My deepest regret is that I have but one life to give for my senior partner.' It was what he'd have expected someone else to say: the junior clerical grades, the assistant magicians, even the associates and the non-equity partners; and the higher the rank and dignity, he couldn't help feeling, the greater the obligation. All fine and splendid, except when it applied to him.

Bloody woman, Colin Gomez thought.

Oh well. He left his office, closing the door behind him, and pottered slowly along the corridor and down the stairs, eventually ending up outside the strongroom. He turned the various keys and recited the various security spells, walked in and nosed around for a bit until he found what he was looking for: a small brown paper bag half-filled with long pointy teeth.

Ironic, he thought, as he locked up behind him. These were the teeth that Emily Spitzer had personally gouged out of the mouth of the last dragon she'd sorted out. According to the strongroom inventory, there were forty-six of them, each one conservatively valued at twelve thousand US dollars. He did the maths and shuddered. It was an awful lot of money. Premium-grade dragons' teeth were greatly in demand, especially these days, with the boom in the private security sector. Phil Hook would skin him alive at the next finance meeting. Maybe it wouldn't need all of them just to get rid of one short girl.

Down two flights of stairs, unlock a huge steel door whose

rusty hinges groaned as he forced it open; down the vertiginous spiral stone staircase that seemed to go on for ever. At last he reached another door: oak studded with ancient hand-forged iron nails, its parched grain scarred with scorch marks and axe cuts, to the point where the little printed notice saying *No admittance* was probably a bit superfluous. This door had no key, because it had no lock. Unnecessary. It was a genuine, original Parker-Shaw Uniface, and existed on one side of the wall only. Colin Gomez laid his hand on the blackened iron latch and pressed down.

CHAPTER TWELVE

The dragon stirred.

Curious animals, dragons. Awake, they have the intelligence of a small rock. Being much closer in evolutionary terms to their dinosaur ancestors than most of their contemporaries in the animal kingdom, they retain the subsidiary brain at the base of the spine, to which the majority of motor functions and other mundane day-to-day concerns are delegated. The tennis-ball-sized lump of grey splodge in their heads barely ticks over during the day; it operates the eyelids, handles sneezing and a few other respiratory odds and ends, and keeps a subconscious track of the stock market and commodity prices, using the inbuilt organic modem located down and a little to the right of the bladder. Otherwise, it just sits there not doing much, until consciousness puts the chairs up on the tables and closes up for the night.

And then the dreams come, flooding the upper brain with thoughts so huge they'd blow out the walls of a human mind: thousand-year thoughts, intricate as clockwork and lace, deep as oceans, teeming with precepts and hypotheses, paradigms, abstracts and equations, concepts so utterly alien to a two-ton forty-foot lizard that it could never begin to understand them in its conscious state. Dragons dream in at least seventeen dimensions, drifting like wind-blown leaves from past to future, soaring like birds over the dividing lines that separate alternate realities, sampling base-eight gravities in continua where sound moves faster than light and the universe isn't so much curved as dimpled, flirting with the possibilities of movement in the z-squared axis, redefining every constant a million times each second. This goes some way towards explaining why dragons love dark, cool places where they can sleep undisturbed, snuggled up on golden batteries from which their forebrains draw the vast quantities of raw power needed to fuel their imaginations; because without the gold, silver, jewels and other isotopes of wealth the dreams simply won't come. Nobody knows why this should be, although accountants seem able to understand it on a purely intuitive level.

Amelia Carrington's dragon was, of course, slightly different from the rest of its kind; hardly surprising, since it had been conceived and born in a vat of green slime in a lock-up garage in Ravenscourt Park. Its dreams were wild, fast and dark, and saturated with disturbing images of its own imminent death. Not that it minded that particularly; when the future is as real and immediate as the present or the past, the end is no more intimidating than any other arbitrary point on the circumference of the circle. What prompted it to stir, shiver and grunt was nothing at all to do with fear, a sensation as irrelevant to dragonkind as income tax. It was something small, a tiny inconsistency, an equation that failed to balance at the twenty thousandth decimal place. A human brain simply couldn't have registered it.

The dragon woke up.

Snarl, it thought. Hungry. Cramp in big flappy flying-with thing. It stretched its neck and snapped up a mutton carcass from the overhead rack so thoughtfully provided by the management, spread and refolded its wings, yawned to the melting point of glass and went back to sleep.

A human. The dragon placed her on the table of its mental centrifuge and spun her until the future separated from the past. The residue was quite interesting; strong influences, restraining rather than inspiring, so that it saw them as clamps and buckles.

The precipitate was a confusing jumble of shapes and colours, red for blood, silver for tears, black for anger and a faintly nauseating pink for the purely human emotion whose name temporarily escaped it. Lots of pink; it tinged the edges of everything, like the marinade in Chinese pork. The dragon wondered how so much emotion could be fitted into such a small container without breaking something.

Its own death. Smaller than it would have expected, rounder and smoother. There would be a moment in a dream when the circle was welded shut. No bad thing, since the dream would go on for ever, uninterrupted by the distractions of consciousness. The human's death, by contrast, was a messy thing, like the frayed end of a broken rope. In fact, there was an unusual quality about it, so different from the sad peterings-out of ordinary humans. It wasn't a whole number, it was a fraction. It was recurring.

None of our business, the dragon thought, because we won't be there to see it. By then, the circle will have closed, excluding all irrelevant data. But still—

The prophecy. The greatest dragon ever born, only the strongest, bravest hero that ever lived will prevail against it. Of course, all prophesies are garbage, apart from the true ones.

The dragon grunted and shuffled about. Under its vast, smooth belly, krugerrands clinked and share certificates crinkled; six dozen infra-red movement sensors woke up, accessed their programming, grumbled and went back to sleep.

And the dream swept on, riding the lightning into far galaxies of intervals, sequences and primes until the human was too small even for a sleeping dragon to see. Humans; so what? Their salvation was their ignorance of their own supreme triviality, without which the sheer bulk of proportion would flatten them into faint smears. In spite of that, however, a flavour of her stayed with it as it danced on a five-thousand-light-year-diameter pinhead. It would know her again when they met, and for the first time the dragon would feel (permeating right through into its inert forebrain) compassion.

*

When is a door not a door? When it's a wall.

The wall opened, and Colin Gomez, of all people, walked in through it. Emily looked up from the corner where she'd been sitting and stared at him for a moment, too stunned to be relieved or angry. Anybody else, but not him—

'What the *hell*,' she demanded, 'is going on?'

He looked at her, and in his eyes she recognised the comforting thought that he wasn't going to have to try and explain himself, make excuses, apologise politely, to somebody who'd be dead in a minute or so. She sprang to her feet, but she wasn't quick enough; he took a paper bag out of his pocket, emptied it on the floor, and dived back through the wall, which healed up as though it had never been breached.

Paper bag, she thought. White things all over the floor; cross between broad beans and bits of dried-up chewing gum. She knew what they were. Not good at all.

The reason why dragons' teeth fetch such a high price on the open market is that, sown like seedcorn on any flat, non-ferrous surface, they sprout into savagely psychotic spectral warriors. There are drawbacks. The warriors come fully armed, but their equipment is hopelessly antiquated – sword, shield, breastplate, helmet, a spear or two if you're lucky but don't count on it – and although they fight with unbelievable ferocity until they run out of enemies or are themselves cut down, they're not bulletproof. Clearly this limits their relevance to modern warfare, and they're chiefly used as assassins, riot police and for crowd control at music festivals. To Emily, armed with nothing but a thermos flask and a plate of cheese sandwiches, they nevertheless posed a serious problem.

'Colin,' she called out. 'Mr Gomez. Get back here *right now*.'

No answer, not that she'd really been expecting one (and besides, could sound pass through that wall? She doubted it). The teeth, meanwhile, were sprouting, little white arms and legs, little bumps, like the knobbles on potatoes, for heads. Spiders, she thought, and she lifted her foot and stamped on the nearest one. The pain was excruciating, even through the sole of her shoe, and the little white thing carried on growing. Oh, she thought.

A plate of sandwiches and a thermos. She could break the plate; that'd give her a sharp edge, and the thermos would just about do as a club, for one hit. It was what Kurt Lundqist or Ricky Wurmtoter or Archie St Clair Lutterworth would've done. Bruno Schlager had taken out a whole platoon of dark elves with a plastic fork, and hadn't the great Nepalese maestro Ram Lal Bahadur once disembowelled twenty Imperial Guards with a comb and a toothbrush?

The first couple of warriors were knee-high now; crash-test dummies with round featureless white heads and faint lines to mark where their armour would be. Two things that Lundqvist, Wurmtoter, Lutterworth, Schlager and Bahadur all had in common. One, they were all men. Two, eventually they were all killed.

Emily stepped back until the wall got in the way. They were at the badly moulded reproduction-terracotta-warrior stage now, just starting to acquire faces, their hair still just a faint pattern of impressed lines. Probably the spectral-warrior equivalent of teenagers, she thought. Yetch.

Now, she thought, would be a really good time for Frank to come through the wall.

So perfect, in fact, would the timing have been that she actually looked round, expecting to see the thin black lines spreading on the whitewashed surface like ink soaking into blotting paper. But they didn't, and while she was looking the other way the first warrior must've finished growing, because when she looked back, there he was, six feet eight of lean muscle, shining armour and gormless expression. He had a short sword in one hand and a round shield about the size of a lollipop lady's sign in the other. He hadn't moved yet.

Right. Here goes. Emily smiled.

'Hello, boys,' she said brightly. 'Who wants a nice cup of tea and a sandwich?'

Of course it shouldn't have worked. If she'd tried it in the practical in her college mid-year exams, they'd have failed her on the spot. Spectral warriors, they'd have told her as they helped her pack, are programmed to be ruthless, unthinking killers. Try that in the field, they'd have told her, and they'll be sending you home in a small plastic bag.

There were twelve of them, all motionless, looking straight at her. She took a deep breath.

– But the other thing about spectral warriors is that, in spite of their unnatural genesis and peremptory growth, they're still basically just soldiers. And what does a soldier do, arriving at a new and unfamiliar posting to find a nice girl handing out tea and sarnies? Cut her head off and jump up and down on her mangled trunk? Don't be silly.

The spectral lance corporal nodded, and slowly extended his new, unused arm. Straight away, Emily wedged the flask top into his hand and poured him some tea.

'Bit of a cock-up with the catering,' she said cheerfully, 'so you'll all have to share. Also, there's no sugar, but I do have some sweeteners.' From her bag she produced a little green plastic tube. She held it over the cup and pressed the lid, discharging little white pellets. 'Pass the cup along,' she said, 'and dig into the sandwiches.'

The lance corporal took a swig of tea and handed the cup on, then reached for a sandwich. For thirty seconds or thereabouts, Emily was kept busy refilling the cup and passing the plate round. Then, orderly as a line of dominoes, the spectral warriors slowly keeled over and crashed to the floor.

Lucky, she thought as she stepped over the lance corporal, that she'd forgotten to return the tranquillisers to store after she'd dealt with the dragon in the National Lombard in Fenchurch Street. Lucky, too, that they'd been the extra-strong concentrated variety – one tablet guaranteed to knock a fully grown manticore out cold for six hours, or your money back and your funeral expenses paid. It was, of course, only a temporary expedient. Sooner or later, they were going to wake up again, and chances were they'd have headaches and be extremely cross with her. Only one thing to do, therefore. She tugged a warrior's sword out of its scabbard and pressed it against his throat. Spiders, she thought.

The sword point wasn't very sharp; designed for strength, presumably. A needle-sharp point would just snap off if you stabbed it against armour. A certain degree of force seemed to be called for.

Right, Emily thought. But there's no tearing hurry. Soon as they start showing signs of waking up, I'll kill the lot of them. Just not yet.

She looked round at the table, where she'd put down the empty plate. It was loaded with fresh sandwiches. She wasn't surprised. The thermos was probably full again, too. If you're planning on keeping a prisoner long-term in a sealed, doorless room, something of the sort is pretty much essential. So, she thought; even if I do slaughter the lot of them, I still won't be getting out of here in a hurry. And Colin Gomez has got the rest of the teeth I pulled out of that dragon, and even if the same trick works a second time, there's only about four tranquillisers left. Yup, still screwed. Just checking.

In which case, why bother scragging the warriors after all? If they came to and killed her, they'd be doing her a favour. Otherwise, all she had to look forward to was staring at the walls and eating sandwiches, until such time as Colin Gomez figured out a way of killing her that she couldn't counter. Wouldn't take him long, but why hang about? Only delaying the inevitable. And besides, she'd died before, and it didn't seem to have done her any harm—

Yes, but that was because Frank Carpenter had been around with his Portable Door; and that was only because Mr Sprague was paying him to save the insurance company the cost of a heavy claim. But Mr Sprague wasn't there any more. Would Frank be along to undo her death if he wasn't getting paid for it? Well, probably he would, if he found out that she'd died. But she couldn't rely on that. Psychology of young men in love: he calls, leaves messages, no reply, so he assumes he's been issued with the regulation cold shoulder and slouches away to wallow in misery for a bit, until some other girl comes along. Somehow, the human race has contrived to find this sort of thing unbearably romantic for thousands of years. As far as Emily was concerned, it wasn't even slightly romantic, just damned inconvenient.

Let the spectral warriors kill her, then? No, absolutely not. Quite apart from the being-dead aspect of it, she was buggered if she was going to let the spiders win. Over her dead body, in fact.

In that case, Emily was either going to have to kill the spectral warriors in their sleep or find a way out of there. She considered the options. The mass-slaughter option had one thing going for it, a quality which the alternative so demonstrably lacked. It could be done. After all, she told herself, it's not as if they're *people*. They're teeth; and if a tooth starts hurting, you trot along to the dentist and have it drilled or pulled. A simple, guilt-free occurrence, and you don't tend to get the ghosts of all your past teeth standing over your bed rattling their fillings at you in your sleep and giving you nightmares.

Correction: they *were* teeth. Not any more, though.

Emily swore, threw the sword across the room and sat down on the floor. All right, she asked herself, what would Captain Picard do in her shoes? Well, obviously he'd engage the warriors in meaningful dialogue, convince them that it was in all their best interests to work together to find an effective but non-violent way of getting out of there, probably involving reconfiguring the biostatic matrix on some handy electronic gadget he just happened to have with him—

Not like that in real life, of course. True, the tube of tranquillisers had been a lucky break. But tranks were the sort of thing she tended to carry about, being an essential commodity in her line of work, so it wasn't the same at all, not *cheating*. And apart from them, everything else she had about her person was just so much useless junk. Look at it, for crying out loud (she started turning out her pockets onto the bare stone floor).

Lipstick. Compact. Three ballpoint pens, two non-functional (but if we could somehow reverse the polarities, we could rig up some kind of interplexing beacon . . .). Kleenex. The silver paper from a roll of Polo mints. A comb. A small cardboard tube.

Emily blinked.

A small cardboard tube: the sort of thing you find behind the lavatory door when an inconsiderate person's been using it before you. Apart from the Blue Peter crew and maybe the Andrex puppy, nobody on earth could have a use for one. Except that she'd seen one just like it – absolutely just like it – in the hands of Frank Carpenter.

Come off it, she said to herself. One bog-roll tube looks pretty much like another. And just because one specimen contains the Portable Door, that doesn't mean they all do. It's just a cardboard tube I must've picked up somewhere, though why on earth I'd want to do that—

She remembered.

The dragon; the same one whose teeth were cluttering up the floor she was sitting on. The dragon who'd turned a billion dollars into ash, but who died guarding this plain brown cardboard cylinder. Now what would a creature devoted to acquiring and hoarding items of great value want with the core out of a toilet roll?

Hardly able to breathe, Emily poked about inside it with her fingertip. There was something in there all right. Something rubbery, thin, rolled up. It could, of course, turn out to be the board from a travelling Ludo set. Only one way to find out.

But it couldn't be the Door, because Frank had it. He'd used it to get in and out of Sprague's office, and when she'd come through into this room it had stayed behind with him, she was absolutely sure about that. Besides – what was she thinking? – if this was the dragon's tube, it had been there in her pocket ever since she'd killed the bloody thing, so Frank couldn't have been using it ever since. The whole point was, there was only one Portable Door in existence.

Only—

She poked a little further, and a corner slid out. Gripping it between forefinger and thumb, she pulled gently. The roll of thin plasticky sheet fell into her lap. She picked it up, and it unrolled like unruly wallpaper.

The Portable Door.

That was the moment when one of the spectral warriors grunted and stretched in his sleep, inadvertently kicking Emily's ankle. She jumped, nearly dropped the Door, juggled with it, caught it and hugged it to her.

Right, she thought. Sod this.

Facing the wall, she pressed the plastic sheet against it. It attached itself immediately, and she watched as it seemed to soak into the plasterwork, leaving behind a rectangle of thin black lines that grew steadily thicker and darker as she looked at them. When is a wall not a wall? Funny you should mention that.

Curiously enough, her door handle was different: an anodised aluminium lever instead of a round brass knob. She reached out, closed her eyes and gripped it. It felt faintly warm.

Where do you want to go today?

Emily hesitated. *Out of here* probably wasn't a precise enough answer. Home? No. Gomez's office, so I can smash his face in? Tempting, but on balance, not a good idea. I can go anywhere I like, she thought: Rome, Lisbon, Marrakesh—

None of the above. The question, she realised, had only one answer because, of course, the Door didn't belong to her. And however nice it was to fantasise about what she'd do if she had a Door of her very own, the fact was that she didn't. Unless, of course, there really were two of them.

Only one way to find out.

Wherever Frank is, Emily thought, and pushed down the handle.

Colin Gomez looked at his watch.

He was pleased at how miserable he felt. It showed character, he thought, to be so upset about killing Emily Spitzer. There had been times over his long years in the profession when he'd wondered if he was growing callous, insensitive to the human cost of doing his job. He'd remember old Mr Kropatchek, the Butcher of Lombard Street, his first boss, a man utterly devoid of compassion and scruple, and just occasionally he wondered if he was turning into him. Apparently not. Marty Kropatchek wouldn't have thought twice about unleashing a whole lower jaw's worth of spectral warriors in Trafalgar Square on New Year's Eve if there'd been money in it, and he certainly wouldn't have agonised about it after the event. Colin, by contrast, had been moping about the place ever since he'd emptied the bag and closed up the basement wall, to the extent that he'd hardly managed to get any work done since. So that was all right.

Twenty minutes: more than enough time for twelve spectral warriors to slaughter one unarmed girl. He sighed and rose from his chair. Better go and tidy up the mess.

There was the small matter of getting rid of the spectral warriors, but he knew how to do that. From the bag on his desk he picked out a dozen teeth. An equal number of warriors from separate sowings will invariably attack each other and, being implacable and perfectly matched, wipe each other out. Expensive – Colin was still dreading what his partners were going to say about it at the next finance meeting; they might even insist that the cost of the warriors should come out of Colin's share of next quarter's profits: bitterly unfair, he'd just have to be stoical about it – but effective, and right now he just wanted the whole wretched business done and out of the way.

Down the stairs, through the big door, down the hateful, vertiginous spiral staircase, never intended to accommodate someone of his weight and girth. He was well aware that the issue of why he'd been kept in the dark about the Portable Door was still entirely unresolved; something else to worry about. It hadn't been a good day, in any respect.

In the top half of the Parker-Shaw Uniface, there's a little sliding panel you can draw back and look in through, the sort of thing you get in prisons. Colin opened it, threw in the handful of teeth, and quickly slammed it shut. Another great merit of the Parker-Shaw is its soundproofing.

He gave it five minutes, more than enough time, then opened the door and went through.

Not a pretty sight. Spectral warriors can take an obscene amount of damage before they die, and Colin Gomez wished he'd had the sense to put his wellington boots on before coming down. A quick headcount; twenty-four of them, only a few still attached to necks. So that was—

Twenty-four.

It was one of those moments when you feel completely hollow, like an egg sucked by a well-instructed grandmother. Two dozen heads; he swallowed hard and inspected them, one by one. It was hard to be sure, the state some of them were in, but he was fairly certain that none of them was Emily's.

He slumped against a wall. Marvellous, he thought. Nigh on three hundred thousand dollars' worth of stock in hand gone down the toilet, and to crown it all, the girl would appear to have escaped.

The practice of magic requires exceptional powers of mental discipline, and these stood Colin Gomez in good stead as he leaned there gazing at the mess. They made it possible for him not to think of what Amelia Carrington was going to say when he told her that he'd failed, again. That was just as well, since the blind panic would have paralysed him, and he needed a clear head—

He looked down at something lying near his feet on the floor. No pun intended, he thought.

Somehow – God only knew how – that bloody Spitzer girl had escaped. Furthermore, she now knew for stone-cold certain that he was out to get her. The chances of her being at her desk at nine sharp tomorrow morning were, therefore, slight. But if she'd done the sensible thing and put as much distance between herself and him as is possible on a curved planet, how the hell was he going to find her and finish the job?

He slid down the wall and sat in something sticky. Amelia

Carrington might just let him off with a reduced profit share and a severe bollocking, *if* he brought Emily's head in a jar along to the meeting. Otherwise, he was done for. And to think, he'd actually been feeling guilty about having her put down. Old Marty had been right. No place for bleeding hearts in the magic business.

Talking of which: he identified the sticky thing he'd been sitting on, picked it off his trouser seat and threw it away.

Finding a competent magical practitioner who doesn't want to be found is the next best thing to impossible. There are wards and cloaks, invisibility charms and stealth locks, and even Krnka's Mirror can be banjaxed if you're savvy enough. Emily Spitzer hadn't had much experience in that area, but she was resourceful, a quick study, and highly motivated; and if she had access to the sort of kit she'd have needed to get out of a self-sealing basement—

Kit like – oh, to take an example completely at random, a Portable Door.

The gurgling noise that the shit makes as it closes over the top of your head is quite unmistakable, and Colin Gomez heard it very clearly. What hurt him most of all was the unfairness of it; because he'd always been a good soldier, a true believer, and in spite of that – maybe, God help him, because of it – he'd been singled out to take the fall in whatever loathsome scheme Amelia Carrington was brewing up. Really, it was more than flesh and blood could bear. It was almost as bad as working for Enron.

Hell hath no fury like a true believer forced to revise his basic assumptions. Standing in the gore-flecked Carringtons basement with the blood of spectral warriors trickling down the inside of his trouser leg, Colin Gomez made his grand renunciation and declaration of war. It was a noble moment and he couldn't help feeling rather good about it, but once the emotion had thinned out a bit he also couldn't help noticing how frail his position was. Such resources as his position as a partner in the firm afforded him couldn't be relied on for much longer; Amelia would be after him first thing in the morning, wanting to be told that Emily was dead, and he knew he wouldn't be able to fend her off for very long. After that, he could only think of one possible ally he could call on. Assuming (sardonic little laugh) that he could find her.

Well. Maybe he couldn't, but a phone signal probably could. Carringtons equipped their staff with Kawaguchiya NP6530s, total network coverage guaranteed *everywhere*; deep in the Earth's magma layer, the craters of the Moon, even railway tunnels. And one thing a girl of Emily's generation would never ever do, no matter what the circumstances, was switch off her mobile.

Colin Gomez took out his pocket diary and looked up her number.

Better, they say, to have loved and lost than never to have loved at all.

Bullshit, Frank reflected, staring at the wooden rafters of the cabin. That's a bit like saying it's better to fall off the roof of a very tall building than to have stayed on the ground.

A man can get sick of the sight of rafters, even his own. But there was nothing else to claim his attention, so he carried on staring.

Love, he thought. What a bloody silly idea. Investing all your hopes, the whole point of living, in someone you've only just met, who you know next to nothing about, is on a par with putting all your money on a racehorse you've picked out of the list in the morning paper using a blindfold and a pin. Before he'd met her – well, his life had been empty and meaningless, but it hadn't really bothered him so terribly much. He'd had the Door, after all; he'd amused himself with sightseeing trips through time and space, earned a little money, done a little collateral good. Now, having loved and lost, he had no interest in metaphysical tourism. No point. The landscape in the background might change, but he'd stay the same. Even the best holiday is no fun if you can't stand the person you go with.

To have loved and lost; it made it sound like a competition – we loved, I lost. If so, then in love as in freestyle knife-fighting, the silver medal isn't worth having. Alternatively, to have lost your love sounds like sheer carelessness. (Where did you have it last? Have you checked all your pockets?) He hadn't mislaid it. It hadn't fallen down the back of the sofa. He'd offered her his heart, and she'd trodden on it.

That's me, Frank thought. Squashed- rather than broken-hearted, with nothing to do and no place to go. That's not tragic, not even sad. It's just plain silly.

He still had the Door. No job running errands for Mr Sprague, though. But so what? The world was full of opportunities. Other insurance companies, for example. Pick one at random – that was how he'd first met George Sprague – make them an offer they couldn't refuse, back to work. And who knew; maybe the genuine girl of his dreams was already there waiting for him, wherever *there* proved to be. More than one of her, even. For all he knew, they were queuing up somewhere, like people waiting to audition for *The X Factor*. Of course, he could stay exactly where he was, staring at rafters until he died of old age. Or he could get up off his arse, unfurl the Door like Columbus's sails, and go exploring for strange new worlds.

Might as well, he decided. Nothing better to do.

Frank stood up and reached in his pocket for the Door. It wasn't there.

In a sense, it was exactly what he'd been hoping for. A few minutes ago, if asked what he wanted most in the world, he'd probably have said, 'To stop moping around thinking about Emily.' Fine; another wish granted ahead of schedule by the genie of the rafters. Thoughts of lost love and post-romantic nihilism evaporated out of his brain like spit on a hot stove.

He performed the frantic, pathetic ballet of the man who's just lost something: the pirouetting round and round, the pocket-patting, the ratting-terrier crouch (bum in the air, head under the sofa), the pacing up and down with eyes glued to the floor, the whole business. But the cabin was very small and very sparsely furnished. If he'd dropped the Door, or if it had fallen out of his pocket, it'd have stood out on his bare, uncluttered floorboards like a haystack in a packet of needles. It wasn't there. It had been there a short while ago, because he'd used it to come home with. But it wasn't there now.

Had to be somewhere. Can't have vanished as if by magic—

Frank closed his eyes and flopped against a wall. By magic was almost certainly how it *had* vanished; basically, the reverse of the procedure by which Dad had come by it in the first place. Looked at from that perspective, there was a kind of beautiful symmetry about it. From every other angle, he was utterly screwed. Not just because he'd lost the only valuable thing he'd ever owned; without it, he was several days' gruelling walk from the nearest source of food, and there wasn't so much as a stale Ritz cracker in the house.

He was looking around for something to prise the floorboards up with when he heard a creak behind him. He looked round, and saw a thin black line running horizontal across the back wall. As he stared at it, two more lines dropped down at each end, forming the outline of a rectangle.

He'd never seen the Door opening from the outside, of course, just as you've never sat in the back seat of your own car. It was only when the handle appeared that he realised what he was looking at.

He started to yelp with joy, then froze. The Door was open-ing. Someone was coming through it.

For one horrible second, he thought it might turn out to be himself. But it wasn't; he'd never have been able to cram his foot into the narrow black court shoe that crossed the threshold into the cabin. But if it wasn't him—

'Hello,' Emily said.

When Frank opened his mouth to reply, he had no idea what was going to come out of it. Could've been 'That's so wonderful, I thought I'd never see it again'; or 'That's so wonderful, I thought I'd never see *you* again' (not his first thought, but valid nonetheless); or, if he'd been up to being cool and laid back about it all, 'Hi, thanks for dropping in'; or even (it was there in his mind) 'Oh God, the place is a real mess, it's just I've been so busy lately'. As it was, he heard himself say, 'It's mine, you can't have it, give it *back*.'

Emily stood perfectly still and looked at him (and he thought, Well, that's buggered that up, well *done*, Frank); because, of course, she'd heard all five versions.

'I'm sorry,' he mumbled, 'I didn't mean—'

She winced, as though he'd shouted in her ear; then she had that let's-get-it-over-with look on her face. 'Frank,' she said, 'there's something you ought to know about me.'

Not what he'd been expecting; in fact, for a moment he forgot all about the Door.

'Oh?' he said. 'Wh—'

'No, please don't say anything,' she snapped. 'Not anything at all, until I've explained.'

'But—'

'*Quiet!*'

She sounded just like his mother. At some point or other, all women do.

'Now then.' Emily perched on the edge of the table and gave him another look, but it wasn't any of the looks in the handbook. 'It's a bit awkward. It's got magic in it, for a start.'

Frank knew he wasn't allowed to speak, but nodding was presumably still permitted. He nodded.

'When you say something—' Pause. 'Basically, it's a side effect of drinking trolls' blood.' He must've pulled a face, because she gave him a don't-be-such-a-cissy look which, he couldn't help thinking, was a little bit much. 'It was an accident,' she went on, 'I was doing a job earlier, a troll cut himself, I must've got a drop of his blood on my finger or something. Anyway,' she continued, 'it means that when you say something – well, I hear it, obviously, but I also hear what you really mean. What you wanted to say but didn't. I can't help it,' she added, 'it's just magic, occupational hazard, and—'

Frank could feel his face burning; the perfect beetroot impersonation. Absolutely no need for her to tell him to be quiet now.

'Well,' she said. 'Now you know. There's an antidote, and I

had a dose before I met you tonight and we went to your Mr Sprague's office, but it sort of wore off, and—'

He didn't need troll's blood to let him know what Emily was feeling, just as you don't need to hear it ticking to know that a black pointy-nosed cylinder with fins is a bomb. It was, after all, exactly how he'd be feeling, in her shoes. Embarrassed, of course. Angry. Stress levels off the dial. And scared.

'Well,' she said. 'Say something.'

'You told me not to.'

'I love you too.'

At which precise moment, Emily's phone rang.

About ringtones. They are, of course, a statement: about who you think you are, who you want to be, who you want other people to think you are, all that. The trouble is, you choose them in quiet, restful moments, when you're generally off your guard. At such a time, your judgement is usually subordinated to your whim, and even a normally rational person is capable of thinking that having your phone warble Crazy Frog or James Blunt is a really fun idea. Or, as in Emily's case, the Laughing Policeman.

She cringed; which is a bit like saying the Second World War was a scuffle. At first, she pretended to ignore it, as if trying to make out that it was something going on in the street outside. Geography was against her there, though. She might just have got away with it if she'd gone with Rutting Stag, but basically she was on a hiding to nothing, and she knew it.

'My phone,' she whimpered. 'Just a second.'

She scrabbled in her pocket and pulled it out, hating it. 'Yes?'

'Emily. Colin Gomez here.'

Colin Gomez had a carrying sort of voice, even over a mobile. Frank nodded, and stood up. 'I'll make us a cup of tea,' he said.

'Hello?' Gomez, sounding faintly querulous. 'Hello, are you there?'

En route to the kettle, Frank stopped and watched Emily. She'd gone ever such a funny colour, and she seemed to have forgotten about breathing and stuff. Then she smiled.

'Mr Gomez,' she said. 'I'm glad you called. I'm going to kill you.'

'What? It's not a terribly good line, you'll have to speak—'

'And when I've done that,' Emily went on, 'I'm going to chop you up into little bits and feed you to the piranhas in Sally Krank's office. Oh, and I quit. Goodbye.'

She stabbed a button so hard that Frank winced. Then she threw the phone across the room. 'Sorry about that,' she said. 'My boss. He tried to murder me earlier. It's all right,' she added, 'you can talk now.'

Frank pressed his lips together and shook his head.

'Please?'

'Yes, but—' And then the Policeman started Laughing again.

'Oh for crying out loud.' Emily lunged across the cabin, snatched up the phone, stabbed it again and snapped, 'What?'

'There's no need to shout,' said Colin Gomez's voice. 'First, I'd like to apologise for what happened earlier.'

'You total fucking ba—'

'And,' Gomez went on, 'I need to know if you still want your job.'

Silence, apart from a faint rumbling from the kettle.

'Hello? Are you still there?'

'Yes, of course I bloody well am. What do you—?'

'I can't explain over the phone,' Gomez said. 'But—' His voice lowered, so that she could barely hear it. 'Let's say there could well be some changes in the way the firm's run, quite soon. Not entirely unconnected with the, um, incident.'

Frank looked at her. Troll's blood, she'd said. Could he really love somebody it was impossible to lie to?

(Yes, he thought.)

'I see,' Emily said. 'Oh, while I think of it, when we went to see Mr Pickersgill, he cut himself.'

'I'm sorry, but I fail to see—'

'Tastes like chicken.'

'Ah.' Long, long silence. 'In which case,' Gomez said brightly, 'you believe me.'

'No choice, really.'

'Excellent. How soon can you be in my office?'

Emily smiled. 'You'd be surprised.'

'Actually, I wouldn't. You've got it, haven't you?'

Her eyebrows shot up, but she replied, 'Long story.' Slight hesitation. 'If I come, you won't try and kill me, will you?'

'No.'

'You're right, actually, it would be. OK, I'll be there.' She stopped, and looked at Frank. 'Soon. Something here I've got to take care of first.'

'Be as quick as you can, then.'

'No,' she said, and hit the button.

They looked at each other. 'Tea's ready,' Frank said.

Emily thought about what Gomez had just said – all of it. Then she dropped the phone on the floor and jumped on it.

'So we won't be interrupted,' she said, and kissed him.

CHAPTER THIRTEEN

Amelia Carrington was waiting for the phone to ring.

To pass the time and take her mind off her own impatience, she flicked through the latest edition of the *New Magical Express*. Researchers in Thailand, she read, were claiming to have proved the existence of a hitherto unknown number somewhere between one and ten. The new number – an integer, of course, not a mere fraction – had so far only been detected as an otherwise inexplicable blip in extrapolated series of intervals, and until it could be properly identified and its value exactly calculated, it was too early to say what practical effect this discovery would have on the day-to-day business of magic.

Amelia raised an eyebrow at that, and made a note on a scrap of paper to have someone look into the possibility of patenting the new number before it passed into the public domain; getting royalties every time someone added up a shopping list or a darts score appealed to her enormously, but not if the cost of enforcing the patent was likely to outweigh the returns. Look what had happened to Schreiber & Deeks in the States when they'd tried to copyright Thursday.

The phone buzzed. She lunged at it and barked, 'Yes?'

Not the call she'd been expecting. Amelia scowled, then said, 'All right, send her in.' A few seconds later, a slim blonde woman with huge eyes and an exaggerated bust walked through the door and perched on the edge of the visitor's chair like a blue tit on a bird table.

'Sarah,' Amelia said. 'What's so important that you had to see me right away?'

A sentient life form would've shrivelled up; but Sarah wasn't a life form. Once, long ago, she'd been one of Amelia's substantial collection of Barbies; the first, in fact, that Amelia had been able to bring to life for more than ten minutes. A simple augmentation charm to bring her up to normal human size, a course of accelerated memory implants and three years at Harvard Business School (where she'd fitted in perfectly) and Sarah was now one of Amelia's most trustworthy and efficient assistants. And she didn't mind holding still while Amelia styled her hair for her, either.

'The bauxite project.'

'Oh yes?'

Sarah looked grave. She couldn't actually adjust her facial expression, which was set forever in the sweet simpering smile she'd been moulded with, but she'd learned to compensate with body language. 'Dennis Tanner,' she said. 'He's trying to double-cross you.'

Amelia smiled. 'Is he really?'

Nod. Sarah had to be careful about that, because her head had a tendency to come off under stress. 'He's been snooping round behind our backs, buying up mineral rights. We don't know where the money's coming from, though we're guessing it's his goblin relations. At any rate, he's got hold of the rights to all the land surrounding our original stake, so if the strike's as big as we think it is—'

'Oh, easily.' Amelia yawned. 'Huge.'

Slight tilt of the head to express puzzlement. 'In that case, he's got us screwed. It's not just the bauxite on what's now his land, there's other issues. Access, water, power cables. Basically, he can stop us dead in our tracks.' Sarah paused; cue reaction, which didn't come. 'I thought you ought to know,' she concluded. 'I thought you'd be—'

Amelia giggled. 'It's all right,' she said. 'All going according to plan. Listen, has he put together a proper consortium, or is it all just handshakes and gentlegoblins' agreements?'

'I'm not sure. I can find out.'

'Yes, please. Quick as you like. And when you know who we should be talking to, offer to sell them our stake.'

Sarah predated the quantum leap in Barbie technology that made it possible for the eyelids to go up and down, but Amelia had had her retro-engineered at great expense. She blinked. 'Excuse me?'

'Be subtle about it, of course. Use intermediaries, so it's not obvious that we're giving in. Make it look like we're being double-crossed by our venture partners, something like that. We've got to be a bit careful, or we'll scare him off.'

'I see.' Barbies don't lie very well. 'How much do we want for it?'

Amelia beamed. 'Lots,' she said. 'Say three times what it's worth. It doesn't actually matter, but if we make him pay through the nose it'll stop him getting too suspicious.' She frowned slightly. 'I do hope you're right and it's the goblins who're financing him. Goblins can be very direct when they're upset with someone, especially when money's involved.'

Shrug. 'Of course. I'll get on it straight away.'

'I know you will,' Amelia said fondly. 'You're a treasure. Oh, and there's a dozen new pairs of shoes for you to try on down in reception.'

Sarah nodded and stood up. 'Colin Gomez wants a word as soon as you're free,' she said. 'He left a message on your voice-mail late last night. Didn't say what it was about.'

Amelia grinned. 'I can guess,' she said. 'All right, thank you.'

Sarah left, and then the phone rang. This time, it was the call.

Amelia gave them their orders, telling them to coordinate with Sarah about timing. 'Whatever you do,' she emphasised, 'don't let it go before she's sold the land to the Tanners. Yes, of course you don't understand, but she does. All right? Fine.'

She put the receiver back carefully, as if afraid of waking it up, then sat back in her chair and breathed deeply. It was, she decided, a wonderful world; a world full of opportunities. A world that needed bauxite, and would very soon find itself paying a lot more for it than it was used to. Her kind of planet, basically.

Assuming that Colin Gomez had finally done as he was told. Her smile flickered briefly, and she picked up the phone. 'Colin?'

'It's you.' His voice was oddly high and strained. 'Sorry, of course it is. Yes, all done.'

'You've killed her, then.'

'Yes.'

'Get in here.'

Short delay, during which Amelia amused herself with the *New Magical Express* crossword. ('Shape-shifting magic of Julia Roberts', six letters beginning with G. Yawn; too easy.) Then Colin came in and flumped down in the spare chair like a sack of worried potatoes.

'With you in a moment – oh.'

Colin looked up at her. 'What?'

'It doesn't fit, there's too many letters. Oh, of course, it's the American edition.' She smiled at him. 'Why can't Americans spell?' she said. 'Never mind. You've killed her at last. Good.'

He nodded. 'It took some doing,' he said. 'I found out why she kept on not staying dead.'

Amelia frowned slightly. 'Really.'

'Yes indeed.'

She waited, but Colin just sat there looking like a fish. 'Well? How was she doing it?'

'It wasn't actually her,' Colin replied. 'She had help. And you'll never guess—'

'Get on with it.'

Colin dabbed a tiny trickle of sweat off the shiny slopes of his forehead. 'It was the insurance people, actually,' he said. 'Because we've got her insured against death in service, like all the junior staff.'

'Have we?' Amelia frowned. 'Yes, I suppose we have. What's that got to do with anything?'

'Well.' Not his usual chatty, hard-to-make-him-shut-up self. More running in fits and starts, like a Land Rover engine. 'The insurance people didn't want to pay out on the claim—'

'Don't take any rubbish from them,' Amelia said sharply.

'No, of course not. But apparently they've hit on a way of not coughing up. They make it so the accident giving rise to the claim never happened.'

Amelia frowned. 'That's impossible.'

For some reason, Colin took a deep breath. 'Not,' he said, 'if they've got a Portable Door.'

The same thought crossed both of their minds simultaneously; Amelia Carrington should've been an actress. 'A what?'

'The Acme Portable Door,' Colin said. 'I'm sure you must've heard of it.'

'What? Oh, *that*. But it doesn't exist, surely. It's a thingummy, urban myth.'

(So that's what all this has been about, Colin thought. I was right.)

'Apparently it does,' Colin said. 'And the idiots at the insurance company got hold of it. Well, not personally. They hired the man who'd got it, as a freelance. And when Spitzer had her accident, falling out of the tree—'

'He made it not happen, I see. How annoying.'

'Quite.'

'But I told you to use the Better Mousetrap.'

'I did. Apparently the Door beats the Mousetrap.'

'Heavens. Well, that's that explained, anyhow. And the Door person saved her again, from the spiders.'

'Yes. And the next time, too. I used dragons' teeth.'

This time, there was no artifice about Amelia's surprise. 'Dragons' teeth? Have you any idea what those things cost?'

Colin couldn't help colouring with shame. 'You did say get the job done. Any means necessary. So I thought—'

'Yes, well. Never mind about that for now.' Pause, while the penny dropped. 'And they didn't work either.'

'No.'

'Extraordinary. So what did you do?'

Colin ran a finger round inside his shirt collar. 'I realised that it had to be the Door,' he said uncomfortably. 'Nothing else could explain it. Once I'd figured that out, of course, it was easy.'

'Was it?'

'Oh yes. I rang Spitzer and told her I knew about the Door, and I was thoroughly fed up with you because you'd made me try and kill her, and I was plotting to get rid of you.'

'Really.'

'It was the only way to get at her, I thought,' Colin said. 'I promised that when you were gone and I was senior partner, I'd give her a partnership too.'

A moment of extremely eloquent silence. 'I see. She accepted.'

'Oh yes. Seemed thrilled at the prospect. So I told her that I'd need the use of the Door if I was going to have any chance of killing you. She wasn't happy about that, but I insisted.'

'Well, of course.'

Colin nodded. 'I arranged a meeting: me, her, and the Door person. And when they arrived, I killed them.'

Amelia hadn't realised she'd been holding her breath. 'Excellent.'

'And I got rid of the Door, as well.'

Time stopped. It was a quite unintentional reflex on Amelia's part, triggered by a combination of shock and fury such as she'd never felt before. Luckily, she realised what she was doing and stopped it before any damage was done, although a lot of scientists subsequently wasted a great deal of time and effort taking their very expensive equipment to bits to see what had gone wrong. 'You did what?' she said quietly.

'Got rid of it,' Colin repeated. 'Well, naturally, the thing's an absolute menace. When you think that an untrained amateur managed to get his hands on it and was actually using it, on a daily basis; it's a miracle we're all still here. So I burned it.'

'You—'

Colin nodded briskly. 'Put a match to it. All gone. Made the world safe for civilisation as we know it, if you care to look at it from that angle.'

He's lying, Amelia's brain shrieked. *Even Colin Gomez couldn't be that colossally stupid.* In which case—

But *was* he lying? As she looked at him, Amelia couldn't be sure. The horrible part of it was, he was actually capable of doing something like that. Basically, she knew, deep down, Colin Gomez was – well, not an idealist, he had his faults but nothing quite as bad as that. Deep down, he was a nice man. He was able to function in business because the little seed of niceness had been overlaid with innumerable layers of obedience, ambition and corporate mentality, making it possible for him to double-think himself into doing practically anything provided his superiors in the chain of command told him to. But in the absence of a relevant direct order – don't destroy the Portable Door, for instance – there was always the danger that his inner niceness might assert itself and take over. And a nice man would realise how dangerous the Door was; just as a nice man, happening to find a nuclear warhead in the street, wouldn't immediately start opening negotiations with well-funded terrorist groups, even though he'd be well aware of how much money they'd give for one. A nice man would hand it in at his local police station.

Which, in this instance, would be me, surely, Amelia thought. 'You burned it,' she repeated.

'Yes.'

'It didn't occur to you to bring it to me.'

'No. I knew you'd want it disposed of as quickly as possible, in case something happened and it fell into the wrong hands.'

Silent as a card-house folding, three-quarters of her grand plan evaporated. All that work, effort, time and expense of spirit. But Amelia rose to the occasion very well. A lesser woman would've wasted yet more time and emotion cursing herself for not telling Colin from the outset that getting hold of the Door was the main objective of the project – because she hadn't trusted him not to keep it for himself, which was the bitter irony of the thing; because clearly she *could* have trusted him. That was obvious, now that it was too late, because if Colin had taken the Door for his own he wouldn't be there in her office, and quite probably neither would she.

Well; too late to do anything about it now. One had to be businesslike, and cutting losses was one of the pillars of commercial wisdom. She wouldn't even have Colin killed, because what good would that do? She'd only have to find someone else to do his job, and he was quite good at it. She made an effort, like a snake shedding its skin, and shrugged off the fury and the despair.

'Quite right,' Amelia said. 'Well done. Get on to the agency and find someone to replace Spitzer. In the meantime, get Atkinson down from Manchester office to cover her workload.' She gave Colin a bright, brittle smile. 'I think that's all for now,' she said. 'See you at the partners' meeting on Friday.'

Colin stirred but didn't get up. 'Just one thing,' he said.

'Mm?'

'The Spitzer girl. Just out of interest. Why did we kill her?'

We, Amelia noted. There you had it, the perfect synthesis of corporate and nice. 'Oh, it's complicated. All to do with a little deal I'm putting together. Nothing in your line.'

'Ah.' He stood up. 'Well, I hope it works out, whatever it is. I'd better be getting on, I've got clients coming in.'

When he'd gone, Amelia counted up to twenty and screamed. It wasn't like her, but then again, neither was failure. And it was her own silly fault, of course, keeping Colin in the dark.

Assuming he'd been telling the truth. She pursed her lips. Since he hadn't already assassinated her, what would he have to gain by pretending to have burned the Door? Nothing sprang to mind. Even so. She picked up the phone.

'Erskine.'

'Gosh.' Silence; then, 'Is that really you?'

'Stop babbling and get in here now.'

He must've run all the way. Amelia hardly had time to fill in four across before he was there, shiny-eyed and trembling slightly. 'Erskine,' she said, carelessly forgetting to tell him to sit down, 'a little job for you. Several, actually.'

'Golly. Thanks.'

'First,' she went on, 'I want you to search Colin Gomez's office from top to bottom. He'll be seeing clients, so he'll be out of the way.'

'Right, yes, certainly, of course. Um, what am I looking for?'

Amelia described the Door. No point telling him what it was. 'And when you've done that,' she said, 'I want you to clear Emily Spitzer's stuff out of her office and put it in store. She's dead.'

'OK.'

'And then,' she went on – it was slightly wearing to be gazed at with such devoted intensity – 'you might as well move your stuff in there.'

'Thanks. Thanks ever so much.'

Sigh. 'You'll be looking after her work until John Atkinson gets here from Manchester. Do you know John? No, I don't suppose you do. Anyhow, just hold the fort till he gets here. Can you manage that?'

'I'll do my very best.'

'Yes, of course you will. Now, was there anything else? Oh yes. The cardboard tube thing might just be in with Emily Spitzer's stuff. Keep an eye open for it, and if you find it, bring it here immediately. Don't stop to ring first, just get yourself in here. Understood?'

'Perfectly.'

'That's all, then.' Amelia looked at him. He'd have to do. 'For now,' she added. 'Right, on your way.'

Busy, busy. No sooner was Erskine out of the door than Sarah called in to say that she'd arranged the sale of the bauxite stake. She'd done well, too. A small enough consolation, now that the Portable Door had apparently slipped through her fingers, but every little bit helped. Look after the billions, and the trillions will look after themselves.

More to the point, though; Amelia dialled a number, tapping her fingers impatiently on the desk until she got an answer.

'It's me,' she said. 'You can let it go now.'

The dragon woke up.

It had no idea where it was, or how it had got there. Since it was awake, however, its new surroundings hardly registered. It moved its head painfully on a cricked neck, following the scent of roast pork until it located a heap of freshly cooked pig carcasses. It ate five and felt better.

Not hungry, it noted with satisfaction. *Go to sleep now.*

It wriggled, but the surface under its belly felt strange. It wasn't the cold, smooth feel of its usual bedding. Not good. It was lying on *stones*—

It shifted, preparing to move, then intuited better of it. Stones, yes, but nice stones. Being a dragon, it could carry out with a brush of its belly scales a valuation more accurate and detailed than anything a trained mineralogist could do with a fully equipped lab and a staff of twenty. *Nice* stones, worth *lots*.

Can sleep now.

Its nose touched its curled-up tail, and it slid into the intersecting matrices of its dreams. Bauxite, it told itself, currently quoted in New York at sixteen, seventeen-point-two in Lisbon, seventeen-point-six in Sydney and London. Meanwhile, the innate sensors in its hindbrain performed their usual miracle of quantity surveying, and reported back a figure which, multiplied by the closing price in Singapore, made it whistle the melting point of iron.

Blessed are the pure in heart, apparently, for they shall see God. Nobody had ever seen fit to tell Erskine this, since it wasn't immediately relevant to his duties, but he'd sort of figured it out for himself, from first principles. Because he'd been good, he'd been chosen by Her for a special mission of great importance. The glow of pride charged him up like an electric current.

Mr Gomez's room. Normally, he wouldn't have dared trespass on a partner's carpet, but a mandate from the highest possible authority made all the difference.

First, the desk. Erskine had been designed to be methodical. First, he took a mental photograph, noting the exact position of everything. It took some doing, because Mr Gomez's desk was a perfect example of dynamic chaos, but Erskine had been specially fitted with an enhanced memory. With the picture saved on his internal screen, he took everything off the desk, stacked it neatly on the floor and put it back again, in the process frisking everything for small cardboard tubes.

No result; so he started on the piles of blue, orange, green and buff folders that covered two-thirds of the floor, the way the oceans cover the planet. Any one of the piles could have been artfully arranged to hide a small cardboard tube. As it turned out, they hadn't, and Erskine moved on to the filing cabinet.

Nothing in the filing cabinet but files; nothing in the files but paper. Next, he examined the pockets of the two coats that hung behind the door. Mostly, they were full of discarded wrappings from extra-strong mint rolls. No cardboard tubes.

He glanced at his watch. Because the firm charged for its services on a time basis, Mr Gomez considered it a point of honour to make any interview with clients last at least an hour. That meant Erskine had a minimum of twenty minutes in hand. Enough time to lift the carpet and prise up the floorboards? Possibly, but he'd be pushing it. Well; he'd just have to work faster.

First, though, there was the walk-in cupboard. He'd left that till last, because it was such an obvious place for hiding stuff. He opened the door, then took a step back.

'Oh,' said Emily Spitzer. 'It's you.'

'Hello,' Erskine replied. 'And it's Mr Arkenstone from the Salt Lake City office, isn't it?'

'What?'

'*Shhh*. Yes, Mr Arkenstone.' Emily looked disconcerted, and also unusually scruffy. Her clothes were a bit rumpled, and her lipstick was smudged. 'From Salt Lake City. I expect you're wondering what we're doing in Mr Gomez's cupboard.'

'Looking for files, presumably,' Erskine replied.

'That's right, yes. Mr Arkenstone needed a file, and I said I'd help him find it.'

'I thought so,' Erskine said. 'Sorry to have disturbed you, only I didn't know you were in there. I'd have knocked if I'd known.'

'Yes, of course you would.'

'Can I help you look?'

'What? No, thanks, it's fine, we can manage.'

'Right you are.' Erskine hesitated. 'Only, I'm supposed to search the cupboard for a small cardboard tube. You haven't seen one in there, have you?'

'A what?'

'Small cardboard tube,' Erskine repeated. 'About so long, with a bit of old plastic sheet inside, though I'm not to touch that. It won't take me two minutes, and I can be looking for your file while I'm at it.'

'Who told you to look for a cardboard tube?' asked Mr Arkenstone. He didn't have an American accent, which was odd if he was from Salt Lake City. Maybe he'd been posted there as part of a management restructuring initiative.

'Ms Carrington,' Erskine replied, trying not to sound too smug about it, but he couldn't resist adding, 'Personally.' The name had the effect he'd expected. Mr Arkenstone looked properly impressed, and even Ms Spitzer raised an eyebrow. 'And I don't want to have to hurry you or anything, but Mr Gomez will be back quite soon, and he's not supposed to know I'm here.'

Mr Arkenstone stood back out of Erskine's way. 'You go ahead,' he said. 'We'll, um, carry on looking for our file when you've finished.'

'Are you sure? I mean, I can easily keep an eye out for it while I'm looking for the tube.'

Ms Spitzer gave Erskine a conspiratorial glance. He was thrilled. He'd never had one before. 'Need to know,' she said, in a loud whisper. 'You understand.'

'Oh, of course.' Erskine nodded seven times. 'Quite. What file, eh?'

'Absolutely. You crack on,' Mr Arkenstone added kindly. 'Don't mind us. We've got all the time in the world.'

There was something in what he'd said that made Ms Spitzer giggle, though she managed to do it with a straight face. 'Thanks,' Erskine said. 'After all, we're all on the same side, aren't we?'

Mr Arkenstone nodded gravely. Ms Spitzer must've got a frog in her throat or something, because she made a little gurgling noise. But not unkindly. In fact, Erskine reflected as he rummaged carefully through the cupboard (no tube; oh well), she was being a good deal nicer to him now than she had been before. It could only be because he'd been blessed with Her special favour. Would it go on like this from now on, he wondered. He hoped so.

And then he froze.

Erskine's first instinct was to hate himself for being so careless. The excitement of it all had got the better of him, and he'd forgotten something that She'd said to him.

I want you to clear Emily Spitzer's stuff out of her office and put it in store. She's dead.

Erskine thought about that. True, the Emily Spitzer with whom he'd just had that extremely pleasant conversation hadn't seemed all that dead to him, but then, who was he to judge? If She said Ms Spitzer had passed away, which of them was more likely to be right, the Creator or the unworthy result of Her labours? But, replied his inner common sense, Ms Spitzer really didn't look terribly dead at all. In which case, maybe it was possible that whoever had told Her about Ms Spitzer's demise had been lying. In which case, She really ought to be told, right away.

Twin forces of incalculable ferocity were tearing Erskine apart: the imperative of letting Her know, just in case someone was trying to deceive Her, and horrified fear of wasting Her time and getting into trouble. For a full ten seconds, he stood quite still, not even breathing, as his wretched mind was bounced backwards and forwards like a tennis ball. His first solo mission, and here he was, messing it up; because whichever course of action he took, it'd be bound to be the wrong one.

But that wasn't the worst of it, even. She'd also told him to search Ms Spitzer's things for the tube, if it wasn't in Mr Gomez's room. And he'd just gone and mentioned to her that he was looking for it. What if she wasn't supposed to have it? In which case, he'd just tipped her off that it had been missed and was being searched for. What a terrible, terrible mess.

Nothing for it; he was going to have to tell Her at once.

Very carefully, Erskine opened the cupboard door and looked out. What he saw made him whimper. The room was empty. Ms Spitzer (and that nice Mr Arkenstone from Salt Lake City office) weren't there any more.

'Who the hell,' Frank asked as they slammed through a fire door, 'was that?'

'Erskine,' Emily told him. 'Long story. In here.'

In Here proved to be a small, dusty room crammed with angle-iron racks filled with dusty files. She closed the door and listened, presumably for sounds of pursuit. There couldn't have been any, because she came away and sat down on the floor, looking exhausted.

'The new kid,' she went on. 'Trainee. Supposed to be going round with me, learning pest control. Coals to Newcastle,' she added bitterly. 'Though there's something a bit bloody odd about him. I've only just figured it out, but it's pretty strange.'

Frank looked at her. 'Well?'

'I can't hear him.' Emily frowned, then shook her head. 'No, that's putting it badly. Look, I told you about the troll's blood, right? Well, when Erskine says something, that's all I hear. Just the words he says out loud. No little voice in my head telling me what he's really thinking. And before you ask,' she added, 'that's downright weird.'

'Is it?'

'Believe me, yes.' She pulled a bewildered face. 'You, Colin Gomez, Emma on reception, everyone I've talked to since it happened. But now I come to think of it, not Erskine. Which,' she added quietly, 'can mean only one thing. He's not human.'

Frank pursed his lips. 'He's a management trainee, right?'

'Yes.'

'Well, then.'

Emily frowned. 'Good point,' she said. 'But no, I don't think so. It's like listening to – oh, I don't know, an insect or something. No,' she added impatiently, 'it's not even that. It's like he's not even *real*.'

Frank considered that. 'You think he's like that whatever-it-was in Mr Sprague's office,' he said. 'The one that turned out to be a hair.'

'Oh God,' Emily said. 'No, I wasn't thinking that, actually. But you could well be right. Something inanimate that she's brought to life.'

Frank mumbled, '*Like I said, management trainee,*' under his breath, but not out loud. 'All right,' he said, 'if that's true, so what? It's no skin off our noses, is it?'

The look Emily gave him started off various trains of thought in his mind. One of them was that if they really had found true love and were going to spend the rest of their lives together, inevitably there were going to be a lot more looks like that and he might as well get used to them.

'He knows I'm alive,' she said. (*Stupid*, she didn't add.) 'And Colin Gomez has just told the Carrington bitch that he killed me.'

'Oh, I see,' Frank said quickly. 'You mean, everything's screwed up.'

'Sort of.'

'Ah.'

'Like,' she went on, 'bang goes our chance of sneaking up on her quietly. She'll know that Colin's lied to her, which means curtains for his palace coup idea. Probably for Colin, too, though I can't say the thought upsets me terribly much.'

Frank frowned. 'You don't really mean that.'

'Yes, I do.'

'Oh. Right, fine.'

Another look. But he wasn't unduly concerned. Close observation of his parents' relationship had led him to the conclusion that an unshakeable belief on the female's part that the male is an idiot is a fundamental ingredient of true love. Odd, he'd always thought, but presumably there was a sound evolutionary reason for it. 'He tried to kill me, for God's sake,' Emily said, maybe a tad defensively. 'And besides, he's a jerk.'

'Quite.'

'Insufferable bloody man. So inconsiderate.'

'Well, there you go.'

'Right.' She scowled. 'No, we can't just let her kill him. Bloody *nuisance*,' she snarled. 'As if we hadn't got enough to do.'

The miracle of troll's blood was something that Frank couldn't really get his head around, though he believed in it. But maybe it wasn't such a miracle after all, because as Emily spoke he could hear her thinking, *and besides, he's promised to make me a partner.* Perhaps at some deep level he was mildly shocked. If so, he overrode the reaction. She might be the most wonderful person in the world and the meaning of his universe, but she was still Corporate. They think differently from the rest of us. 'OK,' he said, 'we'll add saving Colin Gomez to the list, then.'

She shrugged. 'Well, it's only fair. You save your Mr Sprague, I'll save Colin. Assuming,' she went on, 'we both live that long. Come on, we've got to get out of here, before bloody Erskine tells her I'm alive. Typical Colin Gomez,' she sighed bitterly. 'Should've known better than to get involved in any scheme he's responsible for. Get the Door and let's be on our way.'

Frank took the cardboard tube from his pocket and teased the Door out with his fingertips. 'Where to?' he asked.

'What? Oh, anywhere. No, hang on, let me think.' Emily turned her back on him for a moment while he plastered the Door onto the nearest wall. She was thinking: I know precisely where we should go; back in time to the day Amelia Carrington was born – no, I couldn't kill a *baby*, it'd be impossible, spiders or no spiders. All right, nine months earlier, we could kidnap her dad or something, and then it wouldn't really be killing. Except, of course, that it would. The sad fact is, she admitted to herself (blaming the excessive honesty on the troll's blood, but it wasn't really that), it doesn't matter whether we do it here and now or thirty years ago or before she was even born, it's still basically the same thing; and killing dragons is one thing, but *people*—

And besides, she added, if there's no Amelia Carrington there'd be no Carringtons, and I won't get my partnership—

Maybe that one was troll's blood; if so, Emily really wished it hadn't got into her system. You could mess it up a bit with logic, and say that if you made it so that Carringtons never happened you'd be undoing all the good they'd done in the world, all the bank vaults they'd disinfested, all the spiders they'd squashed; that might be true, but it wasn't what was motivating her. Simple facts: she wanted her partnership, but she didn't want to have to kill anybody, even that bitch, in order to get it.

She wanted—

True love should've made that an easy sentence to complete, but it didn't. Yes, all right, she wanted true love, and it was standing by the wall right now looking mildly sheepish, with an I-don't-want-to-rush-you-but-it's-time-we-made-a-move expression on its face. Fine. But she wanted the partnership and the clear conscience *as well*. Picky, but there you go.

'What we need to know,' Emily said firmly, 'is what the Carrington woman's up to. Otherwise we're just chasing our tails.'

'Agreed.' Frank nodded. 'So, how do we find that out?'

Sigh. 'I don't know. I mean, we can be fairly sure that she wanted to get hold of the Door, once she'd figured out it was out there and on the loose, which basically means ever since you saved me from the apple tree. She'd have guessed it had to be the Door, since nothing else could've beaten the Better Mousetrap that Colin used to get rid of me. But that still raises the question of why she had Colin set the Mousetrap for me in the first place.

I mean, what harm did I ever do her? If she wanted to get rid of me, why not just fire me?'

Frank frowned. 'Didn't want to pay redundancy money?'

Emily thought about that. 'Wouldn't put it past her,' she replied. 'But that's not our way in the magic biz, we're sort of above all that kind of thing. There's got to be another reason, something special about *me*—' She broke off. 'And there's nothing special about me, is there?'

'Well—'

'No,' she said quickly, 'there isn't. I'm just an employee. In fact, I'm amazed that she even knew I existed. But there's got to be something about me that'd cause her real problems, get in the way of a big deal or whatever.' She shook her head. 'Well,' she said, 'that's what we've got to find out. And since we can't puzzle it out for ourselves from first principles, we're just going to have to ask someone.'

'Great. Who'd know the answer?'

'Well, she would, obviously. But apart from her—' Emily scowled. 'Nobody,' she said. 'That's the way she does things.'

'And you don't feel like asking her.'

'Not really, no.'

Frank waited for Emily to say something. He was hoping for a short but powerful speech, about how none of this stuff really mattered now that they had each other, and the Door, of course. How they could simply turn their backs on this whole mess, go somewhere and somewhen Amelia Carrington couldn't follow them, and just be happy. Not having the unfair advantage of troll's blood, he couldn't be sure that that was what she was thinking, but he was quietly confident nevertheless. After all, it was what he was thinking, and if they saw the world so differently, how come they were in love? So he waited, thinking: no hurry, she'll say it in a moment or so, she's probably just trying to think of the right words. He waited.

'But,' she said, 'if that's what it takes, we'll bloody well have to ask her.'

'Oh.'

'What?'

'Nothing.'

(Define true love, Frank thought. Specify the levels of love required in order for it to qualify as true. But later; not now.)

'We can use the Door,' Emily was saying. 'If we zoom straight into her office and we're sharp enough about it, we can hit her over the head or something before she's got a chance to do anything horrible to us. And then we can ask her, and—'

'Sorry.'

'What?'

Frank took two steps away from the Door. 'You carry on,' he said. 'Look, you don't need me, I'll probably just be in the way. You hang on to the Door. Let me have it back when you've finished with it. I'll just sort of go away now.'

He started to move but she grabbed his arm. 'You're scared,' she said.

He looked at her. 'You should know,' he said. 'You're the bloody telepath.'

Emily let go of his sleeve. 'What's the matter?' she said. 'Don't you want to help me?'

'Of course. You can have the Door. You don't need me.'

'Look—'

'No, *you* look.' Frank hadn't intended to sound angry. 'More to the point, you listen.' He took another step, then paused. 'You can hear what I'm really saying, right? Fine. That's a great gift, always assuming that you're listening. But I don't think you are, actually. I think you've got more important things on your mind right now. So, fine. You carry on.'

'Frank, she's been trying to kill me—'

He closed his eyes. 'Yes,' he said. 'And that's really bad. She's tried to kill you, for all I know she's killed my friend George, and you reckon she's up to some evil master plan. Whatever. But we're lucky. We don't have to hang around here and be involved. We can piss off through the Door, go anywhere, do anything; we don't have to stay here and have *adventures*. Not,' he added bitterly, 'unless we want to. And I don't. All right?'

'No, it's not all right.' Emily's eyes were bright with anger. 'Oh, I know what you want. You want us to float away into our own little private universe where we can be happy ever after just gazing into each other's eyes, just like,' she heard herself add, as the data flowed undigested from his mind into her mouth, 'just like your rotten mum and dad. You think that's what being in love means, just the two of us for ever, and a wall of magic to keep the nasty world out.'

'Well, yes, actually.'

'Then you're wrong. And so were your stupid parents. They didn't run away because they were in love, they ran away because they couldn't cope. But I'm not them. I can cope. I don't want to live in a bubble, thanks all the bloody same. I want—'

'You want to be a partner before you're thirty.'

Well, Emily thought. I was the one who raised the subject of bubbles; and now the bubble I've been living in has just gone pop. Because he's right, that's what I want. And not just a partner, but a partner in Carringtons, even though it's a nasty, vicious collection of arse-lickers and psychotics who all ought to be put down in the interests of public safety. But that's what I want.

Wanted.

'You make it sound silly,' she said.

Frank shook his head. 'Far be it from me to judge,' he said. 'I mean, I never wanted *anything* till a few days ago, so I'm in no position to make fun of anybody. All I'm saying is, if that's what you really want, you go ahead and get it, and feel free to use the Door if you think it'll help. And then,' he added, not looking at her, 'when you've got what you want and that's out of the way, maybe you'll decide you want something else as well.'

'In a bubble?'

He shrugged. 'Not necessarily. I don't know much about these things – maybe the bubble isn't actually mandatory. But to be honest with you, I can't see how it'd work without one.'

(And he thought: my God, here we are having a serious talk about our relationship, just like they do on the afternoon soaps.

Never thought I'd find myself doing that. Next thing you know, I'll be getting in touch with my inner feelings. Just fancy.)

Emily pulled a face that would've curdled milk. 'I just don't want her to *win*, that's all.'

Frank had been about to leave, but he stopped. There was, after all, a grain of truth in that. Only a grain, but enough for a hard-working oyster to build a pearl around. He turned back and looked her in the eyes. 'Are you really dead set on being a partner?' he said.

'Yes.'

'Fine. Why?'

Excellent question; one she'd never stopped to ask herself. Of course, she knew the answer right away.

'Because it's there,' she said.

At which he nodded. 'Good a reason as any,' he said.

'And because they don't want me to. And so, if I make it, I've won.' Emily frowned, playing back the simultaneous translation in her head. The two voices merged into one. 'Bloody hell,' she said. 'That sounds really silly.'

Frank shrugged. 'People who live in bubbles shouldn't play with needles. Actually,' he went on, 'I'm the one who was being silly. I don't think being in love is a bubble any more. I think it's more like—'

'Well?'

'Like this.'

Emily thought for a moment. Then she said, 'You know what? I'm quite glad I met you. Otherwise—'

'You'd be dead.'

'Yes, but apart from that.'

'Oh.'

So much for having a serious talk about our relationship. Frank thought about his friend Kevin (friend; he was the counter clerk at the Wayatumba general store. He'd spoken to him, what, two dozen times, over the years) who was always having relationships and, inevitably, the concomitant serious talks. It was OK, Kevin told him, once you'd mastered the knack of half-listening, taking in just enough of the gist of what she was saying to enable you to make the appropriate grunting noises at regular intervals, while allowing the rest of your mind to drift away and graze on more interesting topics, such as the All Blacks' chances against Oz on Saturday. If you were really organised, you arranged to have the serious talk in the pub, so you could watch the footie on the big TV over her shoulder.

'Sorry,' Frank said, 'I seem to have lost track. Where did we just get to?'

Emily clicked her tongue at him. 'I think we'd just decided that we're each of us as bad as the other,' she said. 'You've got hopelessly woolly-minded romantic ideas about being in love, and I've spent my whole adult life chasing after a partnership for absolutely the wrong reasons. Something like that, anyhow.'

'Ah, I see. So it's basically a draw.'

'Yes.'

'Fine. Now, can we go, please? Before this mad senior partner of yours comes along and turns us into frogs?'

'Of course. Where do we go?'

Not again. 'Anywhere. Vienna. Dar-es-bloody-Salaam. Let's just *go*.'

Frank reached for the handle of the Door, but before his fingers connected it started to turn. Hang on, he thought, it shouldn't do that. It's never done that before. What's happening?

And then the Door opened.

CHAPTER FOURTEEN

'Hello, you two,' said Amelia Carrington.

Immaculate in a simple grey business suit and almost austerely formal black court shoes, she stepped through the Door, followed by Colin Gomez, with a black eye and his arm in a sling. The Door closed behind them, fell off the wall and rolled itself up. Colin Gomez pounced on it, snatched it up with his good hand and stuffed it in his inside pocket.

Surprisingly, Frank was the first to recover from the shock. He tried to grab Colin, but Emily stopped him by stamping on his foot. 'Don't,' she said urgently. 'They're dangerous.'

Amelia beamed at her. 'She's right, of course,' she said. 'Oh, I know you but you don't know me. Amelia Carrington. And you're Frank Carpenter,' she added, with a subtle blend of curiosity and distaste. 'I know ever such a lot about *you*.'

'Dangerous in what way?' Frank asked. Then he stopped abruptly, as a pain in his head made everything impossible. It only lasted two seconds, but that was long enough.

'Colin,' Amelia said, and without any apparent hesitation Colin Gomez handed her the Door. She produced its cardboard tube out of thin air, tucked it away and handed it back.

'Now then,' Amelia said. 'Let's get this over with as quickly as possible.'

Emily backed away, dragging Frank with her; not that there was anywhere to go. There was a sort of irony in that; your deadly enemy's got the Portable Door, and you honestly believe that running away might help?

'The story so far,' Amelia said, in the manner of someone making a private joke for her own amusement. 'In about ten minutes' time, you two misfits will walk through my office wall. She'll be waving around a magic sword, in the naive belief that I'll be scared of it. You'll try and force me to tell you my evil cunning plan for world domination, and after that you're going to stop me doing it by taking me back through time and marooning me in –' her upper lip curled in involuntary disgust '– 1963. That's because neither of you have got the guts to kill me, but you really think I ought to be got out of the way, for the sake of the planet.'

Emily looked at her. 'That's what we're going to do?'

Amelia nodded. 'It was his idea.'

'Oh.'

'Quite. Of course, it won't work. While you're dithering about being humane, I flatten you both against the wall with Schrödinger's Ferret, and Colin – I've forgiven him, by the way, he's too pathetic to squash, and he does earn the firm a great deal of money – Colin's been hiding behind the filing cabinet all this time, just in case I can't handle you myself, and Erskine comes rushing in from the interview room, and they jump on you.' Amelia frowned. 'At this point, things go slightly wrong. Well, Colin messes them up, actually. Don't you, Colin?'

Gomez nodded sadly. Not that his feelings mattered a damn, but he did seem very unhappy about the whole business.

'Colin,' Amelia went on briskly, 'sees you –' stern glance at Frank, who winced '– picking up a hole-punch, presumably to throw at me. He overreacts – well, you did, you stupid man – and throws a thunderbolt. Only he misses,' Amelia added, frowning. 'And hits Erskine. Nothing left but a smell of burned hair and a brown patch on the wall. Which is why,' she went on, with a faint sigh, 'we're all here. You see, I'm rather fond of Erskine.'

'Really?'

'Yes. He's my dog.'

Short pause, while Emily realised that this wasn't a metaphor. 'Your *dog*?'

Nod. 'Cross between a Jack Russell and a King Charles spaniel; as unlikely a match as – well, you two, but their union was blessed, and my dad gave it to me for my tenth birthday. You can get attached to a dog,' Amelia added, slightly guiltily. 'And besides, he's been very useful. He found you, for instance,' she said, looking at Frank. 'Wonderful nose, he can follow a scent even through a transdimensional vortex. Looking for the Door, of course. I've always wanted it, ever since I was little. I always put it at the top of my Christmas list, but I kept getting ponies instead. Not that a pony can't be made useful—'

Sudden insight illuminated Emily's mind. 'Sally Esteban in Accounts,' she said.

Amelia nodded. 'And Jack Grimminger, at the St Petersburg office. He used to be a dear little Welsh cob, about thirteen-two, and now he's in charge of Corporate Finance in one of the quickest-growing markets in the sector. Gelding, of course, but that just means one less distraction. Anyway, back to Erskine. When all this started I set him to sniff out the Door, and when it opened – you were running one of your errands for poor George Sprague – he nipped through and started following you around. Led me straight to you, bless him. And now silly old Colin's gone and blasted him into his component molecules, and I don't think I could bear to be parted from him, even though he's a complete moron when he's human. So,' she went on, with a cheerful smile, 'I decided to take a leaf out of young Frank's book, use the Door and make the whole ambush incident never happen. Stroke of luck for you, of course.'

Emily frowned. 'Is it?'

'Oh yes. Sorry, forgot. Colin's second thunderbolt took out the pair of you. In about –' glance at watch '– in roughly six minutes' time, so we'd better get a move on, you two will be extremely dead. Or you will have been, only I want my dog back. So instead,' Amelia said grimly, 'I'm going to do to you what you had planned for me. Nineteen sixty-three,' she added, with relish. 'Really, I don't know which of you diabolical geniuses was responsible for choosing the date, but for sheer inventive nastiness, it deserves some kind of award. But that's all right, since I get to reap the benefit of your ingenuity.' She smiled, and gave Emily an appraising look. 'You're going to look so cute in tall white vinyl lace-up boots,' she said. 'Just think of me every time you wear them.'

Emily said a rude word. Amelia grinned. 'Right,' she said. 'Colin, get Erskine in here. He's going with you,' she said casually, 'to make sure that you behave. He'll be coming back later, of course, but you won't.'

Colin was on the phone. A sudden rush, Emily thought, while she's off guard. Their last chance, probably. Heroism. But she'd been in pest control long enough to know that heroism, like true love, usually only makes things different, rather than better. The Sixties, though. Dear God.

'He's on his way up,' Colin said. 'Oh, and Dennis Tanner's downstairs. He insists on seeing you.'

'Tell them I'll be down in a minute,' Amelia replied. 'He's going to be terribly put out when he finds out what I've done to him. All in all, a good, busy day. Well, come on, you two. Colin, stand by in case they try something stupid. Erskine, there you are at last.'

In he bustled, and although in his human form he didn't have a tail to wag Emily found herself wondering how she'd failed to realise that he was a dog all along. It was so blindingly obvious when you looked at him.

'Door, Erskine.'

Immediately, he took a familiar-looking cardboard tube from his pocket, fished out the rolled-up plastic and spread it on the wall. Which was odd, Emily couldn't help thinking, because last time she'd seen it the Door had been in Colin's hand, just before he stowed it away in his pocket.

'Fetch.'

Erskine darted forward, grabbed Emily by the arm and hustled her towards the Door. Frank tensed himself to intervene, then thought of the brown mark on Ms Carrington's office wall. Play for time, he thought; so he said: 'What have you done with George Sprague?'

Amelia shrugged. 'He's in Holding,' she said. 'Down in the cellars somewhere, I imagine. When he wakes up, of course, it'll be in his own bed and he won't remember a thing. Oh, it's all right, you don't have to worry about him. It'd be far too much bother to break in a new insurance account manager. I only needed him to give you a pretext for making up to her.'

Frank discovered the germ of an uncomfortable thought lodged under the dental plate of his mind. 'That was all part of the plan, was it? Us two getting together.'

Amelia nodded. 'So you'd come into my parlour, and bring me the Door. Economy of effort, you see, birds-to-stone ratios. I never begrudge a little added complexity if it means I can eliminate a superfluous ingredient or two.'

'Whatever.' Frank looked at her. At a time like this, he thought, troll's blood would be quite welcome. 'And Emily and me,' he went on, anger just about overriding embarrassment. 'Only, my father told me about love potions and stuff. You didn't—'

'Oh, I *see*.' Amelia giggled. 'No, that wasn't me. Just a bonus, though I suppose it was always on the cards. Put two sad people together in close proximity and add excitement and pressure . . . It won't last, of course,' she added pleasantly. 'I give it six weeks at the outside, and then you'll be wondering what the hell you ever saw in each other. I mean, really. About all you've got in common is that, way back, you're both descended from monkeys.'

Frank nodded. 'Thank you so much,' he said. 'We'll be going now.'

'Splendid. Oh, and if you were thinking that when you get there, you could go round to Daddy's house and murder me in my cot, don't waste your time. You'll only get caught and thrown in prison, if you're lucky, and what kind of a life would that be? Well, goodbye. It's been such fun.'

Frank felt Erskine's grip on his shoulder; surprisingly strong. Six weeks, he thought: well, we'll see about that. Amelia

Carrington may be able to undo the future, but that's no reason to assume that she can predict the past. A hand shoved him between the shoulder blades and he stumbled forward, through the Door.

It swung to behind him, clicked shut, and vanished.

Perhaps it would've given Frank and Emily a small degree of satisfaction to hear Amelia's scream of baffled rage as the Door turned into a blank, featureless wall. But they didn't. By then, they were decades away.

The dragon woke up with a start, and yawned.

A drop of no more than a quarter of a degree in the temperature of the cavern: you'd have needed pretty sophisticated instruments to record it, but it was enough to smash a hole through the dragon's dream and leave it with an uncomfortable hindbrainful of splintered images.

One of the good things about caverns deep underground is that their temperature stays constant: no sun, no wind or rain, roof insulation beyond the dreams of ecology. A quarter-degree fluctuation therefore can only mean that someone up-tunnel has just opened a door.

The dragon's ears went forward. It listened carefully. It heard a pin drop.

Tinkle, went the pin on the tunnel floor. Bump bump bump went the grenade, like Winnie the Pooh going downstairs. The grenadier had done his calculations pretty well. As soon as the grenade skittered into the cavern, it went off.

The roar of the explosion echoed round the cavern for a good three seconds. Not just your ordinary run-of-the-Mills-bomb pineapple; this one had been specially loaded to exacting specifications by Hewitt and Lane of Curzon Street, bespoke munitions makers to the London magic trade. If the blast and shrapnel didn't do the trick, the shock wave, in a confined space like an underground cavern, was guaranteed to break every high-tensile bone in a dragon's body. It had been awarded an unprecedented five stars in *Which Grenade*, June 2005.

The dragon havered. Ever such a lot of dust had come down from the roof. It did its best, but finally it had to give in and sneeze; fortuitously, just as the assault party poked their heads round the tunnel mouth to see if the grenade had done the job.

The dragon turned round three times and went back to sleep.

'Uncle Dennis,' Amelia said. 'How nice to see you again so soon.'

Dennis Tanner sat down without being asked, and put his feet up on the edge of her desk. That made her smile. Defeat has different effects on different people. Some it crushes; others put on an exaggerated show of stroppiness. Amelia had seen defeated men across that same desk enough times to read the body language at a glance.

'It was that bloody Door thing, right?'

She nodded. 'You're terribly clever, Uncle Dennis. Not clever enough,' she added sweetly, 'but don't feel bad about it.' She pushed a box of cigars, which hadn't been there a moment ago, across the desk at him. He picked one out, sniffed it and put it back. 'How did you figure it out?'

'The Carpenter boy came to see me,' Dennis replied. 'Told me about the Mousetrap you'd set for your pest-control girl. Didn't take me long to work out you're the only one who'd be in a position to do that. I knew about the insurance scam that Carpenter was working. What I couldn't get was why you'd want to knock off one of your own employees. Oh, on general principles, yes,' he added. 'When I was at JWW there were times I'd have cheerfully exterminated the lot of 'em. But just the one, and a Mousetrap—' He grinned. 'And then it just sort of clicked. Bait. To make the Door come to you.'

'Very good.' Amelia nodded. 'So, did you come all this way just to—?'

'Properly speaking, of course,' Dennis went on, 'the Door belongs to me. On account of the fact that Frank Carpenter's dad found it in a drawer in his desk at JWW, so it was the firm's property and, since I'm the only surviving partner, it's mine.' He paused. 'But I don't suppose you see it like that, somehow.'

'No.'

'Well, quite. We could have a lawsuit about it, maybe.'

'We could,' Amelia conceded. 'Of course, that'd mean a lot of lawyers getting turned into frogs, but I'm game if you are. Whether they'd still be able to charge you £500 an hour for sitting on lily pads catching flies with their tongues is a moot point, but knowing your luck—'

Dennis grinned. 'Alternatively,' he said, 'we could forget the whole thing, and you could cut me in for the share you promised me in the big bauxite strike.'

'No.'

'Pretty please? Go on, be a sport.'

'No.'

Nod. 'I was hoping you'd say that. I wasn't going to give you a chance, but Mum insisted. Well, thanks for your time.'

Dennis stood up, then stopped. For a moment or so, he seemed to be trying to drag his feet off the floor, like a man trapped in deep mud. Then he sat down again.

'That's just showing off,' he said.

'Uncle Dennis,' Amelia said. 'You didn't come here just to make me an offer that I can't accept. What're you up to?'

Dennis smiled at her. 'You're not going to let me go till I tell you, right?'

'Right.'

'Fine.' He reached for the cigar box, only to find that it was now empty. He snapped his fingers, lit the result and blew smoke across the desk. It stopped in mid-air and vanished. 'You know about the Wayatumba strike, of course.'

'Naturally. Until word gets out about what we've found, it's still officially the biggest bauxite deposit in the world. You gave it to Frank Carpenter's dad.'

'That's right. And now I've got it back.'

Amelia's eyebrows rose. 'Really? How did you manage that?'

'Bought it.'

'Ah. Borrowed money, of course.'

Shrug.

'Don't tell me,' Amelia went on. 'Borrowed family money. Goblins.'

'Sound enough investment,' Dennis replied blandly. 'And, being a naturally subterranean species, we reckon we know a bit about mining and minerals.'

'Indeed,' Amelia said. 'I'm sure they went into it with their beady little red eyes wide open. Presumably this is some sort of declaration of war.'

Dennis nodded. 'Price war,' he said. 'We plan on digging the stuff out in vast quantities and practically giving it away. Which means you'll have to do the same. It'll be a case of who can stand the loss longest, you or us, and then the winner buys out the loser's stake for pennies from the liquidators.'

Amelia sighed. 'Dear Uncle Dennis,' she said. 'You know, sometimes you can be very sweet. But I'm afraid you're wasting your time.'

'You reckon.'

'I know for a fact. We sold all our rights in the new strike this morning.'

Dennis Tanner sat still and quiet long enough for his cigar to burn a neglected quarter-inch. 'That's interesting,' he said eventually.

'Yes. Well, do give my regards to your mother. I must say, she's marvellous for her age. You can get up now, if you want to.'

Dennis shot to his feet, staggered and steadied himself on the back of the chair. 'This whatever-it-is you're up to,' he said. 'Is it connected to the Door, or just sort of running in parallel?'

'That'd be telling,' Amelia said cheerfully. 'Talk to you soon.'

As soon as he'd gone, she relieved her feelings by taking the phone off its cradle and bashing it against the side of the desk until the plastic smashed. Of course, Uncle Dennis couldn't have known that something had gone wrong and the Door had slipped through her fingers. No way. Just talking about it, though, hearing it mentioned, made her want to howl with rage.

For the hundredth time since it had happened, Amelia tried to figure it out.

She hadn't, of course, been entirely honest with Carpenter and the Spitzer girl. Getting Erskine back hadn't been the only reason. She'd have done it anyway: the attempted ambush had forced her hand, but it shouldn't have mattered. As far as she'd been able to tell at the time, it had all worked out just fine. Except that now she was short one Portable Door.

Erskine would be back soon, she reminded herself, and then it wouldn't matter. Then at least she'd have one Door, though two would've been nicer. Where was he, by the way? Bad dog.

Amelia ran through the calculations in her mind.

According to Pereira's Last Theorem, if you used the Door to go back through time and open a Doorway in a wall at precisely the moment when, in the past, the Door was being applied to that same wall, you ought to achieve the Pereira Effect: the Door in the future would interface with its past and self-replicate, leaving you with two Doors.

Done that, Amelia reflected. And the look on Carpenter's face when she'd walked through had been worth it on its own. For a short while, then, she'd had two Doors: the one she'd taken from Carpenter after he'd been thunderbolted during the ambush, and its ten-minutes-earlier past self. But, when Erskine had shoved the troublesome pair through the Door (*a* Door) into the Sixties, and she'd looked in the cardboard tube just in case, there'd been nothing inside it except a little stale air. Infuriating.

So: maybe Pereira had been wrong. His work was, necessarily, entirely theoretical, and perhaps there was a flaw in the maths somewhere. Sums, Amelia was prepared to admit, weren't her strongest suit. Nevertheless, she couldn't help thinking that she'd been cheated somehow.

Anyhow; no use crying over vanished Doors. She comforted herself with the thought of Uncle Dennis explaining to the goblins that he'd just lost all their money. It was possible, of course, that they'd be terribly nice and understanding about it, point out that they'd known the risks when they'd decided to make the investment and urge him not to feel bad about it, because after

all, it's only money, isn't it, and family's so much more important; oh, and look out, low-flying pigs operate in this area. Or
they might tear him into little bits and jump on them.

Poor Uncle Dennis.

The Door opened.

'Look out!' Frank yelled, and he lunged forward and shoved
Erskine aside, just in time to stop him being flattened by a
speeding, brand new Triumph Herald.

'Oh *God*,' he heard Emily say, somewhere behind him. 'It's
true. She really did it.'

Frank looked up and down the street. They weren't in
Cheapside any more. The wall they'd just stepped out of stood
in a leafy suburban street, all very mock Tudor and privet-
hedged. At first glance it wasn't so very different, until he
registered the stuff that wasn't there: no satellite dishes, not
many TV aerials, only a few parked cars instead of a continuous
bumper-to-bumper line. Smoke curled up from many of the
chimneys. Not so very different; but, he had an unpleasant feeling, different enough.

'Emily,' he said. 'Did they have cashpoint machines in the
Sixties?'

'No.'

'Fine. So our plastic's useless, and— Bloody hell, I guess
they're probably still using the old money. You know, shillings
and things.'

'Very interesting, but what's that got to do with—?'

'It means we're penniless, that's all. No money we can actually use. Not our biggest problem, maybe, but—'

'You don't seriously imagine we're going to stay here, do you?'

Frank pulled a face. 'What did you have in mind?'

Emily pushed past him. 'We're going to bash Dog Boy here to
a pulp, take the Door and go back,' she said. 'I assume that's all
right with you.'

She advanced a step or two, then stopped as Erskine made a
deep growling noise that seemed to root her to the spot. It wasn't

a specific threat of any kind, but suddenly she felt extremely reluctant to move.

'Sorry,' Erskine said.

That just seemed to try Emily's patience. 'No, you bloody well aren't,' she said. 'If you were sorry, you'd give us the bloody Door.'

Erskine shook his head miserably. 'I can't,' he said. 'I have to do as I'm told, or She'll be angry.'

'Oh, screw you,' Emily replied. 'Frank, get him.'

There's something about the way a dog growls. Even if it's just one of those little yappy self-propelled-toilet-brush jobs with no visible legs, it makes you stop and think, if only for a split second. Erskine, of course, was an unknown quantity. If he'd been human, the two of them rushing him would've probably been a justifiable business risk. But he wasn't, was he? Human beings can't make a noise like that.

'You're pathetic,' Emily said, sounding rather unconvinced. 'You're not scared of a stupid *dog*, are you?'

'I'm not if you're not.'

She had the grace not to reply. Erskine shifted slightly. The Door, of course, was still there on the wall, slightly ajar. If Frank peered past Erskine's shoulder, he could just about catch a glimpse of forty-five years into the future.

'I really am very sorry,' Erskine said.

'Are you?' Emily scowled at him, but stayed where she was. 'Fine way you've got of showing it.'

'Don't say that,' Erskine practically whimpered. 'I'm not enjoying this, you know. I like to be nice to people, I want to be friends with everybody. But I can't not do what She told me to. I just can't.'

Frank looked at him. 'Let me get this straight,' he said. 'That dog that kept following me around. That was you.'

Erskine couldn't help smiling as he nodded. 'That's right,' he said. 'I had a great time, too.'

'Did you?'

'Oh yes. We went to all different places, with lots of really great smells. You even bought me a little ball that squeaked.'

'Did I? Oh, right, yes. And I saved your life just now,' Frank added sternly.

'Yes. You did.'

'How many times do I have to tell you, don't run out in front of the cars.'

No tail to put between his legs, but Erskine managed to convey the same thing by facial expression alone. 'Sorry.'

'I should've guessed earlier,' Emily was saying. 'I mean, it was pretty bloody obvious, now I come to think of it. I told you, didn't I, about not being able to hear him.' She gave Erskine an extra-special scowl, and he slumped a little.

'And you were nice to me too,' he said.

'Was I?'

'Oh yes. We went to see the spiders together, and then we met that nice troll sort of person, and you let me carry the suitcase and everything.'

'True,' Emily said carefully.

'And in the taxi, you let me sit on the seat.'

'Yes, I did, didn't I?' Emily replied, in a slightly strained voice. 'That's got to count for something surely. In terms of pack loyalty, I mean.'

'Yes, but—'

Frank was about to ask her what she was talking about, but she shushed him. 'Really,' she went on, 'there are times when a person's got to think about stuff like that, and decide for himself exactly whose dog he really is. Isn't that right, Frank?'

'Absolutely.'

'Just think about it,' she went on quickly. 'We didn't turn you into a human and leave you to fend for yourself.'

'Damn straight,' Frank said. 'That's cruelty, if you ask me. A dog is for life, not just for—'

'We didn't send you off trailing someone on your own, not even caring if you came back or not. Surely that's part of the deal. You fetch the stick, we're there to take it when you come back, it's the basic ethical contract between the species. But I don't think *she* sees it like that, somehow.'

'Bet she never bought you a squeaky rabbit,' Frank added scathingly.

'Ball.'

'Whatever. It's the thought that counts.'

'But I *can't*,' Erskine wailed. 'She told me, I've got to leave you here and bring the Door back. I've got to do what She says, or I'll end up in the place where bad dogs go. I don't want to go there, it's scary.'

Emily took a deep breath. 'You could come with us,' she said. 'You could be our – Jesus fucking Christ, I can't believe I'm saying this – you could be *our* dog. We'd look after you. Your own basket by the radiator. Chicken. We'd let you drink dirty rainwater from puddles.'

It was tearing Erskine apart. 'Really?'

'Really.'

'Could I sleep on the bed?'

'No.' Both of them together, like a well-trained chorus. 'But you can roll in all the smelly stuff you like, and we won't make you have a bath.'

There were big fat tears in Erskine's eyes now, and Emily thought, *While he's distracted we could probably jump him. Probably. Possibly. Possibly not.* 'I'm sorry,' Erskine said with a sniff like tearing calico. 'I really, really am. I do like you, both of you, very much.'

'We like you too,' Emily snarled. 'Really we do.'

'But I can't.' Erskine stepped back and put his hand on the knob of the Door. Oh well, Emily thought, and tensed herself for a flying tackle. She was just about to let herself go when Erskine said, 'I could give you the other Door, I suppose, if that'd be any help.'

It was one of those moments when everything seems to stop dead. Nothing moved, no bird sang and the only noise was the faint whine of the Everley Brothers from a distant wireless.

'The other Door,' Emily said.

Erskine nodded. 'Mr Gomez gave it to me when She wasn't looking. I was going to ask him why but he sort of scowled at me, so I didn't.'

'But there can't be another Door,' Frank objected. 'You told me, everybody knows there's only the—'

'Quiet, Frank.' Emily pulled herself together so smoothly that for a moment Frank forgot all about the context and was lost in admiration. 'I think that'd be all right, don't you, Frank? I mean, she didn't say anything at all about the other Door, did she?'

'Nope,' Frank managed to say.

'She just said, take them to nineteen sixty-three and bring the Door back. Not both Doors. Just *the* Door.'

'Absolutely,' Frank put in. 'I heard her say it.'

'I'm sure she'd have said both Doors,' Emily went on pleasantly, 'if it'd been important.'

Erskine frowned. There was something wrong there, he couldn't help thinking. Maybe, he thought, She hadn't known about Mr Gomez giving him the other Door. But no, that couldn't be right. She was, well, *Her*. It went without saying, She knew everything.

'I suppose it'd be all right,' he said doubtfully. 'I mean, I'd still be doing as I was told.'

'Of course you would,' Emily said, trying hard to keep the hunger out of her voice. 'In fact, I'm pretty sure it's what she wants you to do, or else she'd have said bring back both Doors, instead of bring back the Door.'

'But maybe She didn't know that Mr Gomez had given me the other one.'

Emily managed to synthesise a look of shocked amazement. 'But Colin Gomez is on her side,' she said. 'So, naturally, he wouldn't do anything she didn't want him to do. You must see that, surely.'

Despairingly, Erskine looked at Frank, who gave him a slight nod. That decided him. After all, Mr Arkenstone was a nice man, he'd given him the squeaky ball.

All in all, Erskine wished that he could be a dog again. Being human was very exciting, and obviously it was a great honour to be promoted and allowed to walk on his hind legs and wear clothes and everything. But being human was so *difficult*. People made demands of you, and forced you to make awkward choices, and some of them told you one thing and some of them said another, and he couldn't remember the last time anybody had thrown a stick for him or taken him for a walk. Perhaps the simple truth was that he wasn't worthy of promotion.

'All right,' he said miserably, and from his pocket he took the roll of plasticky stuff. A voice at the back of his mind told him that he ought to carry it over in his mouth and lay it at Mr Arkenstone's feet, but he decided to keep it simple, for now. He held it out, and Ms Spitzer snatched it out of his hand.

'Good boy,' she said. '*Good* boy.'

Now that he'd actually done it, Erskine felt much better. 'Thanks,' he said, and turned to walk through the Doorway in the wall behind him. 'I've got to go now,' he said. 'See you.'

'Just a moment.' Emily held out an arm to stop him. 'When you get back, I wouldn't bother mentioning giving us the spare Door.'

That didn't sound right either. 'Really? Are you sure?'

'Better not.'

'Oh.' Erskine wondered about that. 'Why not?'

Ms Spitzer seemed lost for words, but Mr Arkenstone said, 'Well, you know how busy she is. And she doesn't need to be told all the fiddly little details. Just tell her you did as she said, and that'll do fine.'

'Oh. All right, then.'

Erskine was still thinking about it as he stepped over the Door's threshold and came out in the twenty-first century.

'Where the hell have you been?' She asked, sitting upright in her chair with her hand over the mouthpiece of her phone. 'Never mind. Sit still while I finish this call.'

So Erskine sat, while She uncovered the phone and said, 'Sorry about that, now where we? Oh yes. Right. All right, this is what we're going to do.'

Colin Gomez stirred in his chair. For more years than he cared to remember, he'd been happy in that chair. When he was sitting in it, it was like being the captain of a starship, that same balance of being in control and facing a whole galaxy of uncertain but wonderful possibilities, never knowing what extraordinary opportunities the next day might bring. It could be just another day at the office – the bread-and-butter work, the reliable bedrock customers; it could just as easily be the day he made first contact with strange new clients, sought out new work and new ways of charging for it. To that chair for their orders came his loyal crew, hand-picked, dependable, almost as essential to his well-being as the punters themselves, but ready (whether they knew it or not) to be sacrificed for the greater good without a moment's hesitation. As for himself: he liked to tell himself that it was better to be a captain than the admiral of the fleet, anchored to the big desk instead of skirmishing the galaxy questing for new people to do business with. And if he didn't actually believe that, the self-deception was his own precious secret, something to take out and love when nobody was looking—

Now everything had changed. Colin reckoned (though with Amelia Carrington you never *knew*) that he'd got away with it so far. By turning in his unexpected and unwanted allies, he'd clawed back a little bit of her trust. Letting them have the other Door (assuming that Erskine could be relied on; which was a bit like putting your weight on a spun-glass stepladder) meant they'd be back again to help him, any moment now. At which point he'd have to do it: stage his coup, overthrow the government and get himself crowned as the God-emperor of Carringtons.

It wasn't what he'd wanted, except in the safe privacy of his daydream. For one thing, he wasn't entirely sure he was up to the job. Oh, he knew how to win clients and keep them happy, and surely that was all there was to it. But supposing it wasn't? He was dimly aware that there was rather more to it than just doing a good job and finding ways of charging twice as much as it was worth without letting the client find out he'd been scalped. There was – well, *politics*: diplomatic relations with other firms, industrial relations inside the firm itself, all manner of things that called for approaches more cynical and brutal than he was comfortable with. More to the point, he had to get there first; and that would mean bloodshed.

All in all, a bit of a pickle; which was why, for the first time that Colin Gomez could remember, his chair didn't feel right. It sort of caught him in the small of the back.

To distract his mind he turned on his screen and scrolled through the latest news update. The headlines hit him right between the eyes like a stone from a slingshot.

Biggest-ever bauxite find shut down by dragon infestation.

Dennis Tanner was reading the same headline.

He took it well. Instead of falling off his chair or screaming, he stayed perfectly still, as if the screen was a predator who'd pounce on him at the slightest sign of movement.

The bitch, he thought. The *clever* bitch.

The screen told him how the vast new bauxite deposit recently discovered at an undisclosed location on New Zealand's South Island had attracted the unwanted attention of a dragon – also, by some strange coincidence, the largest of its kind ever recorded – bringing the whole project to a standstill. Because of the location's unique geology, access to the deposit was only possible through a large natural cavern, in which the dragon had made its nest. Pest-control teams from leading firms had so far failed to deal with the problem and a halt had been called to further attempts in view of the high attrition rate (follow the hypertext link to find out more about job vacancies in this exciting sector). The implications for the market—

Dennis thumbed off the screen. He didn't need to be told about them.

First, the wonderful investment opportunity into which he'd persuaded his wealthy but vindictive relatives to pour their money now had a bloody great big lizard sitting on it. Wonderful. As if that wasn't bad enough, it was inevitable that the world bauxite market (in which his relatives were already catastrophically committed) was poised to dive like a cormorant. A vast new source of the stuff had been discovered, threatening to flood the market, but for the time being it couldn't be got at; so, until the dragon was dead, only a gibbering idiot would touch bauxite with a ten-foot lance, since there was no way of knowing when the new strike would finally be unlocked. Dennis turned the screen back on and checked out the latest prices in Jakarta and Brisbane. As he'd thought: for the price of a pie and a pint, anybody stupid enough to want to do so could buy himself the bauxite mine of his choice.

He closed his eyes. Dennis wasn't a natural clairvoyant (unlike his Uncle Garforth, banned from every bookmaker's in the Western hemisphere) but he was prepared to predict that by close of trading someone would've been round buying up all those worthless and unwanted mining shares, giving that same someone the next best thing to a world bauxite monopoly and, with it, effective control over that useful commodity's selling price. After that, he had a shrewd suspicion, the dragon's life would be very short. But by then his uncles and aunts and cousins and nephews and nieces would've sold out and be too busy disembowelling Our Dennis to notice they'd been had—

Bloody woman, he thought.

And then, in a moment of perfect clarity, the screen inside his mind cleared, and he understood.

He jumped up out of his chair, scuttled across the room and hauled down a dusty old book from the top shelf of his bookcase. Index: *dragons, prophecies concerning—*

Dennis snapped the book shut, filled his lungs with air and yelled (as all good boys eventually must) for his mother.

At least thirty seconds, possibly forty-five, had passed since Erskine had walked through the wall, but neither Frank nor Emily had spoken. There was too much to say, and not enough of the right kind of words to say it with. Also, as far as Frank was concerned, there was a problem with saying things to her that he couldn't actually hear himself. Hard to pick exactly the right words, under such circumstances—

'Well,' Emily said eventually.

Frank nodded.

'I don't like it here.' She looked round. To Frank, there didn't seem all that much to take exception to. It was just a suburban street, no big deal. But, he reflected, I'm used to being out of my time. Some of my favourite places are in the past: Renaissance Tuscany, Edwardian London, *fin de siècle* Paris. Of course, you wouldn't want to live there.

'Stuff it,' Emily said. 'Let's go home.'

She used the word assuming that Frank knew what it meant. But as far as he was concerned she might just as well have said, 'Let's go to the Hundred Acre Wood and see Pooh and Piglet'; because home was one of those places you grew up believing in, until you slowly came to realise it was just a pretty story. He opened his mouth to reply, then thought better of it, fished in his pocket and took out a slightly grubby envelope and a pen.

OK, that's When, he wrote. *How about Where?*

'Frank, why are you writing – oh,' she added. 'I see. That's—'

No offence. Two fs in offence? *But right now I'd rather you didn't.*

Emily frowned. 'Sure,' she said, 'whatever you like. But—'

Thanks for being so under—

'But,' she repeated firmly, 'it's – well, it's hardly a vote of bloody confidence, is it? I mean, what are you thinking that you don't want me to hear?'

Interesting question; and Frank could think of a lot of other questions that'd crop up sooner or later, if they spent their lives together: *Do you really like my hair this way? You don't mind if I switch over and watch the film, do you? Are you sure you don't mind going to stay at my mother's for the bank holiday?*

Do you still love me?

He wrote: *Where shall we go?*

Another frown. 'Well, the office, naturally. We've got to catch up with bloody Amelia Carrington and help Colin with his Glorious Revolution. Well, haven't we?'

No, Frank thought. *I guess so*, he wrote. So much easier, on paper.

Then a thought struck him. He crossed out what he'd just written –

'Look,' Emily said impatiently, 'how long are you going to keep this up for? Because for one thing, it's bloody inconvenient.'

– and under it, wrote: *Or we could get some allies first. Dennis Tanner.*

'Who? Oh, right, you told me about him. Your dad's old boss. But why would he want to get involved? It's none of his business.'

I don't know any other magicians. Besides, I owe him money. If I can make him think we're going to make a fortune out of this and I can pay him back out of the proceeds—

'Maybe,' she conceded. 'But we don't need him. I know loads of magicians.'

Frank scowled, turned the envelope over and wrote on the back: *Yes. At Carringtons.*

'All right, good point,' Emily agreed reluctantly. 'But I still don't see what—'

You've never met his mother, have you?

'What, Dennis Tanner's mother, you mean? No. At least, I don't think—'

He hesitated, then wrote: *Trust me.*

'Sorry, but your handwriting—'

He frowned, crossed it out and wrote it again, this time in capitals: *TRUST ME.*

'Oh.' She shrugged. 'Fine. And in return, you can bloody well stop writing and *talk* to me. Agreed?'

Frank nodded, and flexed his cramped fingers. 'Agreed,' he said.

Emily glowered at him. 'Do you really want us to run away together and start a new life in Vancouver?'

'Oh for crying out—'

'Sorry. I was just a bit puzzled. I mean, why Vancouver?'

'First place that came to mind. And yes,' he added, 'I think that'd be a very good idea, but we've already been into all this, and you don't want to run away, and I respect your reasons for not wanting to, and—'

'Yes, all right. It'd bad enough just one of you talking quickly.' Emily shook her head. 'I'm sorry,' she said. 'But this means something to me, that's all. So do you,' she added, and it wasn't an afterthought. 'But the two aren't – well, mutually exclusive.' She paused. 'Please?' she added.

Frank was quite shocked at what a difference that word made. 'All right,' he said.

She grinned. 'Can I have that in writing?'

'Look, if you're going to—'

'Sorry. Not the right time. So, if we're going, let's go.'

Frank nodded, and spread the Door against the wall. 'Mostly,' he said, as the lines appeared and spread, 'I want to see if he can clear up a question that's been bothering me.'

She reached for the handle. 'Right. What's that?'

'How did the Door come to be in that bank vault when you killed the dragon?'

Right on the threshold, Emily stopped. 'You know,' she said, 'that's a good question.'

'Isn't it, though. Do you know the answer?'

'No.'

'Fine. In that case—' Frank turned the handle. 'We're off to see the wizard. Well, are you coming, or what?'

He thought *Mr Tanner's office* and stepped over the threshold. At the precise moment when he had one foot in Sixties suburbia and the other in south London forty-five years later, he called back, 'Please just come on and walk through the Door, will you?'

And he heard Emily's voice behind him saying, 'Which one?'

'What do you mean, which—?' he said, and then something bashed him on the head and he went to sleep.

CHAPTER FIFTEEN

Frank woke up and opened his eyes. Looking down at him was the loveliest girl he'd ever seen.

She was pale and fair, with eyes the colour of clear spring skies and a perfect heart-shaped face. She was wearing a flowing white dress that seemed to shimmer faintly, and she was gazing at him with a look of pure, deep compassion. An angel, he thought. I've died, and—

He thought again. 'Knock it off, will you?' he said.

The angel grinned at him. 'Had you going there for a moment, didn't I?' she said, as she transformed into a reassuringly hideous goblin. 'Couldn't resist. Anyhow, you'd better go in and see our Dennis while he's free.'

Frank rubbed the back of his head. 'What hit me?'

'I did,' said Mr Tanner's mother.

'Oh.'

'Thought you were someone else,' she explained.

'Let me guess. Amelia Carrington.'

The goblin grinned approvingly. 'You're smart,' she said. 'Not like your dad, bless him. I always reckoned he was like confectioners' custard, sweet and thick.'

'You thought she'd got hold of the Door.'

'It was a possibility,' Mr Tanner's mother said. 'And not a risk worth taking, if you follow me. Bash first, look to see who it is at your leisure. It's the goblin way.'

'So I imagine.' Frank stood up. His head hurt and he felt woozy and a bit sick. Had Mr Tanner's mother finally hit on the elusive secret of the alcohol-free hangover? he wondered. 'Emily's in there already, I suppose.'

'What?'

'Emily. Emily Spitzer, the girl who was with me.' A horrible thought struck him, though not quite as hard as Mr Tanner's mother had done. 'You didn't bash her too, did you?'

A puzzled look in those small, round red eyes. 'Sorry, dear, who are you talking about?'

Emily woke up.

'Frank?' she called out. Her voice echoed in the darkness. Not a reassuring sound. Something snagged her attention, and she sniffed.

Some smells are unmistakable.

Instinctively, she reached for her tool kit, which wasn't there. A pity. Never go on a job without the proper equipment – it was the first rule of pest control. It's a bit humiliating to have to tell the client that you're just nipping back to the office for a reel of electric cable or a mass spectrometer or an RPG-7 anti-tank rocket. It's really humiliating to get killed.

But she wasn't on a job, was she? Her head was spinning a bit, but not so much that she couldn't remember. She'd been with Frank. They'd been marooned in the Sixties, but they'd talked Erskine into giving them the other Door (what other Door? Skip that for now) and they'd been on their way to see Dennis Tanner, for some reason that she was sure she'd understood at the time. So what was she doing in a dark underground cavern that smelled disconcertingly of dragon?

Interesting question.

Calm down, Emily told herself. Just because a place stinks of dragon, it doesn't necessarily follow that there's a live one in there with you. The pong tends to linger quite some time after the dragon's gone. This could be the strongroom of any one of a number of banks she'd disinfested over the last six months. No way of knowing in the dark, of course.

As if on cue, a light flared, showing her curved rock walls and a low rock ceiling, on which droplets of water sparkled as they dribbled down encrustations of limestone slurry. Being able to see her surroundings should've made her feel better, but it didn't; mostly because the light was red.

When dragons snore, theorists claim, the plasma flares are as hot as the surface of the sun.

She listened, and heard the plop-plop-hiss of droplets of molten stone falling and cooling on the cavern's damp floor. Sooner or later, the walls of a dragon's bedchamber turn to glass, giving their living quarters a decidedly retro-Seventies look.

Oh, Emily thought.

Even in situations as desperate as this, it's possible to keep calm provided you can anaesthetise your mind completely. Let's think, she ordered herself. If there's an unblocked exit in this place, it should be possible to locate it, even in the pitch dark, by the presence of a tell-tale cool draught. A match or lighter flame will quiver slightly, and there you are. Of course, even the slight glow of a match, combined with the smell of burning phosphorus, would wake the dragon up as effectively as a radio alarm clock tuned to Terry Wogan . . .

Her phone. Of course. All she had to do was ring the office, and they'd trace her by her signal and send someone to . . .

All right, Emily thought, weapons. Improvised weapons. Kurt Lundqvist had once killed a dragon in the vaults of the Vatican by forcing it to swallow a crystal-and-gold reliquary from its own hoard, on which it had obligingly choked to death. St John Xavier Willoughby, under similar circumstances in the strongroom of the Credit Lyonnaise in Dijon, had bashed a fifty-foot bull dragon to death with a hastily scooped fistful of krugerrands stuffed inside one of his socks. And hadn't Graziano Fiocchi poisoned the dragon in the stacks of the Uffizi with a lethal cocktail of white lead, cobalt and lapis lazuli scraped from the borders of late-fifteenth-century religious paintings?

Well, she thought, bully for them. They'd had the raw materials to work with. This dragon, by contrast, didn't appear to have acquired a hoard. She reached out and scrabbled on the floor, but felt nothing under her fingers but grime and wet stone. The flare, she remembered, hadn't lit up the whole place with the stunning warm orange of fire reflected in polished gold. No hoard. Very unusual.

(But not, she remembered, unprecedented.)

So: if it wasn't guarding precious metals or artwork, what was it doing here? Emily thought about that for a bit, but soon gave it up as too difficult and also irrelevant. More to the point: what was *she* doing here?

The logical assumption was that someone had brought her there so that the dragon could kill her. Furthermore, given her trade, death by dragon would be readily put down as an unfortunate industrial accident – her own fault, of course, since she'd somehow neglected to bring her tool kit. That fitted in quite neatly, since all Colin Gomez's previous attempts on her life could equally have been passed off as death in the line of duty – the spider, the spectral warriors, not to mention rescuing old Mrs Thompson's cat.

The second Door – now she remembered. Just as Frank had been about to go through, a second Door had opened in the wall. Emily had stopped to stare at it, it had opened, and that was as far as she could recall. Erskine, tortured by conscience and neglected duty? A Colin Gomez quadruple-cross? It could just as easily have been Amelia herself, or one of her many obedient servants. Didn't matter, in any event. It was as obvious as a lorry in a salad bowl that she wasn't getting out of this one, not unless Frank came and rescued her yet again; and in order to do that, he'd have to know where she was, and how, pray, was he supposed to find *that* out? Another advantage of death by dragon is that there's no body. No corpse, no paperwork, no inquest, no insurance claim. She'd simply vanish in a puff of smoke, and the poor lamb wouldn't have a clue where to start looking for her.

Her own stupid, stupid fault, needless to say. If she'd listened to Frank, they'd be in Vancouver right now, with a new life to look forward to. As it was; even if he somehow managed to find out what had happened to her— The picture was clear and sharp in her mind. Frank, stepping through the Door into the cavern, to be greeted by twin blasts of heat so murderous that Arctic pack ice thawed and the sea level rose a quarter-inch all round the world. It'd be mercifully quick, yes, but agonisingly final.

Oh well, she thought. That's that, then.

Emily sorted and catalogued her regrets. They came in a wide variety of sizes and priorities, ranging from not having a child of her own some day down to never finding out if it was really true that dragons set their tails on fire every time they ate beans. Never getting to be a partner was in there, as she'd anticipated, but to her surprise it found its level about halfway down the list, sandwiched between never having been to India and not getting to discover whether Frank snored. So, she reflected, more wryly than bitterly, it really was nothing more than a means of earning a living to her, after all. That said, never landing her toe forcefully on Amelia Carrington's designer-clad arse was in there too, so high up it was practically at the top.

Practically; but not quite. In fact, it had only just scraped bronze. Both the gold and silver medallists, she noted, were directly Frank-related, and Vancouver would've been as good a setting for them as any.

But then again, too few to mention. Now then: should she, out of pure professional pride, carry on hoping and improvising and hiding right to the bitter, fiery end? Or would it be far less hassle just to cough loudly and get it over with?

Then the dragon spoke.

All it actually said was 'Gwmphmtm', followed by a snort and a sharp contorted wriggle, for all the world as though it was trying to yank more than its fair share of a diamond-studded cloth-of-gold duvet. But what it also said was, *She's here.*

Fine, Emily thought. Who's she, then, the cat's mother?

The dragon snuggled its muzzle under its left forepaw and grunted. It also said, *You are here.*

Well, yes. I know that, thank you so much. Look, can we please just get on with it, before I get cramp?

No researcher has ever recorded an instance of a dragon talking in its sleep. By the same token, no researcher has conducted the relevant tests on a dragon born in a vat of green goo and raised to maturity in the time it takes to boil a kettle.

It's all right, the dragon said, *I don't mind. You can only kill this body, which is more of a hindrance than a help. The essential part of me can never die, since it has already dreamed the dream. Please, carry on. In your own time.*

Emily frowned. It struck her that the dragon was a wee bit confused about who was supposed to be killing who.

Oh, there can only be one possible outcome. I have seen it, after all, one single intersection on the circumference of the dream. You are Emily Spitzer. How could you possibly fail?

At this juncture, Emily felt constrained to point out that she'd taken the same attitude to her Biology GCSE and therefore done no revision, with the result that she'd barely scraped a C. Once bitten, no pun intended—

Don't you know? The voice inside the sleepy, grumbling noises sounded faintly amused. *Everybody knows. I've only been alive for a week, and I know.*

Know what, for crying out loud?

The prophecy.

Sorry, you've lost me. What pro—?

Not, perhaps, the right word. Prophecy is a vague, unreliable glimpse through the keyhole of sequential Time. In the dream, it's simply another solidly historical event, something we have known about ever since the day in the mid-Cretaceous period when a recklessly whimsical time traveller fed steroids to a pterodactyl and dragonkind was born. We have preserved it, analysed it, looked back on it in both sorrow and anger. Surely humans know it too.

Some humans, maybe. Not this one.

It is recorded in the dream, the dragon said, *that the greatest dragon of all shall be born not of dragon but of a vat of something a bit like undercooked pea soup; that it shall never see the sun but shall live out its brief span in a cavern, guarding the avatar of wealth known as bauxite; that its dream came to be only because a woman whose name is too unimportant to be remembered wanted to—* Here the words faltered, and instead Emily saw in her mind's eye a complex diagram, colour-coded and plotted on five axes, annotated with notes of commodity prices, hostile takeovers and sine-waves representing mining stocks on the Hang Seng. Anybody else would've assumed it was Damien Hirst trying to be funny with a pack of felt tips, but Emily saw it and understood.

'The bitch,' she said aloud.

Mistake. The dragon quivered, lifted its head, opened one eye and shut it again. By the red glare of its accelerated breathing, Emily watched as it slowly relaxed back into sleep.

Where was I?

The diagram. Amelia Carrington cornering the bauxite market.

Oh yes. It is also recorded in the dream that Emily Spitzer will face the greatest of all dragons in a dark place, and when they fight, she will win. There is no more, since the circle of the dream curves away.

That's, um, fascinating. Does the dream also record how Emily Spitzer manages to kill the greatest dragon of all time armed only with a mobile phone and a roll of peppermints?

Of course.

Well?

The dream also ordains. Don't spoon-feed the lazy cow, make her figure it out for herself.

Ah. The dream sounds suspiciously like my mother.

The dream is all our mothers, and our daughters, and ourselves. How perceptive of you, as a mere human, to have worked that out for yourself.

'Thank you,' Emily said, not really knowing what she was thanking the dragon for, but politeness never does any harm. 'Look, can I have a moment to think about this? It's—'

Of course. Oddly enough, I am in no hurry to be killed. Take all the time you need.

Prophecy, she thought. Well, there were two schools of thought in the profession about prophesy. One held that it was effectively impossible, since nobody could get information from the future without going there, and that could only be done with a Portable Door. The other school replied, Don't ask how, but we just knew you were going to say that.

But supposing there really was a prophecy, clawed down from generation to generation of dragons, and that she was the Emily Spitzer referred to in it, and this was the dragon. If so, she was going to have to fight the bloody thing, and somehow or other she'd win—

No, rewind. What had it actually said? *When they fight, she will win.*

Maybe just sloppy wording, garbled in oral transmission; but—

Excuse me, she thought.

What? Oh, you again. I was circling.

Yes, well, sorry to be a nuisance, only—

I was turning inside the circle of the dream, revolution and evolution within a closed system. Has it never occurred to you that nature abhors a straight line? Throw a stone into the air, and it will rise and fall in a curve, modified by gravity. Is it not mere sloppy thinking to believe that time runs in straight lines, when nothing else in nature does?

Only, Emily interrupted grimly, I was thinking. About the prophecy.

Time runs rings around us all, so that the precise moment of death is also the instant of birth. Can it be a coincidence that we are born screaming? Surely the newborn's howl is nothing but a reaction to the terror of the previous moment, the closing of the diaphragm that will open again a mere moment later –

Yes, Emily insisted, quite, but about this wretched prophecy. You're sure it said *when* they fight, not *if*?

A pointless quibble, since there is no If, in an infinite universe. 'If implies that something may or may not happen, but in Infinity every possibility is realised, and therefore sooner or later, everything happens. 'If', therefore, is just another way of saying 'When', and accordingly—

Whatever. Look, Emily insisted, if it says *when*, then we don't have to fight at all, which means I don't have to find a way of killing you, and you don't have to die. Wouldn't that be better all round, don't you think?

You assert that you may not be my foreordained doom after all? You would contradict that which is established in the patterns of the circle?

Well, I suppose so, yes.

Dream on, girlfriend. It's established, there's nothing anybody can do—

Bullshit. It doesn't say, *Emily Spitzer will face the greatest of all dragons in a dark place, they will fight and she will win.* It says *when they fight.* Difference, see?

Pause; then – *You are suggesting a postponement?*

No. Well, yes, I suppose I am. An indefinite one. A bit like the difference between saying 'You'll die tomorrow' and 'You'll die eventually.'

Thoughtful silence. *There's a difference?*

Oh for crying out— To me, yes. You can please yourself. Only, I'd quite like to get out of here, and I'd much prefer not to have to wake you up and fight you, because I don't particularly want to kill you, and I really don't want you to kill me, so if there's any sort of compromise we can reach—

Why don't you want to kill me? You're a dragonslayer.

Yes, but—

Spiders. The word dragonslayer fills your mind with images of spiders. You crush them because they are – intolerable. Therefore, by the same token. . .

No. Well, it's not the same. I mean, here I am talking to you, it wouldn't feel right. It'd be like, I don't know, murder.

Because we have talked to each other.

(Put like that—)

I guess so, Emily replied awkwardly. I don't know, it's just a silly irrational feeling. Look, you don't want me to kill you, do you?

I take no interest.

What? But you can't—

As far as I'm concerned, it has already happened. And it wasn't so bad. The circle turns. I am still here.

Oh be quiet, you stupid bloody reptile. If I'm not killing you, I'm not killing you. Understood?

If you say so. I was just pointing out an inconsistency—

Then don't.

Fine, as you wish. I have to say, though, that for a dominant species, you have a rather lackadaisical approach to maintaining your dominance. I don't want to kill you because you can talk to me. What kind of attitude is that?

(On the other hand, Emily thought, if I could come up with a way if killing it, at least that'd make it shut up.) Here's the deal, she proposed confidently. Tell me how I can get out of here. I'll go away and promise never to come back. You stay here, snuggle up with your manganese—

Bauxite.

All right, bauxite. Be happy. Live long and prosper, I don't care. I just want to get out of here and carry on with my life.

Do you really?

Yes.

Forgive me for saying so, but that's rather like me asking you what you want for your twelfth birthday, and you replying that you want to be twelve. Your life will carry on regardless of me. Until it stops, of course. In the dream, on the other hand—

For a moment, Emily felt like giving up. If the stupid creature couldn't be bothered to stop talking drivel and cooperate when she was trying to save both their lives— It would've been very different, she admitted, if she'd had a bucketful of industrial-strength SlayMore with her. But she hadn't; and she was stuck in there with it, and from various things it had said she'd got the impression that if it woke up there'd be a little less conversation and a little more action, with consequences that she'd prefer to avoid, even if this daft prophecy thing was true—

Besides, the dragon said, *you can't get out. There's no exit.*

What did you just—?

When they brought you here, they collapsed the only tunnel with explosives. You'd have to dig through I don't know how much rock and rubble, and I don't think you'd be up to the task, not without heavy machinery.

Oh.

Or a whatsitsname.

Portable Door?

Sorry, I don't know what that means. Sort of a bit of rubber mat, rolled up inside a cardboard tube. Is that what you had in mind?

Yes. But I haven't got one.

I haven't, either, not any more. A great shame. It would have solved your problem for you. A remarkable invention, I must say, particularly for a species that doesn't know about the dream. I can't imagine how your people came up with it. Rather like a blind man inventing the camera.

Just a minute. Did you say you haven't got one any more?

Yes.

A sharp, stabbing pain started up in the front of Emily's head. So you did have one once.

Oh yes, though of course I never got around to using it. As far as I was concerned, it was just an extremely valuable object, and as such something desirable in itself, quite apart from what it was capable of doing. Like a pension fund buying up Old Master paintings. Of course, some of the best pension-fund managers in the world are dragons.

You had one once, but you just laid on it.

That's right, yes.

In a bank vault.

Of course. You should know. You were there.

I was? No, wait, hang on. You can't possibly mean—

You were there. You sat in the corridor outside the vault, waiting for me to die. Then – I don't know what happened then, of course, because I died.

You d—

Haven't you been listening? That's why it's really a prophecy, just a memory; a memory of something that has already happened, and which will happen again. Hence, of course, the inherent irony of your profession. Every dragon you've ever killed is me, and everybody who's ever killed a dragon is you. All that talk of circles, you see, was a hint—

'Now just a moment—'

The sound of the words, inadvertently said out loud – said out very loud – hung in the still, dead air for a full three seconds. Then, just as Emily thought *Oh shit*, and started to scramble to her feet, the dragon woke up.

'Slow down,' Dennis Tanner said, 'for crying out loud. Now, where were we? You came through, but the Spitzer chick—'

'Emily,' Frank growled. 'That's her name.'

'Whatever. She didn't follow, and you thought you heard her say *'Which one?'* just as you stepped over the threshold.' Dennis leaned back, bit the end off a cigar and spat it out. 'You realise,' he said bitterly, 'that by law I'm not allowed to smoke in my own bloody office. Health and safety. The only way I can get away with it is by registering this building as an annexe to the Goblin High Commission in Tavistock Square, which makes it diplomatic so I can do what I like. Which one?' he repeated thoughtfully. 'Implying two Doors, yes?'

'I don't know, do I?' Frank snapped. 'Sorry, yes, I suppose so.'

'And Amelia's got one, and that clown Colin Gomez gave you the other.' Dennis Tanner scowled. 'Weird as a barrelful of ferrets, the whole thing. Still, that's the magic business for you. Did your dad ever tell you about the time he took on Countess Judy and the Fey? Now that really was weird, because—'

'No, he didn't, and I'd prefer it if you didn't, either. Look,' Frank said, almost pleading, 'all I know is, she's disappeared and I don't know where to start searching for her. Couldn't you look in a crystal ball or something?'

Dennis Tanner didn't bother to reply to that. 'My guess is,' he said, 'knowing Amelia as I do, that there's more than one bit of nonsense going on here. The thing about her is, she does like to run things together rather than keep them separate. Which explains why she took a fairly roundabout way of getting hold of the Door. A more straightforward person would've traced you to where you live and had someone steal the Door from your pocket while you were asleep. Instead, there's this complicated rigmarole with Better Mousetraps and God knows what. Seems to me,' he went on, 'that the main plan was getting rid of your Emily, and the Door only entered into it – no pun intended – when she refused to stay dead. Soon as Amelia figured out that whoever was saving Emily must be using the Door, she decided it'd be a nice bonus, or maybe she shifted the priorities, put getting the Door ahead of the other scam. But I'm pretty sure the Emily-must-die thing came first.'

'Fascinating,' Frank said, with a certain lack of sincerity. 'But how does that—?'

'Fortuitously,' Dennis Tanner went on, ignoring the interruption, 'I have a pretty good idea of what the main plan is, mostly because I'm in it, right up to my neck. Bauxite.'

'Bless you.'

'It's a mineral,' Dennis said sternly. 'Well, of course, you know that, Paul and Sophie's little boy, of course you do.' He paused, frowned, puffed at the cigar to keep it alight. 'And your Emily was in pest control, right?'

'Yes.'

'I see.' Dennis rubbed his eyelids with his fingertips. 'Now we've got to ask ourselves, why would Amelia want to kill one of her own employees? Actually, that's a pretty dumb question. When I had employees, there were times I'd cheerfully have slaughtered the whole lot of them – particularly,' he added with a grin, 'your parents. But aside from that. If she wanted to get shot of Emily, why not just fire her instead?'

Frank shrugged. 'I hope you're just thinking aloud, rather than hoping I'll contribute something useful,' he said.

'You bet. Same reason I talk to myself a lot: it always pays to talk to the smartest guy present. And the answer is that if she fired her, Emily would probably just go away and get another job with another firm. After all, she's got a living to earn, and I'm assuming she's good at what she does. And we don't go a bundle on references and stuff in this business, so there wouldn't be any of that you'll-never-work-in-this-town-again stuff. No,' Dennis added, blowing smoke out of his nose (blue from the left nostril, red from the right), 'what I'm thinking is this. Amelia didn't want Emily on the staff any more, and she didn't want her to go working for anyone else, either. OK so far?'

'I suppose so. I really don't know enough about—'

'Stay with me,' Dennis said reassuringly. 'I know enough about the trade for both of us. All right,' he went on, 'Let's suppose we're right. Now, then. *Why* would Amelia want those things?'

He looked at Frank, who shook his head. 'You're thinking aloud, remember. I'm just sitting here doing background noises.'

'We're assuming that Emily's good at the job,' Dennis said. 'And we'll also assume there's no internal-political stuff going on, or at least there wasn't when all this started. I'm sure Emily'd have mentioned it, although she might well not have known about it. But anyway. Here's what I think. I think Amelia wanted to make sure that Emily wasn't working in pest control, for Carringtons or anyone else, at a certain point in time, namely now. And – knowing Amelia – I'm prepared to bet that the reason she wanted Emily out was all tied up with the bauxite scam she's working.'

Frank looked at him blankly. 'Why?' he said.

'Ah,' Dennis replied smugly, and he quickly filled Frank in on the background to the new Wayatumba strike and Amelia's aim of cornering the world bauxite market. 'Which dovetails quite plausibly,' he concluded. 'Because on the one hand we've got a missing dragonslayer, and on the other hand we've got this huge scheme resting on the fact that there's a dragon blockading the new bauxite find. And not,' he added, 'just any old dragon. Latest word on the grapevine is, it's taken out five specialist teams that've been sent to get rid of it; and the blokes who got torched were the best in the business, and from what I've gathered, they tried all the approved methods and none of them worked.'

'That's so sad,' Frank grumbled. 'So bloody what?'

'Have I really got to spell it out for you? Amelia wants Emily out of the trade because, for some reason we don't know about, Emily's the only dragonslayer in the business who can zap Amelia's pet dragon. In which case,' Dennis added, jumping to his feet and stuffing things snatched off his desktop into his pockets, 'wherever the dragon is right now would probably be a good place to look for Emily. Of course, she might be a bit two-dimensional by now, since if I'm right Amelia will have sent her in without any useful dragon-killing kit – thinking, Maybe I can't get rid of the stupid girl, but I bet my dragon could, provided Spitzer doesn't have any of her toys with her – so when we get there we may just find a familiar-looking silhouette on a blackened cave-wall.' He frowned at the wretched expression on Frank's face, and went on: 'But maybe you and the Door could do something about that. And of course, ' he added, grinning, 'there's the distinct possibility that it's all some kind of trap, and when we get there we won't live long enough to feel a thing. But what the hell.' The broadest grin Frank had ever seen spread across Dennis Tanner's face. 'When you grow up in the rough and tumble of goblin society,' he said, 'you get to the point where mortal peril is a bit like rain in Manchester: you only notice it when it isn't there any more. Let's go and have a look, shall we? You know,' he added wistfully, 'I've always secretly fancied having a go on that thing.'

'What? Oh, you mean the—'

Dennis nodded. 'And from what you've been telling me, it sounds like my dear mother had it stashed away somewhere all the time and never thought to mention it. And then,' he added bitterly, 'she gave it to your dad, presumably because she felt sorry for him. Can you believe that? Possibly the rarest, most valuable artefact in the world, something I'd have found incredibly useful in my work, and she just gives it away because she feels sorry for the hired help. Fine. She never ever felt sorry for me, though if anybody ever deserved sympathy I'm him.'

'Oh?'

'Growing up with a mother like that? Are you kidding? All right,' Dennis said, bracing himself. 'Let's see it, then.'

Obediently, Frank took out the Door. Dennis stared at it for about three seconds, his face a blank.

'That's it, is it?'

'Yes.'

'My birthright.'

'Well, I suppose you could see it in those terms.'

'It looks like a bit of damp-proof membrane.'

'Yes.'

Dennis shrugged. 'Oh well,' he said. 'Let's go, if we're going.'

But Frank didn't move, and his grip on the Door tightened ever so slightly. 'Just to clarify,' he said. 'You're coming with me to the cave of a giant dragon who's already killed the best dragonslayers in the business, on the off chance that we can rescue my girl. Is that about—?'

Dennis nodded.

'Why?'

'Ah.' Dennis smiled pleasantly. 'Now there,' he said, 'you have the difference between you and your old man; and it's the reason why there may still be just a tiny glimmer of hope for you yet. You're suspicious because you can't see what's in it for me. Your dad would've assumed that I'd seen the light or got religion, and I was helping you out because it's the right thing to do.'

'Yes.'

'Fair enough. What's in it for me is the biggest bauxite strike in history, as against being ripped into little wet shreds by my blood relatives. Good enough reason?'

Frank nodded uncertainly. 'If you say so. I just want to find Emily.'

'Ah, bless.' Mr Tanner shook his head. 'Tell me,' he said. 'Haven't you been tempted to nip forward through that thing – you know, into the future? Take a look at yourself in thirty years' time? You and the missis, nice bungalow somewhere, Volvo, golden retriever, National Trust season tickets, round-robin newsletter tucked in all the Christmas cards, swing on the lawn for when the grandchildren visit. Well?'

'No, actually.'

Mr Tanner nodded. 'Sensible boy,' he said firmly. 'Just because the abyss is there waiting for you, doesn't mean you have to go and stare into it. Oh, nearly forgot.' He pushed past Frank, opened the connecting door and yelled, 'Mother!'

'Oh,' Frank said. 'She's coming too, then.'

Dennis nodded. 'When putting yourself in danger, always bring a weapon. We could take a flame-thrower and a couple of Uzis, but why settle for second-best?'

A stunning brunette in a close-fitting scarlet dress and matching shoes put her head round the door. 'I heard that,' she said.

'Oh for God's sake, Mum. You're not going out looking like that, are you?'

The brunette grinned. 'He used to hate it when I picked him up from school,' she said. '*Mum, why can't you be fat and drained-looking like all the other mummies?* Of course,' she added sweetly, 'you've got all that to look forward to. Come on, then,' she added, standing in front of the closed Door like a cat waiting to be let out. 'Don't just stand there like a prune, our Dennis. We've got work to do.'

For a split second Emily stood staring into a pair of small, round yellow eyes. Then she jumped.

As she landed painfully on one knee, she felt the intolerable heat. The thin stream of white plasma must have missed her by several feet, but she felt the skin on the back of her neck blister and melt. No time to waste on feeling pain. She rolled, scrambled onto her hands and knees and scuttled as fast as she could go away from the direction of the blast.

Fatuous, of course. Hiding from something whose mildest sigh can melt rock is a waste of time and effort. Even if there had been any sort of cover handy, huddling behind it would've been as much use as parrying a lightsabre with a stick of celery.

He's not coming, Emily thought. Time is his oyster, so to speak. If he was coming, he'd be here by now.

Oh well.

The dragon's head turned. She looked up and found herself staring into two huge black nostrils, dark and endless as the mouth of an Underground line where it leaves the platform and vanishes into the cavernous gloom. Any second now, there'd be light at the end of the tunnel: bright, red, and not at all what the original coiner of the phrase had in mind. She felt a stir in the air as the dragon breathed in—

Behind her, something moved. Emily only noticed it subconsciously, since it really couldn't matter, could it?

Wrong. Fingers tipped with bright coral nails clamped tight on her shoulder and jerked her backwards through a doorway, just as the dragon let fly.

She was in his arms.

Well, all right. Unexpected, but – she was actually mildly surprised to discover – really the only place she wanted to be. It had other attractions, of course (no dragon, for example) but the best thing about it was the gentle urgency of the squeeze, and the way he said, 'You're safe.'

'Not a mark on it,' said a woman's voice behind her somewhere. 'Wonderful gadgets, these. Here, I suppose you'd better have it back.'

One of the encircling arms detached itself from the hug for a moment, but not for very long. 'Thanks,' Frank said.

'Don't mention it. So this is your girlfriend, then.' An appraising tone of voice; not impressed.

He let her go. 'Emily, this is Dennis Tanner's mother. She's a goblin.'

She looked over her shoulder. Of course, she knew about goblins. Even so.

'We're in our Dennis's office,' the goblin woman explained. 'We rescued you.' Pause. 'No, really, it was no bother, please don't mention it.'

'Thank you,' Emily said.

The grin on the goblin woman's face had a long and eventful

pedigree. Embedded in it were little fragments of ancient memories – lost travellers seeking shelter from a storm in a mountain cave, in whose shadows lurked a hidden terror; dark, dripping mine shafts where the footfall you hear behind you might not be an echo; a glint of red eyes and soft, vicious laughter on the edge of hearing. Just as well, Emily thought, she's on our side—

'You're welcome,' the goblin woman said. 'Now then, what the hell were you playing at down there? You're supposed to have killed the bloody thing.'

'I'm sorry,' Emily said. 'But I didn't have my stuff with me.'

Derisive snort. 'Oh for crying out loud. If you were really any good, you'd have found a way. I remember Kurt Lundqvist—'

'I'm sorry,' Emily lied. 'But it's not that easy. Besides, I—'

She stopped herself just in time. *Besides, I didn't want to kill it*: not really what her audience wanted to hear, not when they'd just risked their lives rescuing her. There's a time and a place for non-violent conflict-resolution, mutual respect and understanding and David Cameronesque dragon-hugging; this, she felt, wasn't it.

'I was scared,' she said. And that was true, too.

The goblin woman raised an eyebrow. Frank said, 'Well, of course you were. Anybody would've been,' which was sweet but very unhelpful. The little shrivelled man sitting on the edge of the desk was looking at commodity prices on his computer screen.

'Anyway,' Frank said, 'you're safe now, that's all that matters. And I think we should—'

It should have been a tender moment, but Emily wasn't listening. She was too busy staring at the thin black lines appearing on the wall behind her, as if drawn in by an invisible Tony Hatch. Two uprights and a lintel, and a black dot where a doorknob would be.

'Frank,' she said, in a hoarse little voice.

Too late. A Door had opened in the wall, and Amelia Carrington stepped through it.

CHAPTER SIXTEEN

'Let's get this over with quickly, shall we?' Amelia said. 'Boys.'
It says a lot about Amelia Carrington's presence and force of personality that, until she drew attention to them, Frank hadn't noticed her two companions. They were, he guessed, trolls or ogres or something like that: anthropoid, like the better class of ape, but so drastically out of proportion that you'd never be tempted to think of them as human. Not even Walt Disney could have made them cuddly. The overall impression was that they'd been designed by someone who was very good at muscles but had never quite got the hang of heads. The spears and axes gripped in their enormous paws were easily the friendliest things about them. As far as menace went, however, they might as well have been little gambolling puppies, because they added nothing. Compared to Amelia they weren't scary, just quaint.

'Uncle Dennis,' she said. 'Sweet little office you've got here. Auntie Rosie.' She looked straight past Frank as though he wasn't there. 'Emily, dear. I hope you haven't been upsetting my dragon – it cost ever such a lot of money. I'm very disappointed, though, it really should have burned you to a crisp instead of just lying there sleeping like a teenager. I'm going to have to have a serious talk with the supplier about that.' She finally noticed Frank, advanced a step towards him and held out her hand. 'The

Door, please,' she said, and Frank gave it to her, because trying to resist would've been like arguing the toss with gravity.

'I shall deal with Erskine later,' Amelia said, more to herself than to them. 'It's a bad day when you can't even rely on your own dog. Fortunately, Lynford and Gervase here aren't dogs, they're nose-hairs, so I know I can rely on them implicitly.' She nodded her head, and the trolls picked up Dennis, his mother and Frank by their collars and held them a foot off the ground, presumably just to show that they could, since none of them struggled a bit. 'Emily, you're with me,' she said. 'Come along, now.'

So Emily followed her through the Door, and found herself once again in the cellar where she'd encountered the dragon's teeth. Someone had been round with a dustpan and brush and tidied them all away, though there were still a few patches of sawdust with a sort of brown mud seeping through. The trolls came after her, carrying their luggage, which they put down neatly against the wall. 'You're staying here,' Amelia said to them. 'Emily.' She opened the Door again, and Emily followed her through it into a place she didn't recognise. Not somewhere she'd be likely to have forgotten if she'd ever been there before.

It was daylight, but the sky was black and freckled with stars. She stood up to her ankles in fine grey dust, staring at a landscape of rocks and boulders, without the faintest suggestion of green. Directly overhead, huge and yet tiny at the same time, was the round shining blue-green Earth.

'Welcome,' Amelia said, 'to the Moon.'

Oh, Emily thought.

'Now, then,' Amelia went on. 'While I'm here with you, you're quite safe. I brought enough air and gravity with us for five minutes. After that, well—'

Emily listened hard, but there was no simultaneous translation. Amelia, it seemed, was one of those people who says exactly what they're thinking.

'One small step, dear,' she said. 'Which is about all you'll have time for. Oh, before I leave you.'

'Yes?'

'The Macpherson case. Did you ever get around to sending them a bill? Only I can't tell from the file. You always were rather sloppy about credit control, you know.'

'What? Oh, no, sorry. I was meaning to, but—'

A faint tongue-click. 'You never got round to it, quite. Never mind. Apart from that, I have to say, your files are in pretty good order – it won't take your replacement long to get the hang of them. All in all, I'm sorry to lose you, but there you go. Plenty more fish. I was hoping that Erskine could take over from you, but I think I'll have to get an ordinary human after all. Goodbye.'

'Wait,' Emily gasped, but Amelia had already stepped back through the Door and closed it. The thin black lines faded from the boulder in front of her, until it was hard to believe they'd ever been there.

Emily Spitzer, she said to herself, the first girl on the Moon.

Three minutes.

She spent one of them just standing perfectly still and shaking all over, partly because of the cold. The remaining two she wasted seeing if you really could make out the Great Wall of China like you're supposed to be able to. As luck would have it, it was night in Asia just then, and she eventually found what she thought was Japan, though at first she thought it was New Zealand. But if that was Japan, then the sort of semicircular cut-out must be the Yellow Sea, in which case, the Great Wall must be—

But then time ran out.

The trolls left, closing the Door behind them. It vanished, taking the light with it.

For a long time, nobody said anything. Then Mr Tanner's mother swore.

'Where are we?' Frank asked.

Dennis laughed. 'Here,' he said.

'Um. That's not terribly helpful.'

'No.'

'Is there a light-switch anywhere?'

Dennis sighed and muttered something, whereupon the room

filled with pale green light. 'Look around,' he said, 'see the sights. Only you'd better be quick about it, because I can't keep this up for more than ninety seconds.'

Frank saw a table, on which stood a plate of sandwiches and a plastic Coke bottle. That was it. No windows, no other furniture or contents of any kind. No light-switch. No door.

'All done?' The green light faded and died. 'Well,' Dennis went on, 'here we are. Bloody fucking Carpenters,' he added, managing to pack an extraordinary amount of feeling into seven syllables.

'Yes, but where—?'

'It's called a sealed room,' Frank heard Mr Tanner's mother say, and it worried him to hear how subdued she sounded. 'Which describes it pretty well. The plate and the bottle fill up by magic twice a day, so we won't starve to death. We're a long way underground, so the temperature stays more or less the same. I expect if you ask him nicely our Dennis can do the pretty green light from time to time, though since there's nothing to see I don't think there'd be much point. That's it, basically, until we grow old and die. Though,' she added, with a faint wobble in her voice, 'rumour has it that when you're in one of these places, real time doesn't actually pass, so you don't even grow old. Dennis's dad was stuck in one of these for a hundred and fifty years, till your dad let him out, bless him, and when he escaped he didn't look a day older—'

'Oh,' said Frank.

'But it's not all doom and gloom,' Dennis said, with a feather-edge of hysteria in his voice. 'I mean, we can play games to pass the time. How about I Spy? Something beginning with D.'

'Be quiet, Dennis, you're not helping.'

'Be quiet yourself.'

Stunned silence; then, eerie as a banshee's wail, the sound of muffled sobbing. Frank listened to it in fascinated horror, until he heard Dennis say, 'I'm sorry, Mum, I didn't mean—'

Sob, sob, sniffle; and Frank couldn't help wondering if this was the first time that Mr Tanner had ever heard his mother crying. There had been panic in his voice, the sort you'd expect from a man standing on a collapsing bridge. He tried to imagine what it must have been like, growing up with her for a mother. Of course, it would be different for goblins. But not all that different.

'Please don't cry,' he heard Dennis say. 'I didn't mean it, really. I shouldn't have answered you back, it's just that I'm all stressed out with this being-trapped-for-all eternity thing. I'd really like it if you could stop crying now. Please?'

Slowly, sniffs came to outnumber sobs, while Dennis rambled pitifully on through a repeating loop of explanation and apology; and Frank thought, *Trapped in here for ever, with them. Oh boy.*

''Salright,' Mr Tanner's mother snuffled eventually. 'Only you hurt me, our Dennis, you really did. And you were always such a good boy, when you were small. And what about poor little Paul Azog, who's going to look after him while I'm stuck in here? I'll never see my baby boy again, and it's all *his* fault—'

Pitch dark, but Frank just knew that two pairs of very sharp red eyes were fixed on his last known location. Trapped in here for ever with two goblins who hate me.

'Don't blame me,' he snapped, his patience fraying. 'You wanted to come, you volunteered. Bauxite, remember? All that money. I just wanted to rescue the girl I love, but you—'

'Oh be quiet,' said Mr Tanner's mother, and just because her voice was back to its usual peremptory bark Frank was filled with joy. 'Of course it's your fault, for playing around with the bloody Door in the first place. If it'd stayed in New Zealand, nice and safe, none of this would've happened.' Long sigh. 'Actually,' Mr Tanner's mother went on after a moment, 'it's as much my fault as anyone's. Should never have given the stupid thing to your dad in the first place. Of course, he wouldn't have lasted five minutes in the trade without it, and he most definitely wouldn't have got together with your mum. So I guess it serves me right. That's what you're both thinking, isn't it?'

Well, yes, Frank thought. 'No, of course not,' he said briskly. 'It's all that bloody Carrington woman's fault. She started it all, she was the one who tried to kill Emily and kidnapped my friend George and stole the Door and concocted this stupid bauxite thing. So why don't we all stop having a go at each other, get a grip and figure out how we're going to escape. Well? Come on, you two, you're supposed to know about this magic stuff, what's the drill? I mean, do we all say a spell or an incantation or something, or what?'

The long silence that followed was eventually broken by a sigh from Mr Tanner's mother. 'You tell him,' she said.

'Tell me what?'

He heard Dennis clear his throat. 'Yes, there is a way out of here,' Dennis said. 'Tried and tested, it's in all the books, comes up in the final exams most years.'

'Great. What is it?'

'The Portable Door,' Dennis replied. 'And if you haven't got it, then tough. And since there's only two of the bloody things in the world, and that woman's got both of them—'

'Three, actually.'

'—It really isn't a whole lot of . . . what did you just say?'

'Three,' Mr Tanner's mother repeated. 'The original, the new one she's got hold of somehow – Pereira's Last Theorem, presumably, that's how I made my back-up, just before I gave the original to Paul Carpenter.'

Frank opened his mouth but nothing came out; it was Dennis who rasped, '*Back-up?*'

'Yes, that's right. Hence three. She's got two, plus my one.'

'*Mother—*'

'Oh, don't go getting all excited, it's no bloody good to us in here, is it?' Mr Tanner's mother made a strange noise, somewhere between a sigh and a snort. 'What am I going to do with this rare and dangerous magical object, I thought; can't just leave it lying around, someone might pinch it and fuck up the fabric of space/time. No, I thought, I'd better put it somewhere nice and safe until I need it again. So what's what I did. More fool me, really.'

No need of troll's blood to know what Dennis was thinking. 'Somewhere nice and safe,' he said in a strained voice.

'That's right. Well, I could just imagine the fuss you'd have made if you happened to come across it in a drawer somewhere. So I put it in a safe deposit box, in a bank.'

'A bank.' Dennis made the words sound like the death warrant of the universe.

'That's right. The National Lombard in Fenchurch Street. Best security in London, they reckon. If only I'd gone with my instincts and shoved it down my front we'd be out of here by now and ripping bloody Carrington's lungs out with a bent spoon. All in all, it makes me wish I'd never set eyes on the stupid thing in the first place.'

It's not despair that does the real damage, it's hope. Dennis mumbled, 'Well, that's that, then.' His mother found a bit of wall and kicked it for a while, but only because it was there. Then she groped round for the plate of sandwiches and started to munch. 'Well, why not?' she said, with her mouth full. 'I always eat when I'm miserable. Salmon paste,' she added resentfully, after a brief bout of noisy spitting. 'Now that's just plain spiteful.'

After a while, Frank felt his way along the wall to a corner and sat down. Eternity, he thought. Eternity in the dark with the Tanners and salmon-paste sandwiches. Later on, he supposed, he could have a go at slitting his wrists with the Coke bottle or choking to death on sandwich crusts, but he was fairly sure he'd be on to a hiding to nothing. If Mr Tanner's mother was right and you couldn't grow old in here, more than likely you couldn't die, either. Or if he did succeed, what was the betting that Amelia Carrington would zoom in with the Door and bring him back to life? Someone capable of putting salmon paste in their eternally self-replenishing sandwiches wouldn't think twice about doing something like that.

So far he'd managed not to think about Emily, but he knew he couldn't dodge it for ever. Sooner or later he was going to have to face up to – well, what? He'd never see her again. By now, maybe, she was dead— His mind skidded off the word, like tyres on black ice. He'd taken more than his fair share of liberties with death lately; for George Sprague and his shareholders, to begin with, and then for her. Maybe somewhere in the valuable warehouse space behind his eyes he'd got into the way of thinking that it was somehow optional if you were clever enough, like capital gains tax. But now, here he was, for keeps, and if she wasn't dead already she soon would be (in ten minutes, an hour, sixty years, two hundred; what's time anyhow but calibrations on a clock face, artificial and arbitrary?); and that being so, how long would he sit here in the dark before it no longer mattered?

Really don't want to start thinking about that. Frank dragged his mind away, but there wasn't really anything else to think about; nothing that mattered, anyhow. All that was left inside his head was superseded trivia. What's the capital of Paraguay? How does that song go? When was the last time an Australian won Wimbledon? Whatever happened to poor old George? And how did the Door come to be in Emily's pocket when she was stuck in here with the dragon's-teeth people?

Oink, he thought.

Frank held perfectly still and, for some reason, listened. Somewhere in the dark, Dennis Tanner was having a sneezing fit and his mother was eating. Very soft noises, you could easily go mad listening to them.

'Excuse me,' he said.

No reply, so he said it again. 'Excuse me?'

Nothing, apart from Dennis Tanner snuffling through his blocked nose. For some reason it was a rather evocative, poignant sound; mournful, even. While my catarrh gently weeps, and all that.

'Excuse me.'

'What?' Mumbled through a mouthful of half-chewed bread.

'The spare Door,' he said. 'Did you just say you put it in a bank?'

'Mmm.'

'The National—'

'Lombard.'

'Fenchurch Street?'

'M.'

Suddenly, Frank's mind was buzzing. 'Isn't that the bank – oh hell, of course, you wouldn't know.' He didn't feel much like explaining; that would mean going back over ground he'd already covered, when he was bursting to press on with the tantalising new hypothesis growing in his mind. 'Emily had to go to a bank, I think it was in Fenchurch Street, to kill a dragon. When she'd killed it, she found it had burned all the money and papers and stuff, so that all that was left was a cardboard tube which turned out to be the Door. But she didn't know that at the time, of course, so she stuffed it in her pocket and forgot all about it, until that Colin Gomez bloke locked her in here with a load of magic warriors – something to do with teeth I couldn't follow when she told me—'

'Dragon's teeth?'

'I think so. Anyhow, she found the cardboard tube in her pocket with the Door inside it, and by then, of course, she knew what it was and used it to escape. She came to my place in New Zealand, and when she walked in through the wall I'd just found out that the Door wasn't in my jacket pocket. I assumed the Door she used to get away from the teeth people was my Door.' He paused for much-needed breath, then added, 'But what if it wasn't? What if it was this spare Door of yours, which you say you stored in a bank vault? Well?'

Long silence.

'I suppose it's possible,' Mr Tanner's mother said eventually. 'Just, even if you're right, I don't see how it helps matters. It just means your girlfriend nicked my Door. A bit of a liberty, but in the circumstances I don't think I'll be pressing charges.'

Frank squeezed his nails into his palm. She was missing the point, and just at that moment Frank Carpenter was spearheading the movement for the ethical treatment of points. 'If the Door she used wasn't *my* Door, then what happened to it?'

Another silence. Then Dennis said, 'You must've dropped it somewhere.'

Frank shook his head, a futile gesture in the pitch dark. 'Can't have,' he said. 'I was back home, in New Zealand, remember. So I must've had the Door with me when I got there, I must've used it to get home. And she – I mean, your mum – knows what my place is like. Small.'

'Scruffy. Strong smell of mould. You really ought—'

Reminder, if any was needed, that Mr Tanner's mother was as much mother as goblin. 'Well, quite,' Frank snapped. 'What I meant was, though, it's a small place. One room, basically. I'm trying to remember what I did, and I think I just took the Door down off the wall and lay down on the bed.'

'Fine, so that's what you did. And at some point it must have fallen out of your—'

'No,' Frank yelled. 'It couldn't have. Immediately I found it wasn't in my coat pocket, I searched the place from top to bottom. No sign. And it may be scruffy but it isn't cluttered. If the Door had fallen out onto the floor or down the back of a chair, I'd have found it. And I didn't.'

A yawn from Dennis Tanner. 'All right,' he said. 'So whatser-name's Door must've been your Door after all.'

'*No.*' Frank hadn't meant to shout. 'No, how could it have been? How could it have gone back into the past, into that bank vault, under that dragon, all on its bloody lonesome?'

'Magic?' suggested Mr Tanner weakly.

'That's what I assumed at the time,' Frank admitted. 'Weirdness. The kind of shit I've had to get used to putting up with, ever since I fell in with you people. But you're the magic expert. You tell me what sort of magic could've made that happen, and then I'll be convinced. Well?'

'Off the top of my head—'

'Hm?'

'Not possible,' Dennis conceded. 'But this is the Door we're talking about. Really, all we know about the perishing thing is that anything can happen. So—'

'Not possible,' Frank repeated firmly. 'In which case—' A huge thought collided with him. 'No, it couldn't be that, it'd be so—' He tore his jacket off his shoulders, laid it on the floor and started a fingertip search.

'What's he doing, our Dennis?'

'I don't know, it's dark in here.'

'*Christ!*'

Dead silence; then Mr Tanner's mother said, 'Now what's he doing?'

'Ask him yourself, you—'

Frank sat up on his knees, his fingers in his inside coat pocket, the tip of his forefinger thrust into a hole in the lining. He was still dizzy from the nasty bump on the head that the huge thought had given him; maybe that was what made him reluctant to take the next step. Or it could have been fear that he was wrong.

'Dennis.'

'*Shh!*'

Frank pulled himself together. A hole in the pocket of a lined jacket. He knew what happened in those circumstances. 'Anybody got a knife?' he asked.

'A what?'

'Forget it.' With his teeth, he bit into the jacket lining. Not nearly as straightforward as you'd think. Chewy old stuff, polyester. But, after he'd worried at it for a bit, he managed to make a hole big enough to get a finger in, and the rest was quite easy.

'He's tearing up his jacket.'

'Why's he doing that?'

Next, Frank inserted his hand, up to the wrist. Of course, it wouldn't be there. You get these inspirations when you're searching frantically for something; they fit all the known facts and for a while you're all excited and hopeful, but they always turn out to be—

He felt it; the pad on the tip of his left index finger brushed against cardboard.

He froze. Other things besides Door holders are made of cardboard, and he really, really didn't want to get his hopes up. In fact, wriggling his fingers deeper inside the lining and teasing out the cardboard tube was quite possibly the hardest thing he'd ever had to do.

'Got it,' he said.

'Now what's he—?'

'I've got it,' he said again. 'The Door. My Door. It was in my coat, all the time.'

If anybody had told Colin Gomez, a week earlier, that a day would come when he wouldn't feel like working, he'd have laughed out loud. Might as well predict that he'd stop breathing air. For Colin Gomez, the universe was composed of two elements, work and other stuff. He'd never cared much for the latter.

But, as he sat at his desk with a file open in front of him, the words of the letter (from Harlequin and James, a tempting compromise offer in the Northampton beanstalk dispute) seemed to repel him like reversed polarities, and however hard he tried, he couldn't bring himself to read them.

He gave up trying and instead made an attempt to analyse the problem.

A mind like Colin Gomez's can do practically anything with a bunch of facts. Accordingly, he quickly reached the conclusion that he'd done nothing wrong. True, he'd conspired against his senior partner, but he'd only done it for the good of the firm. Also true, he'd subsequently betrayed his fellow conspirators, but he'd only done that out of loyalty to his senior partner. So, he had nothing whatever to feel ashamed about, and plenty to be grateful for. He was still alive. He hadn't been slung out of the partnership. He'd even hedged his bets, in the light of the apparent conflict between his two entirely justified actions, by giving the spare Door to Emily and her young man so that they wouldn't have to spend the rest of their lives horribly backdated, trudging grimly through Beatlemania into the flares-and-sideburns era and then on through monetarism and the noxious Nineties just to get back to where they'd started from.

All bases covered, therefore. He should be feeling properly smug. But he wasn't.

Rationalising his misgivings into pulp should have restored his appetite for work, but when he returned to the letter from Harlequin and James, it continued to avoid him, the communications equivalent of walking straight past him in the street. He had an idea what that meant. Work was shunning him, because on some level somewhere he'd proved himself unworthy of it.

It was just possible, Colin Gomez conceded, that his self-justifications had been just a bit too glib. The death of Emily Spitzer, for example; on the face of it, no big deal. It's the role of management to play chess with the lives of employees, and from time to time in chess you have to sacrifice a pawn or two. There is a difference, however, between letting a pawn be taken and jumping up and down on it till it's reduced to a fine resin dust. Maybe Amelia Carrington had gone too far there, and maybe he shouldn't have been quite so ready to help her.

He thought about that, and dismissed it, remembering instead the first rule of management. Once you start thinking of employees as people, you're screwed.

The problem had to be, therefore, one of his two tactical betrayals. Unsettling: questions of right and wrong, ethical dilemmas, weren't usually a feature of his mental landscape, and detecting the presence of one was like coming across a stranded battleship in the middle of the desert. Still, if it was stopping him from working, it had to be dealt with, quickly.

Colin Gomez's first loyalty was to the firm. The firm and the senior partner were one, an indivisible whole. Therefore his first loyalty was to the senior partner. No question about that.

By the same token, the firm had a right to have the best possible senior partner; and, it went without saying, the best man for the job was himself. Therefore he owed it to the firm to become senior partner. No question about *that*, either. Accordingly (it amazed him, now he came to think about it, that there had ever been any doubt or uncertainty in his mind on this score) Amelia Carrington had to go. Right. Fine.

Except that she was so *scary*. And not scary in the irrational-fear sense, like being afraid of loud noises or cows or the cracks between paving stones. Being afraid of Amelia Carrington was supremely rational, because she killed people.

Awkward.

For a short while, Colin Gomez had allowed himself to believe that the Spitzer child and her curious boyfriend might be able to get rid of Amelia, thanks to the Portable Door. But then it had become apparent that Amelia was way ahead of all of them, and was using them to get her perfectly shaped hands on that remarkable artefact, and he'd quickly purged his mind of dangerous wishful thinking and realigned his loyalties; quickly, and perhaps just in time, or perhaps not. Being realistic, probably not. If he was honest with himself, he had to recognise that he was almost certainly somewhere on her things-to-do list, gradually working his way up to the surface, like a splinter of shrapnel in an old wound.

He sighed. Such a shame that Spitzer and her sidekick were so sadly ineffectual. He'd gambled on them by making the fool Erskine give them the spare Door, but that had been some time ago, and nothing seemed to have happened, so presumably they'd used the Door to run away, as any half-sensible person would. No use pinning any of his dwindling stock of hopes on *them*—

Lines appeared on the wall facing his desk. They could have been stray strands of dust-laden cobweb, except that they were too straight. He lifted his head and stared.

The Door opened.

Colin jumped up, quite an achievement for a man of his bulk. The lunatics, he thought; they can't come here, if she finds out—

But the woman who walked in through the wall wasn't Emily Spitzer, or Amelia Carrington; just some young blonde female. In Colin's world, young women under the age of thirty were divided into two types. The ones who wore suits and carried briefcases were junior staff. The rest were typists, receptionists and office juniors. Neither category was any use except for routine, trivial tasks, and – most definitely – neither category should have the use of rare and powerful magical objects like the Door. In which case—

'Are you Gomez?' said the inexplicable female.

'Yes. Who are—?'

Behind her, someone else. At least he recognised this one: Dennis Tanner, of all people. He'd known Dennis on and off for years, as a fellow professional, and of course he was the principal fall guy in the bauxite scheme. That didn't give him any right to come walking through Doors—

'Where's Emily Spitzer?'

A third voice. Behind Dennis Tanner (how many more of them were there going to be, for pity's sake?) the Carpenter boy. Colin opened and closed his mouth, but no words came out. This was all too much—

'He asked you a question,' said the inappropriate young woman. Colin ignored her. With all this going on, he couldn't be bothered to notice impertinent questions from the secretarial grade. But then she sank her unexpectedly strong fingers into three of his four chins, and he revised his priorities accordingly.

'Don't know,' he gurgled. 'Let go.'

'You're in trouble,' the annoying secretary said, with a disturbing grin. 'First, Carrington knows you gave the spare Door to Frank and Emily. Second, I'm going to throttle you unless you do as you're told. Third, Frank's going to smash your face in for trying to murder his girlfriend. Fourth, our Dennis doesn't like anybody in this firm very much. There's probably a fifth, but I don't think there's enough of you to go round.'

Then she let go, and Colin fell backwards, banging the base of his spine painfully on the edge of the desk. He tried to summon up enough magic for a fireball, but there was something about this terrifying, steel-fingered secretary that drained all the power out of him. He opened his mouth to whimper, but his throat was too badly mauled.

'On the other hand,' the secretary said, 'we could make you senior partner. Would you like that?'

The phone purred. Amelia picked it up.

'Oh, it's you,' she said, with a frown.

She wasn't ready to talk to Colin yet. Not because the actual words she'd be saying were in any way complicated; she was undecided between 'So long, then,' and 'Die, traitor', but it really didn't matter. It was just that she had other, more important things to do first: bauxite things, involving large sums of money.

'Sorry to bother you,' burbled the voice in her ear, 'but I was just wondering. How did you get rid of the Spitzer girl, in the end?'

She frowned. Colin shouldn't want to know that. 'Why?'

'Just interested.'

'Need to know,' Amelia replied shortly. 'Just take it from me, she's gone and she's never coming back. After all,' she added venomously, 'it'd take a Portable Door to save her now, and we've got both of them. Haven't we?'

'Yes, absolutely.'

'Excellent. What did you do with the spare, by the way?'

Click. Colin had hung up on her. Both of Amelia's precision-engineered eyebrows shot up in blank surprise. Then she quietly rearranged her Things To Do list, with Colin's name a bit nearer the top.

She looked back at her screen. Bauxite prices. If they went much lower, they'd come out in Australia. She extended a finger to press a key that would set in motion the necessary sales and purchases, and then she could—

Some invisible vandal was drawing thin black lines on her wall. Amelia lifted her hand away from the keyboard, scooping the elements of fire out of the air like a child clawing snow into a snowball, but before she could let fly, the Door opened.

'Hello,' said Emily Spitzer.

They found him in a poky little office in the annexe. He was stapling together bundles of computer printout, and sorting the bundles into neat piles. He seemed genuinely pleased to see them.

'I'm glad you're all right,' Frank said, surprised to hear himself say it. 'Only, I thought that when Amelia Carrington found out that you'd given me and Emily the other Door, she might have done something nasty to you.'

Erskine frowned. 'Well, I've been sentenced to death,' he said, 'but she was quite nice about it. She said I'd been incredibly stupid rather than actively treacherous, and of course I can see her point. It looks like we both misunderstood what she wanted me to do.'

'But you're still alive,' Frank pointed out.

'For now, yes. She explained about that. She said she's pretty busy right now, but she'll try and fit me in before half past five. So in the meantime I'm making myself useful, filing the Mortensen printouts. I felt it was the least I could do, since she'd been so reasonable about everything. Oh, hello, Mr Tanner, I didn't see you there. I don't suppose you remember me, I'm Ms Carrington's junior assistant. Was,' he added, with a flush of shame. 'I failed her, you see.'

Dennis said something under his breath, but Frank nudged him in the ribs. 'Erskine used to be Amelia's pet dog,' he explained. 'Man's best friend, and all that.'

Erskine nodded eagerly. 'She let me do all sorts of stuff for her,' he said. 'I fetched sticks and made the little rubber ball go squeak, and I always came back when she called, and lately I've been spying,' (he counted the activities off on his fingers as he named them) 'guarding, fetching and carrying, providing back-up, and we did some spider-killing and trollslaying too. It was all very exciting, but then I did the bad thing, so—' He shrugged. 'Anyway, I'm glad you managed to get back from the past all right. Are you going straight back to Salt Lake City?'

'Not quite yet,' Frank said evenly. 'Before I go, I wanted to ask you something.'

'Me? Gosh. Yes, go ahead, fire away.'

Frank drew in a deep breath. On the one hand, he'd never really liked dogs. But— 'I was wondering,' he said, 'which you preferred. Being a dog, I mean, or being a junior management trainee. Just curious, you know.'

Erskine's brows huddled tightly together. 'Actually,' he said, 'I think I preferred being a dog. I mean, all the stuff you humans do is tremendously interesting and exciting. But it's also very confusing, and I don't like that. It means I make mistakes and do bad things, which upsets me.' He simpered a little. 'Actually, I haven't been a very good human, and I reckon I was always a fairly good dog. It's best to stick to what you're good at, I think. So yes, a dog, definitely. Not,' he added with a shy smile, 'that it matters a lot now. I had my chance and—'

'The thing is,' Frank interrupted, 'fairly soon, Amelia Carrington isn't going to be the senior partner here any more. In fact, she may be, um, going away on a long journey, so I was thinking: instead of, well, dying, would you like it if Mr Tanner here turned you back into a dog? He says he knows how to do it, and it won't take a second.'

Erskine's nose twitched. 'Whose dog?'

'What?'

'Whose dog would I be?'

One of those questions that jumps out at you when you aren't expecting it. 'I don't know,' Frank answered. 'Your own dog, I guess.'

But Erskine shook his head. 'You can't be your own dog, it doesn't work like that. I'd have to be *somebody's*, or— No, I think I'd rather be dead than a stray, thanks all the same. But it was very kind of you, and Mr Tanner, too.' And, although he had no tail to wag, he sort of vibrated on the spot while smiling warmly.

Oh for pity's sake, Frank thought. 'You could be my dog,' he made himself say. 'If you wanted, I mean. Rather than being dead.'

'Your—?'

'After all,' Frank ground on, 'you were sort of my dog for a while, when you were trailing round after me, and you weren't that much of a nuisance, I suppose.'

'That's right. You called me Bobby.'

'Quite. And you did rescue Emily and me from the Sixties, so I guess I owe you one.'

'Yes, please.' A huge beam lit up Erskine's face; you could have read small print by it in the dark. 'At least, until Ms Carrington gets back from her long journey. I'd have to go back to being her dog then, of course, it'd only be right. But until then, that'd be super.'

'Fine,' Frank said, muffling a heavy-duty sigh. 'Right then. Dennis, if you wouldn't mind.'

Mr Tanner cleared his throat and lifted his left hand, but before he could go any further, Frank suddenly stopped him.

'Just one other point,' he said, trying to sound casual. 'When you were, um, spying on me.'

'Yes?'

'You're good at that sort of thing, are you? Finding people, sniffing things out. Good nose, I mean. A knack for following a trail.'

'Oh yes,' Erskine said, not without pride. 'I can find most things. I did lots of finding for Ms Carrington, even tricky finding, like across interdimensional barriers and stuff. So long as it's alive, I'm fairly sure I can track it down.'

'I see,' Frank said slowly. 'So if I asked you to find my friend George—'

'I'm sure I could. What does he smell like?'

'Only,' Frank said, 'Ms Carrington sent him somewhere, and I really ought to bring him back again. I don't think he's dead or anything like that, just – well, put somewhere. Is that the sort of thing—?'

'Piece of cake,' Erskine said cheerfully. 'Just give me a sock to sniff, or a shoe, or his favourite chair, and I'll have him for you in no time.'

'Excellent,' Frank said, with a certain degree of genuine authentic sincerity. 'In that case, Dennis, if you wouldn't mind.'

Dennis nodded. A moment later, there was a flash and a sort of sizzling noise—

'It's the same dog,' Dennis observed. 'The one that was following you about, the first time you came round my place.'

'That's him, yes.'

'And he's—' Dennis frowned. 'He's yours now, then.'

'Apparently.'

Dennis clicked his tongue. 'In that case,' he said, 'you should make him get off that chair. Once you start letting them sit on the furniture, they think they own the place.'

'Hello,' Emily said.

It only took Amelia a third of a second to recover. She closed her right hand hard on a fistful of air, squeezing out all the trace elements that wouldn't burn until she was left with a sort of fiery snowball. With a fast, easy movement she hurled it at Emily's face. For a split second, the girl's head was shrouded in roaring flames. But then they went out, leaving no mark or trace of any kind.

'That's not very friendly,' Emily said, taking a step forward. 'Anybody'd think you weren't pleased to see me.'

Amelia threw another fireball. Might as well not have bothered.

'For crying out loud,' Amelia screeched. 'Can't you stay dead for five minutes?'

Emily smiled. 'No,' she said. 'Bet you can, though. Like to find out?'

Amelia was groping under her desk for the panic button. 'Don't you dare threaten me,' she shouted. 'You're just an assistant, you ought to be terrif—' She stopped and froze, as a sensation she hadn't felt for years soaked into her. Fear, she remembered. She'd never liked it much. 'Why aren't you scared of me? Everybody's scared of me.'

'With good reason,' Emily replied placidly. 'Which is why you need to be put down, like a biting dog.' She came a step closer, and Amelia (much to her own surprise) retreated.

'You can't have come back,' Amelia said. 'I've got both Doors.'

'Indeed. Two out of three. Nearly the complete set, but not quite.'

'There's a *third*—'

'Yes.' Emily smiled. 'Thanks to the intelligence and foresight of Dennis Tanner's mother, a splendidly resourceful woman who you completely underestimated. Most people do,' she added. 'Anyway, that was your big mistake. Oh, and I wouldn't rely too much on anybody coming to rescue you. The alarm doesn't work. Well, it does, but Colin Gomez rerouted it to his office. So it's just you and me. Well, go on, then. Fireballs don't seem to do any good, but I'm sure you've got lots of other weapons up your sleeve. Let's see, how about Litvinov's Polecat? Or a nice consequence mine? Or dragons' teeth, even.'

Amelia stared at her warily. 'They won't work, will they? You wouldn't be suggesting them otherwise.'

'No.'

'You're bluffing.'

'Perhaps.'

Rather clumsily, Amelia tugged a few hairs from the top of her head, blew on them and threw them in the air. They changed into giant bats, which flew at Emily's face. She swatted them easily with the back of her hand. They hit the walls and folded up.

'You can't possibly do that,' Amelia protested.

'Can't I?' Emily smiled. 'I kill monsters for a living, remember. And I'm good at it. Maybe you should consider paying me more.'

The next twist of hair turned into three adult male lions. They took one look at Emily and scampered behind the desk, making whimpering noises.

'Try spiders,' Emily suggested. 'I never did like spiders.'

Amelia did just that. The spiders, *Atkinsonii*, each as big as a Great Dane, joined the lions behind the desk. There wasn't really enough room for all of them, but they managed to squeeze in together somehow.

'You can keep that up till you're as bald as a cue ball and it won't do you any good,' Emily said smugly. 'Look, why don't you give Litvinov's Polecat a try? It won't work, of course, but I do so enjoy all the pretty coloured lights. Or, tell you what, how about an inversion grenade? The worst that could happen is that it'd get you too, and you'd hardly feel a thing.'

Amelia had retreated so far that her back was to the wall. The feel of it seemed to calm her down, somehow. 'No, thanks,' she said. 'Your turn. If you're going to attack me, go ahead.'

'Splendid,' Emily said, and clapped her hands together. 'A little bit of backbone, that's what I like to see. Preferably sticking out through the side of your neck.' Faster than Amelia's eye could follow, Emily lunged forward, raised her right hand and slapped her across the face. Amelia howled, tried to retreat, tripped up over her own feet and fell on her bum. 'That *hurt*,' she squealed furiously.

'Yes. Serves you right. Come on, get up. We've got a lot to get through, and I haven't got all day.'

Amelia didn't move. 'There's something wrong about this,' she said quietly. 'This can't be happening. It's all an illusion, it must be.'

'Maybe,' Emily replied, and kicked Amelia hard on the shin. 'Real enough for you?'

Amelia replied with yet another fireball. It missed, bounced off a wall and hit one of the spiders. There was, interestingly, a distinct smell of burning hair.

'The joke is,' Emily said, 'you did it yourself.'

'What?'

'The way you killed me, the last time.' Emily clicked her tongue. 'It was a really neat idea, but it backfired, and now – well, I'm not afraid of you any more. And that's all it takes, you see.'

'Nonsense.' Amelia had gone from terrified to angry without even noticing. 'There's nothing unusual about the lunar atmosphere that could possibly— Or the reduced gravity,' she added, dismissing the thought as quickly as it came. 'I had Simon Aristides in Metaphysics run a thorough computer simulation, and there couldn't possibly be any side effects. You're bluffing again.'

Emily's face was as featureless as East Anglia. 'The Moon,' she said. 'Generally speaking, of course, you're right. But maybe there were other factors you didn't take into account. Oh, I don't know; something to do with the time of day, or perhaps there were significant beryllium deposits just under the surface of that particular crater. Easily overlooked, of course, but—'

'Balls.' Amelia was almost beside herself with fury. 'I checked Simon's results myself, otherwise I wouldn't have gone ahead. You can read his report for yourself if you like – it's just there, on the desk.'

'Is it?'

'Yes. Help yourself,' Amelia added sardonically. 'You won't find—'

'*Thank you.*' Emily swung round and pounced on the desk like a cat, sweeping papers aside until she found what she was looking for. 'That's marvellous,' she added, glancing at the front page before tucking it firmly down the front of her blouse. 'Exactly what we needed to know, and congratulations on being so wonderfully thorough. Oh yes, before I forget.'

Two long strides took her back to where Amelia was kneeling; then she shook herself, like a wet cat, and turned back into a goblin.

'Surprise,' she said.

Amelia stared at her for a moment, then shut her eyes tightly. 'Shit,' she said.

'Quite,' the goblin replied. 'It's like I keep telling our Dennis, never judge by appearances. You'd have thought he'd have got the message, what with being part goblin himself, though of course he can't do the shape-shifting, because of his human side. Ah well,' she added, and booted Amelia in the side of the head, sending her to sleep.

Once she'd made sure that Amelia was out cold, Mr Tanner's mother tied her up securely with a length of computer flex. Then she picked her up and swung her over her shoulder like a sack of coal, checked to make sure the report was still safely wedged down her front, and headed back to the Portable Door in the far wall. On its threshold she paused and turned towards the desk.

'It's all right,' she said. 'You can come out now.'

But the lions and the surviving spider didn't budge; in fact, one of the lions twitched an inch of exposed tail back out of sight behind the leg of the desk. Mr Tanner's mother grinned.

'Talk about a hair of the dog,' she said to herself, and closed the Door behind her.

CHAPTER SEVENTEEN

As one Door closes, another opens.

Thanks to Mr Aristides's superbly detailed report, the timing was flawless, as was the dead-reckoning navigation. Accordingly, Emily was still staring at Honshu under the misapprehension that it was New Zealand's North Island when she felt a tap on her shoulder.

'Hello,' Frank said.

'There you are,' she replied, when her heart had stopped trying to hammer its way out of her chest. 'I was wondering when you were going to show up.'

Frank's eyebrows disappeared into his fringe, like explorers setting off into the rainforest. 'Sorry if I kept you waiting,' he replied.

'Oh, that's all right. I knew you'd come.'

'Did you? I mean, that's very—'

Emily smiled at him. Behind her head, a million stars twinkled inquisitively. 'Pretty safe sort of belief, as such things go. I mean, if I'd been wrong, I wouldn't have had to suffer agonies of disappointment for very long.' She looked past him, at the mountain range that made up the far wall of the crater she stood in. The first girl on the Moon: well, fine. Strange new worlds are where you find them. 'Let's go home, please.'

Frank stood aside so that she could see the Door, set into a giant boulder. It was slightly ajar, and yellow light leaked through the opening. Emily took a step towards it, then stopped.

'There's just one thing,' she said.

Frank stopped dead in his tracks. 'What?'

'That long sort of lacy bit there,' she said, pointing at the Earth. 'That's New Zealand, right? Where you come from.'

He followed her pointing finger and shook his head. 'That's Sumatra, I think. Look, does it really matter? If it's all the same to you, I'd like to get back to a breathable atmosphere.'

Emily shrugged. 'Fine,' she said. 'I was just taking an interest.'

'Just to update you,' Frank said, as they passed through the Door together and came out in Emily's office in the Carringtons building. 'Rosie Tanner's got Amelia Carrington locked up in that doorless cellar place. Dennis Tanner's nipped out to find a chemist's; Rosie got a couple of nasty burns while she was sorting out Amelia, but apparently, since she's a goblin, a dab of Germoline and she'll be right as rain. Colin Gomez,' he went on, closing the Door and rolling it up, 'is staging a rather genteel palace coup, with the aim of getting himself crowned senior partner. Oh, and Erskine's all right. I made up a bed for him in the bottom drawer of a filing cabinet, with a couple of Amelia's cashmere sweaters to lie on. He's going to sniff out George Sprague for me once he's recovered from turning back into a dog again, so that's all right. I think that covers everything.'

'Rosie Tanner,' Emily said, frowning as she sat down in her old, familiar chair. 'Oh, right, the goblin woman.' Slight double take. '*She* managed to get the better of Amelia Carrington? How the hell did she manage that?'

'You don't want to know,' Frank said. 'But it worked. Amelia's safely locked up, and we got the coordinates so I could come and fetch you. Oh, and you owe her a favour.'

Her old familiar chair. When you live in an office (she had a flat, a tiny little thing huddled in the shadow of an enormous mortgage, like a cottage at the foot of Vesuvius, but it was just somewhere she went to sleep), your chair gradually becomes the centre of the universe. It's your triangulation point, where you measure all your distances from. It's where you're to be found, unless you have legitimate business that calls you away. Needless to say, it reflects your status as accurately as the shoulders of a soldier's uniform. Emily's chair swivelled and sort of reclined, though you dared not push your luck unless you really wanted to visit the floor, but it was old and tired, having been handed (so to speak) down in a career of inverse promotions: full equity partner to associate partner to senior assistant to junior assistant, and when Emily, if Emily ever got promoted, it'd descend another rung of the ladder and support the weight of a *junior* junior assistant, until it finally wore out completely and went in the skip. The thing about office chairs is, though, that the more beat-up and rickety they become, the more comfortable they grow and the harder they are to leave. The seat moulds itself to the bum, but the brain and the heart mould themselves to the chair, until it's not quite clear where one ends and the others begin—

'Yes,' Emily said gravely, 'I guess I do. What did she have in mind?'

'Well,' said Frank.

The dragon stirred.

Fluctuations in the dream carried it, like a leaf in a storm. Gusts of memory swept it back into the shared past of all dragonkind, eddies sent it spiralling sideways into the minds of other dragons as they brooded, sulked, hoped, loved and regretted eating cheese. A swirl of vicarious pleasure lifted it up, but then it stalled and felt itself hang in empty air as it registered an unfamiliar presence.

You again, it said.

Me again, replied the human female.

The dragon registered her properly. Emily Spitzer, dragon-slayer; exponent of a necessary function, since dragons hardly ever die of old age or disease, but unless dragons die the dream would be a straight line rather than a circle. *Hello, Emily Spitzer. Have you come to kill me now?*

Sort of, she replied.

The dream filled with strange shapes and rare colours. *Sort of*, the dragon repeated.

Look, said Emily Spitzer, about this prophecy.

Oh yes.

You know more about it than I do, obviously, and Amelia Carrington clearly believed in it, or she wouldn't have gone to all that trouble to get rid of me—

Have you been got rid of, then?

Yes, but I came back. Just *listen* for a moment, will you? The prophecy says that when we fight, I'll win, okay?

Yes. I can show you the place in the dream, if it'd help.

No, really, that's fine. Only, I was thinking. I don't really want to kill you, you see.

Oh. That would be – inconvenient.

The dream flared orange with Emily's irritation. Well, tough. Look, this dream of yours. It's not, well, carved in stone, is it?

Of course not. It exists within the neural pathways of all dragons, comprised of regulated electrical discharges travelling along synaptic—

Oh, be quiet. What I mean is, if we wanted to, we could change it. Right?

Deep, rather revolting green. *Well, in theory—*

Excellent. So, let's fight.

Now you're talking. Just give me a second to wake up, and I'll be ready for you.

No (said Emily Spitzer, the dragonslayer), don't do that. Just tell me if I'm on the right lines, okay? The prophecy says when we fight – fight meaning 'engage in conflict', yes?

I suppose so, dreamt the dragon grudgingly.

Engage in conflict, right. And in this context, presumably, the ownership of great wealth has to be at stake, yes?

It's what we're all about, yes. Otherwise, how do you keep score?

Exactly (thought Emily Spitzer). Keeping score. Now, I'd like you to concentrate, please.

The dragon concentrated; and into the dream came a pair of wooden blocks with holes drilled in them, two matchsticks and a pile of cardboard rectangles with pictures printed on them.

Ready to fight?

Always.

Fine. Now then, the name of the game is cribbage—

'Just to clarify,' Dennis Tanner said, after a long silence. 'You won the new Wayatunga bauxite strike off Amelia Carrington's super-dragon in a game of *cards*?'

Emily was too tired to speak, so she nodded.

'Oh well,' Dennis said. 'It's an approach, I guess. Very eco-friendly and non-violent of you, and you'll probably be getting Christmas cards from Bob Geldof and David Cameron. So,' he added wistfully, 'what're you planning on doing with it, now you've—'

'Already done.' Emily yawned. 'Gave it to your mum. Small token of appreciation.'

'Oh.' Dennis's face registered no visible emotion whatsoever. 'How about the dragon?' he went on (and, tired as she was, Emily recognised a changed subject when she heard one). 'Only it's not really such a good idea to leave something like that just wandering about. You know better than anybody what they're capable of—'

Emily's next yawn registered on seismic instruments all over the world. 'Gone to Vegas,' she mumbled. 'It reckons gambling's the most fun it's had in years and what's the point of having money if you don't spend it? Said something about putting together a dream syndicate of all dragons everywhere. Poor buggers,' she added, 'they'll end up losing the scales off their backs. Still, better than—' Her eyelids drooped, and she fell asleep.

'She'll be all right,' Dennis said, as Frank half-rose from his chair. 'Just tired out, that's all. I mean, what with all the dying she's been doing lately, it's hardly surprising.' He fell silent and sat quietly for a while, staring down at his hands.

Frank waited for a bit, then said, 'The Carrington woman.'

'Locked up in the cellars. Won't be going anywhere in a hurry.'

'Yes, but we can't just leave her there.'

Dennis looked up. 'Yes, we bloody well can. Your girlfriend there may suddenly have turned into a dragon-hugger, but I prefer my pest control traditional, thanks all the same.'

Frank frowned. 'Isn't Amelia Carrington your god-daughter or something?'

'What's that got to do with anything?'

'I just thought—' Frank shrugged. 'Forget it, then. But you can't leave her down there. I've been there, remember. So have you.'

'Fine.' Dennis grinned. 'We'll kill her, then.'

'You can't do—'

'Why not? We don't need her for anything any more. If you don't want anything to do with it, I expect Colin Gomez'll help us out. Jump at the chance, probably.'

Frank shook his head; then a smile crept over his face. 'No,' he said. 'I've got a better idea.'

Amelia Carrington woke up.

Her first reaction was to grab for a handful of fire, just in case the goblin woman was— No, belay that. She wasn't in her office any more. In fact, she wasn't in a building of any sort. She was lying on grass – wet grass, yetch – under a cloudless blue sky.

Does not compute. She sat up, and in doing so she caught sight of her feet. They were bare, and stuck out from under the hem of a flowing, tie-dyed cheesecloth skirt.

A horrible thought struck her. They couldn't have, she thought. The *bastards!*

It was at that point that she became aware that she was not alone. Lying grouped around her on the grass were a number of young men and women. The girls wore kaftans, headbands and big clunky beads, the boys had long hair, beards, and, in the most extreme cases, round rimless spectacles. One of them was strumming a guitar.

The funny smell, Amelia realised later, was patchouli oil.

They couldn't have, she thought. But they could, and they had. Bastards!

Rage flooded into her, and she clenched both hands in the air. True, her real enemies were presumably decades away by now, leaving her Crusoe-stranded in the most unforgivingly alien environment known to mankind, so she couldn't very well firebomb them. But the rage was so strong that it had to be vented somehow. She needed to firebomb *somebody*, or she'd burst.

She looked round and selected two of the hippies at random. After all, she told herself as she squeezed the inert elements out between her fingers, who the hell would miss them?

A male exhibit lifted his head and stared blearily at her. He'd do for one target. Him and that bloody guitarist. She gave the fireballs in her hands a final squeeze for luck, took careful aim and let fly—

(Later, Amelia figured out that someone – Uncle Dennis, most likely, or possibly Colin Gomez – must've put a strong dampening field on her, almost entirely neutralising her magical abilities.)

—releasing two glowing blobs of plasma that drifted slowly up in the air, hung a yard or so off the ground and then popped softly, briefly filling the air with brightly coloured sparks. They swirled for a second or two in the vestigial breeze, glittered, faded and went out.

The bleary-eyed man shook his head, closed his eyes and lay down again, while a girl next to him giggled and said, 'Hey, far out. Can you do that again?'

(In time, of course, the field began to wear off, so that by 1979 Amelia was able to bend spoons, materialise white rabbits out of hats and do physically impossible things with playing cards, coins and bits of string. By then, however, she was quite broken in mind and spirit, and had long since given up any thought of taking revenge or trying to regain her lost power. She was last heard of in 2003, standing unsuccessfully as a Liberal Democrat in a council by-election somewhere in Essex.)

'Oh, go away,' she said, and burst into tears.

*

What else? Oh yes—

'And therefore,' said Colin Gomez, 'in consideration of your dedication and hard work on behalf of the firm over the last three years—'

'Four, actually.' Emily, who'd been tapping her foot impatiently, smiled. 'And while I think of it, troll's blood.'

'I beg your pardon?'

'I absorbed some, a while back. So I know what you're really thinking.'

Mr Gomez went quite pale. 'Oh,' he said. 'Well. Look, do you want to be a partner or not?'

Emily's smile broadened, until it bore a distinct resemblance to the Tanner family grin. 'Yes, please,' she said.

'Fine. In that case, welcome to the—'

'And the same to you too, with knobs on.' Emily closed her eyes, just briefly, then opened them again. 'So that's it, is it? I'm a partner.'

'Yes.'

'Ah.' She frowned. 'You know, I always thought it'd feel different, somehow. I don't know, something like the troll's blood thing. I expected the world would change.'

'I see,' Mr Gomez said carefully. 'Has it?'

'No. But I suppose I had to get here to find that out, didn't I?' Emily shook her head. 'Oh well,' she said. 'Another ambition realised ahead of schedule. True love *and* a partnership. That just leaves the rest of my life to fill with something. Maybe I can take up gardening.'

Mr Gomez was looking at her anxiously, as if waiting for her to pounce. 'Really?' he said at last. 'Troll's blood?'

'Mphm. That troll you sent me to kill. Long story.'

'So you can hear—'

'Yes.'

Mr Gomez nodded slowly four times. Then he reached for a piece of paper and took a pen from his top pocket.

'It's all right,' Emily said, with a sort of exasperated sigh. 'I'm not stopping. I resign.'

The pen made a faint clunking noise as it fell to the desktop. 'You're what?'

'I quit.' Big smile, not even faint traces of a grin in it. 'I wanted to be made a partner, just because – well, because it was there, I guess. But actually *being* one—' She pursed her lips to hold in a giggle. 'No offence,' she said, 'but I don't think so.'

'Oh.' Mr Gomez gazed at her as though she'd suddenly started speaking in tongues. 'Why ever not?'

'Because,' Emily replied sweetly, 'worst-case scenario, I'd turn into Amelia Carrington. Best-case scenario, I'd turn into you.'

'Thank—'

'And in either case,' she went on, 'I think I'd rather be eaten alive by rats. But that's just me, I'm afraid. Not a team player, after all. No, I'm thinking of turning freelance, and anyhow, I've gone off killing dragons. Not that there'll be much call for that soon, if they've really discovered gambling. I have an idea that a few weeks of Internet blackjack will do what generations of hairy men with swords could never quite manage, and there's Progress for you. Anyway, I'm out of here.' She sighed, and gave Mr Gomez a friendly smile. 'Before I go, I'd like to say how much I've enjoyed working with you.'

'Ah, well, and the same—'

'But I promised my mother I'd tell the truth, so I can't. Never mind.' Emily stood up. 'I'd better go,' she said, 'Frank's waiting for me in reception – we're going to find his Mr Sprague and then have lunch. You know, I'm quite sure you'll make a really good senior partner, Mr Gomez. You've got all Amelia Carrington's stupidity and none of her intelligence. I won't bother clearing my desk,' she added. 'There's nothing there I actually want any more. Goodbye.'

She was halfway to the door when Colin said, 'I'm sorry you're leaving. We shall miss you.'

The odd thing was that he said it twice, simultaneously; or at least, that wa how Emily heard it. She stopped and looked back. 'Really?'

'Oh yes,' Colin said. He went on, 'You were always a pleasure to work with and highly conscientious, and I think you'd have had a great future in the profession.' Or rather, he went on, 'You earned us a shitload of money, did all the rotten jobs and never seemed to notice that we were paying you peanuts. Still, you're only a woman, you'd have left sooner or later to have babies, and I can replace you like *that*, so what the hell.'

Emily nodded gravely. 'Thank you,' she said, and left the room.

It took Erskine less than ten minutes to find Mr Sprague. He was in a matchbox in a file in a locked filing cabinet in the junk-furniture collection in the third floor back office, where all the old manual typewriters went to die. Fortunately, Emily knew how to unpack him, and soon she had him back to his normal size without even waking him up.

'Can you make him a couple of inches taller?' Frank asked. 'Only he's been put through a nasty ordeal on my account and I think he deserves some sort of thank-you present.'

'Could do,' Emily replied. 'But then his trousers'll all be too short.'

Frank shrugged. 'I guess,' he said.

They took him back to his office through the Door and left him in his chair, still peacefully sleeping, while Erskine skipped round their heels, wagging his tail. Then they went back through the wall—

'Where are we?' Emily asked.

The Door had opened out of the side of a rusty corrugated-iron shack under a clear blue sky. An empty road stretched out as far as the eye could see in both directions, and in the distance a purple haze masked the peaks of improbably beautiful mountains.

'My favourite place to eat,' Frank said. 'I can particularly recommend the egg and bacon rolls. Actually, that's all there is. Come on.'

They walked round to the front of the shack, where a middle-aged man in a filthy white apron was prodding slices of bacon on a greasy range. 'G'day, Frank,' he said. 'You've been a stranger. Usual?'

Frank nodded. 'And two teas.'

'Coming up.' The man noticed Emily and frowned slightly. 'Who's the—?'

'Her name's Emily. She's English.'

'Ah.'

They took their rolls and their styrofoam cups over to the roadside, where there was a handy anthill to sit on. Far away in the distance, a huge, long lorry shimmered into view through the heat haze. 'Actually,' Frank said, 'you've been here before.'

Emily looked blank. 'Have I?'

Frank nodded and pointed at the ground. 'Down there somewhere. We're directly above the new Wayatumba bauxite strike; you know, the one you gave to Mr Tanner's mum.' He sighed. 'Won't be long now before all this is spoil heaps and loading yards,' he said. 'I thought you might like to see it before it gets trashed. I used to come here a lot at one time.'

Emily stared at him. 'Really? Why?'

'Because, if I set out really early in the morning, I could walk here from home by noon. It was something to do, and it got me out of the house. I didn't like it at home much, you see.' Suddenly he grinned. 'On balance, I think it'll be a good thing,' he said, 'talking to you. It won't matter that I can't find the right words to explain what I mean. You'll know anyway.'

Emily nodded slowly and cleared her mouth of a rather chewy bit of fried egg. 'You think so?' she said. 'Someone else might reckon it'd make any sort of relationship impossible.'

'I've been thinking about that,' Frank said. 'But what the hell. If ever I feel the need to lie to you, I can always put it in writing.'

'But then I'd know—'

He shrugged. 'Quite,' he said. 'Saves time, that's all.' He broke off a corner of his roll and threw it to Erskine, who sniffed at it and backed away. 'Really,' he said, 'I only brought you here because it's lunchtime, and I *like* Herman's egg and bacon rolls. Or I used to, anyway,' he added, as Erskine scuffed up a small hole with his paws and buried the roll-fragment in it. 'Also, there's this general sense I've got of being at the beginning of the rest of our lives. Seemed as good a place to start as any. Did you mean what you said earlier, by the way? About going freelance, I mean.'

Emily nodded absently. 'Probably. I don't want to think about work just now. Let's go somewhere with a beach, and have an ice cream.'

'Good idea,' Frank said. 'I'll just get the—'

Door, he was about to say, but as he opened his mouth he caught sight of two figures walking along the road. There was nothing particularly unusual about them, if you ignored context. One of them was a boy, about fifteen: tall, fair, thin, unfinished-looking, with a small nose and big ears. The other was a girl, about the same age but short and thin, with dark hair. Both of them were in some kind of school uniform, with their shirt-tails hanging out and their ties wrenched sideways, and the girl was reaming dirt from under her fingernails with the cap of a biro. She looked up, caught his eye and said, 'Hello, Frank.'

He stared back at her for three seconds, vaguely aware of Emily's voice saying, 'Somebody you know?' The boy looked at him too, and smiled vaguely.

'It's you,' Frank said.

'Hello, Frank,' the boy replied. 'And this must be Emily. Hello.'

For some reason, that made Emily feel nervous. 'Frank,' she said, 'who are—?'

'What?' Frank seemed to wake up. 'Oh, right, yes. This is Emily Spitzer, we're—' He paused, and went slightly pink. 'Emily,' he went on, 'meet Paul and Sophie Carpenter. My mum and dad.'

At that moment, for some reason, it occurred to Emily to look round. She saw the egg-and-bacon-roll man, Herman or whatever his name was, apparently frozen in the act of breaking an egg into his frying pan. A few feet away from him, a butterfly hung motionless in the still air.

'So,' Frank said, and he felt as though he was trying to hammer the words into a crack in solid rock with his bare hands. 'What are you two doing here?'

The girl scowled; not at anything in particular, just a generalised expression of dissatisfaction. 'We came to see you,' the boy said. 'How's everything, by the way?'

'Oh, fine.'

'You've found true love, then.'

'Yup.'

'That's good. Your mother was saying only the other day, it's about time young Frank found true—'

'You've got to give it back,' the girl interrupted.

Before he said 'Give what back?' Frank already knew the answer.

'The Portable Door, of course,' the girl said. 'You shouldn't have taken it. It's dangerous.'

'It's our fault, really,' the boy said. 'We shouldn't have left it behind, only we didn't have a choice. When we went away, you see, it closed, and we were on the other side . . . Anyhow, we're not blaming you. But your mother's right, I'm afraid. You can't keep it.'

'Oh,' Frank said, as Emily hissed loudly, 'That's your *mother*?'

'Yes,' the girl said, and if there was a hint of he's-mine-you-can't-have-him in her voice, Emily could only deduce it in the normal way, rather than hear the actual words. Whoever or whatever these two were, troll's blood didn't seem to have any effect. Be that as it might, she thought. Although it was utterly true that she didn't just want Frank because of the Door and its endless possibilities, there was no way she was going to let him give it up without a fight. She took a deep breath, looked the girl squarely in the eye and said—

(Later, of course, she kept on asking herself, over and over again, *why?* Just kidding herself, of course. She knew perfectly well why.)

'Go on, Frank,' she said. 'You'd better do as they say.'

Frank shrugged. 'Oh, all right, then,' he said, and he held out the little cardboard tube. The girl snatched it out of his hand, and it went somewhere.

'Thanks, son,' the boy said, with maybe a trace of guilt in his voice. 'Sorry. But you know it makes—'

'And the other one,' the girl interrupted.

Frank nodded, dug in his jacket pocket and produced another cardboard tube. The girl took that one as well. This time Emily watched closely, but she still failed to see where it went.

'You'll be better off without it, I promise you,' the boy went on sadly. 'I know I am. After all – how long's it been now? Oh, yes, silly question, but you know what I mean. It's been ages, and I haven't missed it at all. Never given it a second thought, in fact,' he added; and although the troll's blood wasn't working, Emily didn't need it to hear what he really wanted to say. 'And anyway, you're young, you've got your whole life in front—'

'*And* the other one.'

This time, Frank couldn't help pulling a face. 'Oh for pity's sake, Mum—'

'Give it here. Now.'

Very slowly and reluctantly, Frank knelt down, rolled up his trouser leg and removed a cardboard tube from inside his left sock. He parted with it so reluctantly that Emily reckoned it must have taken the skin off his fingertips. 'There,' he said. 'That's the lot. Promise.'

The girl nodded grimly; the boy gave Frank a faint, weak smile, as if to say *I'm proud of you, son, but we both know what my opinion's worth*. The girl turned her head away and said, 'Come on, Paul, we've got a lot to do. Goodbye, Frank, look after yourself.' Then she gave Emily a long stare, took three paces forward and vanished. A moment later, her voice called out, 'Here, boy'; and Erskine, who'd been curled up fast asleep beside the egg-and-bacon-roll-man's shack, jumped up, sniffed the air, trotted after her with his tail wagging and disappeared too.

'Bye, Mum,' Frank said.

The boy looked as though he was about to follow; then he

stopped and turned back. 'You could always come with us, you know. I mean, yes, we've had our differences, and—'

'Thanks, Dad. But no.'

'Oh.' A tiny pinpoint of despair, small and bright as a distant star, glowed briefly in the boy's eyes. Then he shrugged. 'Well,' he said, 'if ever you change your mind, you know where we are.' Frank nodded, said nothing; the boy forced his mouth into a two-dimensional smile, then turned and looked at Emily. 'Look after him for me, will you? It's his mother, you see, they never really—' He shrugged, turned away, turned back again. 'Nearly forgot,' he said. 'There's forty million US dollars in your name in the First State Bank of Wisconsin. Just a little something left over from the old days, no use to me any more, but for God's sake don't tell your mum, all right?'

Frank nodded. 'Thanks, Dad.'

'That's all right. Sorry about the Doors.'

'Forget it. Bye, Dad.'

'Bye, Frank,' the boy said; then he too walked three paces forward and disappeared.

Behind her, Emily heard the sizzle of an egg landing in hot oil. She looked at Frank, who shook his head slowly.

'My parents,' he said. 'Sorry about that.'

'It's all right, I understand, I know you must be feeling really upset right now but later we'll talk about it and maybe it won't seem so bad,' was what Emily fully intended to say. But there was some sort of glitch in the translation, and what actually came out of her mouth was, 'Forty million *doll*—'

'Yup,' Frank said, then added, 'Better than a kick in the head, I guess.' Then, quite suddenly, he smiled broadly. '*Considerably* better than a kick in the head, actually.'

'No Door, though,' Emily pointed out.

'True.' Frank was grinning so broadly, it was a wonder that his head didn't fall off. 'But what the hell. Emily.'

'Yes?'

'What would you do if you suddenly came into forty million dollars?'

The Better Mousetrap • 345

Emily thought for a moment. 'I think I'd find a dragon who had eighty million dollars and challenge it to a game of gin rummy,' she said.'And then I'd find another dragon with two hundred and forty million and see if it fancied playing whist. And then I'd find two more dragons worth a total of four hundred and eighty million and – you *do* know how to play bridge, don't you?'

Frank smiled at her. With or without a Door he had only one life, and without a purpose, existence is meaningless. But with a purpose—

'No,' he said. 'But I'm sure you can teach me.'

extras

about the author

Tom Holt was born in London in 1961. At Oxford he studied bar billiards, ancient Greek agriculture and the care and feeding of small, temperamental Japanese motorcycle engines; interests which led him, perhaps inevitably, to qualify as a solicitor and emigrate to Somerset, where he specialised in death and taxes for seven years before going straight in 1995. Now a full-time writer, he lives in Chard, Somerset, with his wife, one daughter and the unmistakable scent of blood, wafting in on the breeze from the local meat-packing plant.

For even more madness and TOM-foolery go to www.tom-holt.com

Find out more about Tom Holt and other Orbit authors by registering for the monthly newsletter at www.orbitbooks.net

if you enjoyed

THE BETTER MOUSETRAP

look out for

THE ACCIDENTAL SORCERER

Rogue Agent: Book One

by

K. E. Mills

The entrance to Stuttley's Superior Staff factory, Ottosland's premier staff manufacturer, was guarded by a glass-fronted booth and blocked by a red and blue boom gate. Inside the booth slumped a dyspeptic-looking security guard, dressed in a rumpled green and orange Stuttley's uniform. It didn't suit him. An ash-tipped cigarette drooped from the corner of his mouth and the half-eaten sardine sandwich in his hand leaked tomato sauce onto the floor. He was reading a crumpled, food-stained copy of the previous day's *Ottosland Times*.

After several long moments of not being noticed, Gerald fished out his official identification and pressed it flat to the window, right in front of the guard's face.

"Gerald Dunwoody. Department of Thaumaturgy. I'm here for a snap inspection."

The guard didn't look up. "Izzat right? Nobody tole me."

"Well, no," said Gerald, after another moment. "That's why we call it a 'snap inspection'. On account of it being a surprise."

Reluctantly the guard lifted his rheumy gaze. "Ha ha. Sir."

Gerald smiled around gritted teeth. *It's a job, it's a job, and I'm lucky to have it.* "I understand Stuttley's production foreman is a Mister Harold Stuttley?"

"That's right," said the guard. His attention drifted back to the paper. "He's the owner's cousin. Mr Horace Stuttley's an old man now, don't hardly see him round here no more. Not since his little bit of trouble."

"Really? I'm sorry to hear it." The guard sniffed, inhaled on his cigarette and expelled the smoke in a disinterested cloud. Gerald resisted the urge to bang his head on the glass between them. "So where would I find Foreman Stuttley?"

"Search me," said the guard, shrugging. "On the factory floor, most like. They're doing a run of First Grade staffs today, if memory serves."

Gerald frowned. First Grade staffs were notoriously difficult to forge. Get the etheretic balances wrong in the split-second of alchemical transformation and what you were looking at afterwards, basically, was a huge smoking hole in the ground. And if this guard was any indication, standards at Stuttley's had slipped of late. He rapped his knuckles on the glass.

"I wish to see Harold Stuttley right now, please," he said, briskly official. "According to Department records this operation hasn't returned its signed and witnessed safety statements for two months. I'm afraid that's a clear breach of regulations. There'll be no First Grade staffs rolling off the production line today or any other day unless I'm fully satisfied that all proper precautions and procedures have been observed."

Sighing, the guard put down his soggy sandwich, stubbed out his cigarette, wiped his hands on his trousers and stood. "All right, sir. If you say so."

There was a battered black telephone on the wall of the security booth. The guard dialled a four-digit number, receiver pressed to his ear, and waited. Waited some more. Dragged his sleeve across his moist nose, still waiting, then hung up with an exclamation of disgust. "No answer. Nobody there to hear it, or the bloody thing's on the blink again. Take your pick."

"I'd rather see Harold Stuttley."

The guard heaved another lugubrious sigh. "Right you are, then. Follow me."

Gerald followed, starting to feel a little dyspeptic himself. Honestly, these people! What kind of a business were they running? Security phones that didn't work, essential paperwork that wasn't completed. Didn't they realise they were playing with fire? Even the plainest Third Grade staff was capable of inflicting damage if it wasn't handled carefully in the production phase. Complacency, that was the trouble. Clearly Harold Stuttley had let the prestige and success of his family's world-famous business go to his head. Just because every wizard who was any wizard and could afford the exorbitant price tag wouldn't be caught dead without his Stuttley Staff (patented, copyrighted and limited edition) as part of his sartorial ensemble was no excuse to let safety standards slide.

Bloody hell, he thought, mildly appalled. *Somebody save me. I'm thinking like a civil servant . . .*

The unenthusiastic security guard was leading him down a tree-lined driveway towards a distant high brick wall with a red door in it. The door's paint was cracked and peeling. Above and behind the wall could be seen the slate-grey factory roof, with its chimney stacks belching pale puce smoke. A flock of pigeons wheeling through the blue sky plunged into the coloured effluvium and abruptly turned bright green.

Damn. Obviously Stuttley's thaumaturgical filtering system was on the blink: code violation number two. The unharmed birds flapped away, fading back to white even as he watched, but that wasn't the point. All thaumaturgical by-products were subject to strict legislation. Temporary colour changes were one thing. But what if the next violation resulted in a temporal dislocation? Or a quantifiable matter redistribution? Or worse? There'd be hell to pay. People might get hurt. What was Stuttley's playing at?

Even as he wondered, he felt a shiver like the touch of a thousand spider feet skitter across his skin. The mellow morning was suddenly charged with menace, strobed with shadows.

"Did you feel that?" he asked the guard.

"They don't pay me to feel things, sir," the guard replied over his shoulder.

A sense of unease, like a tiny butterfly, fluttered in the pit of Gerald's stomach. He glanced up, but the sky was still blue and the sun was still shining and birds continued to warble in the trees.

"No. Of course they don't," he replied, and shook his head. It was nothing. Just his stupid over-active imagination getting out of hand again. If he could he'd have it surgically removed. It certainly hadn't done him any favours to date.

He glanced in passing at the nearest tree with its burden of trilling birds, but he couldn't see Reg amongst them. Of course he wouldn't, not if she didn't want to be seen. After yesterday morning's lively discussion about his apparent lack of ambition she'd taken herself off in a huff of ruffled feathers and a cloud of curses and he hadn't laid eyes on her since.

Not that he was worried. This wasn't the first hissy fit she'd thrown and it wouldn't be the last. She'd come back when it suited her. She always did. She just liked to make him squirm.

Well, he wasn't going to. Not this time. No, nor apologise either. For once in her ensorcelled life she was going to admit to being wrong, and that was that. He wasn't unambitious. He just knew his limitations.

Three paces ahead of him the guard stopped at the red door, unhooked a large brass key ring from his belt and fished through its assortment of keys. Finding the one he wanted he stuck it into the lock, jiggled, swore, kicked the door twice, and turned the handle.

"There you are, sir," he said, pushing the door wide then standing back. "I'll let you find your own way round if it's all the same to you. Can't leave my booth unattended for too long. Somebody important might turn up." He smiled, revealing tobacco-yellow teeth.

Gerald looked at him. "Indeed. I'll be sure to mention your enthusiasm in my official report."

The guard did a double take at that, his smile vanishing. With a surly grunt he hooked his bundle of keys back on his belt then folded his arms, radiating offended impatience.

Immediately, Gerald felt guilty. *Oh lord. Now I'm acting like a civil servant!*

Not that there was anything wrong, as such, with public employment. Many fine people were civil servants. Indeed, without them the world would be in a sorry state, he was sure. In fact, the civil service was an honourable institution and he was lucky to be part of it. Only . . . it had never been his ambition to be a wizard who inspected the work of other wizards for Departmental regulation violations. His ambition was to be an inspec*tee*, not an inspec*tor*. Once upon a time he'd thought that dream was reachable.

Now he was a probationary compliance officer in the Minor Infringement Bureau of the Department of Thaumaturgy . . . and dreams were things you had at night after you turned out the lights.

He nodded at the waiting guard. "Thank you."

"Certainly, sir," the guard said sourly.

Well, his day was certainly getting off to a fine start. *And we wonder why people don't like bureaucrats . . .*

With an apologetic smile at the guard he hefted his official briefcase, straightened his official tie, rearranged his expression into one of official rectitude and walked through the open doorway.

And only flinched a little bit as the guard locked the red door behind him.

It's a wizarding job, Gerald, and it's better than the alternative.

Hopefully, if he reminded himself often enough, he'd start to believe that soon.

The factory lay dead ahead, down the end of a short paved pathway. It was a tall, red brick building blinded by a lack of windows. Along its front wall were plastered a plethora of signs: *Danger! Thaumaturgical Emissions! Keep Out! No Admittance Without Permission! All Visitors Report To Security Before Proceeding!*

As he stood there, reading, one of the building's four doors opened and a young woman wearing a singed lab coat and an expression of mild alarm came out.

He approached her, waving. "Excuse me! Excuse me! Can I have a word?"

The young woman saw him, took in his briefcase and the crossed staffs on his tie and moaned. "Oh, no. You're from the Department, aren't you?"

He tried to reassure her with a smile. "Yes, as a matter of fact. Gerald Dunwoody. And you are?"

Looking hunted, she shrank into herself. "Holly," she muttered. "Holly Devree."

He'd been with the Department for a shade under six months and in all that time had been allowed into the field only four times, but he'd worked out by the end of his first site inspection that when it came to the poor sods just following company orders, sympathy earned him far more co-operation than threats. He sagged at the knees, let his shoulders droop and slid his voice into a more intimate, confiding tone.

"Well, Miss Devree – Holly – I can see you're feeling nervous. Please don't. All I need is for you to point me in the direction of your boss, Mr Harold Stuttley."

She cast a dark glance over her shoulder at the factory. "He's in there. And before you see him I want it understood that it's not my fault. It's not Eric's fault, either. Or Bob's. Or Lucius's. It's not any of our faults. We worked hard to get our transmogrifer's licence, okay? And it's not like we're earning squillions, either. The pay's rotten, if you must know. But Stuttley's – they're the best, aren't they?" Without warning, her thin, pale face crumpled. "At least, they used to be the best. When old Mr Horace was in charge. But now . . ."

Fat tears trembled on the ends of her sandycoloured eyelashes. Gerald fished a handkerchief out of his pocket and handed it over. "Yes? Now?"

Blotting her eyes she said, "Everything's different, isn't it? Mr Harold's gone and implemented all these 'cost-cutting' initiatives. Laid off half the Transmogrify team. But the workload hasn't halved, has it? Oh, no. And it's not just us he's laid off, either. He's sacked people in Etheretics, Design, Purchasing, Research and Development – there's not one team hasn't lost folk. Except Sales." Her snubby nose wrinkled in distaste. "Seven new sales reps he's taken on, and they're promising the world, and we're expected to deliver it – except we can't! We're working round the clock and we're still three weeks behind on orders and now Mr Harold's threatening to dock us if we don't catch up!"

"Oh my," he said, and patted her awkwardly on the shoulder. "I'm very sorry to hear this. But at least it explains why the last eight safety reports weren't completed."

"But they were," she whispered, busily strangling her borrowed handkerchief. "Lucius is the most senior technician we've got left, and I know he's been doing them. *And* handing them over to Mr Harold. I've seen it. But what *he's* doing with them I don't know."

Filing them in the nearest waste paper bin, more than likely. "I don't suppose your friend Lucius discussed the reports with you? Or showed them to you?"

Holly Devree's confiding manner shifted suddenly to a cagey caution. The handkerchief disappeared into her lab coat pocket. "Safety reports are confidential."

"Of course, of course," Gerald soothed. "I'm not implying any inappropriate behaviour. But Lucius didn't happen to leave one lying out on a table, did he, where any innocent passer-by might catch a glimpse?"

"I'm sorry," she said, edging away. "I'm on my tea break. We only get ten minutes. Mr Harold's inside if you want to see him. Please don't tell him we talked."

He watched her scuttle like a spooked rabbit, and sighed. Clearly there was more amiss at Stuttley's than a bit of overlooked paperwork. He should get back to the office and tell Mr Scunthorpe. As a probationary compliance officer his duties lay within very strict guidelines. There were other, more senior inspectors for this kind of trouble.

On the other hand, his supervisor was allergic to incomplete reports. Unconfirmed tales out of school from disgruntled employees and nebulous sensations of misgiving from probationary compliance officers bore no resemblance to cold, hard facts. And Mr Scunthorpe was as married to cold, hard facts as he was to Mrs Scunthorpe. More, if Mr Scunthorpe's marital mutterings were anything to go by.

Turning, Gerald stared at the blank-faced factory. He could still feel his inexplicable unease simmering away beneath the surface of his mind. Whatever it was trying to tell him, the news wasn't good. But that wasn't enough. He had to find out exactly *what* had tickled his instincts. And he did have a legitimate place to start, after all: the noncompletion of mandatory safety statements. The infraction was enough to get his foot across the factory threshold. After that, well, it was just a case of following his intuition.

He resolutely ignored the whisper in the back of his mind that said, *Remember what happened the last time you followed your intuition?*

"Oh, bugger off!" he told it, and marched into the fray.

Another pallid employee answered his brisk banging on the nearest door. "Good afternoon," he said, flashing his identification and not giving the lab-coated man a chance to speak. "Gerald Dunwoody, Department of Thaumaturgy, here to see Mr Harold Stuttley on a matter of noncompliance. I'm told he's inside? Excellent. Don't let me keep you from your duties. I'll find my own way around."

The employee gave ground, helpless in the ruthlessly cheerful face of officialdom, and Gerald sailed in. Immediately his nose was clogged with the stink of partially discharged thaumaturgic energy. The air beneath the high factory ceiling was alive with it, crawling and spitting and sparking. The carefully caged lights hummed and buzzed, crackling as firefly filaments of power drifted against their heated bulbs to ignite in a brief, sunlike flare.

A dozen more lab-coated technicians scurried up and down the factory floor, focused on the task at hand. Directly opposite, running the full length of the wall, stood a five-deep row of benches, each one equipped with specially crafted staff cradles. Twenty-five per bench times five benches meant that, if the security guard was right, Stuttley's had one hundred and twenty-five new First Grade staffs ready for completion. The technicians, looking tense and preoccupied, fiddled and twiddled and realigned each uncharged staff in its cradle, assessing every minute adjustment with a hand-held thaumic register. All the muted ticking made the room sound like the demonstration area of a clockmakers' convention.

At either end of the benches towered the etheretic conductors, vast reservoirs of unprocessed thaumaturgic energy. Insulated cables connected them to each other and all the staff cradles, whose conductive surfaces waited patiently for the discharge of raw power that would transform one hundred and twenty-five gold-filigreed five-foot-long spindles of oak into the world's finest, most prestigious, expensive and potentially most dangerous First Grade staffs.

Despite his misgivings he heard himself whimper, just a little. Stuttley First Graders were works of art. Each wrapping of solid gold filigree was unique, its design template destroyed upon completion and never repeated. The rare wizards who could afford the extra astronomical cost had their filigrees designed specifically for them, taking into account personal strengths, family history and specific thaumaturgic signatures. Those staffs came with inbuilt security: it was immediate and spectacularly gruesome death for any wizard other than the rightful owner to attempt the use of them.

Once, a long long time ago, he'd dreamed of owning a First Grade staff. Even though he didn't come from a wizarding family. Even though he'd got his qualifications through a correspondence course. Wizardry cared nothing for family background or the name of the college where you were educated. Wizarding was of the blood and bone, indifferent to pedigrees and bank balances. Some of the world's finest wizards had come from humble origins.

Although . . . not lately. Lately, Ottosland's most powerful and influential wizards came from recognisable families whose names more often than not could also be heard whispered in the nation's corridors of power.

Still. *Technically*, anybody with sufficient aptitude and training could become a First Grade wizard. Social standing might influence your accent but it had nothing to do with raw power. *Technically, even* a tailor's son from Nether Wallop could earn the right to wield a First Grade staff.

Unbidden, his fingers touched his copper-ringed cherrywood Third Grade staff, tucked into its pocket on the inside of his overcoat. It was nothing to be ashamed of. He was the first wizard in the family for umpteen generations, after all. Plenty of people failed even to be awarded a Third Grade licence. For every ten hopefuls identified as potential wizards, only one or two actually survived the rigours of trial and training to receive their precious staff.

And even for Third Grades there was work to be had. Wasn't he living proof? Gerald Dunwoody, after a couple of totally understandable false starts, soon to be a fully qualified compliance officer with the internationally renowned Ottosland Department of Thaumaturgy? Yes, indeed. The sky was the limit. Provided there was a heavy cloud cover. And he was indoors. In a cellar, possibly.

Oh lord, he thought miserably, staring at all those magnificent First Grade staffs. It felt as though his official Departmental tie had tightened to throttling point. *There has to be more to wizarding than this.*

An irate shout rescued him from utter despair. "Oy! You! Who are you and what are you doing in my factory?"

He turned. Marching belligerently towards him, scattering lab coats like so many white mice, was a small persnickety man of sleek middle years, clutching a clipboard and looking so offended even his tea-stained moustache was bristling.

"Ah. Good afternoon," he said, producing his official smile. "Mr Harold Stuttley, I presume?"

The angry little man halted abruptly in front of him, clipboard pressed to his chest like a shield. "And if I am? What of it? Who wants to know?"

Gerald put down his briefcase and took out his identification. Stuttley snatched it from his fingers, glared as though at a mortal insult, then shoved it back. "What's all this bollocks? And who let you in here? We're about to do a run of First Grades. Unauthorised personnel aren't allowed in here when we're running First Grades! How do I know you're not here for a spot of industrial espionage?"

"Because I'm employed by the DoT," he said, pocketing his badge. "And I'm afraid you won't be running anything, Mr Stuttley, until I'm satisfied it's safe to do so. You've not submitted your safety statements for some time now, sir. I'm afraid the Department takes a dim view of that. Now I realise it's probably just an oversight on your part, but even so . . ." He shrugged. "Rules are rules."

Harold Stuttley's pebble-bright eyes bulged. "Want to know what you can do with your rules? You march in here uninvited and then have the hide to tell me when I can and can't conduct my own business? I'll have your job for this!"

Gerald considered him. *Too much bluster. What's he trying to hide?* He let his gaze slide sideways, away from Harold Stuttley's unattractively temper-mottled face. The thaumic emission gauge on the nearest etheretic conductor was stuttering, jittery as an icicle in an earthquake. Flick, flick, flick went the needle, each jump edging closer and closer to the bright red zone marked *Danger*. In his nostrils, the clogging stink of overheated thaumic energy was suddenly stifling.

"Mr Stuttley," he said, "I think you should shut down production right now. There's something wrong here, I can feel it."

Harold Stuttley's eyes nearly popped right out of his head. "Shut down? Are you raving? You're looking at over a million quids' worth of merchandise! All those staffs are bought and paid for, you meddling twit! I'm not about to disappoint my customers for some wet-behind-the-ears stooge from the DoT! Your superiors wouldn't know a safe bit of equipment if it bit them on the arse – and neither would you! Stuttley's has been in business two hundred and forty years, you cretin! We've been making staffs since before your great-grandad was a randy thought in his pa's trousers!"

Gerald winced. By now the air inside the factory was so charged with energy it felt like sandpaper abrading his skin. "Look. I realise it's inconvenient but—"

Harold Stuttley's pointing finger stabbed him in the chest. "It's not happening, son, *that's* what it is. *Inconvenient* is the lawsuit I'll bring against you, your bosses and the whole bleeding Department of Thaumaturgy, you mark my words, if you don't leg it out of here on the double! Interfering with the lawful conduct of business? This is political, this is. Too many wizards buying Stuttley's instead of the cheap muck your precious Department churns out! Well I won't have it, you hear me? Now hop it! Off my premises! Or I'll give you a personal demonstration why Stuttley's staffs are the best in the world!"

Gerald stared. Was the man mad? He couldn't throw out an official Department inspector. He'd have his manufacturing licence revoked. Be brought up on charges. Get sent to prison and be forced to pay a hefty fine.

Little rivers of sweat were pouring down Harold Stuttley's scarlet face and his hands were trembling with rage. Gerald looked more closely. No. Not rage. Terror. Harold Stuttley was beside himself with fear.

He turned and looked at the nearest etheretic conductor. It was sweating too, beads of dark blue moisture forming on its surface, dripping slowly down its sides. Even as he watched, one fat indigo drop of condensed thaumic energy plopped to the factory floor. There was a crack of light and sound. Two preoccupied technicians somersaulted through the air like circus performers, crashed into the wall opposite and collapsed in groaning heaps.

"*Stuttley!*" He grabbed Harold by his lapels and shook him. "Do you see that? Your etheretic containment field is leaking! You have to evacuate! *Now!*"

The rest of the lab coats were congregated about their fallen comrades, fussing and whispering and casting loathing looks in their employer's direction. The acrobatic technicians were both conscious, apparently unbroken, but seemed dazed. Harold Stuttley jumped backwards, tearing himself free of officialdom's grasp.

"Evacuate? Never! We've got a deadline to meet!" He rounded on his employees. "You lot! Back to work! Leave those malingerers where they are, they're all right, they're just winded! Be on their feet in no time − *if* they know what's good for them. Come on! You want to get paid this week or don't you?"

Aghast, Gerald stared at him. The man *was* mad. Even a mere Third Grade wizard like himself knew the dangers of improperly contained thaumic emissions. The entire first year of his correspondence course had dealt with the occupational hazards of wizarding. Some of the illustrations in his handbook had put him off minced meat for *weeks*.

He stepped closer to the factory foreman and lowered his voice. "Mr Stuttley, you're making a very big mistake. Falling behind in your safety statements is one thing. It's a minor infringement. Not worth so much as half a paragraph in *Wizard Weekly's* gossip column. But if you try to run this equipment when clearly it's not correctly calibrated, you could cause a scandal that will spread halfway round the world. You could ruin Stuttley's reputation for years. Maybe forever. Not to mention risk the lives of all your workers. Is that what you want?"

Harold Stuttley swiped his face with his sleeve. "What I want," he said hoarsely, "is for you to get out of here and let me do my job. There's nothing wrong with our equipment, I tell you, it—"

"*Quick, everyone! Run for your lives! The conductors are about to invert!*"

As the technician who'd shouted the warning led the stampede for the nearest door, Gerald spun on his heel and stared at the sweating etheretic conductors. The needles of each thaumic emission gauge were buried deep in the danger zone and the scattered drops of energy had coalesced into foaming indigo streams. They struck the factory floor like lances of fire, blowing holes, scattering splinters. The insulating cables linking the conductors to each other and the benches glowed virulent blue, shimmerings of power wafting off them like heat haze on a dangerous horizon.

Balanced in their cradles, the First Grade staffs began to dance.

"We have to turn off the conductors!" said Gerald. "Before all the staffs are charged at once or the conductors blow – or both! Where are the damper switches, Stuttley?"

But Harold Stuttley was halfway out of the door, his clipboard abandoned on the floor behind him.

Wonderful.

Now the etheretic conductors were humming, a rising song of warning. The air beneath the factory ceiling stirred. Thickened, like curdling cream, and took on a faintly blue cast. He felt every exposed hair on his body stand on end. His throat closed on a gasp as the etheretically burdened atmosphere turned almost unbreathable. Something warm was trickling from his nostrils.

He should run. Now. Without pausing to pick up his briefcase. Those conductors were going to invert any second now, and when they did—

"Bloody *hell*!" he shouted, and leapt for the nearest cable.

It wouldn't disengage. None of the cables would disengage. He ran up and down the benches, tugging and swearing, but the leaking power had fused the cables to the cradles and each other.

He'd have to get the staffs clear before they all got charged.

Stumbling, sweating, parched with terror, he started hauling the gold-filigreed oak spindles out of their cradles. Tossed them behind him like so much inferior firewood, even as the air continued to coalesce and the etheretic conductors juddered and sweated and discharged bolts of indiscriminate power.

In his pocket his modest little cherrywood staff began to glow. It got so hot he had to stop flinging the First Grade staffs around and drag off his coat, because it felt like his leg was burning. Moments after he threw the coat to the floor the wool burst into flames and disintegrated into charred flakes, revealing his smoking staff with its copper bands glowing bright as a furnace.

The First Grade staffs he'd released from confinement leapt about the floor like popcorn on a hotplate. Those still in their cradles began to buzz. On a sobbing breath he continued tearing them free of the benches.

Ten – twenty – thirty: oh lord, he'd never finish in time—

And then the staffs were simply too hot for flesh to touch. As he fell back, scorched and panting, the power's song became a scream. Both thaumic emission gauges exploded, the top of the conductors peeled open like soup cans . . . and a torrent of unprocessed, uncontrolled etheretic energy poured out of the reservoirs and into the remaining First Grade staffs.

The thaumic boom blasted him against the nearest wall so hard he thought for a moment he was dead, but seconds later his blackened vision cleared.

He wished it hadn't.

Terrible arcing lines of indigo power surged around and through the staffs he'd failed to pull free of their conductive cradles. The emptied conductors, ripped apart from the inside out, lay fallen on their sides. Two ragged gaping holes in the ceiling directly overhead spilled sunlight onto the dreadful aftermath of undisciplined thaumic energies. Through them spiralled two thin columns of unfiltered emissions: the leftover power not captured by the staffs escaping into the wider world beyond the factory.

Groaning, Gerald staggered to his feet. If he didn't shut down that self-perpetuating loop of energy pouring through the First Grade staffs it would continue to build and build until it exploded . . . most likely taking half the suburb of Stuttley with it. It wasn't a job for a lowly probationary compliance officer, or a Third Grade wizard who'd received his qualifications from a barely recognised correspondence course. He doubted it was even a job for a First Grade wizard . . . at least, not one working solo. A whole squadron might manage it, at a pinch.

But that was wishful thinking. There wasn't time to contact Mr Scunthorpe and get him to send out a flying squad of Departmental troubleshooters. There was just him. Gerald Dunwoody, wizard Third Grade. Twenty-three years old and scared to death.

So long, life. I hardly lived you . . .

Looming large before him, the howling, writhing mass of

thaumaturgically linked First Grade staffs, bathed in unholy indigo fire. Abandoned on the floor at his feet, his pathetic little cherry-wood staff, as useful now as a piece of straw.

And scattered around him, four of the First Grade staffs he'd managed to rescue before the massive conductor inversion. Rolling idly to and fro they glowed a gentle gold, their filigree activated. They must have been caught in the nimbus of exploding thaumic energy.

Everybody knew that Third Grade wizards didn't have the etheretic chops to handle a First Grade staff. Even using a Second Grader was to risk life, limb and sanity. Attempting to use one of those erratically charged First Graders was proof positive that sanity had left the building.

But he had no choice. This was an emergency and he was the only Department official in sight. Instincts shrieking, fear a gibbering demon on his back, he reached for the nearest activated First Grade staff. If it was one of the special orders, keyed to a specific wizard, then he really was about to breathe his last—

A shock of power slammed through his body. The world pulsed violet, then crimson, then bright and blinding blue, spinning wildly on its axis. Something deep inside his mind torqued. Twisted. Tore. His vision cleared, the mad giddiness stopped, and he was himself again. More or less. *Something* was different, but there was no time to worry or work out what.

Bucking and flailing like a live thing, the staff struggled to join its brethren in the heart of the magical maelstrom. Gerald got his other hand onto it, battling to contain the energy. It felt like standing inside the world's largest waterfall. The staff was channelling the excess energies from the atmosphere, attracting them like a magnet. Pummelled, battered, he wrestled with the flux and flow of power. Poured everything he had into taming the beast in his fists.

But the beast didn't want to be tamed.

Gasping, fighting against being pulled into the maelstrom, he opened his slitted eyes. The etheretic conductors were empty now, their spiralling columns of power collapsed. But the trapped staffs within the indigo firestorm continued to blaze, amplifying and dis-torting the energies they'd consumed. Only minutes remained, surely, before they exploded.

And he had no idea how to stop them.

CHAPTER TWO

Desperate, Gerald tipped back his head and stared through the nearest hole in the factory ceiling. This was no time for pride; he'd take help from anywhere.

"Reg? *Reg!* Are you out there? Can you hear me?"

No reply. Did that mean she was just refusing to answer or was she really not there? Was this the one time she'd actually done what he asked and was keeping her beak out of his business?

Typical.

"Reg, if you're out there I'm sorry, all right? I apologise. I *grovel.* Just – *help!*"

Still no answer. Breathing like a runner on his last legs he ignored the howling pain in his shoulders and wrists and battled the gold-filigreed staff to a temporary standstill. Like a wilful child it fretted and tugged, still trying to join its blazing siblings.

A glimmer of an idea appeared, then, an iceberg emerging out of a fogbank. Staffs were both conduits and reservoirs of power. They were attracted to it like flies to honey. Yes, this staff was already charged – but not completely. And everybody knew that Stuttley's staffs absorbed higher levels of raw thaumic energy than any other brand in the world. So if he could just coax some more of that untamed pulsing power into this activated staff and perhaps one or two others – maybe he could prevent the imminent enormous explosion.

Summoning the last skerricks of his strength, he inched closer to the indigo firestorm. Immediately the staff began to fight him again. He hung on grimly: letting go would be the worst, last mistake of his life. When he was as close to the writhing thaumic energy as he could get without being sucked in, he stopped. Raised the staff above his head. Focused his will, and plunged it end-first into the factory floor.

Where it stuck, quivering.

A questing tendril of thaumic energy licked towards it and, amidst a sizzling crackle, fused with the staff's intricate gold fretwork. More power poured into the tall oak spindle. Gerald watched, the stinking air caught in his throat. If it held . . . if it held . . .

The transfer held.

Staggering, he picked up another partially activated staff and plunged it into the floor two feet along from the first. Within moments it too was siphoning off the lethal, undirected thaumic energy. He did the same to a third staff, then a fourth. A fifth. A sixth. By the time he'd finished, he was looking at a whole row of crackling, power-hazed First Grade staffs and his legs could barely hold him upright. His lungs were a pair of deflated balloons. Indigo spots danced before his eyes. But he'd done it. He'd averted disaster. The suburb of Stuttley and its famous staff factory were saved.

Holly Devree had kept his handkerchief, so he smeared the sweat from his face with one shirt-sleeve and watched, exhausted, as the ferocious thaumic firestorm faded. Smiled, shaking, as the car-battering roar of untrammelled power abated.

Saint Snodgrass's trousers. Had anything like this ever happened before? A Third Grade wizard managing to successfully stymie a major thaumaturgical inversion? He'd never heard of it. As he stood there, gently panting, he let his imagination off its tight leash.

This could be it, Dunwoody. This could be your big chance, finally.

Mr Scunthorpe would have to take him seriously now. Let him off probation early. Possibly even approve a transfer to a different department altogether. Even – miracle of miracles – Research and Development.

The thought of reaching such an exalted height made him dizzy all over again.

With a final whimpering sputter the last randomly dissipated etheretic energies discharged into the staffs he'd plunged into the floor. The benches and staffs still trapped in their conductive cradles disintegrated in a choking cloud of indigo ash.

Despite his exhaustion and his myriad aches and pains, Gerald did a little victory dance.

"Yes! Yes! R and D boys, here I come!"

Then he stopped dancing, because it was that or fall over. Instead he just stood there, eyes closed, heart pounding, revelling in his moment of unexpected triumph.

Breaking the blessed silence, a sound. Thin. Sharp. Dangerous – and escalating. Nervously he opened his eyes. Stared at the militarily upright staffs plunged into the floor. Before he had time to blink, the first one transformed into a narrow blue column of fire. Moments later the second followed suit. Then the rest, one by one, like a row of falling dominoes. The air began to sparkle. The factory floor began to smoke.

He frowned. "Oh." Apparently he'd found the thaumaturgical limit of a Stuttley Superior Staff. *How clever of me*. Research and Development, indeed. "Right. So this would be a good time to run away, yes?"

His wobbly legs answered for him. He had just enough time and wit to grab up his poor little cherrywood staff and reach the nearest door. The blast wave caught him with his fingers still on the handle, tumbled him through the air like so much leaf litter and dropped him from a great height into the middle of an ornamental rose garden.

The last thing he saw, before darkness claimed him, was the irate face of Harold Stuttley.

"You bastard! You *bastard*! I'll have your job for this!"

Mr Scunthorpe folded his hands on top of his desk and shook his head. "Gerald . . . Gerald . . . Gerald . . ."

Gerald winced. "I know, Mr Scunthorpe," he said contritely. "And I'm very sorry. But it wasn't my fault. Honestly."

It was much later. The ambulance officers from the district hospital had fished him out of the rose garden then transported him, over his objections, to the emergency room, where an unsympathetic doctor extracted all the rose thorns from various and delicate parts of his anatomy and pronounced him sound in wind and limb, if deficient in intelligence. Which meant he was free to catch a taxi back to Stuttley's and drive at not much above snail's pace home to the Department of Thaumaturgy so he could make his report.

Unfortunately, Harold Stuttley's tongue had travelled a damned sight faster.

"Not your fault, Gerald?" echoed Mr Scunthorpe, and looked down at the paperwork in front of him. "That's not what the people at Stuttley's are saying. According to them you barged into the middle of a highly sensitive First Grade thaumaturgical transfer, ignored all reasonable warnings and pleas to leave before there was an accident, used your Departmental authority to evict the personnel from their lawful premises and then caused a massive explosion which only by a miracle failed to kill someone, or reduce everything within a radius of three miles to rubble. As it is you totally destroyed the factory, which is going to put back staff production by months. I have to tell you Lord Attaby is profoundly unamused. One of the staffs you blew up had his nephew's name on it."

It took a moment for Gerald's brain to catch up with his ears. When it did, he almost choked. "What? But that's rubbish! Yes, all right, the factory did blow up, but I'm telling you, Mr Scunthorpe, that wasn't my fault! Harold Stuttley caused that! The etheretic conductors failed due to a lack of proper maintenance. They were on the brink of inversion when I got there! Ask the technicians! They'll tell you!"

Mr Scunthorpe tapped his fingernails on the open file. "What I just told you, Gerald, is a summary of their testimony. Theirs and, of course, Mr Harold Stuttley's. He's threatening all kinds of trouble. Lord Attaby is very unhappy."

"But – but—" He clenched his fingers into fists. "I *went* there in the first place because there was a protocol violation. Overdue safety statements. That proves they—"

Mr Scunthorpe's round face was suffused with temper. "All it proves, Mr Dunwoody, is that even the best of companies can fall behind with their paperwork. You were sent to Stuttley's to deliver a polite reminder to this nation's most valuable and prestigious staff manufacturer that the Department of Thaumaturgy looked forward to their prompt provision of all relevant documentation. You were *not* sent there to cause international headlines!"

Mr Dunwoody. Gerald leaned forward, feeling desperate. "But there was a woman! I spoke to her! She said things weren't being done right, she said there was trouble." He scrabbled around in his post-explosion memory. "Devree! That was her name! Find her. *Ask* her. She'll tell you."

Mr Scunthorpe rifled through the sheets of paper in front of him. "Holly Devree?" He extracted a statement, picked up his glasses on their chain around his neck, placed them on his nose and read out loud: "'I don't know what happened. I was on my tea break. I never saw the man from the Department. This means my job, doesn't it? What am I going to do now? I've got a sick mother to support.' Signed: Holly Devree."

"No," he whispered. "That's not how it happened, Mr Scunthorpe. My word as a compliance officer."

"*Probationary* compliance officer," said Mr Scunthorpe, still frowning. "Very well then, Gerald. What's your version of today's unfortunate events?"

Haltingly, feeling as though he'd wandered into somebody else's insane dream, Gerald told him. When he was finished he sat back in his chair again. "And that's the truth, sir. I swear it."

Mr Scunthorpe closed his mouth with a snap. "The truth?"

"Yes, sir."

Mr Scunthorpe's face was so red he could have found work as a traffic light. "You expect me to believe that a Third Grade wizard from Nether Wallop, who got his qualifications from some fourth-rate correspondence course, who got fired from his first job for insubordination and his second for incompetence, not only managed to single-handedly prevent a Level Nine thaumaturgical inversion but did so, moreover, by using the most expensive, the most finely calibrated, the most *lethal* First Grade staffs in the *world*? Is *that* what you expect me to believe?"

"Well," he said, after a moment. "When you put it like that . . ." Then he rallied. "But sir, far-fetched or not that's exactly what happened. I can't explain how, or why, but that's precisely what I did."

"Dunwoody, what you're saying is impossible!" said Mr Scunthorpe, and pounded a fist on his desk. "No Third Grade wizard in history has ever used a First Grade staff without frying himself like bacon. To suggest *you* managed it is to stretch the bounds of credulity across five alternate dimensions!"

The urge to punch Scunthorpe in the nose was almost irresistible. "Are you calling me a liar?"

"I'm calling you a walking disaster!" Scunthorpe retorted. "A carbuncle on the arse of this Department! Do you have any idea of the phone calls I've been getting? Lord Attaby! The Wizard General! *Seven* prime ministers and *two* presidents! And don't get me started on the press!"

Gerald stopped breathing. Scunthorpe was going to fire him. The intention was in the man's glazed eyes and furious, scarlet face. If he was fired from another job it'd be the end of his wizarding career. No one would touch him with a forty-foot barge pole after that. He'd have to go home to Nether Wallop. Beg his cousins for a job in the tailor's shop his father had sold them. They'd give him one, he was family after all, but he'd never hear the end of it.

I'd rather die.

"Let me prove it, Mr Scunthorpe," he said. "Fetch me a First Grade staff and I'll prove I can use one."

"Are you *mad*?" shouted Scunthorpe. "After this afternoon's little exhibition do you think there's a wizard anywhere in the world who'd risk letting you even *look* at his First Grader, let alone touch it? And do you think I'd risk *my* job to ask them?"

"Then how am I supposed to show you I'm telling the truth?"

It was a fair question and Scunthorpe knew it. He snatched a pencil from his desktop and twisted it between his fingers. "I'm telling you, Dunwoody, you won't be let anywhere near a First

Grade staff. But—"The pencil snapped. With enormous forbearance, Scunthorpe placed the two pieces on the blotter. "—*if* you can use a First Grader then a Second Grader shouldn't pose the slightest difficulty." He stood and crossed to the closet in the corner of his office. From it he withdrew four feet of slender, silver-bound Second Grade staff. Holding it reverently, he turned. "Lord Attaby gave me this staff with his own hands, Dunwoody. In recognition of my twenty-five years impeccable service to the Department. If I give it to you, here and now, will you promise not to break it?"

Gerald swallowed, feeling ill. "I can't do that, sir. But I can promise I'll try."

Pale now, and sweating, Scunthorpe nodded. "All right then."

"What do you want me to do?"

"Nothing spectacular!" said Mr Scunthorpe, darkly. "Something simple. Noncombustible." He nodded at the painting on the wall beside him, an insipid rendition of the first opening of Parliament in 1142. "Animate that."

He swallowed a protest. Animation might be noncombustible but it was hardly simple. All right, for a First Grade wizard it was child's play and for a Second it was unlikely to cause a sweat. For a Third Grade wizard, though, animation required a command of etheretic balances that tended to induce piles in the unprepared.

Scunthorpe bared his teeth in a smile. "I take it you do know an appropriate incantation?"

Sarcastic bugger. Yes. As it happened he knew all kinds of high-level incantations, and not all of them entirely . . . legal. Reg had insisted on teaching him dozens, even though his cherrywood staff was totally inadequate when it came to channelling them. Even though he, apparently, was equally inadequate. *Learn them*, she'd insisted. *You never know when one might come in handy*.

Maybe she'd been right after all. Maybe this was one of those times. And anyway, what did he have to lose?

He held out his hand for Scunthorpe's staff. Reluctantly Scunthorpe gave it to him. Closing his eyes, he took a moment to centre himself. To rummage through his collection of interesting but hitherto irrelevant charms and incantations until he found the one that would rescue him from his current predicament.

"Hurry up, Dunwoody," said Scunthorpe. "I've an appointment to see Lord Attaby. Somehow I've got to *explain* all this."

"Yes, sir," he said, still rummaging. Then he recalled a small but effective binding that would set the picture's painted crowd politely clapping.

The silver-chased staff in his hands felt heavy and cool. He couldn't detect the smallest sense of latent power from it. When was the last time Scunthorpe had used it? Or sent it out to be thaumically recharged? God help him if the damned thing had a flat battery—

"Hurry *up*, Dunwoody!" snapped Scunthorpe. "I'm running out of patience!"

"Right," he said, and settled his shoulders. Extended the staff until its tip touched the painting's frame, closed his eyes and in the privacy of his mind uttered the animation binding.

Nothing happened. No burning surge of power through the staff, no giddy-making roil of First Grade thaumic energy in his veins or repeat of that strange torqueing tearing sensation he'd felt in Stuttley's factory. Not even his usual Third Grade tingling. And no sound of tiny painted hands, clapping. No sound at all except for Scunthorpe's stertorous breathing.

He cleared his throat. "Um. Why don't I just try that again?"

Before Scunthorpe could refuse he attempted to animate the painting a second time. Nothing. A third time. Nothing. A fourth ti—

"Forget it!" shouted Scunthorpe, and snatched back his precious silver-filigreed staff. "You're a fraud, Dunwoody! After a performance like that I'm at a loss to understand how you even got your *Third* Grade licence! My Aunt Hildegarde's geriatric cat has more wizarding talent than you!"

Stunned, Gerald stared at the uncooperative painting. Then he fished inside his overcoat and pulled out his slightly singed cherrywood staff. Turning, he snatched the broken pencil pieces from

Scunthorpe's desk, tapped them with his staff and uttered a joining incant, a task so simple it wasn't

even included in the Third Grade examination.

The pencil stayed stubbornly broken.

Oh God. "I don't understand it," he muttered. "I've got nothing. *Nothing.* How can that be? Unless—" Horrified, he stared at Scunthorpe. "Do you think I burned myself out when I short-circuited the inversion? Do you think channelling all that raw thaumic energy through those First Grade staffs somehow used up all my power?"

"All *what* power?" roared Scunthorpe. "You don't *have* any power, Dunwoody! You're the worst excuse for a wizard I ever met! I must've been *mad* the day I took pity and gave you a job! I must've been *raving*! Get out! You're fired!"

Gerald felt his throat close. *Fired.* Again. His stomach heaved. "Mr Scunthorpe, I protest. I didn't do anything wrong. Harold Stuttley's the criminal here, not me. I don't care what he says, I contained that thaumic inversion, I didn't cause it. The resulting explosion was unfortunate but—"

"*Unfortunate?*" Scunthorpe wheezed. "You mean catastrophic! Are you really this naive, Dunwoody? Stuttley's is demanding a parliamentary enquiry! They're threatening to sue the government! They want this entire Department disbanded!"

"But – but that's ridiculous—"

"Of course it's ridiculous!" snapped Scunthorpe. "But that's not the point! The point is that if your head's not rolling down the Department staircase in the next five minutes we will lose control of this situation!"

"And then what? Harold Stuttley gets off scot-free?"

"Never you mind about Harold Stuttley! Forget you ever heard of Harold Stuttley! This isn't about Harold Stuttley, Dunwoody, it's about *you.* Don't you *understand?* You've embarrassed the Department and disgraced your staff. You're finished, do you hear me? *Finished!* So don't stand there staring like a poleaxed bullock! Get out of my office. Get out of the *building.* So that when Lord Attaby demands the privilege of personally kicking you into the street I can put my hand on my heart and say I don't know where you are!"

Gerald shook his head. "This isn't right. I'm not going to take this lying down, Mr Scunthorpe. I'm going to—"

"What?" sneered Scunthorpe. "Demand an enquiry of your own? Go on record claiming you're a better wizard than the likes of Lord Attaby himself? *You?* A correspondence course Third Grader? Well, I suppose you can. If you insist. But you'll never work as a wizard again, Dunwoody. That much I can promise you."

Stung, he looked at his red-faced superior. "I thought I was already finished!"

Abruptly Scunthorpe's manner softened. "You are, son. At least around here. But if you go quietly, no fuss, no indignant, out-landish claims and accusations, lay low for a while, well, I'm sure once the dust has settled, in a few months, a year maybe, some little locum agency somewhere will take you on."

"A year?" He almost laughed. "And what am I supposed to do in the meantime?"

Scunthorpe shook his head. "Sorry. That's not my problem. You should have thought of that before you blew up Stuttley's. Now if I could just have your official badge . . ."